Praise for *Fire &*

The soul of an artist meets a woman who finally admits love into her life—despite subtle signs of trouble. I could hardly put down *Fire & Water*. In one moment I was lost in an artist's dream, in another I was on the edge of my seat. A memorable book by a wordsmith whose language enchants.

—**Linda Joy Myers, PhD**, President of the National
Association of Memoir Writers and author of
Don't Call Me Mother and *Journey of Memoir—A Workbook*

Set between the comfort of an Irish pub and the intellectual buzz of San Francisco's UCSF, *Fire & Water* will take you on a breathless journey. You will find the funniest and most honest best friend you could ever want, passionate sex with the likes of Picasso, and a story that will grab your curiosity and soul. Don't make plans once you turn the first page.

—**Amy Peele**, author of *Aunt Mary's Guide to
Raising Children the Old-Fashioned Way*

This author doesn't flinch. She writes down to the bone, deep into the heart, where blood, tears, and humor pool.

—**Elizabeth Appell**, screenwriter and author of
Lessons from the Gypsy Camp

An uncommon love story told with joy and pathos from a writer of exceptional talent. With fearless examination and a sure sense of pitch and pace, the novel reveals the moral predicament that Kate must ultimately face: can the deepest expression of love become an instrument of its demise?

—**Christie Nelson**, author of
Dreaming Mill Valley and *Woodacre*

FIRE & Water

FIRE & *Water*

Betsy Graziani Fasbinder

Live your story!
Betsy Graziani Fasbinder

SwP
SHE WRITES PRESS

Published 2013
Printed in the United States of America
ISBN: 978-1-938314-14-8
Library of Congress Control Number: 2013931117

For information, address:
She Writes Press
1563 Solano Ave #546
Berkeley, CA 94707

In memory of my brother, whose voice I still hear. How is it that you speak most loudly from the very pages of this book? Perhaps my answers are here.

Johnny, we all miss you and wish you were still here.

*Out beyond ideas of wrongdoing and rightdoing,
there is a field. I'll meet you there.*

—Rumi

Family

"Yo, Murphy. Check it out," Mary K announced as we walked together into the doctors' lounge of UCSF Medical Center. Her raspy voice wore rough New York edges and contradicted her petite frame and freckled face.

Awaiting us were a dozen of our fellow interns and nurses, wearing a rainbow of hospital scrubs and white lab coats, and a few of the friendlier senior staff physicians.

Dahlia de la Rosa, my favorite nurse in pediatrics, pushed a hospital gurney with a huge cake on it. Along with her, carrying an instrument tray, was Andra Littleton, the star among stars of the third-year residents. They were both clad in surgical scrubs, gloves, and masks. The gurney was draped and the cake decorated to look like a pale belly prepared for surgery. Blood-red lettering read, *Way to Make the Cut, Dr. Kowalski and Dr. Murphy.*

Dr. John Marshall, the head of surgery, raised his paper cup and the murmurs of the group came to an instant silence. "This class is an exceptionally fine group of interns. Perhaps the best I've seen in all my years at UCSF," he said. "That is, of course, with the exception of when I was an intern."

The crowd gave a good-natured round of boos.

Another intern hollered, "Your specialty was blood-letting and use of leeches, wasn't it Doc?"

"Watch who you're insulting, Dr. Jones. I haven't signed all of your paperwork yet." Warm laughter rolled through the room. "Dr. Mary Kowalski and Dr. Katherine Murphy have been offered residencies from the likes of Johns Hopkins, UCLA, and Boston General. After considering their prestigious options, they've elected to accept surgical residencies right here at our own UCSF."

A burst of applause sent an unexpected charge through me. Marshall's rare compliments and expectation of perfection gave him a well-earned reputation as a hard-ass, but made the praise that much sweeter.

Dr. Marshall continued, explaining that Mary K would begin her specialty in the organ transplant program while I'd be in pediatric surgery. He bragged about us both until I thought I'd die of embarrassment. "Welcome, both of you, to UCSF." Dr. Marshall lifted his glass a bit higher and the crowd shouted, "Cheers!"

Mary K raised her fists and did an end zone triumph dance while I felt my face get hotter.

Dahlia held a scalpel over the cake. "The patient is prepped, doctors. Vitals are good. Time for a little surgery," she said, her native Mexico accenting her words.

"I think you can handle this one, Murphy," Mary K said, shining her fingernails on the lapel of her lab coat. "This patient doesn't require my level of skill."

I stepped toward the gurney. "If the procedure is too much for you—"

"No, no," Dahlia cried. "Both of you. We want to watch you in action, see if all of this praise is deserved."

Andra offered a scalpel. Cameras flashed while Mary K and I made the ceremonial first cut to the cake.

Suddenly, Mary K stepped aside and pulled off her mask. "I pronounce this patient healed." She dipped her pinky into the icing and took a tiny taste. "And delicious. Nurse, can you take over?"

The crowd laughed and the skirmish for cake began. Mary K inserted her thumb and forefinger into her mouth and delivered a piercing whistle that instantly quieted the crowd. She looked at me, silently offering me the floor. I shook my head. "No," I whispered. "You go."

"Hey Kowalski," one of the interns jeered. "Why don't you stand up so we can see you?" Mary K's diminutive size had been the safest topic for teasing from our fellow interns. Only Mary K could carry off all of her bravado from a barely five-foot frame. Her general prickliness kept people from teasing her about much else.

"Hardy, har. If you mangy state employees could stop stuffing your pieholes for just a minute, I've got a word or two."

The group hissed and booed. "Pipe down," Mary K said. "Murphy and I want to thank you all for this little shindig. Dr. Marshall, we're honored that you would join us. Deciding to stay here at UC was just about the easiest decision I've ever made. Great hospital. Great staff." Mary K paused and looked toward me. "Great friends. And, hey, three thousand miles away from those stinking Yankees. What more can a gal from Queens ask for, huh?" Mary K lifted her water bottle. "To a great institution and a group that should definitely be institutionalized."

The rest of the gathering was a flurry of congratulations and well-wishes from colleagues whose duties demanded that they return quickly back to work. They exited carrying paper plates with gruesome slices of red velvet cake. Celebrations in hospitals are more like drive-bys than parties.

Dahlia offered a plate to Mary K. "You didn't get any cake?"

"None for me, thanks. Trying to keep my girlish figure." She tilted her water bottle, emptying the last of it.

I smiled at Mary K's standard decline of sweets. Meanwhile, I'd eaten my second piece, since at nearly five-foot-ten the term *girlish* hadn't applied to me since I was ten.

As the crowd thinned I spotted Nigel Abbot across the room. His navy blue cashmere blazer and turtleneck seemed assigned from a wardrobe department called to costume a distinguished resident psychiatrist. They went perfectly with his pale complexion, precisely trimmed goatee, and somber but kind expression.

"There's your boyfriend," Mary K whispered, her elbow nudging my side. "Thurstin Howell the Third."

Nigel and I had a loose arrangement—one that we'd tacitly agreed was not for public knowledge. Hospital gossip was rabid once couples formed. We saw each other discreetly. No commitment. No drama. He was kind, easy to talk to, and was one of the few single male residents who hadn't slept with nearly every intern and nurse on staff. While our relationship wasn't exactly the stuff of great romance, it was comfortable and convenient. "Roommate code of silence, remember?" I whispered.

"Fair enough," Mary K said. "Just let me know if Dr. Milquetoast is coming to our place later tonight. He gives some of my dates the creeps. Settle a bet," she said out of the side of her mouth. "If he goes out into the sunlight, does he turn into a pile of ashes?"

I shushed her again as Nigel approached. He held out his hand to Mary K. "Welcome." He offered me a businessy kiss on the cheek. "And you, too, Katherine. I'm so glad you'll both be remaining part of our little UC San Francisco family."

"As long as I don't have to call you Uncle Nigel or anything," Mary K said with a smirk. "So, will I see you at our place,

Murphy? Or—" This was typical Mary K. First she'd nag me about how I needed to get laid now and then and not be so serious. Then, if I did date somebody, he became an object of scorn and ridicule. This had been our pattern since freshman year, undergrad.

I'd not included Nigel in the second celebration my family was putting on for Mary K and me, but we'd arranged to share drinks after. Ours was not a take-him-home-to-meet-the-folks kind of relationship. "I've got some paperwork to tie up in the ER," I said to Mary K. "I'll just meet you there."

Just as Mary K was about to make her escape, Andra Littleton glided toward us, seemingly unaware that every man in the room could not help himself from gaping at her. The willowy blonde, hospital rumor had it, was a former Miss Texas, third runner up for Miss USA.

Mary K fidgeted. "Don't look now, but Barbie is coming over here."

"Andra couldn't be a nicer, smarter person. I don't know why you need to insult her." I grinned, loving watching Mary K lose her composure. Andra made her nervous, and I'd never seen anybody else cause that reaction from her.

Mary K glanced toward the exits as Andra approached. Andra leaned down to Mary K's height and gave her a warm embrace. Mary K was a wild animal caught in a trap. "I'm just so happy you decided on UC," Andra said with her broad smile, deep dimples, and hint of Texas twang. She threw her arms around me.

"I read your article in *The New England Journal of Medicine*." I turned to Mary K. "Did you know that our own Dr. Littleton here has collaborated with a microchip company to develop a new kind of computerized prosthetic hand?"

"Must've missed that one. Congrats," Mary K mumbled as she patted the pocket where she usually kept her cigarettes.

I smiled, remembering I'd seen the journal opened to Andra's article on Mary K's side of the table only a week before.

I'd met Mary K by chance when we were assigned as undergrad freshmen roommates at Stanford. We'd remained roommates and study partners for the nine years since. I'd never seen her nervous around someone, but somehow Andra was different.

Mary K patted her pocket. "I'm gonna step outside."

"Mary K," Andra said, her head tilted to the side. "You're not still smoking, are you?"

"I don't appear to be at the moment, but give me a minute. Thanks for the cake and the hoopla." She delivered a sailor's salute and swept a strand of her strawberry blonde hair behind her ear.

Andra's face looked as though it had just been slapped as she watched Mary K exit, her lips forming a perfect O.

Nigel offered a repeat of his congratulations and left for an appointment.

I licked icing from the edge of my plastic fork.

"Why does Mary K dislike me?" Andra asked.

"That's the way she is with everybody."

"No," Andra said, putting her hands on her hips. "She's gruff with everybody. Surly. Sarcastic. Irreverent. Moody. Crass. Even downright insulting. But she avoids me like I'm a bad smell."

"Well, that begs only one question," I said, trying to suppress a grin. "If Mary K is as vile as you say—and I'm not saying she isn't—what do you care if she dislikes you?" I turned and walked away, happy that I'd added a small wrinkle of confusion to Andra's flawless face.

* * *

Murphy's Pub sits on the edge of Golden Gate Park on Lincoln Avenue. A brass plaque beside the door reads ESTABLISHED BY ANGUS AND ELYSE MURPHY. 1956. Just up the hill on Parnassus Street, UCSF Medical Center peeks over the ever-present fog, watching over Murphy's and San Francisco's Sunset District like a castle overlooking its village. Between Murphy's and UC sits the pale-peach fortress of St. Anne's of the Sunset. The triangle of Murphy's, UCSF, and St. Anne's was my universe growing up. Doctors, nurses, janitors, and priests all found their way down the hill to lift a few at Murphy's.

I pressed my palm against the cool brass push plate of the swinging door. A symphony of sensations greeted me: the fragrant smell of Scotch eggs, hard-boiled and wrapped in sausage; laughter and cheers for whatever sport was on the TV above the bar; the jukebox crooning Dad's favorite ballads. Until I moved to the dorms at Stanford, the only place I'd ever lived was the flat upstairs from the pub. I rarely slept anywhere but my own bed. I was invited to sleepovers now and then, but I always ended up calling my dad to come pick me up. He came and pretended to be mad at me, but whistled all the way home.

Downstairs, the pub served as our parlor. The room was filled with dark fir wainscoting and worn velvet couches. It smelled of smoky scotch and pipe tobacco. Unlike many bars, Murphy's was full of light; the front windows were always clean and clear, covered only by lacy café curtains and blinds that were brought down only after closing. The light found its way to the array of pampered orchids, narcissus, and hyacinths that seemed unbothered by cigarette smoke and loud talk. Thuds of darts and cracks of pool balls were percussion to the musical rise and fall of voices. We served enough food to qualify as a restaurant and kids often joined their parents. Always in residence was one or another stray cat adopted by the bar—or, more likely, fed by my father at the back door and allowed in by the same. They arrived thin and skittish and became fat and lazy. Dad always named them after foods like Tater Chips or Muffin or, when they came in two at a time, Corn Beef and Cabbage or Bubble and Squeak.

Upstairs, our flat looked like most regular apartments, but a couple of decades out of date and perhaps on the wrong side of the Atlantic. Doilies on the arms of overstuffed chairs. A small kitchen with chintz curtains and a matching apron in front of the sink. One small bedroom, one large. A few family photos on the vanity table. Everything was frozen, unchanged after my mother died when I was eight.

The melody of Dad's voice, kissed by the music of his mother Ireland, sang out as I entered, "Ah, there's my Kitten." Dad's dove-gray eyes shimmered under his wiry eyebrows. His shirt gaped a little where his belly spilled over his belt. Though in his mid-sixties and built like a short, stout fireplug, he scampered toward me and gave me a crushing embrace. "Look everybody. Our other guest of honor is here!" He pulled me through the room toward the huge round family booth in the front window where Mary K already sat with a club soda, a plume of cigarette smoke unfurling in front of her. "Look what Mary K brought," Dad said, raising his palm to a new addition to his collection of flowers, a delicate blue bloom growing from a piece of mossy bark. "*Orchidaceae Vanda*. A blue orchid," he beamed. He looked over at Mary K and wagged his finger. "Probably pricey, too. Nothing this one should be spending her hard earned money on."

"Hush, Mr. Murphy. It's rude to talk about the price of a gift."

Alice greeted me next. A cloud of Shalimar reached me just before she did. Her hair color changed with each season and she always stacked it in various architectural shapes made stable by an impenetrable shell of Aqua Net. She'd gone extra blonde for this occasion, and her 'do was elevated to a celebratory height. She was a spectacular show of animal print and spangles, a pink fuzzy sweater with matching lacquered nails, and high heels that made her stand well over six feet tall. Alice was the bar's first employee, brought on to cook. She and my mother had become best friends. I'd been named Katherine Alice Murphy in her honor.

It was Alice who took over all womanly duties after my mom died: cooking, putting my hair in ponytails, buying my clothes and my first Kotex pads, back when they were as big as twin bed mattresses. Alice lived in an apartment just a few doors down from the pub where we had girly slumber parties and watched old movies on her black-and-white TV.

"Katie!" Alice cried, covering my face with lipsticky kisses. "Look at your pink cheeks. Where are your gloves? Did you walk down the hill in this cold?"

She took my coat and tugged me farther into the room.

Ivan Schwartz stepped toward us. He took my hands into his tremulous ones and kissed me, first on one cheek, then the other. In his feathery voice he said, "Katherine. I can scarcely remember a prouder day." His head wobbled as he spoke. Dr. Schwartz had been having his morning coffee and his evening brandy at Murphy's Pub since the day it opened, long before I was born. He'd supervised my homework, coached me through AP chemistry, and helped me write my application to Stanford, his alma mater. Dr. Schwartz had been a respected heart surgeon at UCSF until Parkinson's had robbed him of his steady hands.

"Sure you're proud, you skinny old fart. Who the hell wouldn't be goddamned proud of our Katie and her little dyke friend here!" a slurred voice shouted from the end of the bar.

I winced. I'd never heard Tully utter a mean word to anyone.

And though he had only his usual coffee cup before him, he seemed unfamiliarly drunk. Ironically, though I'd grown up in a bar, drunkenness was rare in the "family."

"Hey, hey there!" Alice scolded.

"That'll be a dollar to you, Tully," Dad said.

Tully tried with all his might to raise his weighty black eyebrows, his thin, rubbery face contorting with his effort. "What do I owe a dollar for?"

"The cussing jar, Tully," Alice said winking a heavily mascaraed eye.

"For what? I didn't say nothing!"

"G.D., Tully," Dad said. "And Katie's right here, plain as the nose. You know the rules. And you ought to pay extra for insulting our guest as well."

"Katie ain't even a kid no more," Tully said in slurred protest. "The rule should only be for kids."

"You don't make the rules, Tully Driscoll," Dad admonished.

"Ah, shit!" Tully slurred, reaching into the front pocket of his paint-splattered jeans.

"*TULLY!*" came the chorus.

"That will be two dollars since you're reaching," said my dad.

Some version of this exchange had occurred nearly every day of my growing up with one or another who had overimbibed or simply forgotten the family language rule.

The cussing jar had once served as my college savings account, but now it lived on as one of the bar's unchanged rituals. Because Dad owned the bar, he got to make the rules. Whenever children were present, no profanity was allowed. He was reasonable. Newcomers got a fair warning. *Hells* and *damns* were often overlooked, but all curses that involved anatomy, sexual acts, the Holy Trinity, or a bodily function were strictly prosecuted. A buck apiece. The f-word was double, and there were a few five-dollar fines for the more colorful ribbons of profanity unfurled during soccer matches and Giants games. The World Series and soccer playoffs were exempt from fines.

Dad shook his head and spoke softly to me. "I'm afraid Tully's pretty deep in his cups tonight," he sighed.

"What got Tully drinking?"

"Oh, today's the anniversary of Maggie's death. Always a hard day for him, poor lad." Maggie had been Tully's wife. They were expecting a baby when she'd discovered her leukemia. He had lost her and their unborn child the year before I was born. I'd been the recipient of Tully's adoration my whole life, inheriting all of the love he'd had for his own wife and child. Tully's tender heart, it seemed, had never completely healed. Dad and Alice had long ago refused to serve Tully anything but coffee, but the other bars in the neighborhood did not have the same arrangement.

Dad clicked his tongue. "Came in tonight with a snootful, hiding a bottle in one of those big pockets of his. Won't give it up. Better he should tie it on here than be out in the streets."

"We didn't have the heart to send him home," Alice added. "He'd feel too bad tomorrow if he missed your celebration."

Mary K stood up and stepped toward Tully at the bar. She pulled a twenty from her pocket, setting it on the bar. "Here you go. I'm feeling pretty good tonight, so the cussing is on me. Knock yourself out."

"Oh Lord," Alice moaned. "No telling what he'll say when it's paid for. I'll put a fresh pot of coffee on, and a Glenfiddich for you, Katie?"

"Sounds great. But only one, then it's coffee for me. I've got a double shift in the ER tomorrow."

Mary K and I sat at the family table while various friends and regulars came by to congratulate us. Dad slid in beside me, Dr. Schwartz across from him.

Tully sloshed his way over to the table and plopped limply in beside Mary K. His eyelids were at half-mast. "Sorry about the dyke comment, there. Alice told me that was inna—innapro—Well, it was rude, now, wasn't it?"

"No harm done," Mary K said. "Say something bad about my Mets and I'll have to slug you, though."

Tully's head swayed on top of his skinny neck. "I just don't get it though. Pretty girl like you. Could have any fella you want."

Mary K grinned at me and patted Tully's shoulder. "That's pretty much what my dad said. Difference is he said it with his boot planted against my butt while he kicked me out."

"Such a pity," Dr. Schwartz said. "It's his loss and our gain, darling."

Mary K gazed across the table to my dad. Her eyes glistened. "Thank you for including me tonight, Mr. Murphy."

Dad blushed. "Oh, go on then. You've become like a second daughter to me, Mary Louise Kowalski."

"Anybody but you called me that, they'd be saying good-bye to their teeth."

Dad pulled his hanky from his pocket and blew his nose with a great honk.

"Train's in," Tully said, raising his coffee mug.

"All aboard!" came the chorus from the bar.

Dad smiled and put his hanky back in his pocket. "Ah, what we won't put up with from family. This here is a patchwork family made of orphans and misfits of all sorts. You're one of us by now, I suppose." Dad nodded toward Tully. "We're a little like the mafia, though. Once you're in, we never let you go."

"Good to know," Mary K said, then sipped her club soda.

Tully lifted his head though his eyes remained closed. "I just don't get it. How is it a pretty girl like you don't like boys?"

Alice stepped to our table carrying a coffee pot. "Ah, shut yer yap, will you? The way you smelly brutes behave sometimes, it's amazing that the species has survived at all. Mary K, I might just have been better off if I was more like you. None of my four husbands was worth his weight in kitty litter."

Tully's head seemed suddenly too heavy to hold up, and it fell to the table with a thud. Alice placed a folded towel under his head. Soon his gravelly snore prompted chuckles. Alice patted his back. "They're so adorable when they're sleeping."

Everyone coaxed stories from Mary K and me about our upcoming positions. They delighted in the details of the kinds of surgeries I'd get to perform, gasped at stories of children with injuries and birth defects. Mary K talked of the newest innovations in liver transplants, to everyone's stunned amazement—none more than Dr. Schwartz. He held up his gnarled, trembling hands. "Oh, what I wouldn't give to be starting out today."

Alice filled my coffee cup. "So when do you girls start your new jobs?"

I took in the rich coffee aroma and looked over at Mary K. "I've got a few more days in my last rotation in the ER," I said. "I'm taking a few weeks off before I start in pediatrics. Never had a vacation."

The conversation meandered until Dr. Schwartz started to make moves toward leaving. He stood between Mary K and me, his curved body hunched over his cane. "Your mother would be so proud, Katherine."

Tully lifted his head and took a slow glance around the table. "Yup, that's the truest words you ever spoke, Ivan." Soon Tully's face scrunched, looking like a crumpled brown bag. He tried to fight tears, but they squeezed from the corners of his wrinkled eyes. "Poor Elyse. Poor Elyse," he wailed hoarsely. He wiped his nose on his sleeve.

13

"All right then, sad sack," Alice said, helping Tully up. "Doesn't a weepy drunk just break your heart?" She appeared like Dorothy, trying to help a limp scarecrow to his feet. "Let's let him sleep it off, shall we?"

My dad scooted out of the booth and tucked his shoulder under Tully's arm. "Come along. There's a cot in the storage room with your name on it."

Suddenly, Tully broke away from Dad and leaned in toward me. His breath reeked of whiskey. Tears streamed down his weathered cheeks. "If Elyse woulda known how great you'd turn out, being a doctor and all, I'm just sure she wouldn'ta taken all of them pills. It's a sorry shame." Tully crumbled and went to his knees, sobbing.

Alice's hand flew to her mouth and her eyes got wide.

"Tully!" Dad nearly yelled, his nostrils flaring, "Just shut your drunken mouth. We've had enough of your palaver for tonight." With a newfound force, Dad took Tully's entire weight and began to drag him away from the table.

Tully shouted over Dad's shoulder. "No, Katie. Elyse shouldn'ta done it. All them pills. She shouldn'ta—"

The stunned faces around the table made me feel hollow inside.

"Never mind Tully," Alice said to me with panic in her eyes. "You know how he is when he's been drinking."

As my dad dragged him away, Tully continued his lament. "Poor Elyse. Poor little Elyse. She shouldn'ta done it, Angus."

Alice and Dr. Schwartz's stunned faces showed that Tully's words were more than drunken blubbering. Mary K's face wore every question that ran through my mind.

When Dad reappeared beside the family table he looked exhausted and defeated. "Kitten," he whispered. I looked up into his soft face, his gray eyes reddened with tears.

My heart turned to lead in my chest, weighted down by the twenty-year-old secret.

"A weak heart," I said. "Mother died of a weak heart. She was fragile. That's what I've always been told." I stared into my dad's eyes, then looked to Alice, who sat with her fingers over her lips. Dr. Schwartz shook his head. Mary K sat in rare stunned silence. "So, is that the truth, Dad? Was it her heart? Or is Tully telling a family secret that everyone but me seems to know?"

Every muscle in my dad's face went slack, and if I hadn't known better, I'd have thought he'd had a stroke. He wiped his lips. I could hear his tight swallow. "Katie, we never meant to—"

The scientist in me wanted to pummel him with questions, probe for details of my mother's death. How did she do it? Why? And I wanted to know about the lie—the conspiracy of lies that had taken place my whole life—that wove a tapestry of myth around all I knew about my mother. But something else took over, overpowering my body, clouding my mind. All I could think of in that instant was escaping. "Let me out of here. I can't breathe," I said, trying to push my way out of the booth.

My dad reached to grab my arm. "Sit down. Let's talk this out."

I jerked my arm away. "You lied to me! Twenty years you lied." The words felt like bullets shooting from my mouth.

Without looking back, I rammed my way through the front door, leaving it swinging in my wake. A cold wind pressed me down as I pounded up the hill, my breaths becoming foggy gusts in front of me. Before I was a block away, Mary K was beside me, her short legs keeping stride with mine. Saying nothing, she walked with me until we reached the front porch of our apartment building twelve blocks up the hill. A friendly bark came from inside, followed by the shrill ringing of the telephone.

Mary K pulled her keys from her pocket and opened the door. I stood on the street below our steps, feeling like a statue—lifeless and stiff. Icy wind whipped my hair around my face and I realized for the first time that I'd left without my coat. My stomach clenched with each ring of the telephone.

"I'm not answering that," I growled.

"Nobody says you have to."

I stared down the hill at the street I'd walked my whole life. Lights glowed from the windows of familiar houses. The N-Judah streetcar snaked its way up Irving Street. But none of it appeared as it usually did. I looked up at Mary K. "Nothing. We're saying nothing about this outside this house."

"Sure, Murphy. Whatever you say."

I felt I was no longer solid, but porous and permeable to the wind. I looked up from the street to Mary K and then down at my watch.

Mary K lifted her hand, Girl Scout-style. "Let's go inside. I'm freezing my ass off here on the stoop and I kind of like my ass the way it is. I've got a beautiful sociology student coming over, and she likes it there, too." Mary K jerked her head in the direction of the door.

I looked down at my watch. "I'm meeting Nigel for drinks," I lied.

"Thought you weren't drinking. Double shift tomorrow?"

I glared up at her. Hot anger was beginning to thaw me. "Just go worry about your coed. I'm a big girl."

"It's your hangover," she said, stepping into the door. She pulled a bulky jacket from the hook just inside and tossed it down. The phone resumed its relentless shrill. I turned and walked toward the streetcar, not sure where I'd let it take me.

Anatomical Distractions

By the time I rose and moved toward the kitchen, Mary K was sitting on the back deck smoking a cigarette. She was not yet wearing her contacts, and the lenses of her glasses were so thick that it seemed impossible that her turned-up nose could support them. The words on her favorite sleeping shirt had faded but remained legible: IT'S A BLACK THANG. YOU JUST WOULDN'T UNDERSTAND.

Watching her, I recalled the first time we met. Dad, Alice, and Tully had just left me alone after I'd insisted I didn't need them to set up my dorm room. I sat in the middle of the room surrounded by boxes, trying it all on, grateful for my fresh start. I wouldn't be little Katie Murphy, the dutiful daughter everybody knew from Murphy's Pub. I was a Stanford pre-med student, a future physician, on a full academic scholarship. I'd be seen as just myself, not narrowed by people seeing me as little Katie Murphy.

I set my boxes in the middle of the dorm room, figuring I should probably wait for my roommate so we could discuss our preferences.

Her sandaled foot entered first, kicking the dorm room door open. A box covered her face and she wore an army surplus rucksack that probably outweighed her. The door flew open too hard and swung back, trapping her freckled, clean-shaven calf. "Fuck! Fuck! Fuck!" she ranted. I instantly calculated six dollars for the cussing jar.

I jumped and held the door.

"Fuck me sideways, that hurt," she said, swooping a strand of strawberry blonde hair behind her ear. Her hair was sleek and shiny—Breck Girl hair. Her eyes were robin's egg blue: one pure color, without flecks or shadows.

"Hey," she said. "I'm Mary K—not like the fucking cosmetics lady with the pink Cadillacs. K is for Kowalski. I guess we're roommates." She looked around the room and stared at my stack of liquor boxes, poised exactly dead center in the room. A knowing grin crossed her face. After dropping the box and letting the rucksack slide to the floor, she extended a hand toward me. I'd never shaken hands with someone my own age, so I froze. She thrust her hand a little closer. "Mary K—and you are?"

"Katie. I mean, Kate Murphy."

"Murphy." She delivered a hearty handshake. Her eyes were rimmed with thick but nearly transparent eyelashes that gave her pretty face an otherworldly look. She wore no makeup, and every visible portion of her was splattered with constellations of golden freckles. She stood not quite five feet and her body swam in oversized overalls, the cuffs rolled up to her calves.

"So," she said, "we've got to get one thing straight before we unpack. I'm going to ask you a question, and depending on the answer, one of us might have to go to the RA for a room change."

Did she already dislike me? How could she know already

that I was such a foreigner to this life? That I'd never flown in an airplane or seen a rock concert. That I was too nerdy and peculiar to have friends in school, that I'd never eaten at a restaurant with linen tablecloths until Dr. Schwartz took me to Alioto's on Fisherman's Wharf for a graduation present. That I'd never kissed a guy.

Her stare was cool steel. "Pre-med or pre-law?" She tapped her foot with impatience.

"Uh, pre-med."

"Thank *God*," she said, her body softening. Mary K spoke with flattened vowels. The toughness of New York had stomped hard on all of her a's and o's. She unzipped her rucksack, pulled out a pack of Marlboros, shook the pack, and held it toward me, retracting it with my decline. She hoisted her petite frame up and sat on the windowsill, her feet resting on what would become her desk. She twisted her lips to the side and blew smoke toward the open window.

Without my willing them to, my eyes found their way to the ABSOLUTELY NO SMOKING IN THE DORMS sign on the back of the door.

A sly grin crossed Mary K's lips. "No way I could bunk with the enemy. Christ, in New York you can't swing a fucking dead cat without hitting a lawyer in the ass. Didn't come three thousand miles to share a room with a lawyer fetus."

As I hung my clothes, I tried to sound casual as I tried to get to know her. "Do you come from a big family?"

She talked about her four brothers, her dad, a garbageman, and her mom, a housewife.

"Are you close?" I asked.

Mary K's head tilted as she selected her words. "I was not exactly a good match for Lila and Henry Kowalski of Queens. Queer doesn't play so well in a Polish Catholic family. They got the priest to try and fix me. I didn't fix so easy, I guess. They

19

pretty much don't want to know anything about me or my life. Unless I come to my senses and decide to love dick."

Her candor both intrigued and unnerved me.

"Babies should be conceived in petri dishes and raised under laboratory conditions until they're eighteen. Then parents and kids would have a mutual say in who they'll share holidays with for the rest of their lives. It'd put shrinks out of business."

"And eliminate stretch marks," I said.

Mary K let out the first bark of the raspy laugh I would come to love. She blew a smoke ring, then pierced it with a stream of straight-blown smoke. "Murphy, you and I will get along just fine."

From the only box she brought, Mary K unpacked a Mets pennant, a transistor radio, a large black ashtray that read THE BUTTS STOP HERE, ATLANTIC CITY, and one framed picture. She planted a kiss onto the glass of the picture. "The man in my life," she said, and then turned it so I could see the photo of a salt-and-pepper-furred dog with legs so long they could have been transplanted from a donor moose onto a dog's body. "Ben Casey," she said, "Some crazy cross between a mastiff and a wolfhound. Shits bigger than you do. Smarter than any dog I've ever known, which is saying a lot. More devoted than any human I know, which doesn't say much at all. You got a dog?"

"No, just a series of stray cats my dad adopts."

"I favor dogs, but cats are cool, too. Any creature that doesn't have the capacity for speech."

I opened my small box of framed pictures. Staring at me from the stack was my mother's shining face and body swollen in late pregnancy—a picture I'd always loved. Alice had also framed a photo that had been taken at high school graduation: Dad with his arm around me, Alice, Tully, and Dr.

Schwartz circling us, pride beaming from all of their faces. My childhood collection of birds' eggs took its place on my shelf.

"Hey, Murphy, feel like getting around town a little? It's my first night in California and all I've seen is the San Jose Airport. I'll split the cab fare with you."

"Sure," I said, "but I've got a car." Cussing jar money had bought me a '66 Volkswagen Bug. Tully had painted it baby blue for me, and Alice had sewn slipcovers for the tattered front seats.

"Lucky me, a roommate with wheels. You cart my ass, I'll spring for gas." Mary K sat on her windowsill and reached into her knapsack. She unbuckled her overalls and slipped the bib down, then tugged the loose waistline down just below her hip, revealing a small patch of the unfreckled flesh of her thigh below her plaid boys' boxer shorts. I averted my eyes, trying to pay attention to making my bed, but at the edge of my vision I could see the syringe Mary K had pulled from her bag.

"Don't worry. I'm not chipping. It's only insulin."

"You're diabetic?"

"You're going to be top of the class, Murphy."

I tried to resist watching Mary K inject herself from the small vial she pulled from a thermos in her pack. I waited for a wince of pain as the needle entered her soft flesh. Her expression unchanged, she took a deeper drag off of her cigarette as she pressed the plunger. She exhaled a smoke stream and reattached her overall bib. "Say, Murphy, I'd appreciate it if this could be between us," she said, jutting her jaw toward the thermos. "It's not really the impression I want to give to the profs around here. People get weird about it. Maybe we could establish some, I don't know, roommate code of silence or something. I'm not much of a blabber, so your secrets are safe with me."

I shrugged, wishing I had a secret for Mary K to keep. "Sure. I understand. We all get a fresh start here, right?"

"True enough."

* * *

Mary K came back into our kitchen after snuffing her cigarette on the porch rail. The breakfast table that had for so long been cluttered with textbooks and medical journals was now clean but for *The New York Times* sports pages, a dish of jellied toast, and an ashtray full of cigarette butts.

"You look like hell. Not like you to be out so late on a school night, Murphy."

"Thanks. You're gorgeous, too," I said. I twisted my unruly swarm of hair into a knot. I perused the limited but orderly contents of our fridge. In the door compartment, insulin bottles, and in a clear jar of isopropyl alcohol floated several hypodermic needles.

One semester in the dorms trying to manage her sugar levels on the carbohydrate-laden cafeteria food was enough for Mary K. We found off-campus housing by the second semester. Over that first Christmas break, we retrieved Ben Casey from her sister's third-floor walk-up in New York and drove him to California in my Bug.

"Your folks called about a hundred times."

I focused on my fridge search.

From under the kitchen table, the now elderly Ben Casey huffed as he rose from beneath Mary K's feet to greet me. I rubbed his slack old jowls. "How are those hips today, huh, buddy?" He let out a little whimper. "Did you inject him yet? He looks pretty stiff this morning."

"We're both rigged up," Mary K said. "He got me up early with the wet-tongue alarm. Had a pretty rugged night." Ben's cold nose found the gap between my pajama waistband and my undershirt. The sound of a sweet soprano voice rang from the shower down the hall, singing "Crocodile Rock."

"Who's this morning's diva?" I asked.

"That would be the aptly named Melody, a lovely ingénue I met at The Lex. A sociology undergrad who wants to change the world. She certainly changed mine last night." Mary K took a long swig from her Mets coffee mug and twitched her eyebrows.

"Don't think you've ever sported a Melody. Am I right?"

"Nope. A personal first. Did have a Harmony once back in high school, though. Sort of seems like I'm balanced out now."

"Anything serious?"

Mary K cut a glance at me.

"Not for you. For her?"

"Melody's a LUG, out for a good time."

"LUG?"

"Jesus, Murphy. How many lesbian bars have I taken you to? LUG. Lesbian Until Graduation. She'll have her flings." Mary K pointed to herself. "*Moi.* Then she'll get an engagement ring for graduation, marry an accountant, get a split-level house in the burbs, and have two-point-five kids. End of story."

Finding a yogurt, I slid into the chair across from Mary K. "Thanks for the *Reader's Digest* version of the LUG life cycle."

Mary K's sun-freckled face broke into a sly grin. She licked her finger and turned the page. "And where were you until the wee hours?"

I shrugged and kept my eyes focused on the inside of my yogurt carton.

"I thought you decided to move on from Nigel Abbot for the fiftieth time."

Nigel and I had spent the whole evening talking about the hospital. I'd mentioned nothing about Tully's drunken announcement, instead welcoming the distraction. At the end of the evening, I'd decided I wasn't up to spending the night, so Nigel had driven me home. "Nigel's easy. Uncomplicated," I said.

"Boring. And if your face tells the story, he's also a bum lay. What was all that about not wanting to lead him on? Give the wrong impression?"

"Nigel is not a bum lay. Not that it's any of your business. Nigel helps me, you know, get some release now and then."

"God, Murphy. You make sex about as erotic as lancing a boil. Don't get me wrong. Nothing wrong with having a fuck buddy. But you come home looking shit-faced with remorse every time. You could use some genuine passion, you know? Some *wow*. Some *pow*. Some *oh-my-God*, even."

"Look, Kowalski, you've got a real grown-up woman, a brilliant, skilled physician, completely enamored of you, though I'm not sure quite why."

"Who, Barbie?"

"That would be Dr. Andra Littleton."

"Ha! You think some Texas beauty queen is the real deal?"

"When you're actually in love with the woman who's in your bed, or when there aren't four different misty-eyed coeds in a given season, I'll listen to your advice on relationships," I said, grabbing a bite of one of her pieces of toast. "Just please tell me I'm not going to have to field calls from a broken-hearted Melody."

Mary K was momentarily distracted by Ben, who plopped his giant head in her lap.

"You're lucky that Ben is such a poor judge of character," I said.

A smirk crossed Mary K's face. "Romance notwithstanding, I have a sterling character. Don't I, Dr. Casey?" Ben lifted his massive salt-and-peppered form from the floor, stood by Mary K's chair, and licked her face. His head was bigger than

Mary K's, and right at her eye level when she sat. "You know, you could ratchet the judgment quotient down a few notches. Since you're still all creamy from a guy you only tolerate for purposes of relief-fucking, I don't know that you've got lots of room here for moral superiority." She mashed her cigarette in the ashtray. "Let's face it. Despite our brilliant medical minds, both of us are completely fuck-tarded. You settle for the likes of the Nigel Abbot, the tofu of sexual passion, instead of having true love. I don't fall in love at all, even when the sex is mind-blowing." Mary K clicked her tongue. "And Miss Melody Truman was certainly mind-blowing. What she lacks in depth and complexity, she makes up for in enthusiasm and joint flexibility—"

"Spare me the details." I looked again at the plate of Mary K's half-eaten toast, glimmering with berry jelly. "What's with the breakfast of champions?"

"Little shaky. No big deal. Sugar levels dipped a bit. But good old Mr. Smuckers here is helping me out."

Upon closer examination, I could see her hands tremble as she held the paper. Her complexion was gray, and dark circles hung like shadows under her eyes. "How low?" I asked.

"Not to worry. It's cool."

Despite her rigorous dietary discipline, her recalcitrant pancreas still kept her sugar levels unpredictable.

"Wipe the worry off your puss, Murphy," she said. "This is just one more little turd float in my personal shit parade. It'll pass."

I reached for her hand. Feigning disgust, she jerked her hand back and wiped it on her shirt. "Hey, I know where those hands have been. And recently, too."

* * *

Near-blistering water poured over my head. I stood still in the steamy shower, trying to wash off the weariness of the night before. Tully's words raked through my brain and the look on my dad's face almost melted me. "Liars!" I said out loud.

I stood until the water began to grow cold. "All right," I shouted in surrender to whatever god reigned over water temperature. "I'm getting out, already!" I'd just turned the water off when I heard a crash and Ben Casey's chesty bark. With a towel flung around me, I ran toward the barking.

Mary K lay ashen on her bedroom floor, a toppled lamp on the rug beside her. I lifted her limp arm, trying to find a pulse. "Mary K!" I shouted. "I'm here. Wake up!" I couldn't find a pulse. Ben Casey let out a low, mournful moan. *Low. She said her sugar was low.* I grabbed the phone before I ran to the fridge. "Stay with her, Ben. I'll be right back." The stately dog lowered his massive head and licked Mary K's face. I returned with orange juice and lifted Mary K's head. Her lips were parted, her jaw slack. The juice I poured dribbled from the corner of her mouth. "Come on, Mary K. DRINK!" As she sipped, I fired our address to the 911 operator.

The ambulance arrived in five minutes, but it seemed like hours had passed.

"She's diabetic. Type 1," I instructed. Soon Mary K's body was on a gurney and they were wheeling her out the front door and into the ambulance.

I grabbed Mary K's emergency card from the desk drawer. "She wants to go to Oakland."

The EMT shook his head. "No way. UC's around the corner."

I thought of the promise I'd made so long ago. Going to the ER would be like taking out a billboard, announcing her condition to the whole hospital.

"SF General then," I barked.

The other EMT opened Mary K's eyelid and shined his pin light beam into her eye. "No time," he said.

"Look," the first EMT said, "we're working to get her stable, but she could go into diabetic coma. That could kill her. The faster we get her into the hospital, the better her chances."

I looked down at my friend, so small and still. "Okay, but I'm going with you."

"You can't go in the ambulance, Miss."

"I'm a doctor. I'm going with you."

The two boy-faced EMTs glanced at each other. One reached out and touched my forearm. "Why don't you get dressed and meet us at the hospital." I looked down to see the towel still wrapped around me.

As the ambulance pulled away, its siren screaming as it went, Ben Casey nudged my hip with his great snout and let out a soft whine.

* * *

From the nurse's station in ICU, I could see into Mary K's room. She lay there looking like Goldilocks in Papa Bear's bed, her face toward the window.

I felt a hand on my shoulder. Andra's eyes were moist, green pools. "How's she doing?"

I sniffed. "Stable. Better than this morning, but it was dicey for a few hours."

"That's good."

"Managed to avoid slipping into a coma. Barely." I'd calculated and recalculated the seconds I'd delayed the ambulance, trying to protect Mary K's secret. It all seemed so foolish now. "So I suppose the news is all over the hospital."

"Like a fire in a hayloft."

"She'll hate that."

Andra gave me a reassuring pat on the forearm. "Let me know if she needs anything."

"You're not going to see her?"

Andra shook her head. "I'm the last person she wants to see right now."

"I'm afraid that line forms right behind me."

After Andra left, I eased my way into Mary K's room. "Hi."

The head of her bed was raised and an untouched tray of food sat on the table in front of her.

"Looks like they're treating you all right."

"Yeah, well. It's a class joint. Any kind of gray vegetable you want." She turned her face back toward the viewless window.

I resisted evaluating the readings of the monitors and instead sat in the visitor's chair.

"Ben okay?" she asked, her voice flat.

"Yeah, Mrs. Koblenz is watching him. Ben's the one that let me know you'd passed out. Probably saved your life."

Mary K gave a small nod. "For about the thousandth time." She coughed and cleared her throat.

"Thirsty?"

"I've got enough fucking nurses. Go home. Take care of my dog."

I fought back tears. "I tried to get them to take you to Oakland, but there wasn't time."

"I'd have fucking died on the Bay Bridge. That would have been a shit-for-brains medical decision."

I sat not knowing whether she was grateful to me or furious. "So now you can go to a doctor on this side of the bay. That'll make things more convenient."

Mary K turned to me, piercing me with an icy stare. "Look, Murphy. I'm not quite ready for your silver lining theories. You got your wallop last night. I got mine today. Life's just a series of nasty crap you've got to deal with and a few pleasant distractions to make you forget and that's as good as it gets. Once I'm out of this bed I'll go through the necessary arrangements to decline my residency here and take the one I was offered in forensic pathology with the coroner's office."

My head was full of buzzing bees. "Wait a minute. You applied for a residency with the coroner?"

"Needed a backup plan. Besides, you know how excited I get around a corpse."

Her words were a sock in my stomach. "Autopsies? You want to do autopsies and tissue scans? With those hands and that mind?"

With a sudden burst Mary K slammed her fist against her table. "Fuck!" She held out her quivering hand, palm down. IV tubes dangled like tendrils. "Would you want me to do a liver transplant on your dad on a bad sugar day, Murphy? Would you? I've been kidding myself. Jesus, you act like I have all the choices you do. I fucking don't, okay?"

Mary K had spent years creating the illusion that nothing at all was wrong with her, so much so that I'd almost come to believe it. I knew what becoming a surgeon meant to me; it had been the focus of all of my energy for so many years. The thought of losing it was too painful to fathom. It was a dream that we had shared for so long. I wanted it almost as much for her as I did for myself.

"Wipe the pity puss, Murphy. Or I swear to God I'll slug it off you."

I swallowed and tried to erase whatever on my face was betraying my thoughts.

The ICU nurse came into the room at a run. "Everything okay in here?"

"Fine," Mary K barked back at her. Cora was a seasoned nurse we'd both met during rotations. She had the tact and good sense not to fawn over Mary K. She checked Mary K's IV lines. "Look, you need to stay calm. You're stable and we're about to transfer you out to the floor. But you still need rest."

"I'm not going to the floor. When I go out of here, I go home."

Cora put her hands on her hips. "We'll just have to talk to your doctor about that."

"I'm my doctor. What do you think of that?"

Cora looked back at me with a smirk. Leaving the room, she said, "Five minutes."

"Do not talk, Murphy. Just do not talk to me."

"But, I'm so sor—"

Mary K shot a glare at me that scalded my skin. She drew ragged breath. "So, did you call your dad?"

I tried to mimic the heat of her searing look. She didn't flinch. "Best defense is a good offense, right?"

"I know it's shitty finding things out the way you did, but what the fuck do you expect? They should tell an eight-year-old her mom croaked herself?"

My mouth suddenly tasted sour. "They lied."

"Everybody lies, Murphy. Either by saying shit or by not saying shit. People lie. That's why I prefer dogs."

"Whose side are you on?"

"I'm Switzerland. Look at me. About the only thing I know is that life's short. Quit acting like a baby. Talk to your folks. They're going crazy."

Just then a young hospital volunteer, probably a high school student doing her community service project, brought in a bouquet of Get Well Soon balloons. With a broad smile and a voice right out of a Disney cartoon, she said, "The tag says they're from the entire intern group."

Mary K's lips pressed together and her eyes narrowed. "Get that shit out of here."

The young volunteer blinked in confusion. "But they're for you, and balloons are okay in ICU. No flowers because of allergies, but—"

"Get—Them—Out."

Balloons bobbing behind her, the volunteer made a hasty exit. Just as I was about to tell her what an ass she was, I spied tears spilling down Mary K's cheeks. She quickly wiped them away with the shoulder of her hospital gown.

It was the first time I'd ever seen her cry. I wanted to hold her, tell her it would all be okay. We'd talk about things— think through all of her options. Make a new plan.

"Out," she whispered, before she resumed staring toward the window.

I began to object, but I knew I had to leave her alone for a while. In the mood she was in, I could see her jumping out of the bed and slapping me senseless.

Unlikely Pairings

I first saw his name on a chart in the spring of 1988: Jacob Bloom. Healthy, thirty-six, and in the ER because a shard of flagstone had hit him in the face and the lens of his glasses had shattered into his eye.

My patient lay flat on an exam table, a bloodstained towel and icepack over his right eye, his other eye closed. A small radio rested on his chest; the wires went to his ears, and his paint-dappled Topsiders swayed with a rhythm I could hear only as a pulsing buzz. His left hand fingered the neck of an air guitar.

I cleared my throat. He looked up at me, his one-eyed gaze lingering somewhere near my lips. He tugged at the cords of his headphones. His mouth widened into a soft grin.

"So, Mr. Bloom, I see you've injured your eye," I said, lowering the bloody towel.

"Wow, Doc, you're really good."

"As a matter of fact, I am," I said, examining the deep gouge under his thick, dark brow. I dismissed his mild flirtation and maintained my focus, trying to ignore his beguiling smile. His eye was filled with blood, and the socket was bruised, not broken.

I applied anesthetic drops and removed a sliver of glass lodged in the corner of his eyelid, then stitched his brow. The glass had nicked his eyeball just millimeters from his cornea.

"See, I'm an artist," he explained with a note of silliness. "And I was a little short on red paint. Inspiration was with me, and well—"

Flirtation felt uncomfortable, like a stiff new pair of jeans. "Human blood, particularly your own, seems a poor paint substitute, Mr. Bloom, if only because of its limited quantity and the obvious outcome of over-use."

"Ah yes, but it causes you to meet such interesting people."

* * *

Two days later, well after dark, I was heading home after a grueling shift in the ER. These were my last days as an intern, and I was distracted with thoughts about what would come next. I stuffed my stethoscope into my lab coat pocket and fumbled for my keys. My Beetle sat like a chariot, waiting for me in the amber glow of the parking garage lights. Icy wind sliced through the garage. I pulled my mother's Irish wool, cable-knit sweater up around my neck. On her it had hung so loosely she'd rolled the sleeves. On me the fit was snug, and the sleeves barely made it to my wrists. Though it had grown tattered with the years, wearing it made me feel close to her, and I couldn't let it go. Cold bit through the thinning yarn.

"Ahoy, Matey," a voice came from behind me.

His wiry silhouette and the dark shadow of his eye patch were all I could see, but I knew instantly that it was Jake Bloom.

"Mr. Bloom, you're looking better than the last time I saw you."

He continued in his pirate voice. "This here ship's got a mighty fine sawbones."

"I hope you've seen your doctor for a follow-up, Mr. Bloom."

"Doctuhs..." he said, now in a comical Yiddish accent. "Have I seen *doctuhs*? I'm filthy with *doctuhs*."

After an especially rugged day in the ER, his playfulness was a balm. "No infection? No problems?"

"Nah, you did a great job," he said, sincerity returning to his natural voice. "Vision's fine—as good as it was before, anyway. I'll come out of this with just a small, manly scar adding character to an otherwise boring face."

His face, dark and expressive, was anything but boring. It was a face that seemed somehow to have more moving parts than most, with twitches and grimaces that formed expressions, instantly animating his every thought.

"Good to hear it, Mr. Bloom. You got lucky." I found my key and readied it for the car door.

"I don't believe in luck. And it's Jake. Mr. Bloom is my father." He feigned a shiver. His unpatched eye found my nametag and he squinted. "K. Murphy, M.D. K? Hmm?"

"Katherine," I surrendered.

"I might've known. Katherine, Kate, Katie. Anything but Kathy." He studied my face. "Fair skin. Dark hair. Irish surname. No, you've never been a Kathy. I'll have to decide what to call you after I know you better."

My face betrayed me again, smiling against my will. Those stiff jeans were beginning to feel more comfortable.

"So, Katherine, Katie, Kate. What are the chances of the beautiful doctor accompanying a one-eyed idiot for some midnight pizza and beer?"

"Really, you shouldn't drink with the medication—"

"I've been off the meds since day one. Brought me down." His face was gentle and inviting. "Besides, nothing says thanks to the doctor who saved your vision like brewed hops and processed carbohydrates topped with animal byproducts."

His eyebrows twitched and his smile gave him a hopeful, eager expression.

A part of me felt cautious—was he just a flirt? A player? There were plenty of those among the doctors and interns. But this felt different, like it wasn't rehearsed or something he did with any woman he met. I was flattered. "Sure," I surrendered. "I didn't get dinner. Pizza would be great."

The Front Room was the hangout for UC med students, not because the food was especially good, but because it was nearby and open late and the beer was cheap. Red and white plastic tablecloths and Chianti bottles cloaked in wax drippings donned each table. Kitschy rubber grapes dangled from the ceiling, and Frank Sinatra posters hung from imitation wood paneling.

After nine on a Sunday night, the place still housed clusters of med students, all wearing scrubs; their way of telling the world they were on the way to becoming "M-Deities," as Mary K called them. We sat in a windowed booth. Mario Lanza sang in the background.

"So, I could ask all the usual stuff," Jake said. "But then you'd have a boring story to tell our grandchildren."

His presumptuousness both irritated me and made my body hum.

When the menu came, Jake pulled a mangled pair of wire-rimmed glasses from his shirt pocket that had an empty lens on the side that covered his patched eye. "First confession of my many flaws," he said. "I'm blind as a bat. Now I'm blind as a one-eyed bat." He looked up at the waiter. "You know what to do."

The waiter nodded and stepped away.

"You're trusting the waiter in this place?" I whispered. "They're used to groups of drunk med students in here."

"It's all taken care of." He grinned. "It seems you're not used

36

to being pampered." I couldn't decide if he was suave or just arrogant.

I picked wax off the Chianti bottle. "This is pampering?"

"A little faith, Dr. Murphy."

"So, what do you do?" I asked. "Are you really an artist, or is that just another of your multiple personalities?"

"All right," he said and leaned back in his chair. "I guess we're going to do the boring first-date stuff after all."

"Who said this was a date?"

"You knew it was a date or you wouldn't be here."

It happened again, that feeling of being caught. He was arrogant, but also self-effacing; cocky, yet wholly vulnerable.

Just then, two plates arrived. In front of me was a delicately thin mini pizza topped with butter-browned scallops, goat cheese, pine nuts, and fresh basil, with a bright yellow nasturtium blossom in the center. Jake's pizza was equally beautiful, with curled pink shrimp sitting atop a spiral of ruby red, roasted tomatoes. The waiter uncorked a bottle of Pinot Grigio and poured two glasses.

I stared at Jake, who wore a smirk. "This is not standard Front Room fare. What, did you hire a chef?"

"In a manner of speaking. Taste it."

I bit into a slice and the rich flavors filled my mouth; the scent of basil was hypnotic.

"And?" Jake looked at me like a puppy awaiting a well-deserved treat.

I took another bite. All I could do was groan.

"I take it you like?"

I opened my eyes, not even aware that I'd closed them, and wiped my lips. "I want the name of your chef."

Jake held out his hand. "Jake Bloom. At your pleasure."

"You?"

"Hey, I brought the good groceries. Tipped the cooks. And *voilà*! They let me play in their sandbox."

"All assuming that I'd agree to come here with you. And what if I'd declined your invitation?"

"Then I'd be sitting here all alone with this great food, weeping into my wine glass. Here," he said, holding up a slice of his pizza. "You have to try this one, too."

I took a scrumptious bite from the slice he held before me. "So?" he asked.

I didn't want him to know I had become entranced, but, though I tried, I was unable to act nonchalant. Being with Jake was unlike any first date I'd ever had, though confessedly my experience was limited. Jake was relentless with his questions throughout the dinner. He wanted to understand me, my thoughts, my life, to know about everyone in my life who loved me. He reached across the table with ease, helping himself to morsels from my plate like we'd known each other for years. He probed until I told all about growing up in San Francisco in my dad's pub, and about the motley family that raised me.

"And your mom?" he asked.

The story I usually told about my mother now had an apocryphal addition, as of a few days before. I'd called my dad to tell him that I needed a break from the pub crowd—some time to sort things out—and I hadn't spoken to him since. "She died when I was little."

Jake stopped chewing and stared at me. "And?"

"What and? There's no *and*."

"Your face says there's an *and*." He wiped his lips with his napkin and tilted his head to one side. "Your words are so— careful. But your face, it shows everything. This isn't old pain. This is a fresher wound."

Suddenly, I felt like I didn't have enough clothes on. I pulled my mom's sweater across my chest.

"We orphans have a way of finding one another, don't you think?"

I'd never thought of myself as an orphan. With so many surrogates who had stepped in after my mother died, a shortage of parental figures had never been a problem. But when I thought about Mary K—my closest friend—we were orphans of sorts, even though her parents were all alive.

"And you?" I asked diverting his inquiry. "How is it that you are an orphan?"

"Oh, now that's a tragic tale. Broken home." He looked up and gave a theatrical sniff and wiped an invisible tear. "Parents divorced when I was three. I grew up with my father. At least, in his custody, accompanied by a parade of stepmothers, each younger than her predecessor. I left home when I was seventeen and the stepmother *du jour* was twenty-three. Figured it was only a matter of time before I passed them up. My mother left when I was small. Died when I was in boarding school. One of my old nannies called to tell me about it. My father... well, now there are not really words to describe him, though many have tried." Jake looked up at me and shrugged. "I believe more in family of choice than family by blood. My dad and I settled into an acceptable distance after a blow-up of biblical proportions. Family is me and Burt for the last ten years. Burt Swift. Great man. Aussie swagger on the outside, pussycat at heart. Brother by choice and partner in crime."

"Yeah, Mary K, my housemate, is like that for me, I guess."

"Is she a doctor, too?"

"Yeah. We've been friends since our undergraduate freshman year. She'll be doing a residency in—" I stopped myself.

Jake stopped eating again and looked into my eyes. "Another fresh wound?"

Before I knew it, I was telling him all about Mary K's diabetes and her decision to decline her residency in transplant.

"She's home from the hospital now. Like it never happened. Won't accept any care at all. But that's Mary K." I struggled for words to define my prickly, affection-intolerant friend. "She's sort of a paradox."

Our conversation drifted, weaving easily between topics of music and art, politics and medicine, and though I was enjoying it, images of one of my ER patients from earlier that day kept popping into my mind.

"What is it?" Jake asked. "Something is troubling you."

I shrugged, trying to appear casual. "Just a little tired, I guess. I had a patient that really got to me today. It happens."

Jake's face was an invitation. "Tell me about today."

The restaurant had nearly cleared, but for a few lingering students sharing a pitcher of beer at the bar.

"An ambulance brought in an unconscious woman, probably a prostitute, found tossed out of a car alongside the 101 freeway. SF General was overloaded, so they brought her to us. She'd been stabbed, her face and throat slashed. We're not a trauma unit, but the EMTs didn't think she'd make it to General. Everyone worked hard on her, but she arrested and we couldn't save her."

Jake's hand rose to his throat and his forehead creased. He seemed to feel the slashes in his own flesh as I spoke.

"Look," I said. "Maybe I shouldn't be telling you this. ER is pretty grisly stuff. I'm around doctors all day. They're thick-skinned and—"

He shook his head. "No, no. Tell me about her. Give me the whole picture. I'm trying to see her."

I hesitated, but his expression compelled me to say more. "She came in with a blood pressure of—"

"No," he whispered. "Not her *medical* picture. Tell me about *her*. Tell me about what you felt trying to help her. I'm trying to imagine doing what you do."

Looking into his open face, telling Jake about this patient felt natural. I'd seen many deaths since starting med school. I kept thinking I'd get used to it. Everyone else seemed to. "She was tiny. Maybe a hundred pounds. Looked about eighteen. She came in as a Jane Doe, so I don't even know her name. I just hope—"

"That she didn't know what had been done to her?"

How had he done it? Finished a sentence I'd barely begun—a thought I'd barely let myself think. My throat tightened.

Jake pulled details from me: the mocha color and buttery texture of her skin; the graceful curve of her shoulder; her lavender nail polish and silver angel ankle bracelet; the Hello Kitty necklace that was covered in her blood.

My medical cohorts had offered their obligatory words of comfort for losing a patient—*best you could do, must've been her time, can't save 'em all.* They'd mouthed sympathies, then quickly changed the topic.

Jake wore the loss of my Jane Doe; it was etched on his face. "Her pain is over now," he said. "It will stay with you a while, I know. Now you're the keeper of the last memory of her."

This simple statement caused me to tear up. Silence lingered between us, not uncomfortably, but like a pleasant fragrance. Unlike my colleagues, Jake cracked no joke to break the tension, didn't change the subject or offer saccharine words of comfort. He simply grieved with me.

I wiped my eyes with my greasy napkin. "Not exactly sanitary."

He smiled kindly and I felt exposed for changing the mood so abruptly.

The waiter brought a tray with three different desserts. "Don't tell me you made these too," I said, grateful for the break.

"'Fraid not. Brought these from Lucca's. This would be cheesecake, chocolate torte with hazelnuts, and tiramisu. I'm guessing the chocolate is your pleasure." Though I said nothing, he smiled. "Chocolate it is."

It made no difference which I'd chosen because we both sank our forks, at will, into all three of the treats.

"So, you're finishing your internship soon. What's next?" he asked, taking a bite of creamy tiramisu.

"Yup, two more days. I'm taking a few weeks off for the first time in my life, and then I begin residency."

Jake froze with instant, unedited pain on his face. "You're not moving away to the Amazon or the Mayo Clinic or something? I don't think I could stand it if you broke my heart so soon."

Coming from anybody else, this intensity would have scared me off. But when I looked into Jake's eyes—or rather his eye—an electric surge coursed through my body. The surge passed between us and hummed distractingly between my legs. I gathered the remnants of my voice. "I'll be staying put at UCSF, pediatric surgical residency for the next five years of my life."

The creases between his brows smoothed, and he wore the face of one who'd just unraveled a mystery. "Right here up the hill from your dad's tavern?"

"Corny, huh? I guess I always pictured myself here."

Jake quieted my explanation with the touch of his hand on mine. "Pediatric surgery?" He fingered his eye patch. "I've been told by more than one person that I needed to grow up. And I needed a surgeon. I guess I lucked into the perfect doc, huh?"

"As long as there are dopes who don't wear safety goggles, surgeons will have job security." I wagged my finger at him.

He tucked my scolding finger gently back with its siblings,

then brought my hand toward his lips. His kiss was tender. "Something you gotta know about me, Kat, before you and I go any further. I always work without a net, whatever I do."

I had to look away, afraid my face would say more than I was ready to tell him. I was falling for this guy. Too soon. Too fast. So unlike myself. Something in me sensed that by falling for him, I was opening a part of myself—a tender, vulnerable part that was altogether new.

Impatient busboys, who'd already turned the chairs upside down onto tables, finally shooed us out. Jake slipped money into their hands as we left. We stood in the frigid night air in front of the restaurant at two in the morning. Our foggy breath hung in front of our faces.

Suddenly, Jake appeared agitated. "Damn!" he huffed, looking around in a panic. "I don't want to go, but—it's kind of weird, I sort of have something urgent I have to do right now."

I was glad that darkness hid my face. "Oh, hey. It's late," I stammered. "I've got work tomorrow—or, today. Thanks for the great food. Hope your eye heals quickly—"

He looked away from me as if his next words were to be found somewhere in the freezing darkness. In the blue light of the winter moon, Jake's profile was in contrast to the silver clouds of his breath. He searched the edges of my face and his fingers brushed my hair away. He looked at the night sky. "I *really* have to go," he said. Then, without another word, he bounded away like a deer frightened by a gunshot, leaving me to walk up the hill to get my car.

* * *

The next day I went through my shift in the ER and then to bed that night with an ache in my belly. I woke berating myself. It was just one stupid date—a diversion. I had my residency to look forward to—a coveted surgical residency at one of the country's leading hospitals. Everything I'd worked toward. Who needed a guy? Who needed some impetuous, flaky guy?

The following day I found myself grasping for the focus that usually came easily. Dad and Alice had both left me messages, and I'd returned their calls. But our conversations had a stiffness that had never been there before. While I knew they'd covered the truth of my mom's death to protect me, the newfound presence of deceit rankled me. Mary K and I saw little of each other because of our schedules. I found I was grateful for the solitude. What little sleep I got was filled with dreams that toggled between fitful and erotic. Whenever there was a lull in the ER, despite my resolve, thoughts of Jake spun webs around my mind.

With patients, I could concentrate. Crisis provides focus. Adrenaline moments upstage all else in the ER: hunger, pain, exhaustion, even passion. But when I was able to tell the wife of a patient that her husband had not had a heart attack, just a simple bout of indigestion, the look on her face made me want to tell Jake all about her. I made mental note of the crinkles at the corners of her eyes and the smell of bath powder when she hugged me in gratitude. Jake would want details.

The next day, my last as an intern, was set aside just to close out charts and tie up loose ends. I got off in the early afternoon. My coat was weak protection against the biting wind. I could not remember ever feeling that cold in San Francisco. Snow fell to a thousand feet and dusted Mt. Tam and Mt. Diablo.

On the hood of my Bug in the parking garage, blowing on his fingers, sat Jake.

"You look like a woman who could use an adventure," he said as I approached. The pleasure in his eyes was like a child's, full of a wonderful secret.

My fatigue vanished. "What? You're taking me to McDonald's for filet mignon and Baked Alaska?"

Until that second, I hadn't noticed his missing eye patch. His eye was still bruised, but his dark brow hid the black stitches I'd sewn. He wore wire-rimmed glasses that gave him a gentle, intellectual look.

Jake brought his fingers to my chin and tilted my face toward his own. He studied me, searching my brow, my hairline, the curve of my jaw, warming each part with his gaze. His forehead pleated, then smoothed. "Your face is even more fascinating in three dimensions."

My lips pulsed, anticipating the kiss I'd hoped for two nights before but only received in my dreams. He winked again, acknowledging he'd seen my *kiss-me* signal. "How about joining me? I've got my own wheels and both of my peepers."

I glanced around the lot.

"Come on. I know this is your last day. No excuses."

I climbed into his Valiant. While it was of similar vintage to my Volkswagen, the Valiant was pristine. Its idle was the soft purr of a kitten, whereas my Bug suffered conniptions seismic enough to remove your fillings.

We drove down Irving Street, toward Ocean Beach, listening to Bach on the radio. Without explanation, Jake pulled his car into a beachfront parking lot. Thick crowds milled around the beach. "I want you to see something," he said.

He pulled a down parka from his back seat and offered it to me. Stepping out of the car, I found myself following throngs of people who were gathering into crowds along the beach. My eyes watered from the wind and cold.

The first group formed a circle. I eased myself in among them, only to see a winding, ten-foot-round gully in the sand. Deep inside was a sculpted, circular river formed of a delicate web of icicles. Icicles—in San Francisco! Onlookers snapped photographs. They murmured and pointed, wearing wonder on their faces. Jake guided me on.

The next sculpture was a round pit dug deep into the sand. The sand started as pale, dry oatmeal on the surface and darkened to a rich mocha color toward the moist center of the hole. A bed of khaki green seaweed lay in the center, a tower built of icicles reaching ten feet high perched atop it. It appeared that it had somehow evolved naturally where it lay. Nature had complied with the artist. The mushroom-gray sky was a background, matte and unobtrusive. Temperatures and the icy beach wind allowed the frozen foreign elements to linger.

I moved down the beach, taking in each of five massive structures formed of natural elements unnaturally arranged. Thick slabs of ice rested on beds of pale beach rocks. Icicles adhered together at their bases formed giant, frozen, dandelion-like starbursts. Towers fashioned of driftwood and shards of ice were trimmed in white seabird feathers. I could barely breathe for how each piece moved me. They were at once whimsical and profound. Simple and perplexing.

At the far end of the beach, away from the observing crowds, sat a gigantic mound of snow. Kids squealed as they rode plastic saucers in crayon colors, thrilled at their unlikely day of sledding by the breaking surf. I'd been on this beach with my dad a thousand times and had never seen or even imagined ice or snow here.

Soon the sun slid down the sky and cast a ginger glow. Campfires blossomed around the beach, far enough away from the frozen sculptures that their melting wasn't hastened, but close enough to make the ice sparkle in the firelight.

We sat next to a small fire away from the crowd. Jake poured green tea from a thermos. In the distance the crack of crumbling icicles pierced the twilight and a moan of disappointment rose from the crowd. Jake smiled. Another crack of ice sounded, followed by another murmur. Inexplicably, an ache formed in my throat and my eyes swelled with warm tears. I seldom cried, and now I'd done it twice in front of Jake. "It's just so sad to see them fade," I said.

Jake wiped my eyes with the soft pad of his thumb. "Oh, but that's part of the whole thing. Their disappearance is as important as is their creation."

Until that instant, I'd assumed Jake had simply brought me to see this incredible exhibit. He had told me he was an artist, but it hadn't occurred to me that this was his installment. I'd pictured paints and canvases in a sloppy studio. Late rent checks and defaulted student loans. "*You* did these. All of this?"

"Well, it only seemed fair." Jake fingered the stitches on his brow. "I've seen your art. Now you've seen mine."

"Please tell me that you photographed them," I pleaded. "So that they're preserved."

"Oh they were photographed. That's what my buddy Burt does. He's a great photographer, and he'll publish them in a coffee table book or calendar or something. He's the entrepreneur who helps me to pay the bills. But photographs are only headstones for pieces that will be dead for me long before the film is developed."

"I'll never forget them."

"Ah, then the day was a success. They'll live forever because they've been witnessed and experienced." He paused. "Like your Jane Doe. That's the only permanence there is. People die. Stones crumble. Canvases decay. Photographs fade. But *experience* reverberates indefinitely."

After the sun went down, the crowd thinned to a few dog-walking couples. Jake and I sat by the last of the campfires while the sea crept in and stole the last remnants of his sculptures. The air became brittle around us, inviting us to sit dangerously close to the fire. He jumped up and retrieved a basket filled with bread, wine, and cheese from his car. "How did you do all of this?"

Jake could barely contain his energy as he explained that his work was about manipulating natural elements without intruding on their beauty. He talked of his nature sculptures in stone and leaves, sand and slate, ice and twigs. He'd spent years walking in remote parts of the world, from Tibet to Afghanistan, from Brazil to The Congo. His voice was pure energy, with not a hint of bragging; he was simply revealing himself. "Usually when I work with ice or snow, I do it where it stays cold. But I've wanted to do something in San Francisco for a while. I moved here to wait for the opportunity. I couldn't get the image of icicles near the Golden Gate out of my head. I like unlikely pairings. I've been waiting for a day cold enough that I thought it might work, so Burt loaded a crew into a helicopter and we went up to Yosemite to gather the elements. Hauled the ice and snow in a freezer truck. Cost a mint, but it was worth it."

He must've left for Yosemite straight from The Front Room. "When did you sleep?" He didn't look a bit tired.

"Sleep is highly overrated." He smiled and sipped his wine.

The silence between us was filled only with the pops from the fire. "I need to tell you something, Kat."

The nickname felt as if it had always been mine. I braced myself. I could no longer pretend he was just some guy. I suddenly had more to lose—now that I'd seen the genius of him.

"Everything changed because I met you." He read the questions forming on my face. "I've never had anyone else's eyes in mind when I constructed pieces before. Never. Ideas just come to me in dreams or when I see shapes or patterns." He pulled me close enough that I could feel the warmth of his breath on my skin. "But with these, I couldn't stop wondering what they'd look like to you. I can't imagine making another piece that you won't see."

We lingered there and I breathed in the salt of the sea,

watching the amber light on his face. Knowing him had changed my work, too. It was impossibly fast, what he felt. But then, I felt it, too. From that moment forward I would want to tell him about every patient, every stitch I sewed, every life and death I witnessed.

I must've nodded, though I can't say I remember it, because his lips found mine. It was nothing like a first kiss. It was more like the inevitable meeting of sea and shore.

"Please say you'll stay with me tonight," he whispered. His eyes were the color of river stones under crystal water; speckled gray and green, with flecks of gold. Sometimes the most luminous stones, when taken from their cool waters, turn out to be just gray rocks. Others glitter with a light of their own. You never know about river stones until you take them home. We walked to the car, the fading firelight behind us.

* * *

Jake's home, a warehouse in San Francisco on Brennan Street, was as unlikely as icicles on Ocean Beach. The graffiti-covered cinderblock exterior and corrugated metal doors disguised the enchantment to be found inside. The industrial elements of a warehouse—concrete floors, exposed pipes, metal catwalks, and cavernous spaces—still remained. The enormous single room was warmed by soft, golden light, though the source of this light was a mystery as I could see no actual fixtures.

What he'd created was so simple. The room was huge but divided into intimate spaces by the placement of sculptures: screens constructed of twigs, woven together so that they appeared constructed by Nature herself; a six-foot sphere formed of shards of gray slate; bougainvillea petals, fuchsia splashes on ebony black wood tabletops.

I trembled both from the cold of the day and from my tingling senses. Jake rolled up paper to light a fire; his breath brought the flame to life. We stood beside the hearth still bundled in our parkas, still wearing the sea. The copper warmth of the flames spilled over us. His kisses tasted of wine. His skin smelled of the salty beach. I lost myself in the textures of him: the stubble of his beard, his calloused hands, and his eyelashes against my cheek. As the room warmed, Jake removed my jacket, then my sweater. One by one we removed our garments, revealing ourselves to one another.

This wasn't like me. I hadn't showered since early morning, and I still wore my scrubs. I didn't have on my date underwear, only everyday cotton panties. I worried about my knobby knees, my appendectomy scar, and my ears that stuck out too far. Jake's beach sculptures and every article in his unimaginable home were things of exquisite beauty. My awkward, imperfect form didn't fit in with his exquisite objects of art.

"Don't hide," he whispered as he peeled the last of my clothes away. He cradled me and leaned me back onto a massive chocolate suede sofa. He unfolded my arms like they were the petals of a flower and laid me back, letting his gaze drift over me. "Just look at you."

I'd had moments in my life when I felt attractive, even pretty on rare occasions. But with Jake, I was beautiful. He lay on his side next to me. His fingers moved in long strokes, studying the contours of my body. I let my gaze follow down the line of his throat, further over the soft mounds of his chest and down to the dark nest of hair between his legs.

He lifted his head, startled by an idea. "Here. Close your eyes."

"What for?"

"Relax. Just close your eyes." His fingers moved over my eyelids. "Keep them closed." I kept my eyes closed as I listened to him move. Next to my breast, where his warm cheek had just been, I felt a weighty, radiating spot of coolness. "Relax.

Just go with it," he urged. As the icy intensity waned, another formed just below it. Then another, down my ribcage on the opposite side of my body. As each cold spot warmed, another one occurred, creating a curved line from my heart, across my torso, down my right thigh, and to my knee. I tried to imagine what Jake was doing. There were no ice cubes around us. No drips of moisture made trails on my body.

I was curious about what he was doing, but my body simply wanted to let go and enjoy the sensations. His sudden intake of breath cued me to open my eyes.

From the suede pillow where my head rested, I viewed the landscape of my own body, now adorned with a curved trail of smooth, black stones that Jake had taken from an earthen bowl. The stones followed the mounds and hollows of me in a winding path, drawing the eye from my heart down to my thighs. I held my breath, trying not to ruin what he'd created. Ebony stones against the white of my skin formed a river-like trail. Arranged from large to small, the stones descended my body. My skin warmed the stones, making them more a part of me. I'd never felt so feminine or so lovely.

"You see, Kat. There's no photograph. No permanent exhibit in a museum. But here you are... a work of art that will last forever."

I couldn't move for fear of ruining what he'd made. One by one, starting from my knee, Jake removed each stone. The warmth of his lips on my skin replaced each stone's weight until I no longer felt the loss of it. He set each one on the floor beside me, creating a perfect spiral. After he lifted the last and largest stone from above my beating heart, he entered me smoothly, silently. His body was not foreign to mine, but a missing part now found.

Immovable Object, Unstoppable Force

Jake and I were together every minute of the next four days. It was as if we'd discovered a new food and couldn't get enough of it. Our lovemaking was ravenous. Our meals took hours. We were insatiable in consuming everything about one another. He savored the details of my growing up in Murphy's Pub and reveled in the descriptions of my family there. When I told him about how I'd just learned about my mother's suicide, the pain of it registered instantly on Jake's face. For the first time, my anger gave way to grief. I wept for my mother's death. I wept for her sad life.

But Jake was not the only glutton. I gobbled the details of his adventurous life. The world travel, the art, the encounters with the cultured and the famous. The loneliness in his childhood—of being shuffled between nannies and shipped off to boarding schools where he went months at a time without family contact—became my loneliness.

I called my dad to let him know he wouldn't be able to reach me at home. When I called Mary K to check in and find out about her health, she told me to stop being her mother hen and asked nothing of my whereabouts—typical Mary K. But for these brief encounters, Jake and I might as well have been on our own planet. In four days, I didn't go home for a change of clothes, though most of our time was spent wearing nothing anyway.

"It's official, I have got to go home for underwear," I said one morning in the clean white light of Jake's bathroom. I pulled my only pair of panties off of the shower rod. "They didn't dry overnight. I can't wear damp underwear."

Jake wrapped himself around me and looked over my shoulder at our shared reflection in the steamy mirror. "I like you without underwear."

"That's a fine arrangement for when we're here, but—"

"Then let's never leave here. I can hold you hostage by keeping possession of your panties." He snatched my underwear from my hand.

"That's sounding a little kinky," I said, laughing. "Is there something about you I should know?" I looked into his reflection, expecting a continuation of our repartee. Jake's playful expression wilted. He pulled away from the mirror and went into the bedroom. When I followed him, he was tucking his wallet into his pocket and gathering his keys.

His crushed look frightened me a little. "Jake, did I insult you?"

But when he looked up, I could see that the boyish mischief had returned to his face. "You just wait right here. I've got some shopping to do."

"But—"

"Ah, ah, ah," he scolded. "I'll hear no objections from a woman wearing no underwear."

He was out the door before I could say another word.

$*\ *\ *$

"Well, look what the storm blew in," Mary K said as she eased into our kitchen. "Just about filed a missing persons report."

"How you feeling?"

"You can stop with the health inquiry already," Mary K grumbled. "Is that actual cooking I see you doing?"

"I felt inspired."

Mary K swung a slow circle around me, her eyes fixed on me. "What's with the fashionable duds? Do my eyes deceive me, or is that an actual label I see on those jeans? And let's see, that fitted shirt is not from the Katherine A. Murphy Rainbow of T-shirts Collection. And are those actual boots? What? No tennies? No clogs?"

I looked into the skillet, suppressing my smile. "I felt like a change."

"'Bout time. Man, you look great."

The truth was that when Jake came back to his loft, he'd brought a dozen string-handled bags from stores I'd seen only from the outside: Saks, Neiman Marcus, and boutiques I'd never even heard of. The bags were filled with finely made slacks, tasteful, feminine lingerie, shoes, even dresses, none of which I'd have ever bought, but I loved each item. Everything he'd chosen fit perfectly, though he'd left with no information about my sizes. Now, standing in my own kitchen and wearing new clothes, I felt stylish, but still comfortable and natural—wholly myself.

Ben Casey sniffed the air, full of the aroma of mushrooms and onions. Mary K hadn't been apart from him in weeks, even sneaking him into the hospital doctor's lounge with her during her shifts. It required a complex conspiracy to keep a dog of that size hidden, but Ben engendered that kind of loyalty. He greeted me with a cold nose on the soft skin near my elbow.

Wind slapped branches and threw rain against the windows of the old Victorian. Though it was late in the afternoon, the room was darkened by the storm outside. A flash of lightning lit the room, followed by a rumble of thunder. Ben whimpered.

I stirred the vegetables, which replied with a hiss, then cracked eggs into a bowl. I was pleased with the perfect semicircle when I folded the omelet over. "You got my messages, right?" I tried to suppress my giddy grin.

"Let's see," she said, pulling a carton of milk from the fridge. She tipped her head back, taking noisy gulps. Wiping her lips with the back of her hand, she hummed a mocking little tune. "I got some rather dopey, giggling messages from someone whose voice sounded just a *little* like yours." She licked her thumb and forefinger, then snatched a sizzling mushroom from the pan. She huffed as she chewed. "Couldn't possibly have been you, though. I distinctly heard a man's naughty, sexy voice in the background. I'm guessing Nigel Abbot's never made those kinds of noises. Nor has he ever put a look like *that* one on your mug."

Guilt panged in my gut. "Let's just leave Nigel out of this, shall we?"

"I like Abbot. He's a stand-up guy. He's just not much once he lies down." Mary K snickered at her own joke.

Mary K replaced the milk carton into the fridge. After lighting a cigarette, she sat in the breakfast nook. "Got enough fixings for a second omelet?"

I nodded and cracked another pair of eggs. She sorted through the mail.

For the first time since I'd known her, I didn't appreciate Mary K's respect for my romantic privacy. I wanted her to riddle me with questions about Jake. I wanted to gush about the new passion I'd experienced, the amazing man I'd just spent four days in bed with whose art had moved me to tears. I felt exhaustion down in my bones while everything but my skeleton buzzed with a new, nameless energy.

Joining Mary K at the table, I pushed the eggs around on my plate. My appetite had flirted with me and then left as my mind and my body tingled with thoughts of Jake. The salty smell of the sea on his skin. The rich burgundy taste of wine on his lips. The fragrance of strong coffee brewing in the morning and the warm impression of his body left on the rumpled sheets beside me while he fixed us breakfast. Just recalling how he touched me aroused me all over again. Suddenly I could feel Mary K's eyes on me, drawing me back into our little kitchen.

"You, Murphy, are positively fuck-drunk." She slapped me on the shoulder. "'Bout time."

"I met somebody," I said.

"No shit."

"Are you going to be around? He's coming over. I'd like you to meet him."

"What, leave now?" Mary K replied. "Wouldn't miss out on meeting the dude that makes you this stupid."

I spent the next several hours pampering myself and the flat. I showered, shaved my legs, lotioned myself everywhere I could reach, and put clean sheets on my bed. Looking around our flat, I saw what I hadn't seen for a long time—a neglected place where two very busy interns lived. After being at Jake's loft, I was nervous bringing him here. The garage sale furniture and bare white walls said nothing about us, or maybe too much. Until I imagined Jake's eyes on it, I hadn't really noticed the shabby details of the surroundings. It was a place I crashed in after double shifts. It was clean and orderly, and I was grateful for that.

Frantically, I dug through drawers and cabinets, finding as many candles as I could. I tossed one of my mother's quilts over the sagging couch. After I'd turned down the lights, lit all of the candles, and tidied the towers of medical books, the place looked presentable. I flicked through the stack of albums. I found my usual favorites trivial and switched the music several more times before I landed on Dinah Washington. Rain thrumming against the windows added a cozy feeling that pleased me.

Ben nuzzled my fingertips. I scratched his ancient jowls. The dog was just about the only genuinely personal touch to be found in the place, and, but for the musky smell emitting from his damp fur, I liked what he added to the ambiance. He let out a soft whimper of appreciation.

When the doorbell rang at six, I couldn't resist one last look in the dining room mirror. I'd tamed some of the wildness of my hair and wore my new soft chinos with a white linen shirt. My pale skin wore a flush I'd seldom seen in my own reflection.

When I opened the door, Jake beamed at me. By his side on the porch sat a huge shopping bag with stringed handles, bulging with flowers. He held a large box, which he leaned back to balance. His jacket's shoulders were darkened with rain and his glasses were fogged. "I can't believe how much I've missed you this afternoon," he said. "I think I'm going through withdrawal." I stood drinking in the comic sweetness of his face, his smile. "Can I come in?"

"Sure. Here, let me take that," I said, grasping the bag. He stepped inside, dripping water onto the entryway rug. He set the box down by the door. "Let me get you a towel." After he'd dried off, he came in and surveyed the room. "Nice place."

"Yeah, right."

"No, really," he said. "I love these great old painted ladies. Great details. Leaded glass diamond windowpanes. Clinker brick fireplace. Most of these have been wrecked with

58

modernizing. It's rare to see one in original form." He walked to the mantle and picked up one of my many bird's eggs.

"Yours?"

I nodded, a little embarrassed at the childhood collection. Now and then I'd find a new one to add to the assortment.

He picked up a second egg, examining it like a jeweler examines a diamond. "Why eggs?"

"Started when I was a kid." I stepped toward him, pressing my cheek against his shoulder. "Each one has evolved to be the maximum thickness that a chick of its particular species can peck through. In other words, it's as strong as it can possibly be for protection, but thin enough to allow escape. And each is designed for its habitat. Rounder eggs are from birds in secure nests. More pointed eggs are for species that lay eggs on rocks or hillsides; they roll in a circle so that they won't get too far from their nests. Evolutionary perfection."

"And beautiful."

I'd never asked myself why I loved the eggs before. I looked with new eyes at the collection. "Yeah. Beautiful."

Ben moseyed over to Jake, gave him a quick sniff, and licked his hand. "How you doing, big guy?" Jake petted Ben's head, which came up to his hip. "Your description didn't do you justice, old man. He's even bigger than you described. I guess that means you're not prone to exaggeration."

"No," Mary K said as she entered the room. "Murphy doesn't tend toward hyperbole." Her hair was loose and shiny. Her blue eyes shone like jewelry.

Jake reached his hand out. "You must be Mary K. I've heard a lot about you. It's a pleasure." Jake flashed Mary K a world-class smile. The two shook hands and Mary K gave Jake a sideways appraisal. "Here," Jake said, "I brought something for you. Sort of a nice-to-meet-you gift. Kat told me what a big animal lover you are."

It seemed odd to me for Mary K to hear Jake's intimate nickname for me. He reached into the shopping bag, set the flowers aside, and pulled out a book of photographs tied with a leather strap. "It's a collection of photographs of artists with their animals. Georgia O'Keefe with her horses. You know, shots like that. It's a first edition given to me by the artist. Richard Avedon. He's a good friend of my friend, Burt. Avedon is a great portrait photographer, and—"

"I know who Richard Avedon is," Mary K interrupted, her voice brittle.

Confusion filled me. What had changed the tone in the room? I didn't have a clue who Richard Avedon was and wondered if he was somehow offensive to Mary K.

"Of course," Jake said. He looked down at the floor. "Anyway, I really enjoyed getting this as a gift, but I'm not one to hold on to things. It deserves a new set of more appreciative eyes."

Jake held the box out to Mary K. She reached into her pocket and grabbed a cigarette, lighting it before taking the box from him. "Thanks," she muttered. "That wasn't necessary. First edition. Sounds a little *valuable*." She set the package, unopened, on a side chair. Her face wore creases of suspicion.

"Gifts are only valuable if they're being enjoyed." Jake reached for my hand and gave it a squeeze. I squirmed involuntarily, realizing that though I'd watched Mary K with dozens of her dates, I'd never been physically demonstrative with a man in front of her. Nigel and I only touched when we were alone.

"There's a wolf in there," Jake continued. "One of old Ben's distant cousins. Ooh, and I almost forgot." He reached into the bag and extracted a cellophane bag filled with dog bone-shaped cookies. "They're from this place on Union Street. They make healthy pet snacks." Jake unwrapped the package and removed a bone, which Ben took delicately into his teeth and began munching.

I wanted to smooth the rough edges of the exchange. "Thanks, Jake. Ben seems to love his treat."

"He's a bit of a snack whore," Mary K replied. "Don't know that gourmet goodies can be fully appreciated by an animal that drinks from the toilet."

Jake pulled two bottles from the bag. "Wine and sparkling water," he announced. "Thought we could share a drink together."

Mary K eyed the water and sent me a piercing glare that said, *You told him, didn't you.* I averted my eyes. So much had gushed out of me since I'd met Jake, I couldn't believe he'd recalled the details of Mary K's health and had brought her something. My cheeks stung. Mary K blew a silver stream of smoke toward me and it could not have sliced me more if it had been a dagger.

Jake filled our glasses. The room was static with awkward small talk. I felt like an ambassador introducing leaders of two warring nations. "So, you're from New York," Jake said.

"Queens," Mary K replied with a flat tone.

"I grew up in Manhattan. I guess we were neighbors."

Mary K took a long drag off of her cigarette. "Queens isn't Manhattan."

Jake's smile faded, but returned a second later. "My father would agree. He's a dyed-in-the-wool Manhattanite."

I straightened with pride. "Jake is an artist. He has a sculpture installed in Central Park, and another near the Met. I saw photos."

Mary K squinted, calculating. "Wait a minute. Are you Jacob *Bloom*?" I started with her recognition. The layers to Jake's fame were just beginning to unfold for me.

"Guilty as charged," Jake said. "But friends call me Jake."

"So your father is Aaron Bloom. Bloom Tower. Bloom Industries. Bloom Symphony Hall."

I felt the fast jerk of my neck as I turned to look at Jake. With all we'd talked about, his father's notable identity had not been mentioned.

"My father and I don't exactly—"

Mary K wore a snide look. "I never thought one of the Kowalski clan would be sharing a Perrier with Bloom Industries in her living room, that's for sure."

"I'm *not* Bloom Industries," Jake said, his voice tinged with the first note of anger I'd ever heard from him.

Mary K read my face. "You didn't know that your new, uh, friend has the single most recognized last name on the Eastern Seaboard? Largest private owner of land in all five boroughs, and God knows where else in the world. Wall Street king. Bloom holds up a little pinky and fifteen waiters piss all over themselves just trying to put a fresh olive in his martini."

Jake's jaw clenched. "That would be my father. Not me."

Of course I recognized Aaron Bloom's name. Nearly anyone in America would know who Aaron Bloom was. I just hadn't put Jake's last name together with the mogul's as Mary K had.

"That's right. That would be the Big Bloom, isn't that what they call him? You're the Little Bloom, right? Oh, now wait a minute, what did I read in the papers back when I was in high school about the mogul and his only son? I was about sixteen. That would have made you, what, maybe twenty-two or so at the time?" Mary K tapped her forefinger on her cheek. Sarcastic words slithered from her lips. "I guess my mind is just too full of medical facts to recall the details. But wasn't it some kind of assault? A gun was involved, wasn't it?"

"That's right," Jake said. His jaw twitched. When he looked at me his eyes had paled.

"Yeah, I remember New York's prince not being charged with anything despite the firing of a weapon. Winged the old man, didn't you?"

Jake's shoulders slumped. "There's a lot more to the story."

"Ain't there always?"

Hot anger burned in me. "That was a long time ago," I said, surprised by my urge to defend Jake. "Jake's told me that he and his father have a tumultuous relationship."

Mary K stood up suddenly, ignoring Jake. "Just pay attention, Murphy," she said, her eyes boring their gaze into mine. "Thanks for the bubbles and the book. Turns out I've got a date after all. I'm sure you guys will enjoy the privacy."

I tried to draw a breath, unsure of what had just happened. Mary K wore a smug grimace. "I won't be home until tomorrow morning—late," she said. "The weather is nasty, so I don't want to bring Ben out into it. Can you keep your eye on the mutt until I'm back? I don't think he should be alone."

I wrestled my confusion. "Don't worry. I'll watch him," I said. On cue, Ben lifted his head.

"I already injected him, but this dampness is really pounding his old bones. He may need another morphine shot before bed."

Before I could respond, Mary K kissed Ben, grabbed her coat, and flew out the door. The candles all flickered with the gust of air that blasted in her wake.

Jake refilled our wine glasses. "Well, that was fun."

"I don't know what got into her."

"I'm kind of used to my family name evoking a certain range of extreme responses."

"You could've told me about that," I said.

"You knew my name."

"You know what I mean." I felt foolish and clueless for not having put the pieces of Jake's identity together on my own.

"What was I supposed to tell you? That my dad is one of the richest motherfuckers ever? That his name is on the side of half a dozen high-rises and twenty different companies?

63

Should I have explained how, when I found out that my dad had bribed a woman he didn't deem *suitable for my station* to break up with me, it enraged me so much that I picked up what I thought was an unloaded pistol from his gun cabinet and aimed it at him in front of about three hundred rich people at a cocktail party? When it went off, I nearly fainted. His influence kept me out of jail, on the condition that I go into inpatient psychiatric care. What would all that have meant, Kat, if I told you?"

"I'll admit, it requires some explanation, but it doesn't have to mean anything. It's just information about who you are, is all. I told you about my family. When I asked you about yours all you said was, *We're not very close.*"

"We're not."

"Why the secrecy?"

"I have no secrets, Kat. I'll tell you anything." Jake ran his fingers through his hair. "I just like it when I meet somebody who doesn't think they already know everything there is to know about me because of my last name. You can't believe everything you read. I'm not my dad. We haven't had contact in years."

"None? No contact at all?"

"He sends fat checks every birthday and Hanukah. I never cash them. That's how we talk. He talks with money. I talk by rejecting it. Not exactly father and son of the year."

"So, the gun. Do you make a habit of shooting people?" My heart hammered against my ribs.

"That was by far the dumbest thing I ever did. My dad is unbelievable. But I wouldn't have intentionally shot him."

"And the psychiatric treatment?"

Jake paused. "I was pretty troubled. After that I broke the connection with my dad. Burt became family. That's what I needed to do to have a good life." Jake reached and took my hand, rubbing my knuckles with his thumb. "My family is—I hope this won't spoil things for us."

An image of my mother's body flashed into my mind—small and fragile, lying in the satin-lined casket at St. Anne's. Knowing that she'd killed herself felt like a shameful, sorrowful stain on what I'd always thought of as my ideal family. "Nobody's family is perfect. I guess yours is just on a grander scale, huh?"

Jake pulled me close. Every part of me softened as I took in the soapy fragrance on his skin. His face was newly shaven, and I missed the stubble that had grown while we'd holed up at his place. I pulled off his glasses and set them on the coffee table. His mouth found surprising locations of excitement: under my chin, on each temple, and at the hollow of my throat.

A sudden burst of light flashed, followed by a growl of thunder, knocking out the power. The house went dark, and Dinah Washington's voice wound to a stop. The room radiated with candlelight from every corner and the flickering glow from the fireplace. Ben Casey's tail thumped a slow rhythm against the floor.

Firelight glowed amber on our skin as Jake unbuttoned my shirt. He cupped my breast in his hand, the warmth of him penetrating deep into me and the cavern where my heart drummed in more and more rapid response to his touch. His lips, his tongue, searched my skin. Soon I found myself naked in the firelight, but without any urge to cover myself.

Hungrily, I opened his shirt, then the buttons on his jeans, glad to see that he was as aroused as I was. Both stripped of our clothing, we melted together in front of the fire. I pleasured in the textures of him—the layer of feathery hair on his chest, the firmness of his thighs. I loved the sound of his panting, a sign of his eagerness for me. "Wait," he said, gasping just a little. He pulled my mouth away from him. "I have to slow down a little."

He laid me back, tucking my hands under each of my hips. "You first. Let me take care of you." My body responded to his touches with shudders of pleasure. Lightning flickered in the distance as if we were creating it.

As my breathing quieted, I watched the rise and fall of Jake's chest. With a smooth motion I rolled on top of him, my legs astride. Our bodies found their synchronized rhythm, our eyes fixed on each other. In the glow of the candlelight his face was a twist of bliss and anguish. His moan drifted into a soft sigh until all tension left his body.

Together we lay, entwined as one form, our bodies distinguishable only by the contrast of his olive skin and the near whiteness of mine. The pop of the fire and the rain against the roof were the only sounds in the room. Jake laughed. "We look like a marble rye," he said as he looked down at our bodies.

"What the hell is a marble rye?"

"Don't tell me I've found myself a real live *shikse*? Do you mean to tell me you've never had a marble rye?"

I shook my head.

"Oy," he exclaimed, donning his old Yiddish accent. "A marble rye is such a marvelous thing it cannot be explained. It's only to be experienced. A beautiful mixture of rich brown rye and creamy white challah woven together, dark and white, in a braid. Just like you and me here." Jake began tickling and kissing me until I could take no more. "I need a bite of this creamy white bread," he said, biting me gently. Suddenly he stopped his silly play and looked up at me. "I can't remember when I've felt so happy."

I pulled him close.

"Oh, yeah," Jake said, then rose from the pallet we'd made on the floor. "I gave everybody presents but you."

I leaned up on one elbow. "I think you just gave me a pretty nice present."

"That was for both of us. This is for you." He slid the box he'd been balancing when he'd arrived across the hardwood floor.

I wrapped myself in a blanket and lifted the flaps on the box. Inside rested the earthen bowl filled with smooth, dark stones that had been on his hearth. He lifted the heavy bowl and placed it on my hearth. I pressed my hands against my heart, unable to speak. I lifted one of the cool stones, running its smoothness against my cheek.

"Don't get all choked up," he said, his eyebrows twitching. "It's just a bowl of rocks."

I pulled him toward me, overwhelmed with feelings I couldn't name.

Jake pushed me away from him.

"What?" I asked. "What's the matter?"

"You wouldn't happen to have a bed anywhere in this joint, would you?"

We laughed together, and I realized Jake had been here for hours but hadn't stepped more than ten feet from the front door. I led him by the hand into my bedroom, where the candles I'd lit hours ago still glowed, each an island in its puddle of melted wax.

* * *

The morning sky, exhausted from its nightlong tantrum, shone brightly through my bedroom window, casting white quadrangles onto the rumpled bed. I slid from beneath the covers and pulled on my robe, then went to find Jake. Already I was familiar with his habit of staying awake after I'd fallen asleep and rising before I did. I heard the soft snap of the door latch and turned to see him coming in the front door, followed by Ben, whose head hung low as he walked.

"Morning," he said, smiling. He carried a cardboard tray with large cups of coffee and a paper bag.

"How long have you been up?" I asked.

"Most of the night. You inspired me. Just had to get to my studio for a little while, but I figured I owed you this." He pulled a large loaf of bread from the bag, dark and light woven around each other. "Marble rye. From Max's Deli."

"But—"

"Don't ask. Just enjoy." He ushered me into the kitchen, where the table was already set with placemats I hadn't seen in years and a single gardenia blossom was floating in a cereal bowl.

I looked around the room and saw that the bouquet he brought had been placed in water glasses all around the kitchen.

"Come on, the bread is still warm."

I sat at the table. He tore off a large hunk of bread, spread a little butter onto it, and tucked a piece of it into my mouth, filling me with its rich, yeasty flavor.

"It's not quite New York," he said. "But it comes close. In honor of our sexy union, I think that marble rye should be our official bread."

"How could I argue with that?" I took another bite and a sip of my coffee. "You remembered cream and sugar."

Jake touched the rim of his glasses with his index finger. "I'm studying you, Dr. Murphy. Not a detail has escaped my bespectacled observation."

As I chewed, I looked over to where Ben Casey lay on the kitchen floor. His rib cage rose and fell with his rapid panting. "Did you bring Ben with you to your studio and the deli?"

"Sure," Jake answered. "He needed to get out and you were still zonked. We hadn't gotten much sleep, so I thought I'd keep Ben from waking you."

My chair moved behind me with a screech. "Did you run him?"

"'Course not. He just rode in the car. He was with me the whole time."

I felt the first flash of anger I'd felt toward Jake. "You shouldn't have taken him. He's been really sick. Mary K would freak."

I felt the dog's nose, expecting its cool wetness, only to find it warm and dry. His tongue lay long and limp, touching the floor. His leg twitched, and he seemed unable to lift his head. "Did he get wet?"

"Kat, it's not even raining any more. I wouldn't—"

"God, Jake!" My brain scrambled for what to do next. "He's not right." I jumped to the cupboard where we kept Ben's medicine and pulled out the syringe. I pulled the plunger, filling the vial with morphine, then flicked it until the bubbles were gone. My fingers found the pulsing artery on the side of his neck. "It's okay, boy," I whispered as I pressed the plunger.

I grabbed the wall phone in the kitchen and began dialing every number I knew, looking for Mary K while Jake looked on in horror and petted Ben. My hands flew through pages of the phone book until I found a listing for The Lex, her favorite bar. "Yep," the bartender said. "She was here last night. Stayed late but was by herself. I think she left at closing time."

Jake fell to his knees beside Ben. "Maybe we ought to take him to the vet."

"No," I snapped. "She wouldn't want that. We've been just making him comfortable. She just doesn't want him to be in pain." I lay down on the floor, placing my head next to Ben's gigantic face. "Hold on, buddy. She'll want to say good-bye to you. Please, please hold on."

Jake scooped Ben up into his arms, grunting under the

dog's weight, and set him on the couch. My mother's quilt lay under him, its threadbare patches mimicking Ben's weariness. We spent the morning there, the three of us—waiting. I kept my eyes on the door, hoping to see Mary K.

* * *

Hours later, I rested my head on Ben's unmoving body.

"What should we do? Should we take Ben's body to the vet?" Jake combed my curls with his fingers.

"No," I sniffed. "She'll want to see him. Why don't you go ahead? Weren't you supposed to meet Burt today?"

"I don't care about that. I'm so sorry about Ben. I didn't know he was that—"

"We've known his time was close for a while." I watched death in the hospital every day without crying, but I couldn't hold my tears as I ran my fingers through Ben's coarse fur. "I think it's better if you go. She'll want to be alone with him. She wouldn't feel comfortable—"

"I'll call later. If you need me for anything, call. Okay? He's a big dog. If you need any help, you know, taking care of him." He kissed my cheek and patted Ben. "Wish I'd known you longer, old man."

I sat alone with Ben's body. I tucked the quilt around him and stroked his fur. I was afraid to leave the room, afraid that Mary K would walk in and find Ben all alone. I tried to squash my anger at Jake. Though he'd meant no harm, he'd been impulsive and presumptuous taking Ben out without asking. I had grown to love that dog in the nine years we'd lived together, but as much as I loved him, I knew Mary K's feelings for him were immeasurable. He was her family.

Finally, at nearly noon, the front door opened. Mary K stood silent at the threshold, her eyes fixed on Ben's body draped in front of me. Color drained from her face and she let her rucksack slip off of her shoulder, onto the floor.

"I tried to find you," I whispered. "I guess you already turned in your pager."

I stood. My urge was to rush and hold my friend in my arms, but with Mary K it was always better to read her for cues when it came to affection. She passed me and sat on the edge of the couch near Ben's body. Resting her head on his shoulder, she buried her face in his fur.

"It was quiet," I said. "He just got quiet and slipped away."

Mary K said nothing.

"He was with us all evening," I said, filling the miserable silence. "He walked in with Jake this morning and just laid down on the kitchen floor—"

Mary K sat up in a shot. "With Jake. What was he doing with Jake? Did he take him out in the rain?"

Instantly, I regretted mentioning Jake. "No, no. It stopped raining by then. Jake just took him out to his studio and to get breakfast, and—"

"You let Ben out with a stranger! How could you?"

"Jake's not a stranger," I said, trying to keep my voice level. "I was asleep and he just took him for a ride—"

"I asked *YOU* to watch him. Not him. If I'd wanted Ben out in the cold, I'd have fucking taken him with me. Jesus, Murphy."

"I'm sorry, but Jake took very good care of him. He really liked Ben, and he—"

"How do you know he liked Ben? He knew him for ten minutes. Ben should have had his last hours with—" Mary K gulped, her lips forming a grimace. "He shouldn't have been out. If he hadn't gone out—"

"I'm so sorry Ben's gone." I reached out to touch my grieving friend. She jerked her arm away.

Mary K's eyes stared straight into mine. "Just shut up."

I was prepared for Mary K's grief, but her anger hit me like a cannonball. "I'm sorry about Ben. Jake and I—"

"You're not getting this, are you? I don't want to hear about Jake. Jake Bloom is a pampered prince. A playboy. Probably a whack job. And now he probably fucking killed my dog."

"What's the matter with you?"

"Let's see, aside from my dead dog, I don't know."

"We've known Ben was going to go soon for a long time. Why are you taking it out on Jake? He couldn't have been nicer to Ben. Brought him treats and stayed with him until the end."

Mary K lifted the cellophane bag of treats and flung them across the room. They scattered like hail on the wood floor. "Fuck Jake Bloom!"

She stomped into her room and slammed the door. Normally, Mary K's temper kept me away. I'd wait until the storm subsided and approach once it was safe again. But this felt different. I followed her steps and opened the bedroom door. "I don't want to fight with you," I said, searching for enough calm to speak. "We have to take care of Ben."

"Ben's already been very well taken care of. I can see that."

"Stop this," I shouted. "Is this about Ben or Jake? Why did you take such an instant dislike to him?"

"If he's so great you'll ride away on a white horse. But I just want to go on record. He's trouble, I'm telling you. I can smell it. You're just too blind to see it. If he's that great, what do you care if I like him or not? "

"I care, all right. I care because I'm really in love with this guy and it would be nice if my best friend at least didn't act like she hates his guts."

"So you're in *love* with him. That's rich. You hardly even know him. He comes in here with all of his bribes to get into the good graces of your friend and her old, dying dog. Don't you think that's just a little much, Murphy? Don't you think that some expensive first edition picture book is just a little *extravagant*? That shit doesn't impress me. He even dressed you up like his little doll, for fuck's sake."

I looked down at the garments I wore, wrinkled and covered with Ben's wiry hair. Just yesterday I'd felt so pretty in them. "Jake is big with the grand gestures. He's an artist. He's exaggerated. And if he comes from as much money as you say, the cost of the gift isn't exactly relevant, now is it? You could at least give the man I'm in love with a chance. And just yesterday you liked the clothes."

"For your information, just because somebody gives you a good tumble or two doesn't mean you're in love with him."

I fumed, feeling the muscles in my jaw clench.

"Don't you think you should know a little about this guy before you fall completely? He's made the New York papers more often than the Mets and the Nicks combined. Did you know he was arrested for going ape-shit and vandalizing The Met? Of course, Daddy's money got him out of that one, too. Oh, and let's see, there were the affairs with international heiresses. And let's not forget about him shooting his old man. Not that half of New York wouldn't throw a parade if Aaron Bloom took an ass cheek full of lead, but that little antic landed your boyfriend in a *serene country setting* for quite a little while. You and me, we'd be in the clink."

"He said you'd do this. That you'd rain a shit storm about what the press had said. He told me all about the incident with the gun. He's hiding nothing."

"Don't be naïve. Even if ninety percent of what I've read is bullshit, the ten percent that's true should be enough to make you run screaming in the other direction. This guy is a serious sack of nuts, even if he is a wonderful fuck."

I crossed my arms in front of my chest. "You're certainly the expert there. All I've heard about for years is your *wonderful fucks*. I've watched your endless parade of air-headed ingénues. Your coke addicts. Biker girls. I've taken their sobbing phone messages and signed for their flower deliveries. I've listened to their giggles and moans through your bedroom walls. I've said nothing. NOTHING!"

I swallowed hard. The force of my words was volcanic. "I've treated each one of your *tumbles* with kindness, probably more than you showed them. And now the first time I actually have somebody who makes me happy, you just shit all over it. Nigel was too boring. Now Jake's too wild. Please, please, Dr. Kowalski. Can you write me the prescription for the perfect man? What's the proper dosage of excitement factor for a lover for me?"

I stood and stared at Mary K, waiting for a response. My pulse pounded in my ears. Rain began to beat hard again against the roof and flow off the eaves of the house, falling past the window in sheets. I waited, breathing hard, for some surrender, some softness in my friend's face. Her lips thinned into a hard, straight line.

Hot raged roiled in my gut. "Maybe it's time I get my own place."

"Maybe it is," Mary K muttered, lighting a cigarette.

"Fine. I'll start packing tomorrow."

"Works for me."

Silence hung between us like rotting meat.

"And don't go blaming Jake because you missed Ben's passing. If you hadn't been such a bitch leaving the house, you might have been here."

"Fuck you, Murphy."

I turned and left the room, slamming the door behind me. I flung myself around my bedroom, gathering a suitcase and throwing items into it. On the way out of the house, I gave Ben one last good-bye stroke.

My car groaned with the first crank of the key. Rain made the windshield a blurry wall. I cranked the car once more, hearing the engine's merciful rumble. With the windshield wipers chasing my pulse rate, I made my way to South of Market, threading my way through the gray, wet streets.

Standing in the pouring rain, I knocked on the corrugated metal door. Jake opened it, his face showing surprise in seeing me.

"Can I come in? I might need to stay a while."

Different Worlds

I spent the next few days at Jake's loft like a featherless bird huddled in the nest of his bed. At first, I slept, waking only briefly, then falling back into near catatonia. Jake sketched in an oversized drawing pad at the other end of the loft. It seemed I had not slept in years and I was making up for it. In twenty-eight years, I could hardly remember a single fight I'd had with a family member or a friend, and now, in a matter of days, I'd had two giant blowouts that had severed me from Mary K and my family. I was ill-equipped for conflict, it left me exhausted. I'd emerge from my murky haze to find Jake in the chair beside the bed, his gaze upon me like a shaft of sunlight that warmed my skin. He'd climb under the white down comforter. I felt drunk, reeling from his touch, his smell, the taste of him, drunk enough that I forgot everything outside of the bed.

Jake prepared beautiful, simple meals, intricately spiced and comforting: gingery lemongrass soup; butter lettuce salads with figs and almonds; jasmine rice and stir-fried vegetables. I'd awaken to the scent of a fresh gardenia on the ebony wood bedside table, white stones arranged in a spiral around it, or miniature landscapes of cinnamon and freshly ground nutmeg raked into serene patterns. Fresh coffee greeted me and I'd find clean sheets on the bed after my bath. Each time I emerged from sleep it was with a new sensation, an image, smell, or taste that reacquainted me with my body. And always, there was his touch.

On the third day, Jake coerced me into going on a walk with him, and then a drive. We watched kids flying kites at the marina. Ate falafel at the Embarcadero. Shared clam chowder at the Cliff House overlooking the beach where I'd first seen his ice sculptures. I sipped wine as we looked out of the picture window from our table. Sea lions waddled on rocks below.

"So," Jake said, dragging crispy fried calamari through cocktail sauce. "Have I ruined things forever between you and Mary K?"

My whole body jerked. "No. Absolutely not. She's stubborn and brash. She's—"

"She's your friend. I know what Burt means to me. It would kill me if something came between us. If she thinks I'm doing that, she's right to hate me. I would." Jake looked up at me through his dark brow. "And she did lose Ben, after all."

"I lost him, too," I said, my voice more petulant than I wanted it to be. I looked down at two squabbling sea lions, barking and biting at one another. "She's just not used to me having someone else. That's all. She's been the one with all of the romance drama. I've never really been—" I looked at the crashing waves below, hoping they would carry the word I searched for. "I know I'm twenty-eight and a doctor and every-thing, but I've never been *serious* about someone." I couldn't say it. I couldn't say I'd never felt in love before—until now.

Jake's face lightened and a smile crossed his lips.

Instant regret climbed over me and I scowled at the waves

for bringing me the wrong words. Heat crawled up my throat and I felt redness blossom on my face.

Jake reached across the table and grabbed my hands. "I'm in love with you too, Kat."

I gazed back down at the foamy waves and this time they brought me words I'd never said before. "I guess I'm in love with you, too." A huge, white wave broke over the rocks and the squabbling sea lions slid into the ocean, where their waddling and fighting became water ballet.

* * *

Once the first week passed at Jake's house, I began to grow restless. I'd started working when I was eight, cleaning up the pub and doing a paper route. Eventually I'd picked up babysitting jobs, until I was old enough to have a W-2 job at sixteen. I had been laser-like in my focus on earning money for college; a dog with a bone, my dad always called me. I could not remember the last time I'd had more than an idle hour in years.

Jake taught me to play. His calm and patience made me comfortable with being quiet. He coaxed stories from me like a magician pulling scarves from his sleeve: one tied to the next and the next. Stories of childhood at the pub became stories about college became stories about my family—about my mother.

One morning as we sat on a cliff in the Marin Headlands, overlooking the Golden Gate, he told me how his dad wanted him to be a businessman, a tycoon like him. His father had never believed in or understood his talent. "He thought my art was some passing hobby. I wasn't interested in the stock market, or sports, or erecting skyscrapers, so he assumed I was gay, which disgusted him. I let him think that for a long time. It took the pressure off."

I looked at him sideways. "I can testify that's not the case."

"It wouldn't matter. He couldn't detest me more if I was a serial killer."

"He doesn't detest you. You're his son."

Jake gave me a look that told me how clueless I was. "He shuffled me from one caregiver to another. He's no father to me." His face was a weaving of anger and grief. "When Burt published the first photographs of my work, I started to get more public notoriety. We got prestigious grants. Obscene commissions from famous buyers. When the art started generating lots of money, my dad thought maybe I was legitimate. But then I started turning down commissions. I never have liked doing art just because someone wants to buy it. Kind of misses the point, really. And it drives Burt crazy, too, because he's always wanting to take care of my future."

"Sounds like Burt's looking out for you."

"Burt's a good man, but the money just doesn't matter that much to me. I already have enough."

I grew itchy talking about money. Student loan payments were crippling. My Bug needed new tires, and the clutch was going bad. Guilt flashed as I thought that it was only rich people who have the luxury of not caring about money. I didn't want to think of Jake as I had some of the trust-fund babies I'd met throughout school—spoiled and entitled, reckless with their privilege.

I shielded my eyes from the bright sun. "I want you to know. I've never loafed or mooched like this before. You're probably used to people who try to take advantage, I mean, I'd like to chip in for the groceries or—"

A shadow crossed Jake's face and creases formed between his brows. "Don't do that." His voice was pinched. "Don't insult yourself or me. Or us. It cheapens what we have." He stood and walked toward the bluff. The wind tossed his hair in every direction at once.

I had that helpless feeling that I had said exactly the wrong thing—again.

I walked up behind him and wrapped my arms around his middle, resting my cheek on his back. "I'm not used to someone spending money on me. The clothes. The restaurants. My family's kind of big on the whole idea of noble poverty. Work ethic and all. I just don't want you to think that I—"

"I'm not my father. Money is just a happy accident, nothing I ever aim for. It means nothing. Wouldn't even happen without Burt. And just because I have money doesn't mean I don't have a work ethic." He turned his gaze to the gray horizon while his icy words cut through me.

It wasn't just that I was uncomfortable talking about money, though surely I was. Other than Nigel, I'd never been close to someone who'd come from wealth, and though I hated to admit it, I'd always felt more comfortable with those who shared my working-class roots. Only people who had a lot of money ever said that it meant nothing. Mary K and I had that in common, and had shared nine years of scraping while we'd watched wealthier classmates float through without our worries. The topic of money—as unfamiliar as it was to me—was near toxic to Jake. Money was intertwined with Aaron Bloom and the two formed a noxious compound, like ammonia and bleach, that choked the tenderness out of Jake.

I wrapped my arms around his waist. "I'm sorry," I whispered. "I guess I'm just used to money being a struggle."

"Me too, Kat," Jake sighed. "Money's always been a struggle, but I never want it to be like that between you and me."

I knew in that moment that Jake and I had a different vocabulary—a whole different language—when it came to money. I was relieved when his body softened and he welcomed my embrace. I rested my head against his back, listening to his heartbeat as it slowed from its galloping rate.

Mary K's words echoed in my head. Was she right? How could I be in love with this man I hardly knew? He came from a different world. Was it just sex? Nothing more than chemistry? Or was I just so in love with the idea of being in love that I was flying past all warning signs about Jake? What did we have in common, after all? His was a world of art and culture with celebrities and tycoons. He'd grown up around fame and money while my whole life took place in the small triangle formed of Murphy's pub, St. Anne's, and UCSF.

With a smooth, gentle motion, Jake turned to me. His eyes glittered. "You must be wondering who the hell I am right now."

His uncanny ability to read my thoughts unsettled me. I tried to erase the uneasiness from my face.

"I've frightened you." He lifted my chin and kissed my lips with such tenderness it felt like a sacrament. "It's just I've spent my whole life living down the shame of my father's legacy. And you're used to a family that loves you utterly and completely. It's just so hard to believe that you might want *me*. With you, I feel rich, *really* rich, for the very first time in my life."

As the words left his lips, it felt as if they were not just his but my words as well. No, this was not just chemistry. Romantic love was just so unfamiliar that I hardly recognized it. But there it was, something I never knew myself capable of feeling; unmistakable, desperate, passionate love. These were riches I'd never imagined.

Family Reunion

In those first idyllic days when Jake and I nested in his loft, I pretended nothing else outside mattered. Day trips around the Bay Area, beautiful meals, and lovemaking were nearly enough distraction. But Jake found ways to remind me of the world I was pretending didn't exist. He'd lure me into talking about Tully driving me to Galileo High School in his beat-up pickup, or Dr. Schwartz's inspiring me to go into medicine. As we cooked together, he'd ask me about Alice's recipes and my dad's favorite Irish dishes and if Mary K ever did any cooking.

"You're about as subtle as a wrecking ball," I said.

"I've been accused of a lot of things. Subtlety isn't among them."

It was a week after Ben died and my fight with Mary K when Jake and I took advantage of a sunny day and drove north to the Napa Valley. In his Valiant, we wove our way from winery to winery. At each vineyard, Jake gathered tidbits of history and winemaking craft from the vintners and service staff, swapping jokes and stories with them like he'd known them for years.

From Napa we drove farther north to Healdsburg's pricey,

upscale version of Mayberry with its quaint storefronts and comfortable benches that invite visitors to linger.

"Is today the day?" Jake asked.

"The day for what?"

"The day you make peace with your family and Mary K."

I stopped walking and yanked my hand from his.

He looked at me, wearing a quizzical look. "That's an expression I haven't seen yet."

"You find this amusing."

"Not at all. Just seeing your face in another kind of light is all."

"And what light would that be? Righteous indignation? Betrayed friend and daughter?"

Jake shrugged.

"Come on. I can take it."

"I'm not sure you can."

Metallic anger singed my tongue. In the years I'd dated Nigel, he'd never once confronted me or challenged my behavior. It also dawned on me that my relationship with my family had been a series of polite exchanges. I'd grown up accepting what I was told as absolute, never questioning or rebelling, even as a teen. My family offered me near limitless adoration. It was an enviable childhood by most people's standards, but by its benign nature, my family life had not equipped me for conflict. I was changing, and Jake was the catalyst.

"I really want to know," I said. "What's my part?"

"All right," he surrendered. "How about being judgmental and stubborn?"

"Hey, I'm the wronged party here. My family lied to me for more than twenty years."

"Your family did what they did for no other reason than to protect you."

"So lying is okay with you."

"Of course not. But malice wasn't the motive."

"I know," I confessed. "It's not their motives that I find fault with. It's just the deceit. And judgmental! When have I ever been judgmental of Mary K? You have no idea what I've tolerated from her over the years. I said nothing while she brought a nine-year parade of lovers through the house. I bring one guy that she has some issues with, and wham!"

"To *tolerate* something implies that it's something you have a judgment about, doesn't it? And didn't you—judge her, I mean? You may not have said anything, but—"

I turned and marched down the sidewalk, my steps soon becoming stomps. Jake kept pace. "She ridiculed Nigel so much I never dared bring him to my house. Then she's all barbed wire and dynamite to the only guy I ever did bring home," I mumbled to myself as I continued to stomp. "And she practically accused you of murdering Ben. Oh, and I suppose it's just fine for her to sleep around with a whole slew of people with absolutely no intention of developing it any deeper."

"That's sort of what I've always done," Jake said. I stopped in my tracks.

"I never intended to get serious about anybody," he said. "I figured the Bloom relationship record wasn't so hot. I met a few women along the way that made me think differently, but just about the time I thought there might be something special, she'd decide I wasn't the guy, or that she needed to focus on her career or something. Only one time I loved someone who really loved me for me, and my dad proved me wrong by buying her away from me."

"He really paid her to leave you?"

"Yeah, well... that's my dad." Jake wore an expression that showed a lifetime of betrayal and disappointment.

"You must have been heartbroken."

"I had my art, my travels. Burt." Jake's gaze was across the square, watching a couple with a double baby stroller navigate the sidewalk, sharing licks off of the same ice cream cone. "Sex is easy, Kat. Love is scary. Mary K's got a hard shell to protect herself. She's had a life-threatening illness since she was a kid and probably always assumed she wasn't going to live very long. She just lost a member of her family. She deserves some slack."

I felt my own hardened shell begin to crack. Saying nothing more, he took my hand and we got into the car.

During the long drive back to the city, the mood in the car was reflective, and fog gathered, complying with our inward thoughts. For the first time in a long time I felt peaceful and calm. But questions loomed in my mind.

We stopped at the vista point on the Marin County side of the Golden Gate, its sturdy towers and graceful arches saffron against the clear blue sky.

"Do you like it?" I asked.

Jake leaned his cheek against the steering wheel and looked at me. "Like what?"

"My face in the new kind of light. Judgmental. Stubborn. And I'm thinking maybe I should add spoiled to the list."

"Judgmental just means you have opinions. Stubborn just means you're willing to stand by them. I'm pretty sure I'm going to like your face in every kind of light."

"But why?" I asked. "Why me?" Jake was handsome. Wealthy. Worldly. Talented. Charismatic. Surely he could choose from among hundreds of women.

Silence ticked by almost audibly in my ears, and I feared he'd be unable to come up with an answer. His gaze was penetrating. "You're unlike any other woman I've ever met. You're impressed only by the things that are impressive instead of the things that someone is born with. You're curious and you actually listen when people talk. You seem to have some sort of internal guidance system about what is right, and it isn't determined by what's fashionable or profitable. You're smarter than you know. Prettier than you think you are—and that's rare. Sexier than I'd imagined. And when you ask me this question, you aren't fishing for compliments."

The shimmering string Jake's words spun around me wove a cocoon that at once made me feel deeply adored and embarrassed.

"And my favorite thing," Jake said, his lips forming a lopsided smile. "Your face is like your personal weather system. It shows every emotion."

I inhaled the salty smell of the air, trying to see myself in the way that Jake had just described me. The knot in my throat kept me from speaking, and Jake's kisses spared me the trouble.

* * *

I sat with Dr. Schwartz, my dad, and Alice at the family table at Murphy's. Mugs of coffee sat before us, and stripes of early morning light slipped through the blinds and onto the weathered tabletop. The faces around me appeared years older than just two weeks earlier.

"Tully?" I asked.

"I'm afraid he's been AWOL since the last night you saw him, Kitten," my dad said, shaking his head. "I called a few of his cousins. Sean over at O'Shea's said he's been in there, hitting it pretty hard and crying in his beer about how he ruined everything."

"I'm worried about him," I said. "What if he gets in an accident?"

"Sean took the keys to his truck," Dad said. "We can thank the stars for that."

Alice stirred sugar into her coffee. "Tully used to drink pretty good before you came along, Katie. But then Elyse appointed him your one-man personal transportation committee. Smart cookie, she was. Then he became the driver for us all with his string of beat-up pickups." Alice shook her head. "Tully knows his way back onto the wagon." Alice's mascara had melted into dark shadows under her eyes. Her blonde bouffant maintained its beauty parlor-perfect shape, though her face appeared wilted and tired.

"It's a terrible burden he's carried, Katherine," Dr. Schwartz said, his head wobbling in involuntary agreement with his words. "He was so special to Elyse. And her to him. Closer than any brother and sister I know. Losing her was one of Tully's biggest blows. He couldn't talk about it for years."

"We were wrong not to tell you," Dad said. His eyelids were swollen, his color gray. He peered into the blackness of his coffee cup. After a while, he drew a deep breath and then found my eyes with his own. Even under his wiry brows and the gentle sag of his eyelids, his eyes were clear and soft. "We always meant to tell you everything, when you were old enough to understand."

I opened my mouth to speak, but Dad kept talking. "You were such a little girl, and it all seemed so big." Dad stopped and cleared his throat. Any pain I felt for myself at that moment paled next to what it felt like to see my dad waging such a struggle.

Dr. Schwartz rested his gnarled fingers on Dad's forearm. "What your father is saying is that we've always meant to talk to you. When you were little the time wasn't right. You were such a brooding teenager, so serious, so alone. You didn't have friends the way other children did. We didn't want to make things harder. I'll have to admit we all lost our courage along the way. And time conspires to bury the best of intentions."

The three of them told the story like a fugue, one voice picking up as the other left off. My mother's depression had started back in Ireland, after losing three brothers in the war. She was a woman of great faith. She prayed and asked for mercy. She went to the priests, who told her to focus on others.

Dr. Schwartz took a sip of his coffee. "Medicine was only beginning to really treat depression in the 1960s. One doctor even told Elyse to take up smoking to settle her nerves. Can you imagine?"

"Poor thing tried it, but the cigarettes only made her sick," Alice added. "She was so much better for a while after you came along." A mysterious cloud passed before Alice's eyes. "I never did see anything that could lift her the way you did, honey. The sad spells came back in full force when you were about two. She'd say, 'How can I be unhappy? I have everything I ever wanted.'"

Dad's face was slack with sadness. "When Elyse told Alice that she was wishing she'd die, well—"

"We knew she needed more help than we could give her," Alice said. "So she went to Langley Porter Hospital."

Tully took her to the hospital whenever she needed to go, still wedded to his role as family driver, and wanting nothing so badly as to see her well again.

Dr. Schwartz sighed. "In those days, they did shock treatments. Elyse was willing to subject herself to anything... because there was you, Katherine. She so wanted to be free of it all. She was afraid that her bleak outlook might affect you. But treatment had been futile. Each time she emerged from treatment, she was thinner and less herself. The last time she came out of the hospital, she seemed better, stronger. We all thought the treatment had finally worked."

Alice sniffed. "We didn't know that she was hiding her

sleeping pill every night. Your dad would only give her one at a time and he kept the bottle locked up, but she was squirreling them away."

The faces around me wore an expression I couldn't name. My curiosity was finally being fed, but with a distasteful meal.

Dad shook his head. "I've always wondered if she seemed happier because she knew she her pain would soon be over."

I ached to comfort my gentle father, but sorrow and curiosity fixed me to the spot where I sat.

"On the last Saturday night of her life, she went to confession, just like always, and when she came home she seemed so at peace," Dad continued. "The next morning she rose early, full of vim. Went to early morning mass. When she got back she cleaned every inch of the flat and the bar. Polished every surface and fluffed every pillow. When she was done, she took you for a romp in the park and came home and made a big family Sunday supper."

I remembered that Sunday. Clear and bright for a February day. It had been so long since I'd seen my mother with enough energy to go for a walk. She pushed me on the swings and we smelled every flower in the Arboretum. She pointed out all of my dad's favorites and told stories of the bouquets of lilies and posies he'd given her when they were courting. She even rode with me on the carousel and made an elaborate meal of roasted lamb with creamed peas and new potatoes, and a fraughan pie for dessert. I willed myself to remember the taste of the tart berries and vanilla cream, the sound of my mother's voice, and her lavender scent. She tucked me into bed that night and we said the Lord's Prayer together. I could still feel her gentle kiss on my forehead.

"She came down the stairs bright and early Monday morning with her coat on and said she'd forgotten something at the church," Alice explained. "Asked me to walk you to school.

'Look after our Katie,' she said. 'Our Katie,' that's what she always called you. Those were the very last words she ever spoke to me." Alice brought her handkerchief to her nose and swiped it under her eyes.

I could feel my breathing quicken, and suddenly felt a chill.

Tully was at the bar extra early for his coffee that morning. Offered to go get whatever she'd left, but my mother would hear nothing of it.

"That has haunted Tully ever since, Kitten. The thoughts of *if only* torture him. Before she left for the church, she swallowed all of those pills she'd been tucking away and marched up the hill to St. Anne's."

Tully had a job painting the church, a job Mother had gotten for him. He found her lying in the church courtyard in the flower bed in front of the statue of the Virgin.

"All those pills in such a little body," Alice said. She dabbed her nose and tucked her handkerchief back into her sleeve.

In a panic, Tully picked up my mother's tiny bird body, carried her to the cab of his truck, and brought her back to the flat.

Dr. Schwartz stilled his quaking hands on his coffee mug. "Tully gave Elyse a final kindness by protecting her privacy and driving her home." He removed his glasses and looked deep into my eyes from under his white eyebrows. "I called my friend at the coroner's office."

From his shirt pocket, Dad pulled a folded piece of paper. Despite its years, the paper was still crisp and white. I unfolded it. At the top it said "Certificate of Death" and bore the embossed seal of the San Francisco office of the coroner. My eyes scanned the contents of black rectangles, filled with off-center, typed words and x's that just missed the centers of tiny boxes. *Gender, female. Age, 42. Height, 4 ft. 11 in., Weight, 91 lbs. Cause of death, Heart Failure due to Barbiturate overdose.*

Because he detected no foul play, Dr. Schwartz's friend had omitted any mention of suicide from the death certificate.

"We just sat with her awhile," Alice said. "Saying good-bye. Then we noticed the card sticking out of her coat pocket. One of those little altar cards with a picture of the Christ child and the Virgin. I'll never forget the words she wrote on the back of that card."

Dad pulled the little altar card from his pocket and passed it to Alice. She stroked the card gently, then passed it to me. A haloed Mary held a glowing infant and wore a beatific smile. I turned the card to see my mother's even, slanted script. *Forgive me.* I brought the card to my cheek, needing to feel her written words against my bare skin.

Dad cleared his throat and took a sip of coffee that must've been stone cold. "I was surely mad as hell at her for leaving us," he said. "But when I sit with the truth of it, ending her life was the only way she was to find an end to her pain. I don't know about the ways of God, but it seems any compassionate Creator would understand and extend His mercy."

Nausea crawled through my belly and my eyes burned. I wanted to cry, but no tears would come. Slapped into awareness, I scooted my way out of the booth.

"But Kitten," my dad said. "There's so much more to talk to you about."

"It's okay," I sighed, looking around the table. "I understand." I leaned down and hugged my dad, then Alice, and reached across the table to touch Dr. Schwartz's hand.

"Sit with us just a while longer," my dad pleaded. "There's more."

"No, Daddy. I've want to go find Tully and thank him for taking such good care of my mother."

"Katie," Alice said, her voice sharp and pointed. "Please. I have so much more I want to say to you."

I stood. "I understand. I understand it all. Why you didn't tell me. Why Tully still cries when we talk about Mother. I just want to go find him." As I exited the bar, all I heard was Alice's voice, saying, "But Katie—" as the door swung closed behind me.

* * *

"Ooh Katie, he's over the moon for you," Alice cooed while we stood at the end of the bar watching Dad pull Jake a thick-headed beer. So much had happened in the two weeks since I'd listened to my family's explanations about my mother's death. "The way he looks at you. I've never seen you so happy," she said.

"I am happy." I was surprised by how easily the words came. The dark cloud of my distance from Mary K was the only remaining shadow. I'd returned to the flat to gather some things, avoiding the times when she might be home. I'd left a check for my half of the rent and utilities.

A sudden burst of laughter erupted from the bar where Jake stood with Tully, Dad, and Dr. Schwartz. "They're like a bunch of boys, aren't they?" I said to Alice.

"If you think they ever grow up, I never taught you a thing, honey." Alice smiled and nudged me with her shoulder.

Alice's eyes shimmered. "Thanks for finding Tully. He belongs here with us." Her mouth opened, then she brought her fingers to her lips as if to stop her words from coming out.

"What?" I asked.

"Nothing, honey. I'm just so glad you're here with us. The last weeks have been so—" Mascara-black tears spilled. "Will you look at me. Blubbering fool."

In the bar that night, it seemed that the jagged edges of the truth about my mother had been wrapped in cotton batting: still sharp, but no longer dangerous.

Alice nudged my shoulder with hers. "You're in love with this one, aren't you?"

"I am."

"It shows all over your face—and his."

"It feels exhilarating, but scary, too."

"Real love is like flying the trapeze without a net, honey. Exciting, but terrifying. I don't know any other way to do it though."

Another crack of laughter exploded from the bar. Dad doubled over, holding his sides. Jake wiped tears. Dr. Schwartz bobbed with an inaudible cackle. Alice nudged me with her elbow. "We'd better get over there. No telling what those boys are up to without a woman around to set them straight."

"Yeah, let's go spoil their fun."

As we approached, their laughter wound down to exhausted sighs. "And just what are you rascals hooting about over here? I thought you were going to raise the roof," Alice scolded.

The men exchanged sheepish looks. Dad straightened up, tucking in his chin. "Jake here brought fortune cookies, that's all."

"Fortune cookies are not that funny," Alice scolded. "What, are they dirty ones?" She snatched a cookie from the bag on the bar and cracked it open. "Don't be afraid of your wild side," she read.

Tully's giggling started them all off again.

Alice folded her arms in front of her chest. "What's so funny about that?"

Jake pressed his palm to his chest. "Just a parlor game, Alice. Something some guys in an Australian bar taught me. You add the words 'in the sack' to whatever you read on the cookie."

"My turn," Tully said, taking a fortune cookie from the bag. "Let's see now, this should be good. Tully looked at the white tag, 'You are a great—'" He stopped, his face looking angry, and crumpled up the paper.

"Come on now," Dad said, snatching the paper from Tully's hand. "You are a great lover of animals," he read. The group burst out in a new roar of laughter.

"Ah, shut up, all of you," Tully barked. "You sound like a bunch of old ladies."

Dr. Schwartz held his chest and took off his glasses. "Ooh," he sighed. "I don't know if my old heart can take much more."

I felt myself smile, not at the silly game, but at the easy camaraderie Jake found with the men of my family.

"This pub is fantastic, Mr. Murphy," Jake said. "Like you moved a bit of Ireland across the pond. Reminds me of a place Burt loves in Australia. He lives in New York now. Says there's not a real pub in the whole city. I can't wait for him to see this."

"It's just home to us," Dad said.

Jake turned to Alice. "So you must have been quite a bit younger than your sister."

Alice's brows twisted in confusion. "I don't have a sister."

"Alice and my mother were close friends, not sisters."

"Just as good as," Alice added.

"Oh, I just assumed—" Jake's expression was hard to read, but he replaced it with a polite smile.

Dad refilled his coffee cup from the carafe on the table. "You're a lucky man, Jake. Going to all of them exotic locations. Seeing all of the beautiful nooks and crannies of God's creation. Why I'm convinced that there are shades of green that can only be seen in Ireland. I'm sure such treasures are unique to all kinds of places on this earth."

Jake stepped toward me and put his arm around my waist. He gave me a look and I replied with a nod. "Speaking of trips to exotic locations, I've got a terrific one coming up. I'm headed to Japan. I've been commissioned to have one of my sculptures cast in bronze for placement in Ueno Park in Tokyo. That's where they hold the largest and most beautiful of the cherry blossom festivals, Mr. Murphy. I've heard how much you admire flowers."

"Oh the *Prunus serrulata*. Nothing prettier," Dad gleamed.

"I was just telling your young man that I'd seen his sand sculptures in Santa Barbara a few years ago, Katherine," Dr. Schwartz said. "Exquisite. And my niece gave me one of the books of photographs of his work for Hanukah last year. Isn't that a coincidence? Your work is extraordinary, Jacob."

"My friend, Burt, photographs the work," Jake said. "He'll be in Japan, too. I've designed something special for the town of Kamakura. At the site of the Great Buddha."

"I've always wanted to see the gardens of Japan," Dad said. "Everyone should grab their chance at seeing the world."

"I agree, Mr. Murphy. That's why I'm so glad Kat has agreed to go along."

Everyone's eyes found me like searchlights on an escapee. "Katie!" Alice cried.

Words poured out of me in a scatter. "It's the perfect time. I've got a few more weeks until my residency. It's been so long since I had any time off. I've never really been anywhere and—look!" I pulled my new passport from my purse. "Jake's administrative assistant in New York expedited a passport."

My dad's eyebrows drew close to each other. "But Japan. Kitten, that's half a world away."

"Don't worry, it's safe," I said.

"Katie, you haven't even been out of the country since you were an infant," Dad said. He turned to Jake. "She was born in Ireland. Did she tell you that? But she's never traveled since."

"All the more reason to go. Like you said, there's a whole world to see."

An uneasy silence replaced the sparkling laughter of only

moments before. "You're not jeopardizing your position at the hospital by leaving, are you?"

"No, Daddy. Of course not," I reassured him, "I've worked it all out."

Dad looked deep into my eyes, searching for something. "There you have it." His words were clipped.

"Dad, I—"

"I think your dad has reservations about you going so far away with someone he's just met. Someone you've not known for very long," Jake said.

Dad looked up, his face wearing surprise at being so easily read. I knew the feeling.

"I'd feel the same way about a daughter of mine. Perhaps you would like to talk privately." Jake took his arm from my shoulder and tapped Tully on the arm. "Dr. Schwartz, why don't you and Tully join me at the backgammon table? I imagine you can teach me a few moves." Jake winked at me and left me there with Dad and Alice.

I turned to my dad. "Is that it?"

"We've only just met Jake. And now you're telling us you're going to another country together? It's all so fast."

"You and Mother went from Ireland to France a month after you met."

"We were married, Katie. And her father nearly turned the dogs on me anyway. This is the first young man you've ever introduced to us. I just think you should know him better before you go gallivanting around the globe."

I couldn't bring myself to say that we'd essentially been living together since we'd met. "I know Jake. And just five minutes ago you seemed to like him fine."

"He seems like a nice lad. That's different than trusting him to take my daughter a world away."

"I'm ten years older than my mother was when you married

her." I looked to Alice for backup, but her face seemed frozen in a shocked expression.

"He comes from a world you know nothing about, Kitten. Money and private jets. His father is—well, a different breed from people like us. People that don't know what it is to wait for what they want, put their shoulder to the wheel."

"He's got nothing to do with his father," I whispered, not wanting Jake to overhear. "He's not like that. And if you want to know the truth, it was Jake that talked me into reconnecting with you in the first place. He said I was being stubborn and judgmental. I can't imagine where I learned that." I wasn't asking permission. This seemed like an argument a teenager would have with her parents.

"Katie," Alice said. Her voice stopped me. "You're acting like a child."

"I didn't act like a child when I was a child. Don't you think it's about time I actually had a little fun?"

"This is more than fun, I can see it in your eyes," Dad said.

"Angus!" Alice's voice was as sharp as a shard of glass.

Dad looked up at her and let out a sigh. "I'm sorry. Your choices are yours to make. This one just isn't like you."

"I'm happy, Dad. Be happy with me." I ached to have my family fall in love with Jake as I had. "I know it seems fast. But we're not children. Haven't I earned the right to have you trust my judgment?"

"I'm always happy when you are, darlin'." He looked back at Alice. "It's your family's job to worry about you. That's all. I suppose it's time for us to respect you as the grown woman you've become."

"Don't worry. I'm fine," I said.

Alice placed her warm hand on my shoulder. "We are happy for you, sweetheart."

We moved over to where Jake and Dr. Schwartz faced off across a backgammon board.

Dad put his hand out to shake Jake's. When Jake clasped his hand, I saw my dad's thick hand squeeze Jake's thinner one and hold on. His voice softened to a whisper. "You're taking some precious cargo on this trip and it's a mighty long way from home. You'll take care of our Katie now, won't you, Jake?" It was clear that my father was not making a request but issuing a threat.

Jake returned my father's handshake. "Don't worry, Mr. Murphy. I work with priceless art every day. I know precious things require great care."

Dad gave a single nod. "There it is, then."

"When do you leave?" Alice asked.

I cringed. "Day after tomorrow."

Dr. Schwartz lifted his glass of cognac. His voice was feathery thin. "Then we barely have time to raise a glass and wish you well," he said. He stood, leaning on his cane. His head came only to my shoulder now that he had grown so hunched. "To our Katherine, all grown up. And to our new friend, Jacob. A wonderful adventure to you both."

My dad looked at me from across the group, his lips smiling but his eyes wearing worry. His brows twitched a little as he raised his mug. "And here's to coming home," he said. "The most precious part of every journey."

"Well said, Angus," Dr. Schwartz said, patting my dad's shoulder. "Well said."

Love Nest

Jake was to have three installations in Japan. One was a simple ceremony, unveiling an enormous bronze piece commissioned by the Japanese Arts Council. It had been cast from one of his original sculptures back in the States, completed over a year before, and shipped to Tokyo. This work was inspired by one of Jake's nature sculptures that a senior executive at Sony had seen Jake create in Australia. Jake dismissed it as "a tombstone for an already dead piece of art." The second installation was to be a more organic, temporary sculpture in the tranquil gardens near the Great Buddha in Kamakura. About this installation, Jake talked almost nonstop. Burt's negotiation and Jake's reputation had created an unprecedented opportunity to create an art experience near the holy shrine. And then there was the third installation, about which I knew virtually nothing. All I knew was that it would be far off in the remote Japanese countryside.

After a nine-hour flight to Tokyo, my eyelids felt like they were lined with sandpaper. Each time I blinked, the scrape was nearly audible. Burt was to meet us at the hotel. He'd arrived weeks before to hire the art students and machinery operators necessary to get the Kamakura installation preparations in place. I later learned that whenever a Jake Bloom exhibit was scheduled anywhere in the world, artists, fans, and students lined up to volunteer to be part of the experience.

Japan, at first glance, seemed more like another planet than another country, and I was an alien species. As we walked through the airport, Jake and I drew stares; the breezy sound of whispers followed us. I felt conspicuous with my pale skin, light eyes, and curls. Jake showed no signs of self-consciousness, moving like a native among the people and even conversing in seemingly fluent Japanese. We rode in a chauffeured car through congested Tokyo. San Francisco was a quaint village by comparison. Hundreds of slate-gray towers reached skyward for the only space to be found. Clotheslines between balconies formed a multicolored spider web. The city boulevards flowed with tiny cars and an ever-flowing river of black-haired pedestrians.

Jake sketched with fury as we rode, just as he had throughout the flight. With his drawing undeterred, he talked and filled me in on the many hats Burt wore as his friend, manager, and partner. Burt was road manager and worked with administrative help in New York to take care of all things logistical: equipment, permits, promotions and PR, visas, money—in short, everything but the actual design of Jake's pieces. More importantly, he was also the sole photographer of Jake's work. Fluent in six languages, functional in several others, Burt was the master communicator who negotiated the way into whatever impossible opportunity Jake dreamed up.

"I can't wait for you to meet Burt. I can't wait for him to meet you," Jake said when we rode the train from Tokyo to Kamakura.

When we stepped out of the car in front of the hotel, no

introduction was needed. The enormous Australian was a red-wood among bonsais. Among the slight, dark-haired Asians on that city sidewalk, Burt Swift was an explosion of color. His sun-bleached hair and ginger beard gave him fiery pirate look, while his beak-like nose appeared sunburned despite the season. "Jake-O!" he shouted. The two men embraced as men do, with vigor and slaps on backs, the brotherly bond they shared emanating from them.

"And this," Jake announced. "This is the wonderful woman I haven't been able to stop talking about."

The Aussie's wide smile narrowed as he looked at me. "Kat, is it?" He extended an enormous hand. I could not remember feeling so small next to anyone before.

"That's what Jake calls me. Actually, it's Katherine. Kate Murphy. I'm glad to meet you."

"Isn't she as beautiful as I said, Burty?"

"Jake, stop it. You're making Burt feel uncomfortable."

After the fiasco with Mary K and Jake, I so wanted Burt to welcome me. I instantly liked his big bear presence and the flat Australian pinch of every vowel he spoke.

"What do you have there?" Burt asked, grimacing toward the pad Jake carried. "What have you done to complicate my life?" Gone was the friendly tone in Burt's voice, and despite his shining eyes, I could see his frustration with Jake. Jake seemed oblivious to the weather change in Burt.

An icy chill drifted over me. "Wait until you see," Jake said, opening his sketchpad. "It all came to me on the flight. It's all right here. You'll see what Kat's inspired. She's my muse, Burty."

Burt looked over at me, then took the sketchbook. "Did you get any sleep on the plane?" he asked Jake.

"I'm too excited to sleep."

Burt looked down his aquiline nose at me, then flipped

through the pages. Jake fidgeted while Burt studied the drawings.

"This is nothing like what we put in the proposal. We had wood and small stones in the garden. This is right in front of the Buddha. They'll never allow it."

"But this is way better than what we proposed. They hired *me*, right? They want my best ideas. How can they not love this?" Jake insisted. "Kat thought they were great, too," he said, winking at me.

Deep lines formed around Burt's eyes and he combed his fingers through his beard. "I'm afraid Kate's endorsement won't mean a lot to the Japanese Arts Council. She's not the one who's got to negotiate an entirely new contract with a bunch of tradition-bound Japanese about their holy shrine."

"Oh come on, Burty. Don't get so worked up. Anyone can see these are better designs. Just work your magic. They'll love it. Don't they always love it?"

"Do you have any idea what it would require to get these changes approved? We're supposed to be ready for an installation in one week. You're talking bloody cranes here, and I don't know how many laborers and tons of stone."

"Just do what you do," Jake said, his voice bright. Jake bounded through the revolving door while hotel employees bowed to greet him. He bowed in return and smiled back at us through the glass.

"Bloody baby," Burt mumbled. "Unreasonable bloody baby."

"He's tired," I said, feeling the itch of discomfort standing with the gigantic stranger and his fuming anger. "He'll be more reasonable after he's slept."

"You've known Jake for what, a few weeks?"

"Yes, but..." I hesitated. "I feel that we know each other really well." The crack in my voice betrayed me.

"You'll have to pardon me for saying this, Kate"—when

Burt said my name, it came out like *Kite*—"and I'm sure you're a very nice lady. But just because you and Jake enjoy a shag, it doesn't mean you *know* him. You'll excuse me, but I've got an impossible job to do."

I stood on the sidewalk, watching Burt clomp away like a Clydesdale through the crowd that divided to clear his path. Too jetlagged and stunned to feel embarrassed, I stood there wondering who would win in a fight, Burt Swift or Mary Kowalski. The answer wasn't so obvious.

* * *

I awoke the next morning to find Jake madly scribbling on a sketchpad at the foot of the tatami mat we'd slept on. He lay on his belly with his feet on his pillow. "Hi," I whispered.

He didn't respond. I spoke a little louder. Still, he didn't turn. I crawled down to lay beside him. He held his right hand up in a stop position while his left continued to sketch. I waited, fascinated by how engrossed he was. I peeked over his shoulder at the drawing of a stately Buddha. In the foreground was a trail of boulders of gradually ascending size that led up to the statue in a curved line. Each stone was oval, but severed by a jagged break that divided it into two pieces. Each half-stone sat beside its mate with a space between the two parts, which created a thin slice of black space, a void between the halves. The darkness between the winding rows of boulders became a line of its own which curved, snake-like, and flowed directly to the serene Buddha. The boulders' path—on an enormous scale—was so clearly reminiscent of the trail of stones Jake had formed on my body the first night we were together that I felt heat rise to my face.

Jake sketched without speaking, then strode out of our suite, his eyes glued to his drawing. He banged on the door across the hall. I stood at our door.

"Burt!" he shouted. Then he banged again. "BURT!" he yelled with more urgency.

Unflustered, Burt opened his door, shirtless, wearing pajama bottoms and holding a cup of tea that seemed too dainty for his bulky hands. He was even more powerfully built than I'd imagined, his barrel chest thick and strong, covered with a copper hair. "Don't get your boxers in a bunch. I'm right here."

"Look," Jake said. "Here it is. This is what we have to do."

Burt examined the paper. "How big are these boulders, mate?"

"The biggest has to be at least six feet across, the smallest about four feet. But we've also got to have lots of stones to select from. The interval of size change must be identical between one pair of stones to the next. And the color. It's got to have that green patina—like aged copper. They've got to look like they've coexisted for centuries, right along with the Kamakura. If I do this right, it'll look like a jade river. Perfect. Minimal. Ancient."

A smirk crossed Burt's lips. "What about the wooden towers you planned—in the garden? This requires equipment, months of planning. And just where in bloody hell I'm I going to come up with—" Burt paused and pointed his finger at the drawing, "—nineteen giant green boulders on an island the size of my fucking forearm? Do you have any foggy idea what this would cost? Or how to crack the buggers open?"

"I don't know. You're the wizard. Work your magic. This is what I'm doing."

The air had become charged with electricity; my stomach clenched.

"We've got PR meetings all week and the Uenu Park unveiling in Tokyo tomorrow," Burt stormed. "I've already arranged everything as per original plan in Kamakura—and it didn't include any giant sodding green rocks."

Jake turned and walked back into our room. Burt followed him, teacup in hand. "Drop the Uenu Park thing. That's bullshit," Jake snapped. "It's a goddamn photo op. I'm here to do art. I'm here to make history."

"It's more than a photo op, friend. That hunk of bronze is your ticket to work in this country. I've worked on this for two years. Cancel one, you can forget the other. This is not a country in which you insult people. Forget about the rocks. We go back to the wooden structures we had planned. That's that."

I watched Jake's wiry body go rigid. His face gathered into an expression that I'd seen on junkies and psychotics I'd treated in the ER. Everything in his appearance became a brewing storm.

"That's not THAT!" Jake picked up the telephone from the dresser top, jerked the wires from the wall, and flung it at Burt. Burt ducked and the phone hit a mirror on the wall behind him, sending glass to the floor in a glittering waterfall. I covered my head and jumped to the other side of the room. I stood, frozen, my body taut like a coil ready to spring. Jake snatched up a long shard of broken mirror and held it, sword-like, toward Burt. Blood soon dripped from the heel of his hand from under his grip.

Burt held up his hand to stop Jake from moving. "Settle down now," he said, his voice low and level.

"I won't settle down!" Jake shouted. He waved his sketch with his left hand. I could see a fat stream of blood spilling from the palm that still clutched the glass, a puddle forming on the rug beneath him. "*This* is it. *This* is the art I came here to do. *This* is what I'm doing. I don't care about the Disneyland shit."

"All right, Jake-O. We'll see what we can get done. Just let go of that glass, all right?" Burt turned and glared at me. I'd hoped for a look of reassurance or kindness. Instead I felt the pierce of his gaze that said, *You shouldn't be here. This is your fault.*

"Just get it done, Burt!" Jake shouted. He flung the sketch toward Burt and it went sailing and landed on the pile of silver mirror slivers; then he dropped the bloodied glass onto the pile. He pounded out of the room and disappeared.

Burt turned to me, his eyes bloodshot. "Did he sleep at all?"

"I don't know. He's always awake by the time I wake up."

At nearly a run, Burt took off behind Jake.

* * *

Several hours later, I sat on the small sofa in the living room of the suite, wrapping Jake's hand in sterile gauze. "Thank God you're left-handed. This is deep. I need to get you to a clinic for stitches. These butterflies won't hold on a palm."

Jake's head hung. "Never mind that." He pulled me toward him. "I'm so sorry, Kat. I'm such an idiot. It's just that—"

I was still trembling. I'd walked the streets alone the entire time Jake had been gone, thinking about what I should do. When I'd returned to the suite, Jake had been curled in a ball on the sofa.

He rested his head on my shoulder. "I'm so sorry. I get an idea and it seems like that's the only idea I can—and I just, I just—I know I scared you."

I pushed him away from me and looked into his eyes. "You did scare me. You really did."

"I'd never hurt Burt. I'd never hurt you. You've got to know that. I—"

I got up from the couch, leaving Jake sitting there. "You need to know one thing about me," I said. "I will never be threatened like that. If I was Burt and you'd held that glass out at me, I'd be gone. I arranged for a car to take me to the airport. I don't belong here."

Jake stood and reached toward me. "Please, Kat. Don't leave. You do belong here. With me." Jake's face was guileless sincerity, melting my resolve.

"Never again, Jake. I swear to God."

"I know. I know." His face was lined with anguish.

At that moment, Burt came back into the room. His fiery eyes had cooled. "You all right, Kate?" he asked. I nodded that I was okay.

Burt slapped Jake's chest with a folder filled with papers. "Well, I've worked your bully miracle," he said. "It took a lot of bowing, a hundred phone calls, and an enormous donation from the president of Sony, whose arse you will take over kissing. I've got your pebbles and your permits. Here's the whole enchilada, Jake-O." Burt grabbed Jake's shirt collar like a bullying older brother. "You do the unveiling at Uenu Park. No objections. And you act like you love that wanking hunk of bronze in the park. You do the press that I know you hate. You shake the hands, you kiss the babies. You change not so much as a molecule of that plan. Then, and only then, we go to Kamakura and you put in your goddamned green rocks. When we come back to Tokyo, you do every ceremony and business dinner."

Jake burst into a smile and flung himself at Burt, then kissed both of Burt's cheeks. "Thank you. Thank you and I'm sorry. I'm so sorry."

Burt shrugged. His eyes stuck on mine. "Forget it, mate. Anything for art, right? Don't get all kissy." Burt smiled at me, but his eyes still wore worry. "Jesus Christ on a raft, I've had girlfriends less trouble than you. And at least with them I usually end up with a wank after they throw such a fuss."

Jake sniffed. "I probably owe you that, too."

"Kiss arses, Jake and you can just keep your mitts off my willie."

Jake laughed, lifted his glasses, and wiped tears from his face. "Just wait, Burt. I'll make it up to you. I promise."

In a quick jerk Burt locked his thick arm around Jake's neck and rubbed his knuckles briskly on his scalp. "Oh, quit your blubbering, you ridiculous baby."

* * *

The days that followed returned us to almost where we'd been before. Gone was the irrational, tantrum-throwing child. Gone was the feral animal that turned dangerous when thwarted. Returned was my gentle lover, my playful, good-humored companion. His wild energy when directed to his work was laser beam-focused. He moved with buoyant cheer. Among the yet unbloomed cherry blossom trees of Ueno Park, he played hacky-sack with the children who gathered to watch the unveiling of his sculpture. The sculpture that he thought so unimportant was a tower of interwoven bronze and copper bamboo stalks, green with patina. The tower reached nearly fifteen feet, but defied both its materials and its size and evoked images of lacy jungle growth.

Jake and I attended formal teas with government and corporate dignitaries and art patrons. He charmed them and caused the same easy laughter that he had with my family at the bar.

Having watched my share of concussive exchanges among doctors, it was surprisingly easy to dismiss the outburst in our suite as the momentary explosion of tension and creativity. Surgeons, the divas of the medical field, are not above bringing nurses to tears by berating them for miniscule imprecision. One surgeon at Stanford, upon being told he'd not been given approval for the surgery he recommended, became so enraged he pushed a conference room table over, causing everyone seated to jump to their feet with coffee down the front of their clothing. He ultimately got his approval, result-ing in the saved life of a newborn. Medical journals later lauded him. Millions in research funding for Stanford's cof-fers quieted the administrators and gave *carte blanche* to the surgeon for future tirades.

Watching Jake's and his crew's execution of his vision in Kamakura provoked the same fascination for me as watching surgery. With ancient shrines and gardens around us, Jake ran his installation like a maestro with an entire orchestra responding to his slightest move. He inspired them to feats they could never have imagined. He insisted on perfection and wouldn't stop until it was achieved. "No, no. This boulder is the wrong shade. I don't care how much it cost to get it here, it's not right."

Burt spoke in soothing tones, delivering his orders in Japanese to the crew of local laborers and art students. The harmony of the team reflected the surroundings, with its tran-quil, reflective ponds and sculpted gardens. Winding paths and graceful willows created an environment that seemed to invite everyone—even the hard-hatted crane operators—to speak in reverent, whispered voices. And the Great Buddha himself drew from me a feeling I'd never had in any cathedral. Looking into his serene face, climbing the steps to stand in the cool shade that he cast, was an experience of quiet power I had never known.

When the installation was finished, I stood gazing at the enormous Buddha, Kamakura, with the giant stones winding up the grassy corridor toward him. The boulders appeared as ancient as the shrine itself; as if they *belonged* exactly where they sat, deposited there by an ancient river. They functioned to guide the viewer's eyes, not just to the Great Buddha but to his holy essence. Though I'd watched with my own eyes the power equipment and a giant auger that had broken each boulder into halves, their splits appeared completely organic. I'd seen the forklifts and cranes and the dozens of muscled men move the great stones, but they now rested there in what seemed like it had been their location for centuries.

Burt ran up to Jake and me as we took in the grand view. "Do you see this?" he said, waving a newspaper. "Word about this installation has exploded like bloody fireworks. Every room within a hundred miles is booked for the duration. The tourism board is saying that they've already gotten hundreds of international calls from people wanting to come see the great Path of Stones." Burt squinted and scanned the paper. "Let's see, they're calling this 'an unforgettable image from one of the most important figures of contemporary art... lofty in beauty, scale, and in the sublimely spiritual impact it makes on those who see it.' Do you hear that, Jake-O?"

Jake shrugged. "I'm glad you're happy, Burty." Jake patted his friend's bulky shoulder.

Burt folded the paper and tucked it under his arm. "I've got to check the answering service. I bet the phones are ringing off the hook."

Seeing a man of Burt's size actually scamper away made both of us laugh. Jake turned to me. "I'm starved. Want to get some lunch?"

The accolades that turned Burt from grumpy to giddy mattered not a whit to Jake. The installation would be disassembled after a few months, though it broke my heart to think about it. Jake's perfect, broken boulders would be moved to a garden elsewhere in the small village of Kamakura, but not near the Buddha where Jake had envisioned them—where they belonged.

I wanted each of his creations to stand so that generations could view them and experience the awe of their simple beauty. Burt seemed to want that, too, and he strived to preserve the grandeur of them as best he could with his camera. Soon the Great Buddha would once again be alone in the maple grove among the ancient temples, as he had been since the thirteenth century. I wondered if he would feel lonely. I wanted to talk about it all with Jake, but whenever I tried, he changed the subject. The experience, though it lingered for me, was over for him. He had moved on.

$$* * *$$

We returned to Tokyo after the Kamakura installation. Jake complied with every one of Burt's demands.

"What next, Mr. Bloom?" one reporter asked in broken English at a press conference. "What is the art will you make after you leave Japan?"

Jake was seated on a stage, behind a table with a linen tablecloth, a spider web of microphones before him. Burt skulked at the side of the room. Jake grinned at me where I sat in the audience. Cameras flashed. "We'll enjoy a few more days in your beautiful country. Then I'll go back to San Francisco, where my dear lady friend's artistry as a surgeon is of much greater importance than what I've done here."

I watched as Burt shook his head, frustrated, I assumed, that Jake would waste an opportunity talking of my work instead of promoting his own.

A diminutive Japanese woman stood. She held a small notepad and spoke in perfect English, in a voice so light that it could have been a child's. "If you please. It has been reported that there was initially great resistance to your work in Kamakura. How did such an enormous vision become reality with so many obstacles in the path?"

"I can answer that question in just two words," Jake said. He paused, and a hush filled the room. Jake shielded his eyes from the light and scanned the room. "Burt Swift. Burt, come on up here."

Jake began to clap and the crowd followed, offering a reserved round of applause. Burt arrived at the front, his face glowing bright pink as Jake waxed on about all that he'd done to make the Path of Stones possible. The questions went on for over an hour.

In our final day in Tokyo, Burt collected his last chit from Jake, requiring him to pose for a formal portrait near his sculpture in Ueno Park. "Okay, but snap fast. I think I've just about paid you off," Jake complained.

Once the last photo was taken, I went to get us coffees before we were to leave the city for a few days of solitude and Jake's final installation. When I returned, I couldn't find Jake anywhere. I searched among the lines of cherry blossom trees, now just beginning to bud, and the picturesque arched wooden bridges and gardens. Afloat on a tranquil reflecting pond were lily pads and lotus blossoms, mirrored images of bamboo stalks, and maples. Finally, I spotted Jake crouched at the water's edge.

Before him was a row of three simple nests constructed of gray twigs, each surrounded by beds of burgundy maple leaves. "Wow," I whispered. "How can you make a cluster of twigs and leaves so beautiful?"

"I didn't make beauty," he said as he stood and turned toward me. "I just made you notice it." He stood and I stepped into his arms. From behind a nearby tree we heard the click of a camera's shutter.

"Goddammit, Burt!" Jake shouted. "Turning into paparazzi doesn't flatter you. Maybe you should work for the *National Enquirer*."

Then we could see that it was not Burt, but dozens of the Japanese press. Cameras clicked and photographers stepped closer to get a glimpse of whatever Jake was creating. He chatted amicably in Japanese. Reporters scribbled notes on small pads.

"Come on, Kat. They want you in the picture."

"No they don't, Jake. They want you, not me."

Jake stepped toward me. "You were the inspiration for the Kamakura piece," he whispered. "I need my muse to be in the photographs."

Tucking my hair behind my ears and licking my lips, I reluctantly moved in to pose alongside Jake. Lenses the length of baseball bats came at us from all directions. I wanted to hide behind Jake, but he pulled me forward, surprising me with a huge, passionate kiss. Clicks and flashes exploded for another round.

* * *

We traveled south and west of Tokyo to the opposite shore of Japan to a village outside of the city of Fukuoka. Burt had arranged for Jake and me to have a few days alone while the stage was set for his final installation.

Jake and I wandered the hills, sometimes together and sometimes separately. The Japanese countryside held all of the serenity that Tokyo lacked. Layers upon layers of jade green hills revealed themselves as morning fog retreated. Sika deer, with their stately antlers and delicate spots, regarded us by pausing their grazing. Green woodpeckers fluttered through tree limbs. The limbs, still winter-bare, reached delicate fingers to what little light they could find.

It became sport for the village children to follow the "mysterious American," as Jake was being called, leaving enough distance between him and themselves so as not to disturb his strange behavior. Children dressed in uniforms and yellow slickers followed Jake like a small band of spies, discovering the surprises he left for them. He arranged feathers, leaves, branches, and pieces of shale—items from their everyday surroundings—into whimsical patterns that delighted them.

On the morning we were to move out to the installation site, I repacked my suitcase with the clothes that our host family had insisted on laundering. My cotton shirts smelled of the verdant hills. As I rearranged my things in my suitcase, I came upon the box of tampons I'd packed for the trip. Holding the unopened box, I calculated. *Not in Japan*, I figured. *Not ever at Jake's house.* The reality of how many days had passed started to sink in. I sat on the edge of the bed and ran my fingers over the pink chenille spread.

How could I be so stupid? I did the math. It had been five months since the last time Nigel and I had sex, and that had always been with protection. I'd used my diaphragm with Jake all but our first night together, nearly five weeks before.

I took a walk into town, intending to buy a home pregnancy test at the local pharmacy. Unable to read the packages, I bought three different items with pictures of women on the box, only to find when I opened them that I'd bought feminine deodorant, vaginal itch cream, and a douche. I laughed at myself—a brittle, mocking laugh, because even without the test, I already knew what it would tell me.

* * *

Jake was oddly silent as we drove on the narrow roads to meet up with Burt and the crew, as well as photographers from *National Geographic*. I wanted to talk to him, but he was concentrating, thinking, I assumed, about his installation. With each passing mile, my resolve not to worry weakened.

All I could do was think and sort through a series of alternate plans and contingencies. I was just starting my residency. Jake and I were so new together. And then there was Jake's explosion in Tokyo. Was this someone ready to be a father? He might not even want children.

I could terminate the pregnancy when I got back to San Francisco. In one semester in the dorms at Stanford, six girls I knew had ended unwanted pregnancies. Shucking the last vestiges of my Catholic upbringing, I had supported them, even accompanying one girl to the clinic for her procedure. I'd uttered only support while silently I'd thought them all foolish for getting themselves into situations where they were forced to make such a terrible choice. Judgmental; Jake was right.

Burt greeted us where the road ended and helped us carry our bags the last quarter mile along a dirt path. He guided us to the trailer that would be our home for the next three days while Jake worked. A second trailer sat perched nearby, with a cluster of three smaller RVs a few hundred yards away. Other than the small encampment, no other sign of human touch could be seen from the lush green hillside. Craggy rocks pierced the thick moss carpet that draped over the gentle slopes. In the distance, all that could be seen were layers of emerald hills, folded upon one another, a thousand shades of green.

"How do you like the digs, mate?" Burt asked, his arms spread wide. "Got you two private quarters." He winked at me. "Sure you don't want to bunk in a frat house, Kate?"

I looked into Burt's face, grateful that he seemed to be growing a little less hostile. "Nope, I think I saw the 'No Stinky Girls Allowed' sign."

Burt sank his hands deep into his pockets. "Oh, I think you smell all right," he said. The corners of his lips turned up just a little. The mountain of a man seemed to be warming to me.

We poked our heads into the mobile home. The kitchen table bore a vase filled with a single green orchid dangling like a hummingbird. I thought of my dad's orchid menagerie back at the pub. "Burt, I'm touched," I said. "I hope it didn't put you to too much trouble."

"Trouble is my job," he said, delivering a little salute from the brim of his World Cup cap. He turned to Jake. "Got a moment?"

The two stepped away. Burt handed Jake what appeared to be a small box. Jake threw his arms around the big Aussie, turned his back to me, then hugged Burt again. Burt wiped his forehead and passed Jake a newspaper. Jake leaned back, laughing. Then Burt handed him a smaller piece of paper. Now Jake parted from Burt in a storm. His arms flailed and he kicked at the ground.

Jake wadded and flung the piece of paper down, wearing fury on his face. Burt's murmurs failed to soothe him. Jake turned and stomped off.

I approached Burt where he stood, the rumpled newspaper in his hand. Jake kicked at the dirt in the distance.

"What is it?"

"I don't know. Maybe I should've waited. I just thought those press guys might bring it up. He'll be in no mood now, and we've got a timeline."

Burt handed me the Lifestyle section of *The New York Times*. On the front page, above the fold, I could see my own face next to Jake's; at our feet, his beautiful nests. The caption read: "Environmental sculptor, newlywed Jake Bloom, with his bride at Tokyo's Ueno Gardens."

"Bride! Who reported us as married?"

"Your marital status got a little lost in the translation, I reckon."

My heart sank into the pit of my gut. I thought of the unopened box of tampons in my suitcase. "And Jake is angry because of this?"

"Jesus, no," Burt groaned. "That bit made him laugh."

Burt hesitated before picking up the paper that Jake had thrown to the ground. He handed it to me. The letterhead read *Western Union*, a telegram addressed to Burt.

> Mr. Swift:
>
> Must rectify impetuous marriage. Will compensate you $100K for your influence. Additional $50K to be offered as motivation to the woman. $100K to her when annulment complete. Keep advised on progress.
>
> —AJB

"AJB? I'm assuming that's Aaron Bloom."

"None other. He's a miserable sod, that one. Jake ignores him, so he tries to buy my influence." Burt's face broke into a wide smile. "Not that I can be bought, mind you. Arrogant prick thinks money can buy anything. It does from some people, and Jake's been betrayed before. Students, employees." Burt peered at me. "Girlfriends. But the bloke thinks only in dollar signs. Jake and I made an agreement years ago that I'd always tell him about his dad's shenanigans. Just keeping my promise."

"I thought they were estranged. Why does Jake care what his father has to say?"

"Usually doesn't. I thought he'd get a laugh like he usually does. This time it wasn't funny. I'd knock me father's block off if he insulted you with such an offer."

I gave him a gentle punch in the shoulder. "And I thought you didn't like me."

"Well, there you go thinking." Burt pulled a cigarette from his pocket and lit it.

"What should I do?" I asked.

"Nothing to do unless you want to make an easy hundred-fifty grand. Jake is accustomed to his father tossing his fat around. He'll be over it soon enough. You're special to him."

"He's special to me, too." We stood there watching the mist crawl to fill the hollows in the hills. It rested in thick flannel tufts amid the shadows of the aging day. In only moments, the foggy layer muted the hills. The world disappeared, and it felt like Burt and I were the only two people in it. "I'm pregnant," I said. My words hung in the air, lingering with the mist.

A single exhalation was the only response.

"I don't know what to do. I was afraid of how Jake would react before. Now this."

"Before you are concerned with Jake's response, you'd best know your own. Don't tell him until you're clear what you want to do. He's like a child that way. Don't mention Disneyland unless you've already got your tickets." Without another word, Burt disappeared into the fog.

I crouched and sat down on the mossy hill. The damp ground soaked the seat of my jeans. The ground was a thick green carpet at my feet. There, tucked near a rock, was a perfect, pale green egg the size of an almond. No sign of a nest or a mother bird to be found. I picked up the egg and held it in my palm. It was cool. Nothing I could do would bring its tiny inhabitant back to life.

Gray darkness fell and cold surrounded me. The smell of smoke from a distant campfire singed the air. Suddenly chilled to my center, I followed my nose through the fog. As the smell of smoke grew stronger, Jake stepped into view carrying a lantern. He pressed his warm lips against my cold ones and tucked my arms into his jacket. His hair smelled of ash. "You're shaking," he said. He guided me across the rocky hillside to the amber blossom of his fire. He poked the flames and added a log.

"I was going to look for you, but you seemed to be enjoying your solitude," he said, stirring the fire. "I've been thinking, Kat. I've spent my whole life living for the moment. Maybe because I never thought I'd ever have a future that mattered. I've traveled light. Kept from getting attached to anyone except Burt. I didn't even like my art to be designed with any future in mind. But I've started looking ahead." Jake's eyes looked straight and true, directly into mine. "I see a future now, but only one with you in it."

Only a few weeks before I'd had a future all mapped out, and now that path seemed irreparably altered. "What about your dad?"

He stirred the fire, sending another swarm of glowing sparks into the night. "My father is not a factor in my life. I just don't want him touching what we have."

It was the second time I'd felt protected.

"I was going to wait, but I can't," he said. From the pocket of his jacket, Jake pulled a small box carved from gleaming cherry wood. "This just arrived. I've been worried all day that it might not get here."

The box was an intricate puzzle, the pieces of which slid apart from one another in one silky motion. Inside, nested in a bed of tiny pink shells, was a ring cast in platinum. I'd never cared about jewelry, but this was a ring unlike anything I'd ever seen. Slim, shimmering, silver twigs formed a nest, a miniscule remembrance of Jake's sculpture next to the reflecting pond in Tokyo. Inside the nest rested a perfect pink pearl.

"I sketched it in Tokyo. An artisan there cast it for me. What do you think?"

Jake's words pulled me back into the body that I didn't know I'd left. "It's magical."

"It's a sculpture of my wish," Jake said. "It's you and me. A nest for each other. Ever since I've known you all I can think about making are serene winding trails and nests. Seems like a sign to me. Maybe my art is actually directing me to you. Marry me, Kat."

His words blasted me from where I sat. My careful plans crumbled around me like so much ash from a glowing ember. A baby and a husband weren't part of my design. I tried to imagine going ahead with my plans—taking those steps without Jake. I blurted for the second time, "I'm pregnant." As the words came out, I knew that I'd decided against any possibility of ending the pregnancy.

Jake sprang up. He jumped, both feet leaving the ground, and landed on the huge rock we'd been sitting on. Like a coyote baying at the moon, Jake let out a loud howl that pierced the night. "Ow, ow ooooooooowww!" Then he grabbed me in his arms and twirled me in the glowing firelight.

"What about my residency? All I've ever wanted was to be a surgeon. I'm so close."

"Marry me, Kat. There are two of us in this. You'll be a surgeon. That's *your* art. I'd never get in the way of that. We've got everything. Thanks to Burt I have enough money so you can work as much or as little as you want. I'll change diapers and make baby food. We'll make a home like I never had, right in San Francisco near your family. We'll surround our baby with love and art and—" He jumped to the top of the rock, flung his arms out wide, and resumed his howling.

"I didn't do this on purpose, Jake. I wouldn't—"

"This is the happiest accident I've ever known," he said. His face glowed.

My brain kept clicking through my list of worries, trying to sink my rising glee. "What about your father?"

"He's never mattered less."

Jake took the cherry wood box that I still held and pulled out the ring. Taking my hand, he pulled me up onto the rock with him. Our bodies pressed against each other. Jake lifted the ring to his lips, warming it with his breath. Then he raised my hand and slipped it onto my finger. "Make us a family, Kat."

My kisses gave my answer for me.

Loose Ends and Love Knots

Once we got home from Japan, I avoided going back to our Haight Street flat until it was unavoidable. I tried to call half-a-dozen times, but Mary K hadn't answered. She had finished her internship rotation at the hospital as well, so I had no other way to reach her.

The house was locked up and she wasn't home when I stopped by. I worked there for hours, sorting through nine years' worth of belongings. Scattered around my room were the casualties of moving—piles of books, clothes, and a huge mound of once valuable items, now debris.

"Looks like you're wrecking the joint," Mary K said, peeking into my room. She entered, doing her best to hide a decided limp.

"Where've you been?"

"Queens. Needed to mend a few fences. Other than that, I've just been ducking your calls."

"So I noticed."

"Thanks for the postcards. And the messages."

I wanted to bridge the chasm of our distance, but didn't know how. Most of all, I wanted to tell her about the baby and how I felt nearly explosive with happiness, despite my earlier panic about the whole thing. An ocean of good news held back behind a dam of unexplainable hesitation. I silently folded clothes into even stacks.

Mary K plopped onto my clothing-strewn bed and picked up a pink cotton peasant blouse from the discard pile. "Geez, it looks like the *Brady Bunch* wardrobe department got barfed up in here."

I threw a balled-up pair of socks at her. "What about you? I seem to remember a lot of army surplus overalls and undershirts."

"Yeah, but I made that work." She scooped the hair from in front of her face, tucked it behind her ear, and delivered a grin.

I closed the box I'd filled. I twisted my hair into a bun, poked a couple of stray pencils into it to secure it, and lay down at the end of the bed.

"Thanks for sending the dogwood tree," she said. "I planted it in the backyard where I scattered Ben's ashes. Dogwood." She gave a one-syllable laugh. "Pretty good. Ben would've liked sleeping under it."

"Mary K, I—"

"Water under the bridge." She looked directly into my eyes for the first time. "You don't have to move, Murphy. It was a bad day."

"I know I don't have to. But maybe it's time."

"I suppose." Mary K surveyed the room. "Wow, a decade worth of shit. I've lived with you longer than I did most of my siblings. How's that for a kick in the head?"

We lay on the bed for a while, eyes to the ceiling. "It's been brought to my attention that I can be a tad harsh when sharing my opinions," she said.

"Who shared that little tidbit with you, and to what funeral home do I send the flowers?"

"My mother is alive and well. No FTD required. Told me that since I was a kid, when I'm hurt or sad I attack the ones I love most."

"Yeah, well, we've all got our flaws. I've recently learned that I'm judgmental and stubborn."

"No kidding."

We lay there quietly, street noise from outside the only sound in the room.

"Ben wasn't your fault. It was a shitty thing to say. He just died, plain and simple. Old dogs die. Maybe he didn't want to die in front of me. You know, to protect me. I'm glad he was with someone who loved him."

I reached across the bed and took her hand. She squeezed mine before she pulled away and searched her pocket for cigarettes. She'd always honored my request not to smoke in my room, but the agreement now seemed moot.

She sat up and struck a match.

"I've been thinking about your residency," I said. "It's discrimination. They can't just dismiss you because they found out about your condition. You've demonstrated impeccable skills. There are laws. The Americans with Disabilities Act. They can't just—"

"Cool your jets, counselor. Nobody at UC dismissed me. I made a choice."

"But—"

"I was kidding myself."

"But how about radiology? There'd be no risk to patients there."

"I'd lose my mind looking at film every day. I want to do surgery, even if it is on corpses. Besides, working with the dead probably takes best advantage of my stellar people skills."

A swell of sadness formed in my chest, thinking of Mary K's talent and of how living patients wouldn't have the benefit of her skills. I wanted cry together over the lost dream, but I knew it would piss her off. I sat up and looked into her eyes.

"Lose the face, Murphy. You're killing me here. The ME's office fits with my sunny disposition. Just do your job right and don't give me any customers. Got it?" Taking a deep inhale from her cigarette, Mary K sat up and pointed to the stack of mail on my side table. "Looks like you've got some pretty ritzy correspondence to open."

On top of the stack sat an envelope with a Park Avenue return address. The paper seemed less like a note than a work of art. Linen letterhead displayed the gold monogram "AJB." The evenly penned black script of the note at first appeared machine-printed, but soon I could see that it was just the most uniform, perfect hand lettering I'd ever seen.

Dear Dr. Murphy,

I determined that the newspaper was in error and that you have not yet married. This pleases me as I now have the opportunity to avert a catastrophe and to prevent you from undue suffering.

My son is not well. Entanglement in his life can bring you nothing but heartache once the first blush has passed. He disregards all help that I offer and rejects any course that would be healthy and productive for him.

As you are a well-educated person, I'm sure that you welcome information to inform your decisions. I am willing to provide full background and will compensate you handsomely for the time and any discomfort you might already have experienced. I've enclosed a business card with my private number. I'll await your call.

With urgency,
Aaron J. Bloom

"Big Bloom, I assume," Mary K sighed.

I handed the note to her and waited for her indignation on my behalf. Finally, she snuffed her cigarette in an empty coffee cup from my nightstand and spoke. "Jesus, you didn't get married, did you?"

"That's what you've got to say?"

"Shocker, Aaron Bloom is a dick. He tries to make a bribe sound like, what... compensation? And I told you his son was a head case." Cigarette smoke added a fragrance to her insult. "Don't tell me you got married."

Every muscle in my body went rigid and my jaw tightened. I added artificial sparkle to my voice. "I didn't, but I'm going to. Next weekend."

As though shot from cannon, Mary K sprang from the bed. She stood with fists clenched, ready to punch anything that moved. "What the fuck, Murphy? You just met this guy. You're just starting your residency. A residency I—anybody would kill for. And you're playing bride? Where's the fire? You act like you're knocked up or something."

I closed my eyes tight enough that I could see bursts of red on the inside of my eyelids. My mouth went dry. I opened my eyes to see Mary K still poised in the same fighting position. "You *are* knocked up. Jesus!" She kicked at a box with the foot she'd been favoring and winced.

"I think *pregnant* would be a better term. But I'd be marrying Jake whether I was pregnant or not. He asked me before he even knew."

"What are you, in a trance or something? You've abandoned every bit of rational thought you've ever had. Of course you're pregnant. That's what happens when you fuck a guy while you're unconscious."

I stood and began flinging clothes into an open box on top of the ones I'd taken such time folding. "This is great coming from somebody who's been through nine years of continuous one-night stands. Pregnancy isn't exactly a concern you've had to face." The words left behind an acrid sting on my tongue.

"Lucky me. I'm a needle-using dyke with a future poking around in rotting corpses. I guess I'm pretty fucking lucky not to have to fear pregnancy. You're throwing everything away."

"Don't pull the pity card in front of me. You're alone by choice."

"What about Nigel? Did you tell him?"

"When have you ever cared about Nigel?"

"Couldn't the kid be his?"

"I think I can track the paternity of my child, thank you."

"And your folks? Did they at least advise you to slow things down?"

I looked away from her. Telling my family about an unplanned pregnancy had felt humiliating. But Jake had also taken my father aside, formally asking for his blessing for our marriage. Though concerned, Dad had come around. Given all of the family secrets that had come out, we had all learned to give each other a lot more leeway and understanding. "They were surprised at first. But they're supportive."

"Of course. What fucking choice is there? I'm the only one telling you the truth. Murphy, I'm begging you. Reconsider. You're probably freaked. But you can have a baby without getting married. You've got family. Friends. A career."

"I've also got Jake. Remember him? The man I'm in love with. The father of my child."

Mary K shook her head and walked toward the bedroom door. She put her hand on the knob. "I'm begging you to think about this. Aaron Bloom may be the world's biggest ass hat, but he also knows some stuff about his kid. You're ignoring every warning here."

"I'm ignoring nothing. Jake and I have no secrets." I looked into my friend's steady gaze. "I'm hoping you'll be there stand up with me at the wedding," I said. "It's at the Palace of Fine Arts on Saturday at two."

"No can do, Murphy. Can't support something I know is doomed. Let me know when you come to your senses."

"So you're not even going to come? After everything we've been through together?" My blood pounded. "You're haven't given Jake a chance. He's high-strung, but the most loving man I've ever met."

"You might want to add 'naïve' to that list of your character flaws."

"You can add 'cynical' and 'paranoid' to yours."

"Done." Mary K opened the bedroom door. "Let me share just one piece of advice, Murphy. I'm pretty goddamn sure that I don't have a tail. But if someone who's known me for nearly a decade, someone I *know* loves me, insists that I do, I'm at least going to take a look at my own ass." She jutted her jaw toward me. "Just turn around and look, Murphy. That's all I'm saying."

The front door slammed. I jammed the remainder of my stuff into the last of the boxes. I crammed the last of the boxes into my Bug and drove away from the flat I'd shared with Mary K. I drove away from that life toward my new life with Jake.

* * *

I stood in my slip and bare feet, studying myself in the mirror of my mother's vanity table. Alice stood beside me in lavender organza. Her hair was a subdued shade of ash blonde and her makeup was soft and subtle. Her face glowed in the golden morning light shining through the windowpanes. She smoothed the front of her dress and then clutched each of her hands. She looked over my shoulder at our reflections in the mirror. "Those fancy beauticians at Niemen Marcus work miracles, huh? Jake may have opened a whole can of worms with that present he gave me. I think some of the mad money I've squirreled away over the years might be going for some new clothes." She shrugged. "Oh well, what have I got to be mad about?" Alice said, looking at me in the mirror.

"I think your makeover is magnificent."

"In my case it was sort of a make-*under*."

"You look beautiful." I envisioned Alice's cast-offs, a pretty colorful donation bagful of spangles and animal prints, arriving at Goodwill.

"Enough about this old bird. This is your day," she said, smiling at my reflection. "You'd better get your dress on. The car will be here any sec. I've never ridden in a limousine that wasn't following a hearse."

My hands went to my hips. "Well *that's* just wrong." Smiles cut through the stiffness of the nervous faces in the mirror.

After Mary K, I'd told no one about the letter Aaron Bloom sent and of the seeds of hesitation it had planted in my heart. I pushed thoughts of it to a dark recess in my mind.

Alice reached to me and tucked one of my stray curls under the lace of my snood. "This is a big day. Elyse would have been so proud."

"I've never said this, but I think of you as my mother, too— along with her." I nodded toward my mother's photo on the vanity. "I suppose I always have. I'd like to think of you as this baby's grandmother. You'll be the only one."

In that second, I could see my future baby cuddling in

Alice's lap, growing up being spoiled with sweets and extra cherries in Shirley Temples—just as I had been.

After a moment we broke from each other and looked at our blotchy faces in the mirror. "Oh Katie, I—"

"What shall the baby call you? Not just Alice. Nana Alice, maybe?"

"Katie, I, oh. I just don't know. I'm just so sorry about it all, and—" Whether it was the pregnancy, the wedding day, or all of the years of Alice's mothering, I felt my whole body swell with love.

"There's nothing more to be sorry about. Nana Alice it is. I think my mother would be pleased."

"I hope so, Katie. I really do."

Alice rested her fingers on the silver-framed photo of my mother, pregnant, glowing with joy, her tiny frame rounded by her sixth month of pregnancy. "I guess there'll soon be a picture of me just like that one, with a huge belly and all."

Alice looked at the photo. "She was so happy that day."

We lingered there, weeping together. "It's official," I said looking back to the mirror. "We're a mess."

"Fear not, I've brought the reinforcements." She pulled a suitcase-size satchel from beside the vanity and began touching up our makeup.

* * *

When we got down to the street, Jake and Dad were leaning against the limousine, swapping stories with the driver. Dad's silver hair shimmered in the morning light, and his suit jacket was the first I'd ever seen him wear that actually buttoned around his middle. As soon as he saw us, his eyes lit up. In his brogue, thickened by sentiment, he said, "Jake, you're not nearly as ugly nor nearly as old as me, but I can tell you that you never did a thing to deserve such a lovely lady."

"Of that I'm certain, Mr. Murphy."

Dad reached up and put his hand on Jake's shoulder. "After today, I'm supposing that Mr. Murphy won't quite work, now will it, Jake? We're family now. You call me what you'd like, Angus or Dad, whichever feels right to you."

Jake wore a face full of boyish delight. "I've never called anybody Dad. I think I'd like that." Jake looked at me, beaming.

My dad's pudgy hand gave Jake's shoulder a squeeze. "Dad it is, then."

The four of us loaded into the back of the limousine and rode through the curving roads of Golden Gate Park. We passed Stow Lake, the Arboretum, and the Japanese Tea Garden. Dad rolled down the window when we came to the conservatory, which appeared like Emerald City. "Oh, look girls, the tulips are full out. How nice of them to show up a little early this year. Isn't it grand?"

We seemed to be going in the direction opposite the Palace of Fine Arts. "Jake, where are we going? We don't want to be late."

"Relax. We've got plenty of time."

The limousine came to a stop on El Camino Del Mar amidst the palatial estates of Sea Cliff, an elite neighborhood at the northernmost tip of San Francisco's peninsula. Each house in Sea Cliff stood proud, adorned in bougainvillea blossoms, climbing roses, or red geraniums flowing from crowded window boxes. Filigreed wrought-iron gates separated grand front doors from the sidewalks. The mansions made the humble clapboard places back in the Sunset District around Dad's pub seem like the houses of the first and second little pigs.

"Thanks, John," Jake said to the driver. "We won't be long."

Jake guided Alice, Dad, and me to the enclosed courtyard of an expansive Mediterranean house. Fuchsia blossoms filling hanging planters dangled like jewelry from the eaves. Flower beds exploded with foxgloves, hyacinth, and roses. The sugary perfume of jasmine filled the courtyard and drew us to the oversized oak door. Dad's eyes bugged out, taking in all of the blossoms. "Will you look at this garden," he sighed. "Why, this has been tended by a hand that knows."

"I'm not up for visiting anybody right now," I whispered to Jake. "I'm already too nervous."

He smiled and opened the front door. "Nobody to visit. I just wanted you to see where we'll be spending our first married night together."

Jake said he'd arranged a local honeymoon because I only had a few more days before my residency started. We stepped into the house, gawking at the massive rooms and high ceilings. I surmised that the owner was a customer of Jake's, because his sculptures sat prominently in the living room. The rooms each burst with an explosion of art of all kinds. In the kitchen, a breakfast nook nestled into one of the bay windows. From the table, through diamond-shaped window panes arranged in an arch, was a view of the Golden Gate Bridge and the Marin Headlands to the north, the vast Pacific to the west. A huge atrium sat across the massive foyer on the other side of the house.

Jake led us all up the grand staircase, showing each room. The master bedroom had rich ebony wood floors; the bed was a huge marshmallow of pillows and down comforters.

We followed Jake like mute zombies, finally ending up in a sunny nursery painted in pale apple green, the entire ceiling filled with delicate, suspended mobiles fashioned of origami leaves hung by filaments so fine that the leaves appeared to float. The mobiles swayed gently as our bodies stirred the air and cast dancing shadows over the crib.

"It's beautiful, Jake. Amazing, really. I would never have thought you could rent this kind of place for a weekend."

"I didn't rent it for a weekend."

"For how long?" I began to panic. The thought of how many thousands of dollars such a place would rent for made me feel weak.

Jake pulled a small box from his tuxedo pocket. "Here. My wedding gift."

Inside the box, on a bed of tiny white pebbles, rested a single key.

Dad and Alice wore faces with stunned expressions. "But Jake, the rent on this place has got to be outrageous. I don't—"

"I bought it. It's my gift to you and to our baby."

I buckled into the willow-wood rocker poised in the corner of the nursery. Jake kneeled beside me. "That's where I want to see you," he said. "I want you and our baby to have this home."

"But this is too much. I'll have to take some time off. My residency doesn't pay a lot and I've got student loans and—"

"It's only money. Burt manages all of that. We'll pay off your loans. Don't worry so much, Kat. Do you like the house?"

I looked over at Alice and then at my dad. I imagined the sound of our baby's laughter coming from the nursery. Jake would use the atrium as a studio. I could see it all. But the whole house was so grand. The bar and the flat upstairs had always felt like plenty to me.

"I'll work right here at home while the baby is little. I'll be Mr. Mom. I can see it all. All of it, right here. Oh Kat, it'll be *perfect*."

* * *

The sorrel dome and curved colonnades of the Palace of Fine Arts admired themselves in the reflection of the lagoon. A breeze swayed the graceful limbs of the willows and carried flower-scented air to greet us as we stepped out of the

136

limousine. The springtime sky had shed all her gray garments and wore celebratory blue. Vivaldi's timeless melodies lauding the season sung from the strings of the violins, cellos, and violas poised between the Corinthian columns of the Roman rotunda. Pink cherry blossom petals carpeted the walkway.

Open to the public, the early spring day had invited tourists to the grassy hills beside the lagoon. They watched our arrival from a polite distance. Dad would walk me down the aisle, and Burt and Alice, our best man and matron of honor, would walk together. Our small gathering of friends waited for us inside.

We stepped from the car onto the grassy bank. Burt was there to greet us, always the consummate events arranger. "Here," he said grinning, holding out a package wrapped in brown paper.

Inside was a black-and-white framed photograph of Jake and me, lying on the soft grass of Japan's countryside. Our bodies were entwined and Jake's hand rested on my belly. No world existed outside our gaze for each other and the baby we knew I held. Titled "The Nest," the picture bore Burt's flourished signature. I couldn't imagine how he'd snapped the picture without us knowing he was there.

"I know you're not much for pictures, Jake-O, but I thought I'd give you your first family portrait."

Jake's eyes moistened. "Beautiful, Burty. Just beautiful."

"Oh Burt," I sighed. He wrapped his massive arm around my shoulder and squeezed. "No crying now or we'll all be a puddle."

The florist stepped toward us, ready with giant bouquets of white tulips for Alice and myself, the one detail my dad insisted upon handling.

"Ah, the *Tulipa* from the family of *Liliaceae*," he sighed when he saw them. "Beautiful, elegant, and graceful. Perfect for my

137

two favorite ladies." Dad lifted the blossoms from their boxes. "The blooms are without fragrance, though. I suppose the Creator didn't want to show off."

With my flowers in hand, I spotted Mary K in the distance. She wore a crisp white shirt and black tuxedo pants, her strawberry strands whipping in the wind. Her tilted gait was more pronounced than a week ago, and she used a cane. She snuffed a cigarette in the grass. I looked at Jake. "Can I have a minute?"

"Of course," he said, kissing my cheek.

✻ ✻ ✻

"Quite the shindig," she said as I approached. "Nice threads."

"You shucked your scrubs."

"I clean up okay."

"The cane? That's just to make me feel sorry for you, I assume."

She shrugged away my inquiry. "Look, Murphy. I'm not wild about this whole wedding. But it's not for me to say, right?"

"No, it's not."

"I figure you've stood by me while I've made my share of mistakes. Even if I think this is fucked up, it's your funeral. I couldn't miss my best friend's funeral, right?"

It was the most left-handed gesture of conciliation I'd ever heard, but perhaps the biggest one I could expect. "I'm glad you're here. It wouldn't have felt right without you." I looked down at the cane. "Are you okay?"

"It's nothing. Just God thumbing his nose at me a little to keep me humble."

"I said some things I regret the other day," I said.

"You said the truth, Murphy. Truth is harsh sometimes. I figure we don't need to be enemies. Friends are too hard to find." She jutted her jaw. "Seems like you should get going. You've got people waiting."

Over Mary K's shoulder, I spied Jake smiling at me in the distance. Mary K turned and looked at Jake. "I think we're holding up the party."

I nodded and walked toward the music. Just then the violin melody shifted seamlessly to *My Wild Irish Rose*. With Alice and Burt ahead of us, I took my dad's arm and followed them into the crowd of our loved ones under the dome of the rotunda.

"Ready, Kitten?" Dad whispered. I realized only then that I'd halted my steps. Together, we walked through the arch of the dome. From the corner of my eye I watched Mary K as she wiped her eyes.

Waterfalls

"I can't believe how good you make food taste."

"I'm not exactly flattered," Jake said, pouring himself a glass of wine. "You'll eat anything since your second trimester started. From the looks of your plate, I think the baby likes morel mushroom risotto."

In the three months since we'd returned from Japan, my appetite had grown right along with my pregnancy. All of my senses were more acute. I could become so overwhelmed by smells that I could barely walk down the detergent aisle in the grocery store, and my taste buds had become highly tuned for nuances of flavors I'd barely noticed before. But Jake's cooking was—just like everything he created—an exquisite work of art. "What are these?" I asked, popping a mysterious item into my mouth.

"You ask after you've already got it in your mouth?" He laughed. "Fried zucchini blossoms."

"It's been frozen burritos and Pop Tarts for me since med school. You're spoiling me."

"That's my job."

"Did you call Burt back?" I asked. "He's left about twenty messages."

"Burt *Schmirt*. I'm at home pampering my pregnant bride. Who cares about some installation in Timbuktu? Besides, I want to finish the garden and have everything perfect for the baby."

The clear June day had shrouded itself in the veil of evening. From the breakfast nook, through the diamond-shaped, leaded glass windows, we could see the sherbet sky to the west and the towers of the Golden Gate Bridge to the east. The green fingers of the Marin Headlands reached toward us from the north.

The house's grandeur made it difficult to think of as my home. Jake placed my collection of birds' eggs on the mantle, including the newest I'd found in Japan, and set the pictures of my mother and the rest of my pub family beside them. The simple objects gave me the comfort of familiarity.

"Tell me about your day," Jake said as he pushed his plate away. He pulled my swollen feet into his lap and kneaded the fatigue away. My daytime world was filled with the bright white light of the OR and hospital corridors. Each night, by candlelight and starlight, Jake listened to the stories of my days. He listened to the details of surgeries, the hospital gossip, and about the children who were my patients.

"Simone is lots better," I told him. "I got to assist while she got her heart valve transplant. It was amazing to see her fingers and toes turn pink when her blood flow improved. You should have seen her mother when we came out of the OR with the good news."

Jake smiled and kneaded the arch of my foot. "Simone, that's a pretty name." He paused, looking thoughtful. "Let's pick the baby's name."

I couldn't help but smile. Jake had a way of reading my thoughts. "I do sort of have an idea for a boy's name. My mother was Elyse Ryan before she married my dad. It might be kind of special to use her name for a *new* life, a happier life. Do you think that's weird because of how she died?"

Jake took my other foot into his hands and pressed his thumbs deep into the arch. "I don't think we should hold it against her that she didn't want to live in pain." He looked up at me with such kindness that I felt I could cry. "Elyse would be a strange name for a boy, though."

I tossed a wadded up dinner napkin toward him. "*Ryan*, you dope."

His smile formed deep parentheses in his slim cheeks. "I think Ryan works for a girl, too. In fact, I like it better. What will your family think?"

I hesitated. "I sort of ran it by them already."

Jake tossed the napkin back toward me. "You sneak. Why do I even try to pretend I have any say? The Murphy clan has voted. Ryan it is. Boy or girl."

He told me of his day, about the flagstone wall he'd built on our steeply sloping hillside and the crew he'd hired to help with the heavy lifting. He described the peppermint, thyme, and lemon basil by their colors, textures, and smells. "Let's take dessert outside. I hooked up the lighting today."

Jake pulled me around the garden, eagerly showing off each nook. He carried a brown bag—a surprise dessert, but I'd already picked up the aroma of rich, dark chocolate. He carried the bag as we toured the garden.

The path was covered with gravel of lapis and green glass pebbles tumbled smooth by the sea. It meandered like a shimmering stream down the hill. Perches and patios interrupted the path, some covered with arbors fashioned from driftwood twigs. Each niche was furnished with chairs and swings he'd created out of gnarled branches. Into the joints of the furniture were wedged polished river stones and shells.

Outside of the baby's nursery, he'd created what he called a "baby garden." It had already begun to blossom and soon would overflow with velvety lambs' ear plants, peppery nasturtiums, pussy willow stalks, pineapple mint, and wild strawberries—all meant to delight our child's every sense. We sat there, amidst the budding plants, and ate almond brownies.

As the light faded, the breeze chilled the night. Jake's voice turned somber. "Do you think the patients remember?"

"Remember what?"

"Do you think the bodies remember what was done to them under anesthesia? Not consciously. But do you think cutting into the body affects the spirit? That it remembers pain that the body doesn't actually experience?"

"I try not to let myself think of that," I said. "It would kill me to think I was hurting those babies." But even as I spoke, I knew the truth. Surgeons don't like to ask themselves these questions. We prefer to be technicians as we work—cool scientists using our skills to do what is necessary to remedy ailments and thwart diseases. We anesthetize bodies and dull memories so that the human hosts of the puzzles we must solve neither experience nor interfere with our work. We omit the more grisly details in our descriptions of what the surgeries will entail: the seared flesh, taped eyelids, restrained limbs, the cruel hooks and blades, and clamps of metal instruments used on tender tissues. We shield ourselves from their faces. Drape all but what we must see to get the job done.

Jake's question would not allow me to omit the truth I'd always feared. "The spirit knows what the body forgets." I swallowed hard. "I've seen it on their faces."

* * *

Each night of that summer, we'd climb the stairs and wrap ourselves around each other. My changing body grew even more sensitive to Jake's touch. Through our open window we breathed the salty air and listened to the foghorns moaning in the distant sea. Our liquid rhythm mimicked the undulating swells of the waves until we drifted off to sleep. I awoke each day to the Spanish chatter of Jake talking to the yard crew he'd hired, and I felt the cool, empty space on Jake's side of the bed.

The garden was complete by midsummer, and I noticed around that time that Jake had begun keeping notes in a leather-bound notebook. He kept it in his back pocket and scribbled and sketched into its pages many times each day. Curiosity made me sneak peeks. He wrote and drew without constraints of direction or legibility. His print swirled around the pages, flowing more like water than words. Like islands, drawings interrupted the river of words. Soon dozens of jam-packed notebooks appeared around the house. I found them tucked between cereal boxes or discarded on the closet floor, disregarded as soon as they were filled.

As the Indian summer days of September arrived, the garden became a bursting, flowering testament to Jake's labors, and my body blossomed right along with it. I started going up the stairs alone at night. "I'll be up in a little while," Jake would say, and then I'd find him in the atrium the next morning wearing his same clothing.

One morning I was shocked to realize how thin and haggard he'd grown. "You've got to get some sleep," I pleaded, "You're going to get sick. Look how thin you're getting." As I grew rounder and my appetite more voracious, Jake grew leaner and his complexion more gray.

He looked up from his notebook. "I'm sorry. It's just when I get an image I sort of have to go with it, you know?"

"I guess I can lose you for a little while for the sake of art. But would you eat something nutritious?" I donned a poor Yiddish accent. "Maybe some chicken soup?"

He pulled me close and rubbed the rounding bump of my tummy with his open palm. "I'll eat some soup, *Bubbie*. For you."

* * *

I started watching Jake more closely over the next weeks. His lithe frame had become taught and bony. His lean face grew gaunt, the hollows under his cheeks deepening in shadow. He wore storm clouds under his eyes. His hair grew into a long, wild, unruly mass. A scraggly beard appeared in uneven patches, and he wore the same clothes for days at a time.

I often rose in the middle of the night to find him hunched over his worktable. His face within inches of its pages, he'd scratch furiously in a notebook with a stubby pencil.

"You need some rest," I finally said one night at three in the morning, handing him a cup of tea. I tugged at one of his curls. "And a haircut."

He didn't move. I repeated myself. "You're exhausted."

"Me? No, never better. Look at this." He splayed his notebook out for me to see. Scrawled in every direction were words and pictures that made no sense. "Do you see it? I've got an idea for how to get perfect sounds," he said. Then he dipped his head back to his page like a hungry dog gnawing a bone.

"The baby is kicking a lot," I said, nudging my belly against him. While his left hand still scribbled, his right stroked my tummy. We'd found out at our last ultrasound that Ryan was a girl, and I could feel her kick a reply to her father's touch. Jake turned and kissed my stomach, then darted to another table.

"I don't know how much longer I'm going to be able to do surgery," I said. "Ryan seems to be coming between me and my patients in the OR."

Jake picked up two broken pieces of rock and stood clacking them together and pausing, then making hasty notes in his book. He picked up another pair of rocks and banged them, followed by another scurry to make a notation.

"Jake, are you listening to me?" He began to search through cupboards for a pallet and paints. He sat down and began squeezing colors from tubes of paint onto the pallet. Had he stopped finding me attractive with my swollen belly and rounding hips? The distance between us felt like a growing, rotten thing—dank and dark. When I left the studio, he didn't even look up.

* * *

One night in late September, I came home late from the hospital. I'd called home several times throughout the day, but had only reached the answering machine. Darkness had fallen, and San Francisco's summer fog had crawled between the houses and the leaning cypress trees. When I pulled up to our house, not a single light shone from any of the windows. No cooking fragrances met me at the door. No fire blossomed in the fireplace. Only the damp chill of the rooms greeted me.

"Jake!" I called. The echo of my voice against the vaulted ceilings replied. I flipped on light switches, looking for a note on the kitchen counter, but I found nothing. I wandered through the rooms and up to our bedroom, where I slid my swollen feet out of my shoes and into a pair of slippers. Then I heard the ear-stinging clang of metal against rock coming from the back of the house and detected the smell of burning leaves.

I called Jake's name from the balcony. All of the landscape lights were on, but I couldn't see him. More harsh pings reverberated from the slope of the yard. I made my way downstairs, outside, and down the path, holding on to the smooth cedar rail to balance my waddling gait.

Jake was halfway down the hill, naked, mud-covered, and cursing. He'd rigged floodlights that blasted the hillside and him with white light, making him appear like an overexposed photograph against the darkness. His hair hung in heavy, sweaty curls around his face. A small fire burned just off the path nearby, and he swung a huge sledgehammer against a stack of stones. A deafening ping rang through the night air as his hammer found its mark.

"Jake, what are you doing? My God, why are you naked?"

The hammer swung again and was met with a loud crack and the sound of rock crumbling to the ground. A dust cloud rose. "There, you sonofabitch!"

"Jake!"

He jumped, falling back a little and nearly losing his footing. "Jesus! You scared the hell out of me."

The fog wrapped me in a cold, moist blanket, making Jake's nakedness seem even more absurd. I surveyed the once-idyllic yard to see rock piles and pulled-up vines surrounded by muddy puddles. The willow furniture lay tossed in a heap. "What have you done?"

He climbed up from the side of the hill to where I stood. His arms waved wildly as he described his vision. His pungent body odor stung my nostrils. "It was all wrong, Kat. It was lifeless. The yard has to have movement and sound. I see that now. We have earth. We have sky. What we need is fire and water. Fire and water together. It'll be *amazing*."

My head pounded with confusion. I pulled my sweater around me, trying in vain to cover my bulging belly. "It was perfect. It was the most beautiful yard I've ever seen. Have you lost your mind?"

"It was dead. DEAD! Now I'm going to put life into it."

"You sound like Dr. Frankenstein." I tried to laugh, but my attempt at a joke didn't sound so funny. The wildness in Jake's eyes terrified me.

"You'll see, Kat. I'm making waterfalls everywhere.

They'll tumble from each of the plateaus. Each one will have a different pitch because of the size, shape, and density of the rocks that the water will flow over and the height of the drop." Jake clicked two pieces of rock together in his hands and a hollow thud sounded. "See, this is granite. It's really dense, so the sound will be deader. I've got soapstone and lava rock. Those are more hollow. It'll be a—a—chorus. Yeah, a chorus on the hillside. The heat and crackle of flame will make it multidimensional." Every movement Jake made was exaggerated and primal—like an animal preparing for a fight. He ran without looking. His limbs flung about as if blown by a hurricane. He ran to a large boulder to make another note in his notebook. Without looking up, he continued to mutter.

His mouth could not spout the words fast enough for his thoughts, and he stammered. He swung his arms. "Imagine water flowing from the Golden Gate. Not real water, of course. That wouldn't do. But the *illusion* of water. Made of crystals or glass or—yeah, then I'll have to find a bigger hill. No, not a hill. A mountain. Half Dome in Yosemite. That's it!"

"Where's this water going to go, Jake? Don't we need some kind of a permit for all of this? Some kind of drainage system? We can't just let water run off the hillside. It'll erode and cause a mudslide."

With a jerk, he pitched a rock off of the hillside. "Permits. Permits are bullshit. You can't get a permit to create. You can't regulate art. Once it's done nobody will care about permits. You'll see." He paced, ranting toward the sky. "It'll take helicopters to make the drop."

"Jake, you're scaring me." My eyes had finally adjusted to the peculiar light, and I took in the extent of the destruction. Ryan was arriving in less than two months. I'd imagined holding our new baby girl, rocking her with the smell of lilac in the air, brushing lambs' ears against her newborn cheeks. With Jake chattering wildly behind me about water volume and stone density, I climbed partway up the hill so that I could see the patio behind the nursery. In place of the baby garden, a pile of rubble and the gangly roots of uprooted plants lay drowning in a pool of mud. In one day he'd destroyed what had taken months to build.

Before I was aware of it, Jake was behind me. "The Golden Gate will be my Sistine Chapel. It'll make this garden seem like nothing."

Fury rose in my throat. "*Nothing*. You're calling this nothing. It was your *everything* all summer. All you talked about. All you could think about. What about all of that talk about sitting out here with our baby? You should have asked me before you tore everything up." Fire raged in my voice. My words ignited an even bigger flame in Jake.

His brows came together into a pointed V and his lips curled in a snarl. "Ask you. I was supposed to *ask* you? Am I supposed to *ask* you every time I want to dig up a few god-damned weeds or move a rock? Did I ask you before I put it in? Why should I ask *you* before I take it out? Do you think Van Gogh *asked* if he could paint fucking sunflowers? Maybe you'd rather he painted daisies or daffodils. If you were Michelangelo's wife, the David would be wearing Bermuda shorts so that no one would be offended."

Some alien force had taken over the body of my husband. I was too stunned to react. The harsh white floodlights cast a strange halo around him, making him unrecognizable. "Stop it. I don't like the way you're talking. I'm tired. I just want to sit down." My voice was shaky and weak.

"You don't like how I talk when *you* don't control it."

"What? What are you—"

"That's right, Kat. I have thoughts and ideas that you don't get to control. I don't have to behave like some domesticated pet. I'm not your fucking houseboy."

"You're talking crazy. Let's just stop before we say something we'll regret."

"Not you, Kat. Perfectly controlled Dr. Murphy. Always calm. Always precise." The stench of his hot breath hit me as he drew his face near mine. Spittle sprayed my face as he shouted. "Everything by the book. Takes no risks. But then, neither does a robot or, or, or a corpse. But a robot never *created* anything. A corpse can't be an artist."

I drew back in silence and turned to walk up the hillside toward the house. With the speed of a pouncing cat, Jake grabbed my shoulder and jerked me back around toward him. Off balance, I stumbled and fell to one knee, cracking it hard against a rock.

Jake hovered over me, screaming. "My ideas can't fit inside a box! You can't expect me to perform like some circus animal. Cooking and planting daisies all day."

My ears rung, my knee throbbed. "I never asked you to—"

He waved his arms as he ranted, his silhouette dark against the stark white light of the floodlights. "No. You never *asked* me. Not you. Not Angus Murphy's Kitten Princess. But you got used to the big house and me as a cabana boy pretty fast, didn't you? And now fucking Burt is calling, telling me we need to generate money like I'm some goddamned ATM machine."

I struggled to stand as fear turned to hot rage. "I never asked you for this house, Jake."

"Fine then!" he shouted even louder. "Fuck this fucking house!" He picked up a grapefruit-sized rock and chucked it up the hill. It landed with a thud. He ran ahead of me toward the house, picked up another rock, and hurled it farther. The large crash of breaking glass pierced the quiet night. His whoops of delight rang out between each of the next dozen crashes while I cowered behind a rock. The backyard lights of our neighbors flashed on.

I crouched on the hillside. Jake's wild ranting and maniacal laughter were punctuated by the explosions of breaking glass. I clung to the rock, its cold penetrating my bones. Moisture seeped into my slippers. I shivered uncontrollably.

Sirens wailed in the distance. They grew louder, and then I saw the flash of red lights against our neighbor's house.

Jake screamed obscenities. A voice came from the side of the house, amplified by a bullhorn. "This is the police. Please put your hands up."

I scurried, as much as my pregnant form and my throbbing knee would allow, to the top of the hill to see Jake screaming. "Fuck you! Get out of my house! You've got no right to be here!" Then he hurled another rock, shattering another window. "Get off my property!"

From behind me on the hillside the small fire grew larger and flames licked the night sky. "Drop what you're holding and put your hands up," the bullhorn voice said in clipped, flat tones. Firefighters crashed through the wrought-iron gate and ran past Jake with hoses.

Jake cocked his arm back, ready to fling another rock. Broken glass was strewn over the back patio and his feet were bloody. Glass shimmered in the scanning beams of flashing red lights. "Drop it and put your hands up," the voice repeated.

"Jake! Stop!" I shrieked. I ran toward him, waving my arms, glass crunching under my slippers. "Don't shoot! Don't shoot!" My abdominal muscles tugged under the weight of my belly as I ran.

Just as I reached Jake, he hurled another rock, this one landing in the bushes. He searched madly to refill his hand. I ran to him, grabbing his arms, trying to wrap his nude body with my sweater. "Stop Jake. Stop. You could get shot here. For God's sake!"

"Yes. For God's sake is right. I'm doing God's work here. Don't you see?" He pushed me aside. I fell backward, landing on my rear end in the mud.

Before I could get up, two uniformed police officers jumped from the shadows to tackle Jake. He thrashed as they wrestled him to the ground; all the while he screamed curses and struggled against their hold. A third man in a paramedic's uniform came to my side. "Don't move. Are you all right, ma'am?"

"Don't hurt him," I pleaded. "He's not well." A young officer offered me his hand and helped me climb out of the mud. My mind was a swirl of fury, confusion, and terror. I stepped to where the police held Jake, the knee of one of the officers on his back. Jake lay face down on the ground. He turned his head and spat an angry spray of dirt and saliva at the other officer, who promptly clicked his wrists into handcuffs. "Fucking cops!" Jake screeched. The flames of the fire had died and only black smoke continued to rise. "Fucking art killers, all of you!" Jake raged.

I knelt beside him, picking up his broken glasses. I wanted to calm his thrashing body and plead for him to return to the Jake that I knew. EMTs arrived and rolled a gurney through the side gate, crunching over broken glass. "Where are you taking him?"

"Langley Porter." For the first time, my fear gave way to humiliation. I'd worked with cops and EMTs a thousand times in my professional life, handling addicts, criminals, and mentally ill patients and their families. Now I was the one being "handled" while the father of my child's fate was being determined.

"Not Langley Porter," I snapped. "Take him to General." I

thought of Nigel and the other people I knew at UC's mental health facility. I couldn't bear the thought of knowing that my colleagues would see Jake as he now appeared. Shame slapped me for thinking about my image when the man I loved was being put into restraints.

"Most people prefer Langley Porter, but whatever you say."

"Don't let them take me!" Jake screamed. "They'll kill me! They'll kill my art, Kat. Don't let them take me. They drug away the spark."

Despite restraints, Jake continued to buck and jerk. The officers tightened their holds, twisting his arms behind him. Nausea rolled through me.

Jake continued to shout. "They'll kill my art. Don't let them—"

I was barely aware of the barrage of questions from the EMT as I watched Jake's gurney getting loaded into the ambulance. *Was he taking any narcotics? PCP? Hallucinogens? Prescription medications? Allergies? History of mental illness or violence?*

"None," I said. "PCP, God no. He doesn't use drugs. He— he's fine. He just hasn't been sleeping."

Now Jake was strapped to the gurney and thrashing wildly. His mouth was agape in a contorted maw. He howled, tears running down his face, repeating, "Don't let them! They'll kill it! They'll kill the spark! Hide the notebooks! Hide them all!" His eyes, amber and glowing, found mine through the open door of the wagon. "The spirit will remember what they do to my body. You know it will, Kat."

The doors to the wagon slammed shut. The two police cars and the ambulance threw beams of flashing red lights around the neighborhood. Neighbors, some in street clothes, others in pajamas and robes, were gathered around. I'd seen some of them watering their lawns or walking their dogs, but knew few of their names. I wanted to hide my face. I wanted to scream at them to go back to their houses.

"Show's over folks," an officer said. "Let's clear the street." The onlookers drifted back to their houses.

Only then did I look down to see the bloody, torn leg of my mud-covered pants. My knee throbbed.

"That doesn't look so good," said a young policeman. He was holding a clipboard and a pen.

"It's just a bump. Where's he going?"

"We called in a 5150, that's a—"

"I know what it is," I interrupted. "Jake's not dangerous. He's the gentlest man I've ever known. He just hasn't been sleeping." Even as I said them, my words sounded ridiculous.

"It seems that there are about fifty rocks in your house, a fire in your yard, and a pile of broken glass that might imply he's dangerous. Your knee doesn't look so good, either. Safe people don't push pregnant women on a hillside."

"I fell!" I snapped. "I'm just clumsy right now with the pregnancy. Jake wouldn't hurt me on purpose." Images of battered women I'd treated in the ER over the years flashed into my head. My credibility was sinking fast.

As the taillights of the ambulance disappeared into the fog, my heart grew leaden. I tried to reconcile the two Jakes: the one who created exquisite beauty and the feral animal who now rode in the ambulance.

I started my old Volkswagen, ready to follow the ambulance to go to San Francisco General. I shivered as I waited for the nearly dead heater to warm up. Ryan flopped wildly in my belly. "Calm down, little one," I whispered. "We'll get this all figured out."

Doctors and Patience

"Yo, Murphy, what brings a nice pregnant girl like you down to the city morgue?" Mary K shouted over the screaming wails of The Grateful Dead in the background. Jerry Garcia's guitar solo ricocheted off the shiny white subway tiles and stainless steel surfaces.

"You know me. Never could resist a good cadaver!" I yelled, covering my ears and poking my head through the examining room door. My status as a doctor had afforded me entry only after Mary K had assured the receptionist that I had sense enough not to touch medical evidence.

The truth was, I couldn't stand being at my house with the broken glass and the backyard a muddy shambles. I'd spent the morning hobbling around the house on my sore knee, then hiring a window company from Oakland. Any construction crew in San Francisco was bound to know Tully or someone else from the pub. I needed to sort out my own thoughts about Jake without having to manage the worry of my family. If I was honest with myself, pride prevented me from calling them, too. The crew boarded up the whole back of the house to keep the weather out. Inside, behind the wood-covered windows, all

I could think about was my trusted friend. I decided that my pride was dispensable and steeled myself to confide in Mary K.

I called first thing in the morning for a squeeze-in visit with my OB, Sylvia Rodriguez, just as a precaution, and was comforted by Ryan's strong heartbeat. Dr. Rodriguez also examined my knee, just a simple laceration and a nasty bruise.

Every time I closed my eyes I saw Jake's sinewy body shimmering with perspiration, silver-gray against the night sky, and that maniacal look on his face. The shattering of glass. The smell of burning leaves. Flashing red lights. Jake's mouth, an open canyon of agony, begging me not to let them take away his *spark*.

I recalled Mary K's warnings the first night she'd met Jake. She'd warned me that he was a "nut job," that I was being a fool not to look at the facts. Then there was Aaron Bloom's letter, warning me that Jake was "not well." And in Japan I'd witnessed for myself the first hint of what lurked beneath Jake's brilliance and kindness. He'd explained it all away; and I'd let him. And now I was married, carrying Jake's baby. If I stood still, the panic about it all might swallow me. Watching Mary K work calmed me in some bizarre way, bringing me back to the world of medicine—something I understood.

Mary K stepped back from the gray body that rested on the table in front of her and removed her face mask and the clear plastic goggles that covered her glasses. Her golden freckles seemed somehow too vibrant for the surroundings. The torso of the thin, bald man was splayed open from the throat to the groin. A tidy row of instruments sat on a tray beside him. She clicked off the tape deck with her elbow.

"I don't want to interrupt if you're in the middle of somebody."

"Nice to hear a voice. My patients are cooperative, but limited in conversation skills."

I stepped from behind the door, unable to walk without a limp.

"What the hell happened to you?"

"I was a little jealous of all the attention you were getting for being a gimp," I said. "Thought I'd garner a little sympathy, get myself a few excused days off from the hospital."

Mary K removed her rubber gloves with a snap. "No kidding, Murphy. What happened?" Her face was pinched with suspicion.

The smell of formaldehyde overpowered me. I swallowed hard and breathed through my mouth. "Just a little clumsiness in the garden," I said. "It'll be okay in a few days. Who's your friend?" I asked nodding toward the eviscerated patient.

"This dashing figure is Mr. Wilson. Step on up. Mr. Wilson likes meeting new people." Gnarled fingers of cancer gripped the liver and stomach and had sent their tendrils throughout the abdomen. Mary K had begun her perfect, even stitches in the horizontal line of the collarbone, which would eventually meet with the vertical line that ran down the torso.

"Cause of death initially assumed to be heart failure as a complication of cancer," she explained. "Lucky guy. If his heart hadn't given out he could have lingered for years. Died quicker than they thought, so I'm making sure nobody helped Mr. Wilson here along. Me, I'd exit long before the cancer had its way. This shit makes you a real fan of the Dr. Kevorkians of the world. Nobody should have to live in that kind of agony."

"How are you handling all of this?" I asked, looking around the sterile room.

"The meat locker? It's all right. I like working with the dead. They so seldom piss me off." A sideways smile crossed her lips and her eyebrows twitched. "Let's go outside. I need a smoke."

The noon sun shone brilliant on Bryant Street. The sidewalk was littered with fast-food wrappers, broken bottles, and the occasional used condom. Bus exhaust and sewer fumes filled the air. Mary K lit her cigarette and twisted her mouth to blow the smoke away from me—a courtesy my pregnancy invited. A dirt-crusted woman with matted hair, wearing layers of coats, pushed a shopping cart filled with unidentifiable items, all separately wrapped in white plastic bags.

"Hey, Irene. I got you some smokes," Mary K said, holding a pack of Marlboros out to the timid woman. She snatched them from Mary K's hand and shuffled away. "You're welcome, Irene."

"How do you know her name?"

"On her good days, she talks." Mary K took another drag from her cigarette. "I was impressed in there. You haven't gone soft, Murphy. Hardly flinched when you saw the filleted corpse and the bucket of viscera at the end of the table."

"If this was my first trimester, you'd have seen some of my viscera right beside it."

"Wow, I can't believe how, you know, how pregnant you are."

I looked down at my expanded form. "I'm a Clydesdale."

"I didn't say you were big enough to eat hay and shit in the streets. You're what, twenty-eight weeks?"

I nodded. "I can't even stop to think about how huge I'll be when I'm full-term. But tell me the full story on *your* leg."

"Neuropathy. Can't feel the bottom of my foot enough to know where I'm stepping. Cane is more spectacle than I'd like, but better than falling on my face. But this is boring. What brings you down here?"

I'd rehearsed all morning. Even at the risk of the world's largest I-told-you-so, I needed to confide in someone. Burt came to mind first, but he was out of the country, scouting new sites for Jake's installations. I gnawed on the one fingernail that remained long enough to grasp with my teeth. "What," I said, "I can't just drop in on an old friend and make her buy me lunch?" I couldn't believe the small talk that was coming out of my mouth when I had such big things to say.

We walked to a corner deli and sat at a sidewalk table. We chatted about work, the new puppy Mary K was considering adopting, my pregnancy symptoms—all chitchat. While Mary K joked about the scrotal piercings and anal tattoos of her patients and the gallows-humored antics of her pathology colleagues, I fashioned my face into a smile but rehearsed what I was going to say. *You were right. Jake really is sicker than I thought. He's in a psychiatric ward at General and I don't know what to do.* But even as I turned the words over in my head, a putrid cocktail of shame and pride halted their arrival to my lips.

"I know you're supposed to be glowing and all being pregnant, but you sort of look like shit."

"Thanks a lot. I didn't get a lot of sleep."

"Baby's good though, right?"

"Baby's perfect," I sighed, comforting myself.

"I'm glad you came. I've been trying to muster up the courage to talk to you about something." Mary K poked at the remnants of her salad with her fork. "I need to ask you a big favor. If you can't, it's cool. I can make other arrangements."

I could not remember Mary K ever overtly asking for a favor. She took a long drag off of her cigarette. She squinted and cast her gaze across the street, where Irene had now reappeared with her shopping cart. "It's this fucking foot thing. Neuropathy is only part of the problem. Looks like I'm going to need some surgery. I was wondering if you could bring me home from the hospital and stay at my place for a few days while I recover. If you're not feeling too pregnant. No physical labor, just supervision. "

"Surgery? What kind of surgery?" I felt the sinking feeling of knowing what I'd rather not know. Mary K had been hiding big issues with small talk, too. Her diabetes had always been aggressive and unpredictable. Despite a near-perfect diet, an ideal weight, plenty of exercise, and strict adherence to her insulin program, her disease had always outwitted her.

She gave me a quick glance. "Wipe off the pity puss, Murphy. Jesus, that face could make somebody feel like she's dying. It's just my foot. That's all they're taking."

I straightened my face into my best clinical, neutral expression. "You've gotten a second opinion?"

"And a third, and a fourth. I kept trying to get an opinion I liked, but they were all the same. It's been gangrenous twice and it's about to get there again. The devil I'm bargaining with seems to deal only in extremities. If I want to stay alive, I have to give up the foot. Period. End of story."

All of this had taken place during my whirlwind with Jake. Between work, Jake, and getting ready for the baby, I'd been unaware that her health had slipped. Countless rounds of antibiotics hadn't touched the infection. She could no longer feel any of the toes on her left foot and she ran frequent fevers.

"The hope is that they'll be able to remove just the ball of the foot, or even just the toes, so that I can have a modified walk without crutches."

"It's not fair."

"Diabetes is a heartless motherfucker. I just decided yesterday to go through with it. Surgery is tomorrow. I came in today to dot the i's and cross the t's on Mr. Wilson. Tried to get myself to call you all week, but here you are."

Visions of Mary K running on the Stanford soccer field and tossing a Frisbee to Ben Casey flashed through my mind. "Who's your surgeon?"

"John Marshall."

"He's the best," I said.

"I was going to ask if I could stay at your house, but I'd really rather be at our place. Usually I'd have to stay in the big house for at least a week. Marshall said he'd let me go home sooner when I said I might be able to have you stay with me, especially because the place is ninety seconds from the door to the ER. I'll be in the hospital a couple of days. I can hire a nurse during the day, but I'd rather not have a stranger sleeping there, you know? You can have your old room. And if you want, Bloom could come, too."

The thought of where Jake was sleeping made my stomach turn over. "No, I can come. Sounds like you need more than a few days."

"It'll be all I can stand of your mother-henning. As soon as I can get back and forth to the can I'm kicking you out. Got it?"

"Does your family know?"

"I'll tell them about it after."

I nodded, knowing that Mary K's pride wouldn't let her contact the family that had virtually disowned her.

"I decided to start my maternity leave early. You're looking at someone gainfully unemployed for the moment," I said. "Cancel the day nurse. I can just stay at your place. I can lie around there as easily as anywhere."

"No way. Bloom would hate me even more than he already does for taking you away fulltime."

"Jake doesn't hate you." I considered the opening, but took a sip of my iced tea and swirled the ice around in circles with the straw instead. "He's going to be away for awhile. I was a little nervous about staying in that big house alone anyway, so the timing is perfect." This was just the first of the half-truths I would tell about Jake.

The crinkles around her eyes smoothed. "You're a pal. I promise not to be a pain in the ass. Bring a buttload of videos so you can stay off that knee. But none of those arty flicks rich with symbolism."

"Car chases and fart comedies. Got it. But I'm not so optimistic about you not being a pain in the ass unless UC's transplant crew has started doing personality transplants."

A wide grin crossed Mary K's lips. "Fuck you, Murphy. Fuck you very much."

The rattling noise of Irene's shopping cart reached us as she crossed the street toward our table. The stench of stale urine, alcohol, and body odor preceded Irene's arrival. Mary K held up a brown paper bag. "Here's your sandwich, Irene," she said in a hushed voice. "I'm going to be gone for a while, so I gave Salvador inside some money. He'll give you two sandwiches each day, and a pack of cigs, and coffee every morning while I'm gone. All paid for. All you've got to do is knock on the back door. Got it?"

The leather-faced woman nodded, but did not take the bag from Mary K's hand. Only when Mary K set it down on the table did Irene snatch it. Then she turned away, shuffling as she pushed her cart.

"You're welcome, Irene. Every day, now. Don't forget. When I get back, you'll fill me in on all the neighborhood gossip, right?"

Mary K looked back toward me. "Wipe the grin off your face, will you?"

"You're a lot nicer than most people know."

"Shut up, Murphy. Just finish your sandwich. I've got to go in and close up Mr. Wilson before the funeral home comes and your farting around with that club sandwich is going to make me late."

"I love you, you know that, right?"

"Don't get all gushy on me. I've got a date with a stiff."

* * *

My knee shot with pain each time I pressed in the clutch on the old Bug, so I decided I'd leave it at home and take cabs between San Francisco General, where Jake was hospitalized, and UCSF, where Mary K was staying. For the first time, the new car Tully'd been trying to talk me into getting started to sound pretty good. I slept—or tried to—in my old room in the flat that Mary K and I had shared. I spent my days going back and forth between UCSF and General and my nights with sleep eluding me.

When I pressed the button for the seventh floor in the elevator at General, I sensed the gaze of the nurses next to me. In most buildings, the top floor is the penthouse, reserved for the most prestigious of guests. At General, it's the locked psychiatric unit. Dread settled upon me. All night and all morning I'd feared they would not let me see Jake. But now the idea of seeing him made me nauseous and weak. The father of my child was now someone I feared. When the elevator doors opened, I threw my shoulders back, picked up my chin, and walked straight to the counter. I spoke through the hole in the Plexiglas wall. "I'm here to see Jake Bloom."

After signing forms promising that I wasn't carrying any sharp objects, matches, weapons, or medications, and surrendering my bag for a search, the receptionist instructed me to wait for an escort to Jake's room. I waited on a shiny, blue, plastic couch that seemed more like a bathroom fixture than a piece of furniture.

The limp-faced stares of patients meandering around me set me on edge. Some wore hospital gowns with loose-hanging robes. One man murmured to himself. A waifish blonde wore bright white gauze around her wrists.

A nurse escorted me to Jake's room. He was small and frail in his bed. The cold fluorescent lights gave his skin a jaundiced pallor. He appeared to be sleeping.

The nurse told me he'd been given Haldal at admission, and at first it had had no effect. With a second dose, the delusions and paranoia had subsided just enough that he'd become enraged at where he'd been taken. A heavy dose of Klonapin had made his speech thick and his movements sluggish, but had succeeded in calming him.

I eased onto the side of his bed. His eyes blinked lazily. When he saw me, pools formed along his lower eyelids. "Oh God, Kat. Did I hurt you?" His voice was hoarse. I couldn't speak.

"Did I hurt you?" His remorse-filled eyes pleaded with me. "The baby. Is she okay? God. Please tell me she's okay."

I combed his thick curls with my fingers. This was my Jake—my tender lover, my playmate, my friend. This was the man who tasted every kind of leaf in the baby garden making sure none were too spicy for a tender tongue.

"She's fine. We're both fine."

He pulled me toward him, his face resting in the crook of my neck. "Forgive me, Kat. Forgive me. I was just so— I just had these ideas in my mind and I couldn't—"

"Shh. It's all right now. It's over."

He melted into agonized sobs.

As Jake wept, his body jerked in deep spasms while his hands clung, claw-like, to the sleeves of my sweater. I looked up in desperation at the nurse who'd accompanied me into his room.

"You all right, Mr. Bloom?" she asked.

Jake kept sobbing.

She made a notation in his chart and changed an IV bag that hung above his head. She whispered, "Give him a little while. It's all just sinking in for him."

I wondered how long it would take for it all to sink in for me. When the nurse left the room, I felt overexposed and vulnerable.

Jake finally calmed, I assumed because of whatever was in the IV bag. Even through the fog of medication, his begging continued. "Take me home, Kat. Take me out of here. This place is for crazy people. I can't stand the sounds I hear through the walls. I want to crawl into our bed and hold you. Everything makes sense when you're holding me."

"We need to get you strong."

"Anything. Just get me out of here."

The last of Jake's words were sluggish. I could see him fighting to keep his eyelids open. Soon the hold he had around me wilted and he withered back into the mattress. I watched the fluttery movement of his eyes under his closed eyelids. I pulled away and leaned over him, kissing his forehead, then slipped out of his room.

* * *

Back at UCSF, I listened to Mary K's soft snoring. She'd been in recovery for a couple of hours. I'd already read the hospital's outdated magazines, as well as the book I'd brought on breastfeeding and sleeping tips for parents of newborns. My mind was a constant hum. I turned the pages of my book, but didn't remember anything I'd read. Mary K stirred and moaned. She whispered a raspy request for a drink.

"Only a sip." I raised a cup with a bent straw to her dry lips.

She swallowed. "All of it?" she whispered without opening her eyes.

"No, just a sip."

"All of the foot, Murphy." Her eyes were slits.

I nodded. "Yes. And your shin. They saved your knee, though. Andra says it'll make fitting a prosthesis much easier."

"Damn," she whispered, closing her eyes. "Littleton knows about all of this?"

"Hospital grapevine. She came to see you earlier, but you were still asleep."

Mary K turned her face to the wall. "Let me be alone for a while, Murphy."

"But—"

"I won't get all morose on you after this. But I've got to have a little while, can you give me that?"

I kissed her forehead. "Sure. I'll come back later."

"Tomorrow," she said without turning toward me. "Come back tomorrow to take me home. I don't want to stay here." Her shoulder rose and fell with a deep sigh. "Being a patient blows."

* * *

"But I'm ready to come home right now," Jake said, looking out the window of his hospital room. "I don't belong here. Kat. The people in here are crazy. One guy is convinced he killed Judy Garland. One woman thinks she's Queen Victoria and eats her own shit. Surely you don't think that I'm—"

"No, Jake, no."

"Well *they* do. They can't keep me against my will. It's not like I'm going to go spray a McDonald's full of bullets or something. I broke a few fucking windows. Windows in my own house!"

The pounding in my chest startled me; the baby rolled in response to what must have been a surge of adrenaline. For two days, Jake had been so calm, so *himself*, but the doctor's suggestion that he stay another two weeks had revealed shadows of the feral creature within. Between Mary K and Jake both busting for a premature discharge, I felt like screaming. But Mary K's discharge didn't fill me with dread.

168

Suddenly, he put both hands on my shoulders and looked into my eyes. "Please don't tell me you think I'm one of these people."

I looked down, thinking about the janitor who'd been cleaning smeared feces from the wall when I came in that afternoon. Surely Jake, the multilingual, world-recognized artist—the man who'd wooed Japanese officials and charmed my family, the father of my child—could not belong with these people.

"No, of course not. But you're not well enough to come home."

He clutched my arm and brought his face up close to mine. "I'm me again. We're going to be fine. I just let myself get too run down. I lost track of you. You're my touchstone."

Running between the two hospitals, I'd not mentioned Mary K's surgery to Jake, and my initial intention of confiding in Mary K about Jake seemed pointless in light of what she was going through. I'd spent the past days trying not to look at the vacant spot at the end of Mary K's left leg and enduring her snapping at me if I inquired how she was feeling. She accepted little help and had threatened to kick me out, as she'd promised, but she also seemed glad I was there. I had been with Jake during visiting hours. Each night it grew harder to leave him behind. As Jake returned to his former self, I'd begun to feel a softening of the hard stone that had been lodged in my chest. But now Jake was frightened me all over again.

I pressed my palm against my belly, feeling what I thought was a knee or an elbow as it traveled across my abdomen. Jake knelt by where I sat and pressed his cheek against me. The baby instantly calmed and focused her bubbly movements to where Jake's cheek rested.

"It's okay, Ryan," Jake said. "I promise I'll be a good daddy."

* * *

My body had become a timepiece, a countdown for the arrival of a monumental change in my life. Sharing this baby with Jake had once seemed like the happiest possibility I'd ever known, but now the idea of my baby being born struck terror in my heart.

In all the hours of sitting with Mary K while she recovered, watching movies and eating meals, I'd formed the thoughts in my mind a dozen times. But any time I tried to confide in her, a dry and brittle crust formed over the words and they lodged in my throat. I told myself it was because of her health—the time just wasn't right—but in truth, I knew that Mary K would only tell me that Jake was crazy and that I should get out.

I went to Murphy's Pub, thinking I'd talk to my family. But once I got there, my loved ones swarmed me with hugs and pats to my growing belly. Alice had crocheted booties. Dad was building a rocking horse that Tully would paint in circus colors. Dr. Schwartz grew wistful and reminisced about when I was little. Days passed, and still I couldn't tell them about Jake's condition.

My family would flock to my support and I knew that. Mary K would defend me with ferocious protectiveness. But none of them really understood Jake or how we loved each other. I felt utterly alone.

Back in my office at UC, I found myself longing for someone who understood Jake, someone who could help me think clearly. In the privacy that my cubby of an office offered, I dialed the number of Jake's administrative assistant in New York to find out how to reach Burt.

When I finally reached him at a hotel in British Columbia, Canada, Burt's voice nearly burst through the telephone with exuberance. "Hey Kiddo! Your voice is a lovely song for these weary ears." We'd talked on a number of occasions when Jake had dodged his calls, and we'd developed a playful repartee over the months. "How's the little nipper?"

"Hi Burt," I said. I swallowed, trying to summon the next phrases I'd vowed I would not squelch. I couldn't talk about the baby. My silence sent a signal for me.

"Kate, what's wrong? Are you okay? Is the baby all right?"

They were simple questions, yet the fact that Burt was the first person to ask them of me sent me into a fit of unexpected sobs. I covered my mouth with my palm, trying to stifle the sound of my weeping.

"Oh, darlin', what is it?"

Finally, everything I'd been holding in came bursting from me, a tsunami of words fueled by a storm of panic. I told him about Jake's descent, his obsessive drawing, his sleeplessness. Then I described that horrible night in our garden and his current condition in the psychiatric ward at General.

After listening to the whole, sordid tale, Burt finally sighed. "I'm so sorry, Kate. I really thought this might be behind us."

I spilled every unspoken thought I'd had for weeks. Everything about Jake. Everything about Mary K. Burt listened to it all with the patience of a priest in confessional. "Oh me," he sighed.

"What am I going to do, Burty? The baby will be here so soon. They want to put Jake on lithium. They want to put him in long-term care. He's furious. I don't know—" I swallowed and summoned up some of the words that scared me most. "I'm so afraid."

"Shh," he whispered, "It'll look better soon, I promise." His soothing words calmed me. "I'll have his medical records forwarded and give a release to his psychiatrist in New York so he can talk to your guy there. That will help them with the treatment plan and keep them from misdiagnosing. I still have a durable power of attorney, so a phone call will do it. I'll be on the next flight to San Fran. Not to worry."

I pummeled Burt with questions about Jake's history. Hospitalizations. Breakdowns. He'd had a few, some attributable to impetuous youth, others sounding more ominous, but nothing sounded quite as bad as what I'd witnessed. And Jake, long ago severed from his own family, had trusted Burt with power of attorney to take care of him. "I don't want people to hate Jake," I admitted.

I heard what sounded like a soft growl through the phone, a sound I'd learn indicated that Burt was thinking and selecting his words carefully. "Jake Bloom is my dearest friend. This is a rough patch. He's had them before, but no matter what, he's still Jake. He just needs our help to come back. That's all. A psych ward must be making him batty. He needs to be home with us, the ones who love him and understand him."

My throat ached and I could barely swallow. "Thank you," I croaked. "Thank you, Burt." The telephone's mechanical sound whirred in my ear. "Burt. Do you think I'm crazy to be with him?"

Seconds thrummed by. "Love is equal parts miracle and insanity. Jake is a windstorm you'll have to weather, but he's also the best, most loyal friend I've ever known. I think you'd be mad not to love him, too." Burt cleared his throat and I wondered if his eyes were damp as he spoke. "I'll see you tomorrow night, kiddo. Just have a good meal so that nipper can grow good and strong."

I listened to the dial tone for a while, unable to hang up and sever the connection to Burt. I rested my head on my desk. Exhaustion was heavy blanket and sleep soon fell upon me.

* * *

"Thank you for agreeing to meet with me, Dr. Murphy." The whites of Dr. Bhanu Gupta's eyes stood out against his charcoal skin, giving him a look of constant surprise. The slight man stood in front of his dented metal desk and held out a plastic chair for me. "I must say that it is against my recommendation that your husband leave the hospital right now. I have told him this." The music of his native India gave everything Dr. Gupta said an anti-rhythmic lilt that was at once melodic and a little frantic. "While his progress has been remarkable, I am not yet confident that his mood is fully stable. He could be benefiting from an extended stay in a therapeutic setting."

I pushed down the sense of panic that rose in me when I thought of taking Jake home. Sitting with Dr. Gupta, humiliation brought heat to my face. Under normal circumstances, he would be my colleague, not someone treating a member of my family. I donned my most professional demeanor, smiling and modulating my voice. "With all due respect, you can't seriously believe that my husband belongs in this population. He was depleted, sleep-deprived, and severely dehydrated. What he needed was rest and fluids, and this week in the hospital has given him that. He's agreed to use medication as necessary to regulate his sleep. He's no longer dangerous or delusional." What I said was factually accurate, but the falseness of my bravado rang in my ears. I heard myself fighting for something I wasn't even sure I wanted.

Dr. Gupta's voice was gentle and patient, somewhere between the Dalai Lama and Yoda. "Dr. Cohen was very thorough in her assessment and recommendations over the phone. I concur with you and with her. Mr. Bloom's current mental status does not qualify him to be kept against his will. His condition is improved. But he has declined the full medication regimen that is indicated."

"You mentioned lithium. You can't be serious. He's not a

psychotic. He's obsessive, and that gets compounded when he's depleted. After this week of rest, he's back to his normal self." The voice that emerged from me was one I recognized; one that argued treatment plans in utilization review meetings. But in those meetings my voice was buoyed by confidence in the truth. In Gupta's office, it was all façade.

From a silver pot etched with filigree, Dr. Gupta poured tawny tea into a porcelain cup. In the shabby surroundings, the tea service seemed strangely civilized. He nodded to me, offering a cup, and I shook my head. "I know this is a matter of great tenderness, Dr. Murphy. Your husband's diagnostic picture is addressed only partly with rest. With manic-depressive illness, the cycle is bound to return. Whereas in a state of hypomania he can be productive and even creative, this episode of psychosis exceeded the definition of simple hypomania. Without medication, a return to this psychotic state is, well—" Dr. Gupta's inky black eyes found mine. "Please forgive me, but the return of his mania is inevitable, and his history, as described to me by Dr. Cohen, would indicate that, untreated, it can become even more severe."

Those words, *manic-depressive illness, psychotic episode*, made Jake seem like some kind of a monster. Ryan would be here in just weeks, and the thought of Jake in his current state, with our newborn, made my hands shake. Though everything that the kind doctor was saying made logical sense, accepting the idea that what Jake was suffering from was a mental illness felt like swallowing broken glass. "You don't know Jake. I've never met anyone more energetic in my life. To be manic-depressive, you have to have depression. Depression doesn't begin to describe him. He's talented, intelligent, decent, gentle, loving. The medication they gave him when he got in here made him a zombie. He can't stand that." I heard the defensiveness in my voice. "He's an artist. If he hadn't ever had a grandiose thought, he wouldn't have been able to create the art that he has. If grandiosity is illness, three-quarters of the surgeons I work with should be on lithium."

"I am a great admirer of your husband's work. Certainly no one would want to medicate that away. Often the spark of such magnificent artistic creativity is accompanied by a, how shall I say—" the doctor stroked his chin with slim fingers, "—a *flame* of madness. This disorder is baffling, especially when patients are so intelligent and talented. He could go years without an episode."

"With all due respect, I'm worried about his state of mind if he stays *here* for long. Jake simply does not belong here." I stood and snatched up my purse and drew in a slow breath to calm myself. "Our baby will be born soon, and we want to go home and focus on that. A healthy focus and proper diet and sleep are what Jake needs. I can monitor his medications and insist that he see you for follow-ups."

Dr. Gupta stood and extended his hand with its bird-thin wrist toward me. "I can see that you and your husband have made your decision. I will sign his discharge papers, with the notation that you have declined the recommended treatment and that discharge is against physician recommendations. I am concerned about your managing him alone, Dr. Murphy. Not that you aren't perfectly competent, of course, but given your pregnancy, I—" He paused and looked deep into my eyes. "I am here if you need anything."

"His friend—our friend—Burt, will be here tomorrow," I said. "We'll be fine."

How many times had I given this very lecture to patients leaving the hospital? I'd written AMA—*Against Medical Advice*—into charts to cover hospital liability and to leave a trail of information for whatever doctors would inherit the case when, inevitably, the uncooperative patient returned.

My gut tightened. This doctor was wrong. He'd seen Jake in his worst moment. He just didn't know the Jake I knew.

* * *

The next day, Jake lingered for a moment at our front door. His chin sank to his chest and his hair hid his face.

"Don't worry. It's all been fixed," I said, rubbing his shoulder. "The glass is all back and the carpets are cleaned. It'll take your touch to get it back to what it was, but the garden is back in order. The crew was able to salvage most of the plants and the furniture was unharmed."

"I don't care about the house." He wrapped his arms around me and swayed, bringing his lips to the nape of my throat. "I could've lost you," he whispered. "Nothing else matters, but if I lost you and the baby I'd just want to die."

"We're here. We're not going anywhere."

The warm light of the house welcomed us and drew us toward its glow. Now, back in the beautiful piece of art that Jake had made for me, I finally felt at home. The beveled glass in the kitchen windowpanes fractured the light into ribbons of color that danced on the wall and floor, tugging us toward the kitchen with its northwesterly view. The towers of the Golden Gate Bridge, anchors of strength and beauty, reminded me of all that remained unchanged.

We exchanged polite formalities as we settled, bad movie dialogue between strangers not knowing what to say. Only when we went into the kitchen did something familiar begin to emerge. Jake hunted in the cupboards and refrigerator. I sorted the mail. After a few moments, a soft hissing sound came from a skillet on the stove and the smell of warm butter filled the room.

"There's not too much to pick from in the fridge," Jake said when he brought our plates to the table. "But I can make eggs."

He set my plate in front of me and my stomach growled in response. The caramelized onions and tangy Swiss cheese made my taste buds vibrate with pleasure. Before I knew it my plate was empty, and I looked up to see Jake, chin in hand, watching me, a serene smile on his lips.

"What?" I said, my voice muffled. "I can't help it. The baby was hungry."

He reached and took my cheek in his hand and pulled me toward him. "It'll be okay, Kat. I'll do everything to make it okay."

Swimming Among the Stars

In the first weeks after Jake returned home from the hospital, he honored the distance I silently demanded. During the days we exchanged fleeting, tender affections. At night, we slept in the same bed but with a canyon between us.

I tried to confide in Mary K or my family, but each time the words turned to dust in my throat. When I thought of how the story might sound out loud, I could imagine only one reply from Mary K: *What are you—nuts? Get the hell out, Murphy.*

Jake took responsibility for everything and agreed to a course of medication. He saw Dr. Gupta twice a week. What more could I expect? If he suffered from Parkinson's or Alzheimer's, or cancer, I'd stay beside him. I tried to stay peaceful for Ryan, my little, unhatched bird.

As I entered my third trimester, Jake reemerged as an artist, the buds of ideas beginning to take form through the thinning fog of medication. Burt arranged a sizable commission in British Columbia. It would be two-and-a-half days of work without any guidelines or limitations, with a public showing at the end of the third day. Photographs of the installation would be featured in *Art Nomad*. VIPs had been invited to see the installation and attend a reception afterward.

My OB okayed me to fly through my seventh month. "We need this trip, for us," Jake pleaded. "I'm back to myself. I've been home for nearly a month. For us, Kat?"

* * *

From the window of a small private plane, the chain of British Columbia's clear blue lakes was a string of sapphires among emerald hills.

Burt met us at an airport owned by a group of wealthy Canadian businessmen, one of whom was on the Arts Council and owned the plane. Burt gave me a warm embrace. "How's the little nipper?"

"Fine," I sighed.

Burt had stayed with us at our house the first two weeks Jake was home from the hospital. Somewhere along the line, Burt had become not just the best friend of my husband, but a friend to me. He was the only person who understood what Jake and I had been through.

"Hey there, Jake-O," Burt said extending his hand. Though the two men were about the same height, Jake was a willow and Burt a mountain. "Feeling all right, mate? This isn't too soon?" he asked.

Jake's eyes jumped to mine. "We're good, Burty."

"Good to hear it," Burt said, his enormous hand resting like a rib eye on Jake's shoulder. "So here's how it goes. Our hosts are putting you two up at a private villa. Staff will deliver meals, but promise to remain otherwise invisible. It won't be a bunch of blue bloods wanting to constantly rub your elbows."

"Thanks for that," Jake said.

"Private beach on a little lake all to yourselves," Burt continued. "You'll have to do some hobnobbing at a party the evening of the installation, but that's it."

"Sounds perfect," I said. Jake put his arm around my ever-widening waist.

"How's the old percolator?" Burt asked tapping Jake on the temple. "Got your vision yet, mate?"

Jake's face broke into a grin. "Burt can't just trust the process. Always wants to know the plan. But what would be the fun in that?"

"Fun, ha! I just wish your *process* happened more than a few hours before I have to fly a crew to the site, that's all. I've reserved forklifts and dozers from a local contractor, have art interns at the ready—whatever your *process* might require. We've got three days of clear weather for you to work your brilliance."

"Poor Burty," Jake cooed. "Carries all the worries for us." Jake turned to Burt. "Cancel it all. No equipment. No materials. Keep the volunteers for gathering natural elements, but they've got to make themselves silent and invisible while I work. Just you, your wading boots, and your silly old camera. Kat and our little passenger are my muses, and nature has provided all I'll need."

Burt's eyes glistened under his golden brows and he clutched at his chest. "Leave the rest to you? Those words'll be the death of me, mate."

* * *

I woke the next morning to a pink dawn and an empty bed. A note rested on Jake's pillow. *Gone to work. Ordered room service. It's waiting in the kitchen for my girls. Eat up. Call this number for a ride. Love, love, love.*

In the quiet, the fears that I'd been squelching seeped into my waking thoughts. Jake was fine now, back to himself. But I could not pretend I hadn't seen the other part of him. This man—this amazing, adoring man—had disintegrated into the feral creature I'd witnessed amidst the wreckage of our garden. But I also could not deny that I loved him, helplessly, and that we were about to have a child. My mind churned with Burt's reassurances that Jake had long periods, years, without episodes of any kind, and then years more where only mild episodes occurred. *Yes,* I reassured myself. *We can control this.*

I hurried through a shower and munched on fresh croissants, then got a ride to the first in the chain of pristine lakes. Tucking myself behind a cluster of birch trees near the shore, I was out of Jake's sight. For two full days—time that passed unmeasured—I watched with fascination. Burt wandered nearby, his camera ready. Burt and Jake walked on parallel paths toward their own version of art; Jake creating the sculpture that would last only an instant, and Burt making it last on film. At times over the two days I'd sleep or take slow walks, but whenever I returned to my perch, I was entranced anew. Art students scampered like silent stagehands, gathering all manner of twig, flower, shell, feather, and stone, keeping a wide distance between themselves and Jake. Birds chirped in the trees and fat bumblebees buzzed, but no human sounds could be heard.

While he sculpted, Jake was oblivious to anything other than the visual poetry he created. He walked barefoot along the shore of the lake, his pants legs rolled up. He kicked the water. He gathered leaves and petals of spring wildflowers, tucking them into a huge burlap pouch that dangled from his belt. Occasionally he'd squat or sit, examining whatever he'd discovered so closely it seemed he might pull out a jeweler's eyepiece. He arranged what he found into patterns on the shore. All the while, Burt snapped photographs.

On breaks, Jake emerged from his trance and bounded over to me, checking on my comfort, kissing my belly, bringing me small flowers and shells he'd found until I'd amassed a collection of treasures. On the second morning, he came to me with a surprise, appearing very much like a little boy with a secret. Finally, he pulled his hand from behind his back. In his open palm rested a tiny gray egg with green specks.

"Look, Kat," he said grinning. "Now that I have you I find these abandoned everywhere. Like you said. They're about a perfectly designed future. About potential."

Ryan made a gentle roll within me, reminding me that she was *our* little hatchling. I tucked myself into Jake's arms and pulled his hand to my side. Together we stood, relishing together in our daughter's movements.

At lunchtime on the third workday, Jake looked in my direction, and for the first time he called me into the field of his work. "Kat, come look!"

It was my first close look at the works he'd created. I wandered along the shore for my own private showing of what the crowd of invited guests would tour in just hours. Trails of yellow-green leaves and blue flower petals wove together in a serpentine chain that led to another chain formed of gray birch bark and black twigs. The bark and twigs led to a series of stacked stones. One stone was coated in fuchsia flower petals, standing out from the otherwise gray-toned wall.

Each piece drew me forward, beckoning me to take in the whimsy and beauty of the next. Each sculpture was so simple, yet they were nothing that anyone but Jake could have created. The pieces wouldn't endure beyond the next rain, but for this instant they filled me with a sense of peace I couldn't find words to explain. How could I not be in love with the man who created such things of beauty? This was his essence. That rest was only a symptom—an illness that required a remedy.

I came to the last section of beach before the forest overtook the path. Here were sculptures I had not observed from my perch. Carved ridges in the sand formed two sets of spirals like nautilus shells, each more than eight feet in diameter. One was lined with birch bark and thousands of black and white feathers. The second was the same size and shape, lined with blue flower petals—intricate and ingenious. Where the two circles came together, the edges of them intertwined, a blending of the blacks and whites along with pink, blue, and yellow flower petals. I found myself breathing hard, tears threatening to spill. I knew as soon as I stepped close to it that this was Jake's sculpture of our family. Jake was all color, and I so black and white. Between us, an image of perfect balance united us.

From behind me, Burt's rich baritone broke the silence of my thoughts. "I never know what it's going to be, but it's always bloody brilliant." He snapped another photograph of Jake in the distance, then he turned the camera onto me and clicked it before I had a chance to turn away.

"He's a lucky bastard, that one," Burt sighed. "I've never seen him happier. He's ass over tin pot for you." He raked his fingers through his beard as though he might find his next words hiding in there somehow. "I know you've been through a bad patch. But Jake's the most luminous, life-loving bloke I know."

I looked back down at the spirals of lake water at my feet and then at Jake flinging rocks into the quiet pool of water. His voice rang with unbridled glee. "Kat, come look! You won't believe the beautiful splashes!"

Burt chuckled. "That is a one-of-a-kind wild dingo we've got on our hands."

"One of a kind," I said.

* * *

Once Jake had finished creating his sculptures, he had nothing more to do with them. Never once did I see him look at the critically acclaimed photographs Burt had taken of his work, nor at the articles of praise for his artistry. After each of his installations, Jake seemed relieved when wind or rain or surf reclaimed the elements of his art and returned them to the place from which they'd been borrowed.

We attended a lakeside gala in a giant white tent full of Canadian, American, and European dignitaries. Tables flowed with elaborate hors d'oeuvres, and champagne was served by black-and-white clad waiters. A string quartet offered Mozart and Bach in the background while guests mingled.

Jake pasted on a thin smile on as he posed for photographs with wealthy art patrons who trapped him in tedious conversations. His forced tolerance showed only slightly in the distracted look in his eyes. The only people at the party in whom he showed any authentic interest were a pair of attending children. By that point in the evening, my feet had swollen so that they seemed like over-risen dough erupting from my shoes. Heartburn ached in my chest. I found a comfortable chair, fished a TUMS from my purse, and watched Jake's animated exchange with the children.

"How do you get that stuff to stick together like that?" asked a chubby girl with chocolate at the corners of her mouth.

Jake squatted down so that his eyes and the girl's were only inches apart. "What do you guess?"

"Very sticky glue. Or maybe tiny little nails."

An ivory-skinned girl of about eight, obviously the younger girl's older sister, chimed in. "It's not glue or nails. I think you just find the way to stack things so they'll be balanced just so."

Jake looked up at me and smiled.

"But what I don't know," the older girl continued, "is how you get the leaves and petals to stick to the rocks and twigs."

Jake leaned in toward her and beckoned the smaller sister over with his finger. "Promise to tell no one?" he whispered. The children nodded, their faces shimmering with the glee of the secret. "I spit on them," Jake said. "My entire career as an artist is reliant upon really good loogie-making."

The girls giggled and scrunched their noses.

Jake began to feign a cough and continued speaking with a falsely raspy voice. "By the end of a three long days of work it feels like I've been eating nothing but crackers and sand. I'm practically all out of spit and so thirsty I think I might die."

He stood with a sudden jerk and leaned his head back, emptying his water glass with a single gulp. Then he snatched the ginger ale glasses that the children held and gulped them down. The well-cultured girls seemed both shocked and delighted by this small bit of bad behavior.

At first, I felt my muscles tighten. Was Jake losing control again? But almost as soon as the thought came to me he looked over at me, his eyes glistening in mischievous delight. This was the Jake I loved—well-bred enough to know how to behave among aristocrats, but too irreverent and spontaneous to obey their rules of decorum. Jake grabbed a water pitcher and tipped it to his mouth until ice and water showered over him, watering down his clothing and making a huge puddle at his feet. The stuffy party guests, and especially the two children, were nearly in fits, the bigger girl covering her mouth with her hand in giddy horror. Burt's hearty laugh joined the chorus of chuckles from the crowd.

After the crowd's gasps and laughter died down, the wide-eyed younger girl asked in the coolest possible of voices, "So have you drunk enough now to do art again, Mr. Bloom?"

"Only if you'll do it with me, and only if you call me Jake."

A dignified couple wearing a shared pink of embarrassment

came to stand by the girls. "Mr. Bloom, we're so sorry if our girls have intruded," said the girls' father.

"Are you kidding? They're making this into a party for me. Do you mind if we do a little project together? We'll go outside to forage for materials, but we'll be right back."

The girls' pretty mother glowed. "Oh my, well. We'd be honored. But only if you don't mind."

"You in?" he asked the girls.

They nodded in a vigorous unison.

"All right then." Jake turned to Burt, who had stepped closer to the commotion. "Burty, I have an idea. Can you get my burlap bag and have some of the interns bring the extra piles of materials up here? Now, let's see," he said to the children. "You're my partners in this project and I don't even have your names."

The older sister stood straighter, as if only then remembering her breeding. "Melinda Wesley, and this is my sister, Sarah."

"All right then. Melinda and Sarah, I'll only do this if it's all of us working together. Your ideas too. Full-on partners. Deal?"

The two girls began to jump up and down.

The three exploded from the tent. Their squeals provided great entertainment to the crowd. Partygoers decorated in silk and jewels suddenly became children themselves, trying to sneak peeks at the scavenging committee. Jake and the girls returned barefooted, creating muddy footprints on the shiny parquet floor of the tent, with Jake's burlap bag bulging and armloads of sticks and flowers. Scanning the room, Jake spied the flower arrangements that covered the tent posts and snatched them, plucking their petals from the stems. Whispers traveled like electricity. With great noise, Jake and the girls spat on flower petals and leaves, wrapping them around twigs and stones and forming stacks in the middle of the tent. Jake pulled off his jacket and tie, flinging them aside. The children's dresses were covered in mud, their socks and shoes nowhere to be seen. The hypnotized crowd looked on while Burt skirted the edge of the tented room, snapping photographs and laughing. The musicians stopped playing and the waiters stopped serving, equally rapt by the spectacle.

Instructing waiters to pull linens from vacated tables, Jake had them create a curtain that covered the last of bits of their work. Whispers permeated the scrim. The crowd waited. Jake called for a ladder and one was promptly fetched.

Jake and the girls emerged from behind the curtain and a hush fell on the crowd. "Go ahead, Melinda," Jake urged.

Wringing her hands in front of her, with a tremble in her voice, the girl announced, "As a thank-you for this lovely party, we present you with—" she looked at Jake, who smiled and nodded, "—a one-of-a-kind Wesley, Bloom, and Wesley production."

"Go ahead, Sarah, you say the rest," Jake said, smiling.

The younger girl stepped forward, held her arms wide, and announced, "We now present to you, 'Rainbow to Heaven.'" She curtsied, then added, "The title was my idea." The room erupted with laughter and applause.

The waiters dropped the makeshift curtains. Standing before us was a nearly eight-feet-high tower fashioned of stacked sticks, each one wrapped in leaves and flower petals: a perfect, vertical rainbow, deep purple at its base and red at its top, with bands of petal-formed rainbow colors in order in between. A pool of multicolored petals surrounded the struc-ture—a sea of color from which the delicate tower seemed to rise.

Applause burst again from the crowd and Jake joined hands with the girls as they all took a bow. Jake had become the Pied Piper, creating a parade that every child and every adult would want to follow. Watching him, I could only imagine how our daughter would adore him.

The remainder of the evening was transformed from a stuffy event to lively party. Jake took me in his arms and began to sway. Over his shoulder I saw that couples had joined us. Waiters hustled to move tables aside to create an impromptu dance floor, and the orchestra abandoned their classical playlist and played great standards that lent themselves to dancing.

"The Way You Look Tonight" wafted through the white tent. "Tired?" Jake whispered in my ear.

"I keep thinking I should be, but then something happens that gives me another wind."

"Damn. I was hoping for an excuse for an immediate departure."

I looked over to see Sarah and Melinda peering dreamily at Jake. "It seems I've got some competition for your affections. You were great with those girls."

"They saved me. I was going to scratch out my own eyes if I had to listen to any more mind-numbing conversation about the status of the arts in North America. Kids are the truest artists. Just think, in a few weeks we'll have our own daughter around to inspire us all the time."

I watched Burt as he danced with a young museum curator. Over her shoulder he gave me a look that said, *See, I told you he was something.*

* * *

Back at our cabin, Jake and I sat on the back porch overlooking the lake. I wrapped my shoulders with a soft quilt against the night chill. The cloudless night sky was inky black, bejeweled with brilliant white stars. A single bullfrog made commentary with a bellowing croak. Jake pulled my feet into his lap and rubbed my throbbing arches.

"You've been a great sport. Three days of boredom and a night of elbow rubbing. More than any man should ever ask of a pregnant wife."

"I loved every second of it," I said, surprising myself. "But you can keep rubbing my feet if you feel guilty."

Jake stood. "Will you look at that? Oh my God, Kat."

I stood beside him, peering over the black silhouettes of the trees near the balcony. The lake before us was still, a flawless mirror for the star-filled sky. The water met the sky at the lake's edges, forming an uninterrupted blanket of stars above and below us, and the water became a bottomless lake of stars.

Jake grabbed my hand and a blanket. "Let's go."

"But—"

"No buts. You have to come."

Jake led me down the steps of our porch to the lake's shore. At the water's edge he pulled off his glasses, his shirt, and then his pants. He laid his glasses on top of his clothing on the shore. "Come on."

I scanned the scene around us. Seeing no sign of anyone, I dropped the quilt.

Jake pressed his lips against my bare shoulder, then unzipped my dress, letting it fall to my feet. "But it'll get dirty."

"Shh." He tossed my dress and undergarments onto the quilt. We waded into the lake. The warmth of Jake's skin was a cocoon in the cold water around me. I was buoyant, freed from the weight of my body. The swelling of my feet and the heaviness of my breasts had been lifted.

Jake stroked my skin, kissing my lips and face, and I felt my body soften to welcome him. Despite the chill of the water, I felt my own heat rising. His fingertips found the source of my warmth beneath the water's surface, causing my breath to catch.

"Be still," he said.

In the stillness, I could hear my pulse pounding in my ears. With each slowing beat I could feel myself release the anger and fear that had nearly consumed me for weeks. The images of Jake, wild and dangerous, or helpless in the hospital restraints, now seemed almost as though I'd dreamed them all and then awakened to this tender sweetness. I was all body, all sensation, freed of the mental noise of worry. Everything in me wanted to writhe with him, to create currents of our own.

"Look. Just look."

The water on Jake's skin reflected starlight, and when I looked down at my own body I saw that I, too, wore a silky garment of glittering light. We were swimming among the stars.

"This is the best moment of my life," Jake said, his voice not so much made up of words, but more an exhalation of a thought.

We stood there wrapped together until the cold began to penetrate and I started to shiver.

"Let's go back to where it's warm," he said.

"But I don't want to leave this. I've never seen anything like it. I wish we could photograph it."

"We don't need a picture. This is ours forever."

* * *

Back in the warmth of our bed we made love for the first time since Jake had come home from the hospital. I'd had no champagne, but felt drunk with all that my senses had absorbed. His skin smelled of the lake's fresh moss. Eyes closed, I could still feel the cool of the water and see the shimmer of starlight on my skin.

We lay together, all breath and heartbeats until the bullfrog resumed his call. After we rested there a while, I found a whisper. "I've been so scared."

"I'm not just sorry. I'm so far past sorry that the light from sorry doesn't even shine on where I am."

"We can't let you get tired like that. We can't let you get so run down that it brings on—you know."

Jake turned onto his back and I could see the strength of his profile. "I wasn't just tired, Kat. You know that, don't you?"

I nodded.

"I want to promise you only moments like this one. I want to make our life with our daughter perfect."

Perfect. I thought of how my own father tried to make my childhood *perfect*. How I'd had a *perfect* plan for my life and career. "That's not realistic. There will be dirty diapers and sleepless nights and fevers. We'll catch her ditching school and leaving her room a mess. We'll get tired and crabby. Things can't be perfect all of the time. We'll fight and disappoint each other and—"

His eyes pleaded with me. "But all of that stuff *is* perfect, Kat. That's all of the stuff I never had. I just don't want to be a disaster as a husband and a dad... as a person."

Jake's upbringing had been privileged: the best schools, homes all over the world, servants. But he'd never had any semblance of family life. My patchwork family was flawed, but I'd grown up surrounded with people who loved me, even lied to protect me.

"I'm scared too," I confessed. "I don't know how to play with children the way you do. I was a serious kid. I studied and obeyed the rules. I don't know if I'll be a good mother."

"Maybe between the two of us we've got enough to be one really good parent."

"It'll take the both of us. Together."

Jake wrapped his body around mine. "Together."

Monday's Child

Once we got home from Canada, we settled into a nesting routine, readying ourselves for Ryan's arrival. The garden had grown lush, its blossoms and leaves erasing any visible memory of destruction. I hung the photograph that Burt had given us in Ryan's nursery so we'd see it whenever we sat in the rocker. Sometimes, as I waited for her birth, I sat and gazed at it; The Nest, he'd called it, and I rubbed my belly talking to my little hatchling.

One November morning, I went downstairs to find Jake working early in his studio. Morning cast a hazy white light over him as he hunched over his drafting table. My hair, damp from showering, rested heavy and cold against my cotton maternity shirt. I stepped close enough to Jake that the fragrance of his shampoo met me, but he seemed not to notice that I'd entered the room.

"Whatcha up to?" I asked.

He flinched, startled by my voice, and then settled. "Morning, sleepyhead." His supple lips found mine. "Mmm. If I'd known you were going to feel so nice, I'd have woken you up for a little playtime before I came down to work. But you looked so cute with that line of drool between your mouth and the pillow."

"Very nice, making fun of a pregnant lady."

Ryan, due in just three weeks, banged around inside as she always did when Jake was near. He pressed his cheek against her. "Morning, lamb," he whispered.

"All right, you two. Enough roughhousing."

As Jake sipped his coffee, I snatched a peek over his shoulder at his colorful drawing. Under a moody sky stood the Golden Gate Bridge. The bridge's towers appeared just as they did in the view from our kitchen window—powerful and dramatic, persimmon against a dove-gray sky. My heart clutched as I took in the surreal additions Jake had made to the landmark. Interwoven strands formed a web that draped from the bridge's span. The net was adorned with thousands of what appeared to be shimmering, irregular glass shards in blues, greens, and silvers. Like a jeweled jigsaw puzzle, the waterfall cascaded into the bay below. The flow was punctuated by blooms of red-orange flame, with fire and water blending together.

"What do you have there?" I asked, trying to keep my voice light.

"Just some images that keep coming to me. Every night in my dreams I—" Jake stopped, suddenly reading my face. "Relax will you? This is just how I work."

I wanted to ask more—to pick and make sure he was not launching back into the obsessions of fire and water from two months before. Questions were a logjam in my mind.

Jake rested his head against my heart. "You have every right to be nervous. You did have a husband that went pyro and got shipped to the nuthouse." He looked up, traced the flesh of my lower lip with his thumb, and then kissed me. His voice was tender. "You should dry your hair. It's chilly out. You don't want to catch a cold."

"Old wives' tale," I whispered. "Temperature has nothing to do with viral transmission."

Jake had remained true to his word. He ate well, put on weight, slept regularly, and had regular sessions with Dr. Gupta to monitor medication. He resumed his role as my companion and passionate lover, making me feel sexy and adored despite my expanding girth—or even because of it.

"Tully's due. Ready for car shopping?"

Jake had convinced me that my old Bug wasn't safe for the baby. He had already sold his Valiant as a show of solidarity. I found myself hesitating to get rid of the old car. Senseless and sentimental. It had outlived its practicality. But I'd left so much of my life behind by adding Jake and a baby to the mix. My body was morphing into something I hardly recognized. And now, being off of work, the Bug and my little collection of eggs felt like the last bits of my old self.

I pointed to the drawing that lay on Jake's drafting table. "Something I should worry about?"

"We're in a great place again, aren't we, Kat? You can't freak out every time I draw something. Tully will be here any minute."

I nodded, pushing doubt aside to look into the soft greens and golds of his eyes, which were magnified by the lenses of his glasses. "No one in our family has ever bought a new car. They depreciate by 30 percent as soon as you drive them off the lot, you know. I'm not getting something with a lot of doodads on it."

"You are definitely Angus Murphy's daughter." Jake donned his comically accurate imitation of my dad's brogue. "The Murphys certainly give every wee penny a mighty tussle before it leaves their purses. They surely do." He rubbed both palms against my belly. "My sensible wife. At least get power windows. Tully's been talking for a week about how he's never driven a car with power windows."

"Whose car is this, mine or Tully's?"

195

The doorbell rang. Jake grinned. "Your answer's at the door."

I opened the door to see Tully wearing a crumpled tweed jacket with an extra wide clip-on tie, carrying a battered briefcase jammed full of glossy brochures. His wiry hair had been slicked down with some manner of gelatinous goo and his chin, shorn clean of its customary stubble, was speckled with crimson nicks. "Ready to go, Katie?"

The salesmen couldn't have known what was about to hit them.

* * *

"SURPRISE!"

The shout that greeted me when I opened my front door nearly knocked me over. I looked around the foyer, taking in the smiling faces of a dozen wonderful women in my life.

After my heart rate slowed to a gallop, I noticed Tully next to me, his lean face stretched into a Stan Laurel grin. He'd insisted on going to nearly every car lot in San Mateo and South San Francisco, eventually endorsing a new Volvo wagon, a deeply discounted end-of-the-year model—with power windows.

"You sneak," I said, giving him a punch to the shoulder. His skinny chest expanded under his clip-on tie.

Jake gave me a quick kiss. "Gotcha," he said. "Tully and I are outta here. Off to watch the Niners game at the pub."

"Don't worry, Katie. No drinking. Scouts' honor," Tully said, crossing his heart with his forefinger.

Alice, right up front, stood beaming, surrounded by a few of my fellow former interns and nurses. From the back of the crowd, Mary K delivered an off-center smile. I resisted my urge to let my eyes travel down to the dangling leg of her jeans. She had not yet healed fully enough to wear a prosthesis. Beside

Mary K, tall and golden with a wide smile, Andra Littleton stood holding a huge bouquet of yellow roses.

"Look who I invited to the party," Mary K said. For a split second, she seemed almost nervous.

The afternoon was a flurry of gifts and food, laughter and swapping of stories of motherhood. Amidst the festivities, Andra and Mary K held hands while Alice kept refilling her own wine glass.

Soon the guests were gone, but for Andra, Mary K, and Alice.

Alice raised her glass and, in a voice louder than seemed necessary, she offered a toast. "To our little Katie," she slurred. "All grown up and having a daughter. And I'm going to be Nana Alice!" Alice suddenly held her finger to her lips. "Shh," she said. "That was a little loud."

"Here honey, why don't you sit down for a while?" I said.

Alice looked deep into my eyes. "My little Katie," she repeated. "And I'm—" Alice sniffed and began to bawl. "I just wanted you to be a happy little girl. That's all I ever wanted. I'm so sorry, Katie."

I'd never seen Alice drunk. I kissed her and helped her to sit on the sofa. I stepped toward Mary K.

"Sheesh," Mary K whispered. "Alice is feeling no pain."

"It's not like her," I whispered, watching Alice as she folded baby clothes into a tidy stack.

"We'll take her on home," Andra offered. "After we help with the last of the clean-up."

"It's all done," I smiled. "That swarm of women did everything but shampoo the carpets and reshingle the roof."

They offered to stay until Jake got home, but I was exhausted and ready for bed. Alice had drooped onto the sofa.

"Come on, sweetie," Andra said in sweet Texas tones. She helped Alice to her feet.

Alice cupped my chin in her hand, speaking groggily. "I just can't believe it, Katie. I can't believe my little Katie will soon be a mother." With that, she broke into a blubbering mess, her words almost as wet as her face. "I just love you so much, Katie. I just never thought—"

Mary K shrugged. "Sentimental drunks."

As I held the front door, I looked into Andra's shining face. She'd always been beautiful, but there was something more. Mary K looked happier than I'd seen her in months—years, maybe. "You two look really happy," I said. "I'm glad."

Andra glanced toward Mary K. "I've lived in a lot of places. I think I've finally found home."

Mary K pulled a cigarette from behind her ear as they ushered Alice toward Andra's car. "There's no place like home, right?"

As they pulled away I checked my watch. Eight-thirty. Jake would tease me for pooping out so early, but I headed straight to bed, where I fell into a soft sleep.

* * *

I jerked awake with pain, deep and sharp, gripping me low in my belly. I waited until the vise released its grip. The room was dark. Jake's side of the bed was empty and the covers lay smooth. The numbers on my bedside clock glowed one-thirty.

I inched my way across the bedroom and out into the hall. The glass of the atrium reflected only moonlight from the window. "Jake," I called. Only my own voice echoed a reply. I called his name twice more before another wave of pain grabbed me.

I dialed Murphy's Pub. "Katie, hi!" The music of Mike's voice was light and playful.

"Hi, Mike. Can I talk to Jake?"

"Sorry Katie, he left early this afternoon. Just after the game started. Smart guy, left before the Niners went straight

into the shitter. Oops, sorry. Guess I owe the cussin' jar, huh?"
Mike's warm belly laugh came over the phone.

Another pain gripped me and I gasped.

"Everything okay, Katie?"

"Just fine." I steadied my voice. I really didn't want to discuss my labor pains or my AWOL husband with the weekend bartender.

"Do you want me to wake your dad? He went upstairs a few hours ago, but maybe Jake told him where he was off to."

"No, I'll call tomorrow."

As I set the phone back in its cradle, another contraction grabbed me. *Where is Jake?* Pain grabbed my lower back and left me breathless until it subsided. I brushed my teeth and dressed.

I waited for the next wave of pain to come and go, then stepped into the garage. When I flipped on the light, my new Volvo gleamed, making the empty gap beside it seem that much more vacant. Jake had taken the Bug. Now panic took a bigger hold, making my heart beat wildly and scattering my thoughts into a torrent.

Focus. I had to focus.

I called my doctor's exchange. I gave the details of how far I'd progressed. Contractions were about twenty minutes apart. Suddenly, it felt frightening to be alone in the house.

After another hour had passed, my labor was progressing, and my fury was rising along with it. When my doctor called back, she urged me not to wait any longer. She'd be waiting for me at the hospital. I called for a cab. Throwing a coat around my shoulders, I paced and peered through the window, the increasing grip of contractions causing me to lean against the wall for support.

I waited another fifteen minutes before I grabbed the keys to my new car.

* * *

It felt odd to be on the other side of the hospital experience: the tedious questions at intake, the confirmation of my birth date, insurance information, and recitation of everything I'd eaten. After registration, I was finally in the family birthing room. The mechanics of a regular hospital room had been softened by pastel wallpaper and comfortable furniture for family members.

"Who can I call for you, Dr. Murphy? You're eight centimeters dilated. Your delivering physician will be here any minute." Maggie Simon was a seasoned delivery nurse I'd met during my labor and delivery rotation. I was pleased to be in such experienced hands.

"Please, call me Kate," I said to Maggie. "You've just felt my cervix. I think we can abandon the formality of—" A contraction stopped me from finishing my sentence.

I'd given up dialing home after a dozen tries and couldn't bring myself to call my dad or Mary K. What would I say? *I'm in labor and Jake's missing.*

I panted through the next wave until the grab in my abdomen released. "I can't imagine what's keeping Jake."

Maggie removed her rubber gloves and tossed them in the trash. She covered my exposed body with the crisp sheet and patted my knee in reassurance. "Well I'm not going anywhere. I'll be your honorary girlfriend. How's that?"

I nodded, afraid that if I spoke a sob would escape.

* * *

I held Ryan in my arms, amazed at the miracle of her. The light of mid-morning shone bright in the room, letting me discover each detail. Thick, dark hair covered her head, and impossibly long fingers reached outside of her blanket. Her eyelids fluttered, revealing smoky gray eyes, then closed again as she stretched in a yawn.

My delivering physician had come and gone, a phantom in a mask. She had been called to another delivery and it was once again just Maggie in the family birthing room with Ryan and me.

"I never get tired of seeing these little ones arrive." The nurse tilted her head and looked at her watch. "November tenth. That makes her a Scorpio. And let's see, Monday's child. But she doesn't look full of woe to me. Definitely full of grace or fair of face."

Despite her being only a few hours old, I recognized on Ryan the shape of Jake's brow. *Not Monday's child. Not a life full of woe*, I silently vowed. I looked into Maggie's tired eyes. "Thanks for staying past your shift."

Maggie gave a nod and stepped toward the door. "No sassing your mom now, Ryan. She's had a pretty tough night. Sleep, Kate. It may be your last chance. We put the batteries in them when we discharge."

When the door closed behind her, I allowed my false smile to fade.

* * *

I sensed Jake's presence before I opened my eyes. His eyes were bloodshot. On his brow, above his glasses, an angry purple bruise was forming, and his chin was scraped and bloody. His hair was matted with dried blood over one ear, and his hand was wrapped with white gauze stained crimson.

He leaned toward me but I turned my face away from him. I forced down the hot urge to reach up and slap him. The first glimpse of him brought relief, then fury hit. I wanted to scream, *Where the hell have you been?*

Jake pulled back, his eyes darting between my face and my deflated belly. "Oh God, Kat. You're so strong. You must've been so scared. I flew over here as soon as I got home and got your messages. I saw Ryan. They're getting her ready to bring in here. She's perfect."

My words came out like whole notes, one to a measure. "Where. Have. You. Been?"

"An accident. I had an accident in Sausalito. The Bug rolled over into a ravine. I don't know how long I was out. I—"

As Jake explained, I saw the pictures in my mind. My old Bug, flipped over, mangled and smashed. Jake, hanging upside down from the makeshift seatbelt, unconscious, his face bleeding. He'd had an accident. He'd been unconscious. How could I be angry at him? Then it dawned on me. Sausalito— not exactly on the way from Murphy's to our house. Mike said he'd left the bar just after the game started. Where had he been all afternoon and all night?

"I had to show them myself. It's for our future. Ryan's future. This will be the most amazing installation yet."

"Show who *what*?"

"I met this guy at Murphy's who works for the Golden Gate Bridge commission. He knows Mayor Agnos and Governor Deukmejian. They were meeting up in Sausalito today, having dinner. I knew if they heard my idea they could pull strings and—"

"Strings, what strings? Strings for what?"

"Once they saw how amazing it could be, I was sure they'd grant the permits."

I sat up with a jerk. "This is about the waterfall? We're here again, Jake. The Golden Gate? Your drawing? You said that was nothing to worry about!"

"But Kat, they listened. They loved the idea. I sketched it for them right on the tablecloth. George Deukmejian knew my work. He thinks if we can work out the logistics with traffic and permits and safety that it would be spectacular. Burt's great at that stuff. This is for us. For Ryan."

"If it was so perfect, why did you sneak out of the bar where I thought you were without calling?"

"I didn't know I was going until I met the guy at Murphy's. I should have called, but I didn't want to get you excited if it didn't pan out. You've been looking at me like I'm a monster or a crazy man every time I draw anything. I planned on being back before you woke and you never would have missed me, but on the way back I—"

"But what? What!" A hysterical ping had entered my voice. Suddenly the smell of Jake's sweat and the trickle of dried blood on his brow infuriated me.

"I know I messed up. Isn't missing my daughter being born punishment enough? I'll never get that back." His eyes became the green of a stormy sea against the red lightning of his bloodshot whites. I pressed my palm against Jake's chest and pushed him. "Don't try to make me feel sorry for you." He tried to lean toward me, but I kept my hand splayed like a starfish on his sternum. "I can't live like this. Never knowing when you're going to let your impulses dictate your behavior." I pushed him further away. "I just can't."

"It was an *accident*. I had a car accident. I'd never leave you alone on purpose."

My voice was alien and cold. "Get *out*, Jake! Just leave me alone. Do us both—Do all three of us a favor and just walk away. I can't count on you."

He covered his face with both hands. My face and lips had turned to stone, rigid and unmoving. I didn't care about his accident. Didn't care that he probably needed stitches in the scalp wound that was still bleeding.

He pulled my fingers to his lips, kissing them over and over again. "I know you're upset. You've got every right. But this should be the happiest day of our lives. I haven't even *met* our daughter and already I know I'd die for her."

"It's not that easy. I was all alone. *We* were all alone. How can I ever trust you again? I can't live this way. *Leave.* Just leave us alone."

Jake's pleading was interrupted by the slight opening of the door. From behind it peeked my father's bushy brows. "There they are," he sang. "There's the beautiful mother and the proud papa." He pushed the door open and Alice entered behind him carrying a bouquet of flowers with an "It's a Girl" balloon bobbing overhead. Maggie had done one last service for me by calling my dad at the pub, but their cheerful arrival was a mismatch for what was transpiring between Jake and me.

The room seemed suddenly absent of air.

"We took a look at little Ryan through the window," Alice said. "She's just a perfect angel." Through her makeup, Alice's face showed the ashy remnants of a hangover.

I couldn't take it all in. Only hours before, I'd delivered my baby, feeling utterly alone—a nurse as proxy for my husband—too embarrassed to call anyone who knew me. Now the same room held a celebration of new life and my injured husband, who I had just told to leave my life.

Dad leaned over the bedside and kissed me, first on one cheek and then on the other. "How's *my* little girl?"

"I'm fine, Daddy."

Alice threw her arms around Jake with giddy laughter. "Can you believe it? You have a baby girl. You're a *daddy*." Then she pulled back and took in the view of Jake's bloody brow. "Dear God. What happened?"

In a flurry of explanation, Jake told about his accident and sobbed as he talked of missing Ryan's arrival. Alice soothed him with pats and hugs.

Jake looked back at me over Alice's shoulder, his mouth crimped in anguish. "*I'm so sorry,*" mouthed his lips. My furious pulse pounded in my temples. Just as Alice pulled away from Jake, a nurse came into the room pushing a Plexiglas bassinette. The pink card at the foot of the bassinette read, "Bloom, Girl." Her face peeked out from under the tiny pink stocking cap, her lips and tongue sucking hungrily. I recognized the nurse, Ginny Hatfield, who'd looked over several of my infants after surgery. "Hi, Dr. Murphy. I see you've done a little overtime here at the hospital. You do nice work." She pushed the bassinet between Jake and me.

Alice held her elbows tight to her sides and her hands fluttered in rapid, silent applause. "Look who's here. Just look who's here, Angus. Isn't she just an angel?"

Jake's tortured gaze fell onto Ryan, who squeaked and gurgled. At first, when she opened them, her eyes scanned around the room, unable to fix on anything in particular. Then Jake leaned toward her. As soon as he drew close to her, Ryan's movement stopped and her eyes fixed on Jake. Ryan's gaze remained locked to Jake's and neither made a sound.

"Now *there's* a baby who knows her daddy," Ginny said. "I'll let you all visit, then I'll want to let Ryan learn how to belly up to the bar." My breasts throbbed in agreement with Ginny's assessment as she left the room.

Alice and Dad twittered as they inched closer to Ryan. They cooed and declared every inch of her beautiful and perfect. Dad spoke in a hush, his chin dimpling to stop his tears. "Isn't she grand? Just look at those wee hands," he said, holding Ryan's long, slim fingers between his thick ones. He pulled a hanky from his back pocket and blew his nose with his customary honk.

"Train's in," Alice said with a smile.

"All aboard," Dad replied. He gave Jake's back a hearty pat.

Alice pulled her Kodak Instamatic from her pocket book. "Say cheese!" She snapped, the light flashed, and the flashcube rotated, ready for another picture of the perfect family on its happiest day. "And to think," Alice said, her lips drawn down, "on this very night little Ryan could have lost her daddy. It could have been such a sad, sad day. Look at you, Jake with blood all over his face. And here you are. A happy little family."

My gut twisted into a fist. Alice demonstrated all of the sympathy I should have been feeling for Jake. This was a *normal* reaction to hearing someone was in an accident.

Ryan squeaked a whimper, her body contracting into a tight little ball. Soon her face contorted and reddened. A strangled cry erupted. Such a pained sound out of such a little form. Her crying sparked an ache deep within me that told me I'd do anything I could to keep this little being from knowing pain.

Jake looked up at me, his face pleading. *Don't do this. Don't take everything away.* In my cells, in my bones, in the marrow that flowed though them, I knew that keeping Ryan from Jake would kill him as surely as if I drove a scalpel through his heart.

"That's your cue, Daddy," Alice said, her head nodding toward Ryan.

He sat motionless, seeming paralyzed between his urge to embrace his baby daughter and facing my fury. And what had he done, really? He'd followed a lead that could make an artistic vision a reality. He'd dined with the mayor and the governor. And he'd had a car accident after which he'd come to the hospital, bloody, to be at my side. What was so wrong?

With each pulse I could see that Jake was waiting for my cue. I licked my lips and was surprised to find them wet and salty. I nodded ever so slightly and sensed the instant, palpable relief of Jake's exhale. That nod was his green light, his permission to enter the threesome of *us*.

Jake parted Ryan's blanket with fingers still covered with dried blood. His face softened into a look of adoration. "Look at her. Just look." As soon as Jake's fingers touched Ryan, her crying stopped. "Hi, sweet one," he whispered. He picked her up, his two elegant hands forming a nest. "I'm your impulsive, irresponsible, unforgivable daddy." He held Ryan as though he'd never done anything his whole life but hold babies.

Alice snapped another picture. She and my dad were so overwhelmed with Ryan's arrival, they seemed unaware of what brewed beneath the surface between Jake and me. Perhaps the worst of the storm had passed. Alice linked her arm into my dad's. "A loving father is the best gift a mother can give to a daughter, Katie. Ryan is a lucky girl."

Perfectly Lovely Funeral

After Ryan was born, Jake devoted himself to proving that he could and would be the loving father and husband he had promised to be. At first, I thought this would last just a few weeks, until the next flight of fancy distracted him. But the weeks turned into months and the months rolled smoothly into years. I completed my five-year surgical residency and was offered a pediatric surgery fellowship at UCSF. In so many ways, our life together was idyllic.

One day, after a long day in the OR, my whole body felt like one big bruise. The metallic odor of anesthesia still lingered in my nostrils, and the muscles in my shoulders were ropy braids. I came home and opened my front door to find Ryan standing at attention, waiting in the entryway. She gripped the thick stalk of a yellow dinner-plate dahlia while the thumb of her other hand rested against her moist lips. Chestnut curls escaped her barrettes. The mere sight of her made every ache disappear.

"Hi, Noodle, is that beautiful flower for me?" I asked, holding the door with my foot while I balanced packages.

She put a hand on her hip, a gesture that made her look more like a teenager than a five-year-old. "Mommy, did you forget about Nana Alice's birthday party?"

"I absolutely did not," I said, nodding my head toward a pink bakery box cradled in my arms. "Saint Honoré cake, just as you requested."

The scents of garlic and rosemary mixed with burning mesquite wood wafted through the house from the patio outside the kitchen. Fleetwood Mac's "Don't Stop" blared from the stereo. From the patio, Jake's whistling accompaniment trilled high above the melody.

The dahlia tottered above Ryan's head like an umbrella in a wind, each sway sending another trickle of yellow petals fluttering to the floor beside her feet. "Wow," I said. "That one's as big as a pizza."

"Mommy, you told me not to 'zaggerate."

"Right you are. But it is pretty big. It does seem to be raining petals, though."

The garden was one among many of Ryan and Jake's collaborations. The hillside was lusher than ever, each tier its own world. In every nook, simple sculptures awaited discovery. The hillside that had once been a scene of such destruction now boasted figs, tomatoes, melons, and even olives—all of which nurserymen had said had little hope of success in the foggiest, most coastal climate in San Francisco. Jake disregarded the rules of growing climates in the same way he ignored people who told him that he wouldn't be able to execute a design.

From the day of her birth, Jake became the gardener that tended the budding blossom of Ryan; nurtured her with affection; stimulated her growth with constant exposure to ideas and experiences; cultivated her imagination by asking her opinions and welcoming her choices. For the first year after she was born, I was fiendishly protective—fearful that Jake's mania might flower again. I monitored his mood, his medication, his appointments with Dr. Gupta. And Jake complied. By the second year and into the third, I relaxed. Science had won. We had slain the monster of Jake's mania, subdued it into submission.

Jake had erupted with only minor flares of temper—particularly about his art. But it all seemed more artistic temperament than anything that smacked of the mania I'd witnessed nearly six years before. The sway of our daily life lulled me back into the trust I'd once known.

Ryan at age five stood as tall as most second-graders. Her passport had been stamped with the insignias of fifteen countries. She'd seen wild elephants, the Egyptian pyramids, and the Great Wall, and had crested Machu Picchu in a backpack on Jake's shoulders. Though I knew I should discourage it, her thumb-sucking seemed the only remaining remnant of a babyhood that had gone by too quickly.

"Daddy made swish-kebab. He's on the patio cooking them." Another flurry of petals fell as Ryan's arms waved. Her eyes, river stone calico like Jake's, made me feel as if I could fall straight into them and lose myself.

"We used our cucumbers from the garden and made that yummy sauce you like, Mommy."

"Tzatziki?"

"And I painted placemats for everybody."

I bent down and kissed her silky cheek. "That's *shish*-kebab, by the way," I said heading up the stairs. "Would you tell Daddy I'm home and that I will greet him after my shower when I don't smell like old socks and vitamin bottles?"

Ryan pinched her nose and giggled.

Climbing the stairs, I freed my hair from its ponytail

and tried to run my fingers through the snarled curls. Just then, Ryan's icy shriek filled the house. I flew down the stairs, expecting to find her bleeding and broken in the foyer. Instead, she stood screaming, staring at the petal-less stalk she held.

"It's gone! My flower is gone!"

I tried to wrap my arms around her, but she pushed me away.

"Don't worry. We'll pick another flower."

"But that one was the *perfect* one."

"All living things die, darling. You know that. It's part of nature."

Instead of being quieted by my explanation, Ryan's wails grew louder until I thought my eyes would explode.

"We'll get another flower. There are lots of beautiful ones out there. Nana Alice won't even have to know about this one."

Ryan squinted at me, delivering a steely stare. "*I'll* know," she said, her voice a razor's edge. "I can't give another flower when I know this was the best one."

My temples banged. "Clearly it was not the best one, Ryan, because it's all over the floor."

She covered her face with her hands and I wasn't sure if she was crying or plotting my murder. "Ryan, that's enough. Everyone will be here soon. You don't want our guests to see you acting like this."

"You don't even *care* about the flower. If my flower was in your hospital you would care if it died."

Ryan was willful, but not usually a brat. "Do you need to take a nap?" I snapped. Suddenly Jake appeared beside us, barbecue tongs in hand. The fear on his face told me he'd envisioned the same broken child that I had.

"It's dead," Ryan cried, fat tears rolling down her creamy cheeks. She collapsed into a heap on the floor, laying her head on the blanket of petals that had fallen there.

Jake knelt down beside our crumbled daughter and lifted the bloomless stalk. "Oh, it's not dead, Ryan."

Her cries stopped and she lifted her head. "Mommy said it's dead. It's *nature*. Everything dies. She told me."

Jake looked up at me and shrugged an apology. His voice was calm and kind. "Mommy is right, of course. She is very smart about science. I always consult with her on such matters. But dying is partly science and partly how you choose to look at it."

Ryan's face showed her puzzling over the new idea.

"The flower isn't what it was," Jake explained. "It is dead in a certain way. But now it's something else and so it's alive in a brand new way. Close your eyes."

Ryan closed her eyes without hesitation, her pink eyelids and feathery lashes flickering.

"Can you see the flower now?" Jake asked.

She nodded.

"As long as you can see it," he said, "it's alive in the most important way."

Ryan opened her eyes, her dark lashes spiky with moisture. "But now I don't have a present. And it was the most beautiful one, Daddy. I can't give another flower."

"Absolutely not," Jake said. "Another flower won't do when you know that one was perfect." He hadn't even heard her and he'd repeated almost her exact words. Jake looked around the foyer; he picked up an urn that rested in one corner and retrieved a cluster of long, twisted willow branches that he and Ryan had gathered earlier in the day. He licked his thumb and pressed it against one of the fallen petals, and then he pressed it onto the shaft of a branch, wrapping it in brilliant yellow.

Ryan's eyebrows climbed and Jake's gaze met hers. "Daddy, maybe we could make Nana some golden branches if we get

213

some more petals from the garden. And the red ones, too. There are lots on the ground. We can put them in one of the stones that we carved into vases. Like a bouquet, but *way* better."

Jake looked up at me over his shoulder. "If Mommy will stir the polenta, then you and I can make a present, but we'll have to work very fast."

Ryan clapped her hands, then she began scooping the petals into a pile. Jake made a hammock of the front of his shirt and Ryan filled it with her gatherings. He looked up at me. "Welcome home."

"Mommy wasn't going to let you see her until she wasn't stinky," Ryan said with mischief in her voice.

"Tattletale," I teased. I turned to Jake. "Did you hear from Burt?"

"He's having dinner with the governor and he'll call with the good news. It's all ready but the contract." Jake smiled, and his face seemed more relaxed than it had in days. He'd been tense and short-tempered awaiting the final signatures approving his grand installation on the Golden Gate. What had at first seemed like a ludicrous idea was now coming to fruition—just as the Path of Stones had six years before. "This is my calling, Kat. This is the art I was born to do."

"If this approval doesn't happen, there will be other installations."

"There *are* no other installations," he snapped. "This one *will* happen."

Ryan continued gathering petals. "The Golden Gate Bridge is Daddy's perfect flower, Mommy."

"I know, baby. I just—"

"A quick stir of the polenta and then your well-deserved shower," Jake said. "Everything else is ready for the invasion from Murphy's Pub."

"I'll kiss you when I've washed the hospital from my skin."

"Can't wait. Hey Noodle, we'd better get moving on this present," Jake said to Ryan.

They began to walk to the studio, each carrying petals in the hems of their shirts. "I love you, Daddy," she cooed.

"I love you more," he said, his words striking the match to their ritual game.

"No," Ryan grumbled, "I love *you* more."

As they walked, the exchange continued for another few rounds until Ryan was shouting and Jake was singing his reply, infuriating her further. Sometimes Jake carried on with the game until the playful banter became so competitive that Ryan cried tears of frustration.

"Jake, please!" I called out. "We've already had one meltdown."

As they went into the studio, I overheard him whisper, "But I do love you more."

* * *

As I stirred, the bubbling polenta batter reminded me of Alice teaching me how to tell when the oatmeal was done. *It's done when it blows you kisses*, she'd said. I'd stand on a stool over the oatmeal pot and listen for the soft *pah* of the thick porridge. Along with the *pah-p-p-pah* of the polenta, Ryan's happy sounds erupted from Jake's studio.

As I stirred, my eyes filled with tears. Jake could console Ryan in ways I never could. Scientific explanations about the how and the why of things always comforted me. I gave her the information she asked for, but Jake soothed her. He was patient and playful. He never needed to scold her because she existed to please him, while she fought with me over every bedtime and wardrobe decision. His kisses on her scuffs and scrapes brought instant healing that nothing I learned in medical school could offer. I repaired other people's children every day—sutured their wounds, aligned their malformed bones—but I felt ill-equipped when it came to my own child.

I felt ashamed of my small jealousy. This was what every mother wanted, an adoring daddy for their daughters. A tear tumbled down my cheek and fell into the pot that I stirred. The polenta, in return, blew me a kiss. *Pah.*

* * *

"Jake, that might be the finest supper that ever crossed these lips." Dad's eyes sparkled as he raised his coffee cup.

Alice lifted a glass of ruby wine. Jake had selected special bottles for the occasion. "I won't say it doesn't taste lovely, Jake—it's delicious. But the best thing of all is that someone is serving it to me instead of the other way around. I think I'd be giddy over Kool-Aid if someone else poured it."

Jake raised his glass. "The credit for the meal must be shared. Ryan helped with every detail, down to selecting the cake. And all of the herbs and vegetables came from her garden."

"Mommy stirred the polenta," Ryan said.

Jake grinned and cut his eyes toward Tully and Dr. Schwartz.

Tully's rubbery face twisted into a grimace. "Was that yellow stuff with black speckles in it the polenta?" Snickers rose from around the table.

Jake stroked my forearm with his fingers. "As a chef, my darling, you make a wonderful surgeon."

"I'd like it on record that I've never once represented myself as a chef."

"Never you mind, Katherine," Dr. Schwartz said, bringing his napkin to the corner of his mouth with jerky movements. "Your skills are utilized in the OR."

Tully stirred the black and yellow mess on his plate. "Just

so she don't cook in there." It felt fun to be part of this big family of teasing, even if I was the butt of the joke.

"And they wouldn't want *me* doing surgery on their kids," Jake said in my defense. "While I marinated lamb, she saved a baby's life. What's a little burnt polenta?"

"You get *my* present after dishes," Ryan said to Alice, barely able to contain herself.

The doorbell interrupted the conversation.

Jake pushed his chair from the table. "Excuse the interruption. Burt was due to call with the good news. I bet he came with champagne." Jake looked at me and pressed his palm against his chest. "This is it."

As Jake left to answer the door, I explained the awaited call. Burt and Jake had worked relentlessly to get all of the permits for the Golden Gate Bridge installation. I now understood that all of Jake's major installations seemed absurd at first. But it was exactly his imagining of the unimaginable that made him the artist that he was.

Jake and Burt had climbed up every state and federal ladder, wooing officials, securing insurance, obtaining clearances. Burt already had publishers salivating over the future photographs of the installation. They'd secured grant money from individuals, corporations, and foundations—more than enough to fund the project and pay them all handsomely; but that had been the easy part.

"They're down to one last hurdle," I explained. "All they need is the final approval from the state legislation. The approval has to go through the city, the military, the police and the CHP, the mayor, and the governor."

Dr. Schwartz stirred his coffee. "Won't it be magnificent to have one of Jake's installations right here in our back yard? And one of such significance."

"I'd have quit after the first twenty-five no's," Alice said. "I guess that's why I pull beers for a living, huh? Nobody says no to that."

Alice and I began to clear the dishes until Jake's shouting brought us to a halt. "Goddammit! That's *BULLSHIT!*"

Burt's soft murmurs hummed under Jake's shouts.

We all stood up from the table at once and gathered in the foyer. The stream of profanity unfurled around us.

"You're fucking kidding me!" Jake shouted as he burst out from his studio. Burt followed. Jake paced and waved his arms. "They're fucking idiots, Burt! We'll sue their asses off! Get a court order! This is not fucking happening!"

I felt my face redden at Jake's tantrum and profanity in front of Ryan and my family.

"They'll let you do the water image," Burt soothed, "but no fire. They want no risk to the bridge."

"But without the fire, it's just some pretty picture. It's fire and water together. Don't they see that?"

"No fire, Jake-O. Final word."

Jake picked up an intricately carved alabaster vase, given to him by an Egyptian ambassador, and flung it to the floor without hesitation. We all jumped with the impact of the crash.

"Daddy!" Ryan cried. My dad scooped Ryan into his arms and she covered her ears.

"Jake," I whispered, stepping toward him. "Settle down. You're scaring Ryan."

"No fucking WAY!" he shouted, ignoring me. He kicked at the pile of splintered alabaster, sending it rattling across the tile.

"Jake, stop it! You're acting like a child!"

Burt held out his hand, traffic-cop style, and stopped me in my tracks. The look on his face told me it wasn't safe to step closer.

"*Idiots.* Small-minded idiots," Jake fumed. He paced like a cougar in a cage. "We've worked too fucking hard. This installation will happen. It's what I was born to do."

Burt shook his head. "I'm afraid not, mate. They didn't just say no, they passed a bloody ordinance against us. There'll be staggering fines for any crew or engineer or crane operator that helps us. Nobody is going to risk his own nuggets for our project. We can't exactly sneak onto the bridge with a three-ton web of glass, now can we, mate? It's over."

"We've been told no before," Jake yelled. "We've *always* been able to convince them."

"Not this time, mate. This time no is no."

"Did that fucking milquetoast governor see what I did at the Great Wall? They let me work in mainland China! In front of the pyramids? The Kamakura? Does he think his little bridge is more important than all of those?" Jake shouted. "No, goddamn it! This is NOT the end."

Burt's head bowed and his eyes closed.

Alice managed a feeble smile. Her voice was tender as she spoke. "Maybe you could do your art on another bridge. I know it will be beautiful wherever it is."

Like an explosion, Jake lunged toward Alice. "Beautiful?" Jake shouted. "You think I was just trying to make something *beautiful*?"

"I—"

"Oh, let's go make a *pretty* sculpture, Burt," Jake mocked, sarcasm dripping from his words. "Maybe we can hang twinkle lights from Half Dome. Or maybe I can cut giant gingham bows to decorate Alcatraz. Better yet, we can hot-glue rhinestones to Coit Tower. It'll look like a giant spangled dildo. Wouldn't that be pretty?"

I wanted to shake him, to say or do something that would snap him back into the sweet man that made shish kebab and gathered dahlia petals to soothe his daughter. "Jake, stop it!" I shouted. Alice's mouth was agape with shock and confusion. He'd never before spoken an unkind word to her.

"Enough!" Dad handed Ryan over to Alice and stepped toward Jake with his chest out. His nostrils flared. "That'll do now, son. I know you're upset, but I'll not have you talking to Alice that way and scaring the child. There's no cause here to take out your frustrations on those that love you."

In the brief silence that followed, I could hear Ryan whimpering in Alice's arms. I scanned the bewildered faces in the foyer. Tully studied his shoes, shaking his head. Dr. Schwartz hunched over his cane and gazed unblinkingly at Jake. Fury and shame braided themselves together and wound around my throat, threatening to cut off my air.

Burt extended his palm toward Jake and walked with the pensive steps of a lion tamer. "Let's step into the studio, mate. No need to upset the child."

Jake's lip curled in snide disgust. "It's Ryan who should be the most upset. She's the one growing up in a world void of vision."

I wanted to snatch Ryan into my arms and run. Ryan huddled in Alice's arms, sucking her thumb. Jake stepped toward us and put his face close to Ryan's. "This is a nightmare and a travesty, Ryan. We can circle this day on the calendar. It's the day that art officially *died*."

Ryan lifted her head and removed her thumb from her mouth. "But, Daddy, nothing dies, it just changes. You said." Ryan, her eyes wide and her face guileless, looked at her father wearing nothing but radiant adoration. Jake hung his head.

The tastes of rosemary, garlic, and red wine that had been so pleasant only moments before now soured in my mouth. Jake's shoulders began to spasm, and I thought at first that he was crying. Just as I began to step toward him, a bitter cackle escaped his throat. When he raised his head he wore an expression on his face that made the flesh on my arms crawl.

His voice was singsongy baby talk, a tone we never used with Ryan, even when she'd been a baby. "Well, Ryan. Now you'll know what *dead* really is. The state of California has officially killed art." His words and tone of voice were absurd. He was performing some perverse kind of theater. I wanted the curtain to come down, the show to be over. Jake turned and pounded into his studio, his grand stage exit.

Burt nodded to the group. "Perhaps it's best if we give Jake some time alone."

I stroked the soft skin on the side of Ryan's neck. "Daddy's just upset, Noodle. He'll feel better later." Ryan tucked her thumb into her mouth and nodded.

"I'm sorry," I said to Dad and Alice. "I'm so embarrassed. It was supposed to be such a lovely birthday for you, Alice."

Dad pulled me to him and kissed my cheek. "It was a huge disappointment for Jake. We all know that. It'll blow over."

Alice nodded. "Things will look better in the morning. Burt's right. Maybe it's better if we all go on home. How about if Ryan spends the night with me at my apartment?"

I nodded, relieved at the thought of having Ryan and everyone else out of the fray.

"Maybe you too, Kitten," Dad said. "Why don't you come too? Burt will mind Jake, here. It'll give him a chance to cool off."

I shook my head though I craved wearing soft pajamas and having Alice make me cocoa with marshmallows. "No, Daddy. I'll be fine."

"I'll stay here, Mr. Murphy," Burt reassured. "Jake and I have weathered a few storms together. I know how to sail into the wind."

As the group organized a plan, Jake reemerged from his

studio carrying a heavy, round, stone vase filled with twisted willow branches, each wrapped in flower petals. Jake was energized, his stride confident, his face full of light and humor.

A peace offering, I thought. He'd come to his senses.

Ryan slid down from Alice's arms and moved toward Jake. "Here's the present I made for you, Nana. It's from flowers in our garden and—"

Jake held the vase toward Ryan and then looked at Alice, cocking his head to one side. One eyebrow raised, his face twisted and oddly asymmetrical. "This is *beautiful*, Alice, isn't it?"

"Why, y-y-yes. It is. Ryan, that's a wonderful—"

"Lovely, sweetheart," Dad said.

Then a shadow of sadistic glee crossed Jake's face. He stepped back and dropped his arms, the stone vase hanging like a pendulum. Like an Olympic discus thrower, he began to spin his body, his outstretched hands clasping the heavy vase.

"Jake, NO!" Burt shouted, trying to get close, but he was forced back by the treacherous centrifuge that Jake had become. "Look out!"

With wild fury, Jake released the stone, flinging it toward the atrium. It soared through the air like a canon ball. Burt shielded my huddling family with his massive body. The crash exploded. Metal framing that had held the atrium glass hung snarled into menacing silver claws.

Ryan's scream was like one in a horror movie. Everyone gasped, and I pulled Ryan toward me and covered her body with mine. We all froze in shocked silence—everyone but Jake.

Enlivened by the clamor, Jake scampered into the doorway of the atrium, picking up the petal-covered twigs that lay scattered there. "See, it *seems* art lives on after carnage, Ryan. But it doesn't." He first ran his fingers over the branches, stripping them of their colored petals, then he crumbled the brittle twigs and sprinkled them onto the pile of glass.

Ryan melted to my feet, her body convulsing with sobs.

I bent down, stroking her back with my palm. "Jake, stop!"

"I've just come to my senses about what the world really values. And there you have it." He spread his arms wide, displaying the whole picture of what he'd created. "Here is my last masterpiece. Burt, get your camera. We're calling it 'Scene of the Crime in California, Governor Pete Wilson Murders Art.'" Jake leaned over, taking an exaggerated bow.

I tried to urge Jake to stop. "This is ridiculous. We can talk about this calmly."

"Ridiculous!" he screamed. "How can I listen to you, of all people, talk about what is *ridiculous*. You've spent the last thirty-three years not knowing that that woman is your mother. I saw it the first time I laid eyes on her." He pointed at Alice. He looked over at Ryan, his eyes fiery, his lips thinned to a straight line. "Get a good look at your grandmother, Ryan. You'll look just like her in about fifty years. Minus the hairspray and bad eyeliner, I hope."

"Jake! Shut up!" I screamed.

"Come on. Look at her bone structure. Look at your hands. How can I listen to a word you ever say when you volunteer to be so oblivious to what's right in front of you?"

I turned around, looking at the stunned faces of my family. Burt wore a mask of horror and sorrow. Ryan huddled at my feet. Tully and Dr. Schwartz looked down at the floor. Alice, with blackened tears streaming down her cheeks, looked directly at me. Like Ryan's flower petals all fallen from their stalk, the pieces of me had fluttered to the ground.

I stood between two oncoming storms, not knowing which one would slam into me first. A lifetime passed before Jake stepped through the archway to the dining room table, grabbed an open bottle of the wine from the table, and lifted it to his lips. He tilted his head back and chugged the bottle.

He bowed again as he passed us, then sauntered up the stairs waving the bottle above his head. Without looking back at those left standing in the wreckage, he raised the bottle again in a grand salute. We all watched as he ascended the stairs with a swagger. With a musical sound in his voice, he pronounced, "It's been a perfectly lovely funeral. So glad we have good wine to mark the occasion." Then he disappeared into our bedroom and slammed the door behind him.

Jake left us all in his wake at the bottom of the stairs, casualties of his cruelty. I whipped my head around and looked at the four I'd always called my family.

I picked Ryan up from the floor and she tucked her head into my neck. Dr. Schwartz shook his head in disbelief. Tully wiped tears with the shoulder of his shirt.

It was my dad who broke the miserable silence. "Let's sit down and talk," he murmured.

My gaze bounced between Dad's eyes and Alice's. An avalanche of questions poured through my mind, but when I looked at Alice only one thought would fully form. "It's true?" My gut was broiling, and I feared I'd throw up. I stared at Alice. Her face had lost all color but for the black smears under her eyes. She looked back and forth in panic between my dad and me.

When I finally looked over at the time-carved face of Dr. Schwartz, it told me all that I needed to know. What Jake said was true. The old man's eyes, magnified by the thick lenses of his glasses, looked straight into mine. "Katherine, none of this was meant to hurt you."

I could only whisper for fear that I would scream. Only one word could fully form. "Again? We're here again with another set of lies? Why?" I asked, looking at them all.

"Katie," Tully said, reaching out to touch me. "Everybody here loves you."

As I picked Ryan up, I felt an odd, ironic laugh erupting from my chest. My husband—who loved me—had just had just exploded, traumatizing everyone, including his daughter. My family—who loved me—had just been revealed in another web of lifelong lies. But it was Ryan's warm, trembling body in my arms that turned my laughter into a sob. "Isn't this a pathetic bit of déjà vu?" I hissed.

Burt stepped toward me and lowered his voice to a whisper. "I'll take care of Jake. Why don't you just take Ryan and go with your family. You all have a lot to talk about." His amber eyes were steady and calm.

"Please, Katie. We can fix this," Tully pleaded. His twitched as he spoke.

I shook my head and held Ryan close.

My dad pulled a handkerchief from his pants pocket and swiped it across his nose.

"Just like Tully said, Kitten. Everybody loves you. We'll all sit down tomorrow and—"

With a snap, I turned my head toward him. Though I spoke softly so that I'd not frighten Ryan any further, my whispered words were broken glass. "Not tomorrow." I felt my face turn to stone as I turned it toward Alice and my dad. "Right now I just need to take care of my daughter. She's had enough drama for one night. She needs to be in her own bed. Burt will take care of Jake."

My dad nodded. "Of course, Kitten. And when you're ready, we're all right where we've always been."

Ryan trembled in my arms as I carried her up the stairs. I laid her into her bed and wrapped my body around hers and listened to the low rumble of voices in the hallway; first my father's, then Burt's, then my dad's again. Whatever was exchanged, I soon heard the coughing engine of Tully's truck pulling away from the house, and finally the rich resonance of Burt's voice—soothing, pleading—coming from the master bedroom, and Jake's screamed replies. I closed Ryan's bedroom door and pressed the play button of the tape player by her bed. Jerry Garcia's sweet, gravelly voice with David Grisman's tender harmony singing "Teddy Bears' Picnic" muted the sound from outside the room.

As the music played, Ryan's sobs turned into whimpers, then fitful sleep. Burying my face in Ryan's thick curls, my thoughts were huge metal doors slamming closed, one after another. Was anyone who I thought they were? *No.* Another door clanged shut. I was alone. I could trust no one.

Like a Stone

In the days after Jake's explosion, he became a hollow shell—lethargic and impossible to rouse. Burt slept in our guest room and we took turns staying with Jake.

I tried to keep Ryan's life as normal as possible given the absurd events of our family. She went to kindergarten and afterschool care. On weekends, Burt took her on outings to Golden Gate Park or the zoo. Somehow Burt could buoy his energy to be playful with Ryan in a way that grief and worry did not allow me to do.

I was a seabird caught in a viscous oil spill, my wings too coated with sludge to let me fly. I was full of questions: Had my dad had an affair with Alice? Did my mother know? Why did they keep it from me for so long? What should I do about Jake?

Burt took on the job of contacting Dr. Gupta—a task my pride prevented me from doing. I'd ignored his medical advice, minimized his diagnosis, and disregarded his recommendations. I feared he saw me as just another wife in denial, or worse, an arrogant physician who thought myself above his advice. Perhaps I was both. Jake refused to see Dr. Gupta, of course. And because he had not threatened any violence and had not articulated any immediate intent to do harm to himself, Dr. Gupta's hands were tied. Throwing a vase at a wall, shocking though it was, did not constitute a threat, and Jake ate and drank just enough that he wasn't considered a passive danger to himself. He was too sick to function, but not sick enough to hospitalize against his will.

Each evening, after acting her normal, cheerful self for most of the day, Ryan would melt down: wanting Jake to give her a bath, read her a story, or simply respond to her. She wanted to see my dad and Alice, to go to the pub and have Shirley Temples with Tully and Dr. Schwartz. No amount of explanation would appease her.

Keeping Ryan at a well guarded-distance from Jake worked at first, but she soon grew more insistent, and it seemed that the mystery of her daddy behind the bedroom door was more upsetting than actually seeing him. Eventually, I relented.

Standing at Jake's bedside with Burt and me looking on, Ryan pleaded with Jake. "Come on, Daddy. Let's go to hunt for shells or work in our garden."

Jake's face remained buried under his sweat-stained pillows.

"I love you, Daddy," Ryan whispered. Then she waited, her thumb resting near her lips; the fingers of her other hand twisting strands of her dark curls. Clock ticks screamed as I waited for him to reply to her. "You're supposed to say I love you *more*. You're *ruining* it!" she cried. Frustration formed in blotches on her pale skin. Jake remained motionless but for the tightening of the creases around his closed eyes. He wanted to respond to her, I could see that. He was as powerless to move as a quadriplegic trying to move unwilling limbs.

Burt looked on, his face wearing a mixed expression of sorrow and frustration. "All right then," he said to Ryan.

"Time to head off to school. Fill that noggin with all sorts of new things to tell your daddy about when you get home."

Ryan scrunched her face. "Daddy's a better teacher. I want to stay home and learn from him. They're learning baby stuff at school."

"Daddy's still not feeling well," I said as I pulled her away from him. "He's very tired." After everything I'd learned about my family, I vowed not to lie to Ryan. But still, I heard the echo of my father's long-ago words. *You're mother is tired, darlin'. Let's give her a rest now.*

Two weeks passed—then three. Jake slept continuously. Soon I avoided our bedroom, sleeping sometimes with Ryan, sometimes on the couch in my scrubs or whatever clothes I'd been wearing. I'd wake to the smell of bacon or pancakes and the sounds of Burt and Ryan talking in the kitchen, and I'd find I'd been covered with an extra blanket at some time during the night.

Then the bills began to arrive: late notices, months-overdue payments for shipments of several tons of tinted glass and thousands of feet of cable; invoices for electronics and chemical compounds; penalties for unpaid balances; and, most baffling of all, fees for helicopter flying lessons from a private airport in Santa Rosa. The totals were as staggering as the materials were mysterious—over four hundred thousand at my first tally, and I had no way of knowing if there was more.

Burt and I sat at the kitchen table after Ryan went to bed. A boxful of bills and receipts I'd collected from Jake's studio sat before us. Burt paged through the piles of papers. "It looks like he wasn't waiting on the okay for the installation. Sneaky bugger."

"How could I be so stupid? I've never kept track of our money. He's always just told me it was all taken care of. How could I let this happen?"

"If you want to kick anybody, kick me. I ought to have known. Jake's gone money wild before. He's seemed so much better since you got married. Stable. Happy. Of course, I wasn't monitoring your personal accounts. With Jake, money has always been the canary in the mine shaft."

"How could I have simply let my whole financial life be invisible to me? Look at this," I said, holding up a statement. "He mortgaged the house and has been spending the cash. He hasn't paid the mortgage for four months. We're in default. They're about to start foreclosure proceedings. Our savings is empty. Ryan's college fund is closed out."

"Don't worry. I've got a rainy day fund that will help some."

"No," I said, shaking my head. "This is my penalty for being so damned oblivious. It seems to be my strong suit. I can't take your money."

"I'm not offering charity, here. It's Jake's money. The income from the books and posters has never been of interest to him, but I've never felt right about calling it all mine. I've set aside 50 percent of all royalties in accounts for him for years. He doesn't know." Burt looked over at me, his face stony but a smile in his eyes. "It's a rather tidy sum."

I looked into Burt's ruddy face. He shrugged.

"You've been taking care of Jake a long time."

Burt shrugged his beefy shoulders once more. "He's a big bother, that one."

"And what about you? What about your life? Your art? Jake said you used to paint. Isn't it sort of unsatisfying to have your art be all about Jake's now?"

"My art?" Burt shook his head, dismissing the phrase somehow. "I can snap a pretty good pic now and then and I've had a little luck sloshing paint on canvas. Don't get me wrong, I'm not falsely modest or anything. I wasn't bad. But the first time I saw Jake's work, I knew I was in the presence of something extraordinary. I'm a good artist. He's a genius. I just had to be part of that." Burt's eyes drifted to the staircase that led up to the bedroom. "Someone like Jake needs people who love him enough to keep everything from going up in flames."

"Is that what we're doing? Fighting fires? I guess my little family drama even threw some gasoline on the blaze, just for a little extra fun."

"I'm sorry, Kate. About your family. About Jake." Burt crossed his arms in front of his chest and gazed out the window toward the Golden Gate Bridge. He said nothing more.

* * *

When Ryan got up the next Saturday morning I asked Burt to take her on an outing so that I could go to the hospital. We hired a nurse from a home healthcare service to stay with Jake. All of us needed to get out of that house. "Any change?" he asked as he poured us both a cup of coffee.

I stirred cream into the rich blackness of my cup. "This is going on and on."

"He'll snap out of it," Burt said. "Once he gets another idea for a project, he'll be back to his old self. Off to Katmandu or somewhere. Before you know it, you'll be spatting with him because he wants to take Ryan to a leper colony in India."

Ryan stepped into the kitchen, carrying her love-worn stuffed lamb. I stretched my face into a stiff smile. "Morning, Noodle."

"I want to go to a leopard colony," she said, rubbing sleep from her eyes.

"Not today," Burt said with a warm smile. "Today you and I go to the zoo. Do you think your old Uncle Burt will be brave enough to stay in the lion house while they feed them today?"

Ryan brought her shoulders to her ears. "They're so loud and scary when they're waiting for their food. I think you can do it. I *love* it when they roar. It makes electricity in me. Can Daddy go too?"

"Another day. But let's see if I can be as brave as you, shall we? I can't have you telling everybody in San Francisco that Burt Swift is a big fraidy cat, now can I?"

"Thanks for—"

Burt placed his huge hand over his heart, quieting my words. "My pleasure." He turned to Ryan. "Come on, little one. Let's go face those pussycats."

✳ ✳ ✳

Three weeks after Jake's breakdown, I decided to go back to work full-time. I had patients and surgeries scheduled, and my uselessness with Jake was a vulture feeding on my flesh. I needed to feel effective at something. At my urging, Burt went to back to New York to complete the publication of a collection of photographs of Jake's work on beaches. "It should generate some income, Katie."

He pulled me into an embrace, engulfing me in his massive chest. I leaned against him, thankful for his sturdiness. "No one but you could have been here for Jake. For me," I said. "I'm just so embarrassed. The money. My family—"

Burt looked down at me. "Not to worry. You take care of yourself and that little one. Let me worry about the business bits. Jake, well, he'll pull out of this. I know it."

As Burt's cab pulled away from the house, loneliness and shame crept over me, viscous and honey-thick.

Later, I found myself sifting through childhood photographs feeling in my gut a tangle of anger, foolishness, and rage. Jake was right. My blindness had been voluntary. The mirror had told me the truth my whole life. Its reflected image bore no resemblance to Elyse Ryan Murphy, with her petite frame and delicate features. Now, looking at the mirror,

my every feature—my coarse, dark hair, my height, the pale-
ness of my skin—mocked my denial of the facts. Alice's reflection, stripped of its heavy makeup and bleached hair, looked
back at me. I had accepted without question the myth of who
I was. Jake had recognized it the first time he'd walked into
Murphy's when he'd assumed Alice was my mother's sister.

The hospital was the only place where I felt normal. The
needs of my patients gave me a heroic excuse to leave the
house. I assuaged my guilt by telling myself that my patients
needed me.

Allison Bennett, four months old, provided ample distraction. A combination of birth defects and a twisted bowel had
left her in constant pain. Surgery was risky. But a shortened
life with a colostomy bag didn't seem much future for her.

Once in my scrubs, I prepped for surgery. Fingertips,
knuckles, between each digit, palms, wrists, arms, elbows.
Each body part, fifteen strokes with antimicrobial soap. The
counting of strokes was my pre-surgery mantra—a rosary-
like ritual that allowed me to block whatever thoughts followed me into the scrub room.

On this day, the ritual brought special comfort. I was win-
ning a war against unseen bacterial enemies, foiling their
planned attacks before the first strike and finding their hiding
places. With each stroke, I annihilated thousands of micro-
scopic adversaries, like some allopathic superhero. In the OR
I was a warrior, strong and fearless, vanquishing my enemy.

It was so simple. I only had to open bodies and repair the
broken parts—correct an evolutionary mishap with established protocol. The outcome could be measured. During
surgery, nothing else existed, only the beeps and buzzes of
monitors and the voiced instructions for instruments and
updates on readings. The rest of the world fell away. No
broken husband. No debt. No lying family members. There

was not even a Ryan. Had I flown to the moon, I could not have been farther away from my life.

As I stepped out of the OR, the baby's family rushed toward me. "It went well," I reassured them. "We removed the malformed section of bowel. Now that there's a healthy connection, her digestive tract looks good. We'll have to watch really closely for infection, so it isn't all over yet." I pulled off my surgical cap and shook my hair loose. "With any luck, though, you'll be up to your elbows in poopy diapers before you know it."

Allison's dad wiped tears from his eyes while her mother nearly collapsed from relief. "Thank you, Dr. Murphy," the exhausted mom warbled through her tears. "How can we thank you?"

"Just bring me some cake from her first birthday party. I'm partial to cream cheese frosting." As I walked away, I longed for the usual feeling of elation I had after giving a family good news. Parents of a sick child normally filled me with gratitude for all that I had. I'd go home and hold Ryan's perfect little body close to mine and say a prayer of gratitude to a god I wasn't sure I believed in. But on this day, all I could feel was a pathetic kind of jealousy. Even with the enormous hardship they were facing, this family was lucky: their problem could be fixed.

* * *

Finally, I could avoid the conversation with Dr. Gupta no longer. My fear eventually trumped my arrogance, and I went to see the gentle doctor. "I've never seen him like this," I explained. He poured tea for both of us from the filigreed teapot I'd seen the first time I was in his office more than five years before. "He's so... dead."

"Does he respond when you speak to him?"

"Only in groans and complaints if I open the shades or turn on the lights. When I talk, he barely looks up, and when he does, he looks like an animal that's been beaten senseless. He eats almost nothing. Hardly speaks. He's lost weight."

"As have you, Dr. Murphy."

I pulled my jacket around me, avoiding the deep black pools of his eyes.

"Can you get him to come to my office?" Dr. Gupta asked.

"I consider it a major coup when I get him to take in some liquids. I'm desperate here. Can you please come to the house?"

"I'm not being confident that would be the best thing." The musical inflection of Dr. Gupta's Indian accent again made me think of Yoda—wise and comical at the same time. If only he had Yoda's powers.

"If it's a matter of money—"

"Please, Dr. Murphy. Money is not at issue. I'm reluctant to be indulging this depression. There's an ethical issue as well." He held up the sugar bowl, and my nod cued him to add two lumps to my cup. "My services are voluntary, and he has declined them. If I come to him, he will have no reason to pull himself forward the next time he suffers an episode of depression."

"The *next* time!" The shriek in my voice surprised me. I breathed to steady myself. "Dr. Gupta, I'd like to prevent a next time."

"Yes, I see. Dr. Murphy, please be hearing me. This will be much more manageable if you begin to view your husband's manic depression not as a series of single, surprising events, but as a chronic illness. It can be managed with consistent medication. This will make these episodes more infrequent and less severe. But recurrence is likely, if not inevitable. While it has been nearly six years since his last serious episode, we should view this as a period of dormancy—a remission, of sorts—for his mental illness."

Dr. Gupta's words were a flock of bats, dark and menacing. *Manic Depression. Chronic Illness. Recurrence.*

"I'm sure you have seen families who have a member with a chronic illness—diabetes or multiple sclerosis. It is challenging to see a disorder like your husband's illness in the same light as physical illness. Maybe even more challenging for a physician. It seems to us that the patient is not really ill when his body appears healthy. It takes a great deal of support and treatment for families to weather mental illness together."

Mental illness. Those two words were smoldering lumps of coal that I was forced to swallow. Those were the words that people used to describe the rag-clad people—toothless, unwashed, and smelling of urine—pushing shopping carts on Market Street like Mary K's Irene. I felt sucker-punched by this recurrence of Jake's illness, infuriated that I'd allowed myself to be lulled into the illusion that it had simply disappeared, and more furious still that Ryan's world had been irrevocably altered by the waking of the sleeping lion.

Dr. Gupta continued, but his voice became only a distant hum in my ear. I thought of Jake, his scraggly beard and his thin body curled in the twisted sheets. He had been a loving husband and doting father for more than five years. How could I reconcile that with what waited for me at home?

"Why does he go off of his medication? He's brilliant. He's got to know this will happen."

"Many creative people with this disorder believe they lose their creativity when they are medicated. The mania, as awful as it can be, is a wild party that they once enjoyed and to which they want to return. After long periods of stability, they trick themselves and think that they can manage without the medication. Not unlike an alcoholic who, after a long period of sobriety, begins to think that he can handle a drink now and then."

Tully's sweet face popped into my mind. How many times had he gone on the wagon? How many times had he sworn that he was done with liquor? And Mary K, but for her smoking, had done everything to manage her diabetes, only to be outwitted by it.

I left Dr. Gupta's office with the feeling that I'd just been issued a life sentence to a prison I'd chosen myself—with Ryan as my cellmate.

✳ ✳ ✳

That night I slept, or tried to, on the suede chaise in front of the fireplace. I could no longer bear sharing a bed with Jake, so unresponsive, so dead to me. As I lay and watched morning's light spill into the room, a pounding came from the front door.

When I opened it, Mary K stood on the stoop, her expression a mixture of anger and concern. Mary K was just another one of the people I'd been avoiding. She'd been right about him, and I couldn't face her.

She held up a large bag of bagels and a cardboard carton containing two cups of Peet's coffee. "I come bearing breakfast." She scanned me from head to toe. "From the looks of you, a meal is long overdue."

I wrapped my arms tighter around myself and watched a car pass on the road.

"You gonna let me in, or are we going to stand on the stoop all day?"

I followed her to the kitchen. The prosthesis that Andra had developed for her left her with a near-perfect gait, no obvious sign of a limp. Saying nothing, Mary K practically pushed me into a chair and began slicing bagels. The smell of toasting bagels made my stomach growl. I couldn't remember the last time I'd had an appetite. Her silence let me know that Mary K had not just dropped over for a social call.

After she'd spread cream cheese and lox on two bagels and sprinkled capers onto mine, she brought two plates to the table and sat across from me. "So, Alice called." Suddenly I felt hollow, and my appetite faded.

"She's worried about you. Wondered if we'd talked."

I pushed my plate to the center of the table. "Yeah, well, I'm sure she gave you quite an earful. You can just take your I-told-you-so bagels and go."

"Really, Murphy? That's what you think I'm here for? I left a couple of messages last week, but figured you were busy. I was up to my ass in stiffs, so until Alice called, I hadn't really noticed that it was so long since we talked. Your dad and Alice are worried sick. You need to call."

Rage made all my muscles clench. "I don't need you to tell me when I should talk to my family."

"Apparently you do. Of all of your many annoying traits, this withdrawal thing you do is by far the most annoying. Are you so dedicated to being a superwoman that you can't let people help you? Jesus, I thought I was a prideful pain in the ass. But you take the cake. But never mind all that. Your dad's been trying to reach you for three days. Did you listen to any of the messages?"

"I unplugged the phone."

"It's Dr. Schwartz."

Her words were a spear that pierced though my defensive shield. I covered my mouth with my hand.

"I know you're going through a lot right now. But I—"

"They told you all of it, then? About what happened with Jake? Alice?"

Mary K nodded, and I was oddly relieved at not having to tell her everything.

"That's some tough shit, for sure. Timing sucks, but I thought you ought to know about Dr. Schwartz. I think you really need to see him. I don't think there's much time."

An image of Dr. Schwartz's tremulous limbs and his valiant fight against Parkinson's flashed in my mind. "Where is he? At UC?"

"At his house. Your family is there with him." It was hard to read the expression on Mary K's face. Was she hiding the worst from me? Of course Dr. Schwartz would stay in his home. That would be his way.

"Ryan's at an overnight. Thank God. The home nurse is here. Let's just go?"

"Done," Mary K said. "But first, you need to eat a bagel with me. You won't do anybody any good if you pass out. Eat, then take a shower. Then we'll go."

My friend's kind smile quelled my anger. She pushed my plate back toward me. "Come on. It's the seedy kind. Your favorite."

"Thanks," I said.

"Skip it, Murphy. This spread set me back twenty-two-fifty, so eat up." She took an enormous bite of her bagel. Her cheek bulged as she chewed.

Before I knew it, the bagel on my plate had disappeared.

Promises Kept

Mary K drove me to Lincoln Avenue and parked her car in front of Dr. Schwartz's house. With dread for what I'd find, I climbed the stairs to my mentor's flat where I'd spent so many afterschool hours as he quizzed me for chemistry and biology exams and prepped me for my SATs, then my MCATs. The thought of losing this sweet, humble, brilliant man made me feel hollow inside. I turned to Mary K on the steps behind me, trying to will myself to ring the bell.

"Go on," my friend urged, grinding her cigarette with her toe. "I'm not getting any younger here."

Alice opened the door. "Katie!" she cried. "How lovely it is to see you." She seemed to struggle, resisting the urge for a customary hug.

"How is he?" I whispered.

Alice's face changed from delight to a question mark and she glanced at Mary K. Just then, I heard the mixed voices of Tully, Dad, and Dr. Schwartz coming from his parlor.

I stepped through the archway into the so-familiar book-lined room with the smell of old books and furniture polish greeting me at entry. Keats, Dylan Thomas, Czeslaw Milosz, and Wordsworth stood sentry from the shelves where Dr. Schwartz had tried to woo me into their pages. Instead I'd always gravitated to Darwin's *Evolution of a Species* and *Gray's Anatomy*, where more measurable, predictable answers could be found. These shelves had provided me so many answers as a child, but now the room was filled with only questions. There, sitting around the coffee table, sat my dad, Tully, and a surprisingly upright Ivan Schwartz.

"Oh, Kitten. I—" my dad began to say.

"What the hell?" I interrupted. I scanned the faces then turned to Mary K, whose eyes were cast toward the floor.

"I thought you said he was sick. That there wasn't much time."

"Technically, I didn't say anybody was sick. All I said was Dr. Schwartz needed to see you. And he does. And don't you think enough time has been wasted already?"

"So now you're lying to me, too?" I reached toward the doorknob.

"Come on, Murphy," Mary K whispered, resting her hand on my forearm. "You haven't exactly been a fountain of whole truths yourself lately. I couldn't think of any other way to get this reunion going."

I shot daggers with my eyes to the rest of the room's inhabitants. "I suppose you all had a good laugh planning this little ruse."

Mary K squeezed my arm. "Nope. This one you can blame completely on me. I just told them I had invited you over."

"Another lie," I barked. "This is getting to be quite a habit."

"How's Jake?" Tully asked.

"Jim Dandy," I said, sarcasm dripping from my words. Tully's face registered the blow with a wince.

Dad set the coffee on the table. "I know you're angry. But your friend got us together so that we could talk. And I, for one, am grateful she did."

A hot lava of rage rose into my throat. "There's nothing to talk about."

Like a sprung steel trap, Dad flung his leg and kicked the coffee table. Coffee splashed onto the table's surface. "Goddamn it to hell, Katie! Can you set your fool pride aside for just one minute?"

Frozen, I stared into my dad's reddened face, then caught glimpses of Tully and Alice, whose eyes were bugging out. I'd never heard my father utter a curse word in my life, much less directed at me.

As if moving through water, Dr. Schwartz's twisted hand raised, silencing us all. In his cobwebbed voice, he whispered, "Listen, Katherine. You must listen."

My father squirmed and cleared his throat. He, Tully, and Alice exchanged glances. silently obtaining each other's consent. Mary K's face wore my own curiosity and trepidation. "We should have told you the whole thing back when you learned about Elyse's death."

Though Dr. Schwartz's voice was breathy, his words still bore their usual sureness. "Time conspires to bury the best of intentions, dear Katherine. And cowardice takes advantage."

Tully patted my dad's back, and it seemed to strengthen him. We all settled into seats; Alice poured coffee for Mary K and me and wiped what Dad had spilled.

Dad spoke first. "When I courted your mother back in Kilkenny, the war had ended and I'd done my two tours of duty. She'd lost all three of her brothers in that war. She was just eighteen. Wanted a family right away. A little joy to offset all of that sorrow. Shortly after we married, she was expecting. Our joy faded when that wee spirit went on back to heaven just a month before he was to be born."

I chewed the snags of skin around my thumbnail, enough to taste the salt of my own blood.

"We laid him to rest in the Ryan family cemetery in a casket no bigger than a whiskey box." Dad looked deep into my eyes. "That tiny headstone was joined by three others just like it in two years' time."

I couldn't look at Alice.

"We moved here to the States," Dad said. "There was too much sadness on that hill for us. I wasn't so much help to her in those times. Spent a fair amount of my time in my cups, I'm afraid. A lot of the soldiers came home that way."

I felt the question that must have shown on my face. "Oh, I tipped the whiskey pretty good in those days, I did. But we made promises when we crossed the Atlantic that we'd leave all of that behind us. Her sadness and my drinking."

Tully nodded knowingly.

My dad continued with some of the parts of the story I had known since childhood. Alice had been part of St. Anne's greeting committee and had welcomed them into the neighborhood. They busied themselves with starting the pub. Alice soon became the first employee and the younger sister Elyse never had. Tully put the first coat of paint on the walls of the pub. Dr. Schwartz was the first paying customer. "It's his dollar bill in the frame behind the bar," Dad said. "These three became our family."

Dr. Schwartz's gauzy words came between thin breaths. "When my Ruth passed on, I was lost. A widower, no children. Elyse and Alice helped me so much."

"We worked hard and life was good," Dad continued, "but Elyse noticed time passing. Every month her womb was empty she seemed to get smaller. Her nerves grew more ragged. She prayed for a baby every day and every night. Then finally we found out she was expecting. I never saw her face happier."

Tully lifted his chin, his face washed with happiness. "She truly glowed, didn't she, Angus? As her belly got rounder, her smile got brighter." I recalled the photograph on my mantle. If pure joy could be captured on film, it was on that black-and-white picture of a mother-to-be.

"But it wasn't to be," Dad sighed. "That child was born with his heart as still as a winter midnight. When the doctor told her that there'd be no more babies—well, I surely thought it would kill her."

I looked at my dad. "So what? You slept with her friend so she could have a baby?"

Alice's jaw fell, her mouth hanging agape. "Katie, no. Is that what you thought?"

I sank deeper into my chair.

"No, Katie. No. Your father loved your mother, and Elyse was like a sister to me." Though still confused, I relaxed a little with this one fear eliminated. Picking up the baton of the story, Alice continued telling of some pieces of her life that I knew, but others that were new to me. "About that time my last marriage ended. You know me. I never had any luck at love. Married a con man, two drunkards, and a man with a temper."

Tully's fingers wadded into fists. "That old fart Father Fahey sent Alice back to that rat bastard, Clive. Even when he beat her bloody." A look of sisterly love passed from Alice to Tully.

Alice tilted her head and looked deeper into my eyes. "I was angry. Foolish. Lonely. Making nothing but bad choices. I met a tall, good-looking fella. Charlie Crowe. A businessman from Minnesota. He was charming and funny." Alice shrugged. "Married." She seemed to scan my face for disapproval. "Well, nature and bad judgment sort of took over, and—"

Dr. Schwartz stepped in when words failed Alice. "This part you don't know, Katherine. Alice found out she was expecting just a few months after Elyse delivered her stillborn child."

Alice's words scrambled out of her mouth. "I couldn't break up a family, Katie. Charlie had three little ones at home. I never even told him. And an unmarried woman, a Catholic, just didn't go and have a baby on her own back then and—"

Their voices, like a fugue, took turns rendering each part, revising my biography with every sentence. Before Alice was showing, she and Elyse went to Dublin. They told everyone at St. Anne's and the pub that Elyse was expecting again and wanted to go back to her homeland to deliver. "Another cluster of fibs, I'm afraid," Alice sighed.

Dr. Schwartz gave them money enough for transportation, to live on for six months, and to cover Alice's medical care. Alice looked lovingly at Dr. Schwartz. Her eyes glistened. "He said he'd never gotten the chance to provide for his own baby, so he'd like to help welcome this one into the world." Alice told the midwife who delivered me that her name was Elyse Murphy and that her husband was "across the pond," waiting to hear of the blessed arrival.

Alice looked into my eyes. "Elyse and I came back here and let everyone believe you'd been born to her."

"So you were ashamed," I said. "You lied to protect your reputation. You lied to me my whole life."

"To protect myself, yes," Alice said, nodding. "That's part of the truth. But it's the smallest part. It was to protect you, too. I wanted you to have every chance. I wanted you to have a father."

"So you're not even my father," I said, willing tears away.

"But I am. As surely as if my blood ran through your veins, I'm your father, Kitten. Always will be."

"Blood isn't everything," Tully said.

"That's it, then? What else? What other lies have I been told? I want it all out right now."

"That's all of it, Katie." Tully said. "They say in AA that you're only as sick as your secrets. If that's true, then the four of us here just got a lot healthier."

"But why?" I asked. "Why didn't you tell me six years ago, when I learned about Mother's suicide?" I looked at Alice. "I had a right to know that you were my—that Ryan has a living grandmother."

"Everything in me wanted to tell you. That morning of your wedding and again at the baby shower before Ryan was born, I almost did. But then I remembered."

"You mean you lost your nerve." My jaw muscles clenched as I probed Alice's dewy eyes.

"No," Alice said. "I remembered the promise we made to your mother."

Tully chimed in. "We promised Elyse you'd grow up as her daughter and she promised Alice that she'd always have a place in your life."

Dr. Schwartz's convulsive movements announced that he wanted to speak. "You must choose how to view this new information. Either you've been betrayed in the cruelest of ways..." The seconds whirred while he tried to still himself enough to speak. "Or the people around you... flawed humans that we are... made enormous sacrifices on your behalf and now look to you for forgiveness and understanding."

"You can hate us all, Kitten. But I swear on all that is holy that we've not withheld another thing from you. The only shared blood in this room is between you and Alice, but the rest of us are all family just the same."

My mind raced through a catalogue of images. Tully teaching me to ride a bike; Dad collecting flowers and birds' eggs with me in the park; Alice sewing jumpers for me; Dr. Schwartz teaching me how to divide fractions. Burt and Mary K now served those roles for Ryan, while her father, the one whose blood ran through her veins, lay in a darkened cocoon of isolation and her mother was barely holding herself together.

I sat there immobile and wishing that I could turn back the clock. I wanted to travel back to the time before I knew that even my most trusted relationships included deceit. I wanted Ryan to be an innocent toddler again, and for Jake to be her adoring daddy. I looked at the frail, tremulous shell of the wise and brilliant man I'd loved my whole life—the man I now knew had provided support to me even before I was born. I looked into Angus Murphy's dove-gray eyes and saw nothing but the love and kindness that had always meant "father" to me. Tully's basset-hound face drooped, weighted by the worry that something had irreparably changed between us.

But it was Alice's face that held my gaze for what seemed an eternity. When I tried to envision her at my age, pregnant and afraid, I could see only my own image in her face. I too had found myself unexpectedly pregnant, as she had. But unlike her, I'd had all that I'd needed to make whatever choice I'd wanted for my child. And even now I didn't know if the choices I'd made were good ones. Alice had been a mother to me in every possible way—perhaps a better one that I was being to Ryan— and now I understood what she'd sacrificed on my behalf.

Mary K nudged me with her shoulder. "So how long am I going to be in the doghouse?"

"Hard to say," I said, trying to maintain the anger I'd felt when I hit the door. But even then I could feel the cooling of my rage. The fixed yardstick by which I'd always measured things like truth, family, and loyalty had turned to rubber, flexible for changing circumstances. My scientific method for determining right from wrong, wise from foolish, was failing me, giving me unpredictable results.

"That's okay," Mary K replied with a second nudge. "I don't

mind it in the doghouse for awhile. It's where some of my best friends hang out. Just remember to throw a dog a bone now and then, will ya', Murphy?"

As if mocking me, the well-thumbed copy of Rumi's *The Book of Love* sitting on the end table next to Dr. Schwartz came into my vision. The words that my mentor had read to me so many times, urging me to take them in, only to have them categorically dismissed, began to reel around in my mind. "Out beyond ideas of wrongdoing and rightdoing/ there is a field. I'll meet you there."

Even the Sufi mystic was conspiring with my family, urging me to understand and forgive.

Body Art

After that morning at Dr. Schwartz's house, I began to take Ryan back to the pub. She seemed relieved to be out of the oppressive darkness of our house with Jake's shadow hovering silently from behind the closed bedroom door.

One night Ryan asked if she could stay at Nana Alice's. I couldn't think of a reason to say no. After that, Tully started picking her up each day after kindergarten. They shared grilled cheese sandwiches at the pub and she spent afternoons in the park with my dad or cooking with Alice. Their kindness cracked through my frosty facade.

With Ryan at the pub, I was spared her questions about Jake's continued seclusion. I called her each afternoon from the hospital. "Granddad is taking me to Chinatown," Ryan would chirp over the phone. "We'll go to the fortune cookie factory and then for dim sum. And tomorrow we're going to a puppet theater…"

As she spoke, I noticed that Ryan had stopped asking about Jake.

The home-health nurse stayed with Jake during the days and into the evenings. Consuelo, a sixty-year-old grandmother from El Salvador, was competent enough for the job, and her limited English let her be a presence without requiring me to communicate much. She served as a glorified babysitter and assuager of guilt for my ever-elongating hospital hours. I managed to see Jake for only a few minutes a day, an arrangement that brought me a salty cocktail of relief and guilt.

Burt called every day or two, but I found it hard to confess to him how much I avoided spending time at home. I talked mostly of Ryan, and Burt talked of his days in his studio in New York.

"I owe it all to you, Kate. I hadn't picked up a brush in years, and now I can't remember why I ever stopped. And you won't believe this, but I ran into an old friend who owns a gallery. He wants me to have a show of my new work."

It was the first light news I'd had in a long time. "That's so great! I'd love to see it. Give me the date and I'll be on the first plane to New York."

"No need," he said. The tone of his voice hinted at the huge smile I knew he must be wearing. "The bloke I ran into is from San Francisco. His gallery is on Chestnut Street. Tell Jake to get his bony arse out of bed. I expect him to give a rousing toast at my opening."

"I'll do that," I said.

* * *

It's easy to hide at a teaching hospital. Everyone in the corridors looks ragged and wears bags under their eyes. Everybody works crazy hours. I appeared normal there.

Allison Bennett had been transferred to the pediatric floor after being in the ICU for nearly a week. No infections, no complications. She was pink and perfect, her incision a precise line I hoped would hide under a bikini some day. My paperwork was more caught up than any physician's in the history of UCSF, and my excuses for sixteen-hour shifts were fading.

252

"On your way home, Dr. Murphy? I think you've checked that baby a thousand times today." Dahlia de la Rosa asked. She was my favorite nurse on the pediatric floor.

"Like you haven't cuddled her every chance you got."

Dahlia smiled coyly. "Can I help it if I like them best when they're preverbal?"

"When do you get off?"

"Don't you know I live here?" she said with a sassy smirk. "This is the only place I can hide from my husband and kids. I'd come here even if they didn't pay me."

I grinned, pretending we were sharing the same joke, and slid Allison's chart back into the rack. "I'm sure the chief administrator would be willing to take that arrangement."

"Enjoy things while you only have one. You and Jake might even still have a shot at a romantic evening now and then, not that I remember what that is."

I wiped my eyes with the heels of my hands. "Romance is about the last thing on my mind right now, Dahlia."

"Don't let this place take you over, Kate. It will, you know."

I closed my eyes. As if it were a movie being shown on the inside of my own eyelids, I saw Jake hurling the stone vase. Then the scene shifted to the terror on Ryan's face.

Fear clutched my heart. What if the spark in Ryan was born of the inferno of her father's mania? Was she destined, imprisoned by her genetic code, to suffer the same creativity and the same madness? She was a fiery child, crazy smart, imaginative, and obstinate.

"Kate?" Dahlia said, touching my shoulder with her hand. "Are you all right?"

I used every muscle in my face to torture it into a smile. "I guess you're right, Dahlia. I've been in this place too long. You can stick a fork in me, 'cause I am done."

"Go home, Dr. Murphy. You're no good to anybody here."

* * *

My head throbbed as I unlocked the front door of my house. It was almost noon. When I opened the door and walked toward the stairs, I expected Consuelo's usual *"The Meester, he is esleeping."* Instead, the gentle ping of metal against glass drew me to the kitchen. Jake sat at the kitchen table, a half-eaten bowl of cereal and a gallon of milk in front of him. His face was thin but shaven, and he wore his glasses for the first time since he'd taken to his bed.

Lazarus, arisen from his tomb.

This was what I'd been waiting for. The veil had lifted, just as Gupta had said it would, and the light had returned to his eyes; I could see it. He was back. But excitement only flickered and then faded.

I should have been kissing him, thanking divine forces for bringing him back to life. I should feel something. Elation? Rage? Anything. Instead, I felt only deadness—the same deadness I'd witnessed in Jake for weeks. I opened my mouth to tell him that it was all over, that I had to leave him and take Ryan with me for our own survival. I didn't want apologies or remorse. I didn't want explanations or promises. Not this time.

He stood. He wrapped his arms around me, his fingers combing through my hair. I leaned on him, more out of exhaustion than affection. "I thought for a minute that you'd left for good," he said, his voice catching. "You'd have every right." He rocked me as we stood there. "Please don't hate me," he whispered.

My molars could have broken under the pressure of my bite. "I don't hate you, Jake." And I didn't. I'd missed him too—*this* him.

I pulled myself away from him and looked into his mossy eyes, made greener by their reddened edges. He was so fragile, so filled with remorse. His wan appearance and the desperation in his eyes were like those of patients in the oncology wards.

Thoughts formed and melted and formed again in my pounding head. Words withered. "Ryan and I can't go through this again. You need to know how much this hurt us."

Jake hung his head. "I don't want to hurt you." He stepped close to me and rested his head on my shoulder. Part of me wanted to step away, while another wanted to enfold him in my arms. He'd missed so much: Ryan losing her first tooth and then her second; Burt getting his gallery show; my reunion with my family.

"I know," I sighed. "You have to stay on your meds. And not just until the dark mood passes. Forever."

He sniffed and wiped his nose with the edge of his sweatshirt sleeve. "I know, Kat. I know. I started taking them again two weeks ago. I'll take them every day. I think that's what helped me get enough energy to get out of bed."

"Where's Consuelo?" I asked, suddenly aware of her absence.

"I paid her and let her go."

"Let her go? You shouldn't be alone."

"I don't need a babysitter. All she did was drive me nuts with the Spanish soap operas." He shrugged. "Maybe those damned *novelas* actually got me up."

I searched his face for any hint of the feral cat or surly hermit. Instead I saw the tender expression, his kind, loving eyes. "Where's Ryan?"

"School right now. Then my dad will pick her up and keep her at the pub until I pick her up tonight. She's kind of the bridge right now between us all." Jake gave a half-smile.

The shrill tone of my pager sliced the air between us. I

recognized the number as the nurse's station in pediatrics. I stepped to the phone in the kitchen and Jake slumped back into his chair, drained of all of the energy he'd had a moment ago.

"Dr. Murphy returning a page."

Dahlia's voice was controlled alarm. "Kate. I'm glad I've found you. It's Allison. She spiked a temp of 105 and she's been seizing."

"I'm there."

I turned to Jake. "You'll be all right here?"

"I'm fine. Go, your patient needs you."

* * *

"She's still febrile, Dr. Murphy. She's having no urinary output. Toxicology came back gram positive. Her breathing is labored." Nora Martin, a pediatric ICU nurse, wore a sleek ponytail and scrubs covered in multi-colored kittens. Nora checked the tubing to Allison's IV. She stroked her sweaty forehead with her fingers. The baby's face was swollen with edema and her fingers fattened with fluid retention. Her tiny arm was strapped down, keeping her from pulling out the IV that pierced her dimpled hand.

"Dammit. I thought we'd avoided infection," I said.

Nora continued to stroke the baby's face. Allison's puckered lips began to suck. "I've got cucumbers in my fridge older than her."

"Remind me not to have a salad at your house." We shared half-smiles and resumed examining Allison's chart. "Her parents?"

"In the waiting room. Completely freaking out."

My tiny patient lay in her crib, her rag doll body limp. "Hang in there, Allison." Even as I spoke the words, my hope faded.

After sitting with the Bennetts and explaining the

toxicology results, every intervention we could try, and the likelihood of their effects, I spent the rest of the afternoon watching Allison fighting her battle. None of the IV fluids, antibiotics, or analgesics reduced her fever. She did not respond to alcohol rubs or ice baths. By late in the day she was in respiratory distress.

Finally, cardiac arrest obliterated the last of our hope.

* * *

"Hi, Mommy," Ryan's voice was as cheerful as Minnie Mouse's.

"Hi, honey," I said into my office phone. I had to hear her voice. I could envision her tucked into the same nest of quilts I'd slept under a hundred times in Alice's bed when I was little.

"Alice said we could paint our toenails tonight."

I pushed aside a stack of research articles on pediatric infection control. I'd been searching for something I might have missed in Allison's post-op medication regimen.

"We had the best day. I helped Grandpa put some new records in the jukebox and then Uncle Tully took me to stir paint for a real fancy house he's painting and..."

Ryan's story meandered as she rendered all of the details of her day. I uh-huhed enough to sound interested, but could think of little else but Allison as the nurses removed the last of the equipment, preparing her body for its transport to the morgue. Allison had never crawled, had never eaten solid food. I suddenly ached to touch Ryan's curls and smell her sweet, powdered skin.

"How's Daddy? Is he still sleeping?" Ryan asked.

"He got up and ate three bowls of cereal today."

"Maybe he'll make something new in the garden."

"Maybe so, honey. He misses you."

"I miss him too. Tell him I found some raven feathers today. Tell him we have to use them for our garden sculptures."

"I'll tell him. I love you, Noodle."

"I love you more," Ryan announced, then her giggle rang over the phone lines. The phone clicked in my ear, declaring her the winner of the game she and Jake so often played.

Watching the grief etched on the Bennetts' faces shamed me. I couldn't let myself imagine Ryan hooked up to IVs. Couldn't let myself think of a scalpel slicing the smooth skin on her perfect tummy.

I walked over the waxed floors of the hospital corridor, into the sluggish elevator and out to the garage. All I wanted was to go home and hold Jake in my arms and tell him about the feathers our daughter would bring him. I missed my companion, my friend, my lover. I needed to tell him about Allison and have him comfort me.

Never again would I take Jake's health for granted. I could no longer trust him to keep his medication regimen stable over time. Despite its hibernation, the sleeping lion of Jake's mental illness had been awakened, and I could no longer deny its existence.

* * *

The porch light glowed. I carried freshly made wonton soup from The Pot and Pan on 7th Avenue, our favorite chicken soup substitute. Our version of penicillin, its rich broth had nursed our colds countless times. When I opened the door, dozens of white candles in the stucco niches of the living room made the place seem like midnight mass at St. Anne's on Christmas Eve. James Taylor crooned softly in the background. I set the soup on the entryway table.

On the coffee table sat an open bottle of merlot, a vintage Jake and I had discovered on a romantic drive through the Napa Valley. A single ruby glass was poured. Next to it stood a vase filled with a bouquet of creamy white orchids, with rich purple veins through the petals—an intricate web of capillaries. The blossoms dangled, each one an origami bird. The color in the veins in each blossom matched the wine so precisely that it seemed the orchids had bled themselves into the glass.

I sipped the wine and moved toward the stairs.

"Jake, I brought penicillin!" I sang up the stairwell. In the kitchen, every dish had been washed. The counter sparkled, and the stale smell of the trash can had been replaced by the antiseptic odors of cleansers. Around the house, dead plant leaves were nipped, and the pile of ashes was gone from the fireplace. My blankets and pillows were put away, and the chenille throw was returned to the chocolate brown chaise. I brushed my fingers across the butter-soft suede, recalling the first night that Jake and I had made love there. On the hearth sat the earthen bowl of black stones, solid reminders of a gossamer memory.

I called up the stairs. "Did you hire a cleaning crew or what?"

Only James Taylor's voice replied. "*I fix broken hearts Baby, I'm your handyman.*"

"Jake?" I called. The wood floors of the stairs gleamed and smelled of lemon; the upstairs hallway was free of the clutter that I'd ignored for weeks.

An uneasy itch began at the nape of my neck and crawled over my scalp. I stepped into our bedroom. It was immaculate. The bed that had been Jake's lair for weeks was now a fluffy, white invitation. Candlelight flickered in the breeze from the open window. A foghorn moaned from the distant sea. I walked through the room to the master bath. My breath grew shallow and my heart began to race. "Jake?"

Candles glowed—the only light in the room. The glass of the mirror was clear of the steam that usually gathered during baths. I looked along the tile floor to the glistening white of the claw-foot tub.

"Jake?" My voice was a surprising whisper. I could see only the top of his head. He'd fallen asleep in the bath. Hadn't I done the same a thousand times? But over his shoulder I could see no shimmering surface of water.

I inched toward him. Jake lay naked in the waterless tub. From his throat to the tops of his feet was a latticework of shallow incisions. Scarlet rivulets trickled in a perfect cross-hatch pattern over his shaved body. The blood flowed across his torso, weaving another layer of pattern over the slices. His genitals were covered with trickles of blood, a woven pattern that covered him completely. Blood flowed from his wrists, gouged from the heel of each hand to the crooks of his elbows. He rested in a bloody lake the same hue of the wine in the glass downstairs. On his face, Jake wore an expression of beatific peace: no flicker of his eyelids, no twitch of his lips. From behind his hip peeked the shiny silver edge of a scalpel. I could smell the earthy richness of his blood.

The sound of my own gasp jerked me into motion from my split-second paralysis. I yanked towels from the rod and twisted them into tourniquets. His body was cool, but not cold. I pressed my hand against his carotid artery to find a pulse. "Jake! Jake!" I closed my eyes to concentrate. I felt again for a pulse. "Jake!" Had I felt it? It was faint, but yes, there had been a tiny throb beneath my fingers. I bolted to the bedroom and grabbed the phone. My blood-covered fingers found the nine, then the one. After one more press, I somehow managed to give the location and medical status of the patient in my bathroom.

Later I would absorb the beautiful horror he'd created—as intricate as any of his installations, as awe-inspiring as any of his sculptures. He'd transformed himself. He'd become the finely formed orchid in a porcelain vase, his own body one of his exquisite manipulations of nature.

He had become his own work of art.

As I watched the EMTs rush Jake toward the ambulance, I looked down for the first time at my blood-soaked clothes. "Take him to General. Ask for Dr. Gupta to be called."

I drove behind the flashing red light of the ambulance reciting a silent prayer. *Please, please. Please—let him die.*

Serenity

From the barstool that I had always considered Dr. Schwartz's spot, I signaled for Mike to replenish my glass. I'd taken to occupying the stool nightly since Jake's suicide attempt. Once he was medically stable, he had been transferred from San Francisco General to Serenity Glen, an inpatient psychiatric hospital in Napa County.

All I could tell Ryan was that Jake needed to go away for a while to rest. Mary K, Burt, and my pub family knew Jake was voluntarily hospitalized, though I couldn't bring myself to tell anyone about finding Jake in the bathtub afloat in a lake of his own blood. To escape the torture of my own memories, I worked longer and longer days and parked myself at the bar each night.

Murphy's Pub had become home again. Tully picked Ryan up from school. Dr. Schwartz helped her with her science fair project. Alice and Dad took care of her each afternoon, fed her supper, and tucked her into bed, often before I ever got there. Once I'd gotten drunk enough that my mind was too soggy to form cogent thoughts, I crawled into my childhood bed beside her.

I'd established a new routine.

Mike brought the bottle of Glenfiddich and a sour expression. "Two fingers, Mikey. On second thought, just leave the bottle, will you?" Lines of disapproval cut through Mike's usually smiling face. It grew easier to ignore his expression after the third or fourth drink.

Tully sat beside me. Mike refilled his coffee cup and the two exchanged furtive looks.

"I saw that," I said to their reflections in the mirror behind the bar, and I raised my glass in a mock toast.

Dad walked in from the storage room carrying a huge bag of peanuts. He took a quick assessment of the beverages in front of Tully and me. "There's plenty of stew left," he said to me. "You might want to eat a little something. Your stomach will be kinder to you in the morning."

On days I didn't have surgery, I'd drive to Napa to the ironically named Serenity Glen. At first, Jake was either morose and wept most of the time or he seemed lost in a fog—a stupor of sedatives. A hard shell grew around my heart, and rather than behaving like a visiting loved one, I was the consulting physician inquiring about his care, his medication, and the treatment plan. I'd sit with Jake for an hour—all I could tolerate—and then drive back to Murphy's. This went on for weeks.

Our house was a sticky web of memories, and I went there only to gather the growing pile of bills and late notices. With the huge mortgage and the past-due bills, the fees for Serenity Glen, it became apparent that maintaining our Sea Cliff home—even with Burt's secret nest egg—was no longer possible. I put it up for sale.

As weeks wore on, Ryan's mood shifted. Usually happy and energetic, she became irritable and demanding. I was the recipient of her worst explosions of temper. She wanted to see Jake, to talk to him on the phone, and I was the obstacle. "He can't be reached by phone," I'd explain. Yet another of the half-truths I'd begun to tell. As she grew moodier and threw more tantrums, it got easier to justify leaving her with my family. She was happier with them.

"Have you talked to Jake?" Dad asked as he filled the first row of peanut bowls.

I tilted my glass, finding the tinkle of ice cubes satisfying. "I don't really want to talk about Jake." Despite my reunion with my family, something in me couldn't tell them the gritty truth about Jake. Perhaps I felt that if I said it, actually formed words and shared them with someone else, it would make it all the more real. In an alcoholic haze, I could pretend otherwise.

Dad and Tully exchanged glances. "Did Ryan go up to bed, Kitten?"

"Alice is reading her a story," Mike answered.

"Where the Wild Things Are," Tully explained. "You always loved that one, Katie."

I took another warm gulp of scotch. "It's all about a kid who feels he's treated unfairly by his mother. Perfect."

"Things are topsy-turvy," Tully reassured me. "It'll get better. You'll see."

"She's just taking out her frustrations on you, that's all," Dad said. "Once Jake is back home and feeling right as rain again, she'll be back to her sweet self."

I tossed the rest of my drink to the back of my throat and lifted the bottle. "Hey, why shouldn't Ryan hate me? I'm just the one earning a paycheck. Oh, and I'm selling the only home she's ever known."

Dad filled a beer pitcher with water and began watering his orchids. "So it's final then, about the house?" I nodded. "What a shame. Such a beautiful place."

"It's too much house. It was a ridiculous, impulsive purchase," I snapped.

Tully stirred sugar into his cup. "I know it's hard with Jake now and all. Well, I've saved a few nickels. I could help you out a little, if you need it, Katie."

"And I've always got some mad money," Dad chimed in. "Maybe just to tide you over."

I put up my hand. "I didn't ask for your money." A doctor's salary should be plenty, but Jake's debts were choking me. "We need to learn what it's like to live on what I actually earn. The house is unrealistic. I'll just have to live with Ryan hating me right now."

Dad shook his head and watered his flowers.

"I'm not the bad guy, you know," I grumbled.

"Kitten, everybody needs a little help now and then. Nobody is here to judge."

"Aren't you?"

I grabbed my glass and the bottle and moved to a table at the back of the bar.

* * *

The next thing I knew, morning light sliced through the window of my childhood room. Ryan and Alice's voices rang from the kitchen. "*And the green grass grew all around all around*," they sang.

The smell of pancakes turned my stomach and my mouth felt like a nest of cobwebs. I pulled the covers up over my pounding head.

"*And the green grass grew all around.*"

I made my way to the kitchen. Ryan stood on a step stool beside the stove. When I tried to hug her, she snapped at me. "We're cooking. You're going to make me get burned." I folded myself into a chair at the table.

"Want a Mickey Mouse pancake?" Alice asked, her tone clipped and formal as she assessed my hung-over demeanor.

Shaking my head felt like moving a boulder.

"Feeling well this morning, Katie?"

"Tip top." I rested my forehead on the heels of my hands, hoping to stop the imminent explosion. "I've got to get some things done at our house tonight. How about we stay there tonight, Noodle? Besides, it's pretty crowded with the two of us in that small bed."

"I want to get some stuff from Daddy's studio. I have an idea for a project that I want to make for him. He'll be surprised when he comes home from his trip and he sees it."

I didn't correct Ryan's assumption that Jake was traveling. "Sure," I muttered. "Be sure and take care of Daddy."

Alice's eyebrows climbed high on her forehead. "I think I'll leave the breakfast dishes for you, Katie." She wiped her hands on a towel and folded it just a little more precisely than necessary. She kissed the top of Ryan's head. "You have a good day at school, Sweetheart." Ryan threw her arms around Alice's waist and squeezed. "Bye, Nana." Alice descended the stairs without saying anything more to me.

"Let me dry that hair, Ryan. You can't go to school with a wet head. I don't want you getting sick."

Ryan tilted her head and put her hands on her hips. "It's a myth that you get sick from having wet hair. You told me, Mommy. It's only viruses, diseases, and bacteria that get you sick."

"Drat," I said, poking her ribs with my finger. "Foiled by my own words. Let me towel it off."

"I already did that," she said. Her face was crumpled in a scowl. "Stop telling me what to do!"

"It would help me a lot if you'd be less grumpy with me."

Ryan replied by flouncing off into our bedroom.

I followed her. Ryan's bedside lamp glowed, and with the

curtains drawn, the light from the lamp still shone. She'd insisted that I bring the lamp from her bedroom at home. Jake had created it for her from shells they'd collected. Unlit, it appeared as a simple lamp—a long cylinder decorated with shells. But when illuminated, it cast a panorama of shadows onto the walls and ceiling, the dark and light creating a scene of woodland animals—deer, birds, butterflies and squirrels— clustered together in a forest full of trees and blossoms. I'd tried for years to see the pattern when the lamp was off, but could see only the shells.

Ryan plopped onto the bed and looked up at the ceiling. "Daddy's not working on a job, is he?"

I lay down beside her and looked up at the shadowy menagerie. "No, not exactly."

"Is he still as sick as he was?"

"They're just figuring out what medicine can help him the most."

"He takes a lot of medicines."

"Sometimes it takes a while for doctors to figure out what kind works the best. Every person's body is different."

"Daddy said that the shot he gives himself makes him feel better."

"Daddy doesn't take shots," I said. "Just pills."

"I don't know how he sticks himself like that. I hate getting shots."

I sat up like with a jerk. "You saw Daddy give himself a shot? When?"

A cloud crossed over Ryan's face. "I didn't *see* him give a shot. I found a bag with his shotters in it when I was looking for paints. A long time ago. Before I started kindergarten. He told me not to touch it because his medicine could make me sick."

"Where, Ryan? Where did you find his—his *shotters*?"

"In that black cabinet in his studio. Don't get mad. Daddy

told me not to tell you because you'd get mad that I touched his shotter and that he should have locked it up better."

Snatching her little hands into mine, I searched for any signs of needle pricks. It was irrational—she'd been in school for months—but panic had taken over my actions. "Ryan, did you stick yourself with Daddy's needle?" My voice was ragged and sharp-edged. My head pounded both from a hangover and from the adrenaline coursing through me. "Ryan, did you stick yourself anywhere?"

Tears pooled in her eyes. "No, Mommy."

I closed my eyes and pressed my palm to the top of my head, which felt as though it might just blow off any second. *What more? How else can Jake screw up our lives?* "Listen carefully. Did you touch the needles at all? Did you cut yourself or—"

"No. I promise. I only opened the bag and saw them. Then I asked Daddy about them. Don't be mad at me."

I scooped Ryan into my arms and clutched her to my chest. "I'm not mad at you."

"You're squishing me, Mommy."

I released the clenching grip and rocked her. "I don't want you to ever touch medicine that you find again. If you find anything, don't worry Daddy about it. You come to me. I know how to handle medicine, okay?"

I lay down again beside Ryan and wrapped my body around hers. We rested there among the shadowy woodland creatures. I missed the Jake who made the magical night-light for his baby girl. I missed the Jake who touched me and made the rest of the world disappear—who could rearrange pebbles on a beach and create art. I missed my friend.

Ryan finally said, "Mommy, I think I'm going to be late for school."

* * *

After I dropped Ryan off at school, I drove to Sea Cliff. I foraged through Jake's studio like a dog digging for bones. I thought I'd been through everything looking for bills, but under stacks of paint, tools, and layers of canvas, I unearthed a leather satchel. I opened a bag and revealed a lighter, a strip of rubber tubing, a collection of syringes, wads of foil, clumpy white powder in a sandwich bag, and a bent spoon scorched on the bottom.

How long had he been using, what? *Heroin? Speed?* Could he have exposed me through our lovemaking to whatever bacterial or viral nightmare these needles might have introduced to his body? And what about Ryan? What if she had handled these needles and was too scared to confess the truth?

I'd been in med school when the AIDS epidemic had exploded. Over the course of my career, my needle handling had become fanatical. I'd worked with infected children; I'd attended the funeral of a Stanford surgeon who'd been infected during surgery.

I jumped from where I was sitting and grabbed one of Jake's wooden mallets from his worktable. I wanted to smash it all—the syringes, the lighter—then pound the spoon until it was a jagged wad. My whole life had been about repairing things, preserving health, mending that which was broken or diseased. But I wanted to destroy something.

Like the blue of a sky after a storm, clarity came to me, stopping me mid-motion. Jake hadn't done any of these things to hurt me or Ryan. Just as my life had been about reparation, his was about creation. He lived for the quick gasp of breath that occurred when someone saw one of the pieces he'd created. In that gasp he felt alive and his life had meaning.

Illicit drugs had been part of how he'd kept the lion hibernating. How he'd coped with his immense sensitivities. Though he was credited with enormous creativity, Jake actually lacked the kind of imagination it took to live daily life with its compromises and mediocrity. When he could not create, his only option was to destroy—mostly himself.

I set the mallet on the worktable. With the precision I used when handling surgical instruments, I placed the items back into the satchel, zipped it shut, and returned it to its dark hiding spot.

* * *

On my drives to Napa to see Jake, I took in the once spring-green hills of wine country. They had baked all summer and dried to tawny blonde in the rainless days of August. Layer after layer of hills lounged like a pride of lions in repose. I braved the feline guardians each day to enter Jake's lair, never quite knowing what I would meet there.

For the first weeks he was a lamb, remorseful, tearful, and filled with apology. Then he began to pace like a caged cat. We sat together on the plastic cafeteria chairs, our dinner trays touching. Jake swirled mashed potatoes with his fork, the tension in his shoulders making him appear ready to pounce.

"What are you telling Ryan?" he eventually asked.

"The truth—limited. That you're taking a break. Resting, trying to get stronger. Trying to find medicine that helps. Once we figure out exactly what we're going to do, Dr. Malmstrom can help us figure out how to talk to Ryan."

Jeanine Malmstrom was the psychiatrist on staff at Serenity Glen. She'd insisted on my participation in some of Jake's sessions. Though it felt like rubbing my skin with sand-paper, I'd participated, stoically, in each session—if only to comply with the medical advice.

Jake rammed his tray into mine. Apple juice and decaf coffee sloshed the sides of their plastic cups. "No shrink can teach us how to talk to Ryan. Do you hear yourself? Fuck!"

"Dr. Malmstrom says you're doing much better."

"Exactly what is *better*, Kat? *Better* than what, exactly?" His words were bullets.

I scanned the room to see all eyes fixed on us. "Jake, stop it."

"Stop what? Stop expressing what I feel? That's all they have me do all goddamn day. The truth? I feel nothing. Nothing! They've got me so medicated I can't get a morning hard-on. Is that what you want, Kat? Maybe I could be like a neutered house pet. One of your dad's fat cats, maybe. Or better yet a goldfish. A goldfish doesn't get overstimulated. And if it does, well *Whoooosh*. You can just give it the old flusheroo."

"Lower your voice."

"As soon as I form a creative thought, it disappears like, like, like vapor." Jake's hands were frantic birds above his head. "I'm not even who I am anymore!"

"Calm down," I whispered, looking around at the dining hall full of onlookers. "Why don't you take part in the art therapy program here? Dr. Malmstrom says that using your talents could be a vehicle to helping you to feel better."

"Gluing Popsicle sticks together? Jesus! You said my art was what got me into this shit hole."

"Not your art. Your *obsession*." Venom sharpened my words.

"If it's not obsession, it's not art. Maybe you want watercolors of barns or baskets of lemons. Macaroni necklaces."

"I don't deserve to be the whipping boy for your bad mood today."

"Don't you? I think you *do* deserve it. It's your fault I'm in this place."

I folded my paper napkin, set it on my tray, and stood up. "I'll see you on a day when you can be civilized."

Jake stood, knocking his plastic chair over with a clang. "You don't get to just leave," he ranted. "You don't get to just walk out when you don't like what I'm saying."

A broad-shouldered man with "Serenity Glen" embroidered on his blue polo shirt stepped toward us. "Everything okay here?"

"Fine," Jake shouted. "Just a little marital communication. You're all about *communication* in this place, right?"

"Why don't we take this into a private room, Jake?" the attendant said calmly.

My face burned in the gaze of other patients and their visitors.

"We have no secrets in here, do we, folks?" Jake pointed his finger at a mousy woman hiding behind her stringy hair. "We hear everything in group, don't we, Marcia?" She peered up from under her hair curtain. "We know all about Marcia here giving blow jobs for coke. Nick here, he thinks he's Jesus when he's off his meds, and Grayson over there is pretty sure they poison the oatmeal. You might just be right there, Grayson. I had some suspicious lumps in my bowl last week and I haven't taken a shit in four days."

The orderly took Jake by the elbow. "Let's get you back to your room."

Jake jerked his arm away and stepped back. "The first complete thought I've expressed since I got in here and now they want to SHUT ME UP!"

"Jake, people are staring."

"That's all you care about. What people think," he said, his arms flung wide. "What do you care what a bunch of nut-jobs and drug addicts think, Kat? You put me in this funhouse. This is what you get."

Fury rose from my gut and I clenched my jaw to stop its escape. I spoke in measured, flattened tones. "You're here because of *your* choices, Jake. Not mine. You went off your medication. You put yourself into a heroin-induced stupor. You cut yourself to ribbons."

He stared at me, his eyes feral and probing, finding my fear. "*My* choice was to die. You're the one who pulled me back into this nightmare." He turned to the group. "Shall we give the heroic Dr. Murphy a round of applause?"

One tremulous man stopped rocking himself and clapped.

I fled the room with Jake ranting behind me.

* * *

"You must be psychic. I was going to call you today." Mary K pulled off her surgical gloves and mask and stepped out from behind the body she was examining—a Latino man of about forty, riddled with gunshot wounds. Mary K wore her sleek hair pulled back and tucked into a blue paper cap. "What brings you down to the meat market?"

Jake had been at Serenity Glen for two weeks. Pride and shame took turns in preventing me from confiding in Mary K about the full details.

"What's Ryan up to?"

"She's at the Aquarium with my dad."

"Nice. How's Bloom?"

"Still in treatment. Looks like your patient had a pretty bad day," I said, nodding to the corpse.

Mary K's glare let me know she recognized my avoidance of her question. "Yeah, Mr. Aguilar here has seen better days. Most people would think that the holes in his head and body were the cause of death. Take a look."

As I stepped forward I heard a jingling sound coming from Mary K's small adjoining office. On a large dog bed stood black fur ball of a puppy that seemed more mop than dog. His tail wagged and he let out a single yip. Mary K snapped her fingers and the pup sat down, awaiting his next command.

"And who's this?" I asked, approaching the dog. His tail wagged faster as I scratched behind his ears.

"Murphy, meet our newest junior medical examiner, Welby. As in Marcus Welby, MD. But he doesn't stand on ceremony. Welby will do."

"What's his breed?" I asked.

"Welby here is a three-month-old BBM," Mary K said with a smile. "That's a basic black mutt. Picked him up at a shelter."

"I thought Andra was against getting a dog until you got a place with a yard."

"Yeah, well... What's missing, Dr. Murphy?" Mary K said, jutting her jaw toward the corpse.

I patted the pup and looked up. Mary K was quizzing me, just as she had all through med school. "No blood."

"Yup. They shot him up after he croaked. I'll likely find a belly full of pills."

"Why would someone try to make a suicide look like a murder? Isn't it usually the other way around?"

"Insurance is null for suicide, not murder. People really should consult a medical examiner before they try this shit." She tossed her gloves into a wastebasket and reached into her pocket. Pulling out a dog treat, she bent down on one knee and scratched the puppy on his head. She stood. "I'm glad you stopped by. How about you buy Welby and me some lunch? The yogurt in the fridge with the lab specimens isn't calling my name right now."

At the deli down the street, Mary K ordered a plate of meatballs, a salad, and a club sandwich for Irene. The deli owner threw in a beef bone for Welby.

We sat at our usual outdoor table and the homeless woman began circling with her shopping cart. Welby, tethered to Mary K's chair under the table, gnawed happily on his bone.

"Hey, Irene," Mary K shouted. "I'm setting your sandwich on this next table, but to get it you have to say hello to me and my friend here." She turned toward me. "Irene and I are working on greetings and salutations." She turned back to the frightened woman. "Murphy here sprang for the grub, so a thank-you would be in order. That's a few words in exchange for a triple-decker sandwich *with* bacon."

The dirt-crusted woman muttered her disgust.

"That's the deal. Six words. Hello Mary K. Hello Murphy. Thank you. Then lunch is yours. If you squeeze in a nice-to-meetcha, there's a lemon bar in it for you as a bonus."

We began eating. Irene paced.

"Come on," I said. "I don't want her go hungry just because she can't say a few words."

"She will not miss out on bacon. Trust me, Murphy. She can do this. She talks with me now and then. Bums my cigs. Real conversations on her good days. Used to be a legal secretary before she lost her marbles. Has an adult son and a sister who try to take her home, but she ends up back here talking to the cast of thousands in her head. I talked to a social worker at the shelter. If she learns to have remotely normal exchanges with people and takes her meds they could place her in a group home."

I studied Irene as she struggled between the lure of the sandwich and her revulsion for human interaction. I tried to imagine the legal secretary walking in the financial district wearing a suit, stockings, and clean hair, but all I could see were the tattered clothes and the filth, the missing teeth and the matted hair. I thought of Jake, before dining with diplomats and celebrities, now in a facility with bandaged forearms.

"I've decided it's time to buy a house," Mary K said. "Welby needs a yard, and it seems stupid to pay more rent. There's a fixer down the street from me at a good price."

"You and Andra are moving up in the world, huh? Buying a house together, that's big."

Mary K looked across the street, following Irene with her eyes. "Nope. Going solo. Littleton's getting a place of her own."

I examined her face for any signal of what had happened, but saw nothing. "But you two are so good together."

"It's good until it's not, right?" Mary K picked a carrot slice out of her salad and tossed it up, catching it in her mouth. "You know what a dyke brings to a second date, right?" She paused. "A U-Haul." She picked more items from her salad. "Things were just a little too intense, you know? I'm not really the relationship type."

"You okay?"

She reached down and petted Welby's head. "We're good."

"So a house, huh?"

"Welby pisses on the stairs in the morning on the way down for a walk. Three stories is a lot to ask of a puppy bladder."

"Ryan's going to flip when she sees him."

"When I see how cool that kid is, I think maybe you made the right choice about Bloom after all. Kills me to admit it, but he's a pretty smokin' dad. I know he's struggling now. But you two seem to be handling it all. My hat's off. For better, for worse, right?" Mary K pulled a pack of cigarettes from her pocket, shook one free of the pack, and lit it up. With a satisfied sigh, she blew a stream of smoke away from Welby and out into the street.

I didn't know what to say. I'd spent six years defending Jake against Mary K's blistering assaults. I'd come to confess that she'd been right about him, and that I was leaving him. Now Mary K, of all people, was reminding me of what I loved most about Jake.

"What did you want to talk about? You came all the way down here to the you-stab-em, we-slab-em department for something."

I took a drink of my iced tea. "Soccer," I said. "Ryan's league has an opening for a one-footed, chain-smoking soccer coach. I thought you might be interested."

"You're on. I *rule* at soccer."

Irene sauntered over, pushing her cart with a regal air. She lifted her chin as she grew closer, looking down her nose at us. In a singsongy voice she said, "Hello Mary K. Hello Murphy. Thank you." Then she snatched the sandwich and began to scurry away. Suddenly she turned and looked at me with wild animal eyes. "Nice to meet you," she growled.

Mary K slapped her hand on the table, making Welby jump. "Good night, Irene! That lemon bar will be waiting for you right here, baby. Right here." Mary K looked at me with a look of triumph and raised her eyebrow. "Was I right, Murphy? Or was I right?"

"What can I say, Kowalski? You were right."

* * *

Once the levels on his medication began to reach efficacy, I could see Jake returning to his normal self.

"Take a walk with me?" he asked one day after he'd been there nearly two months.

Fear must have splashed across my face, because I could read the hurt on his. The thought of being alone with Jake gave me an unexpected sense of panic.

"It's okay, Kat. I'm good today."

We walked through downtown Napa and got gelato, each taking tastes of the other's treat as we walked. He hung on every detail about Ryan. We laughed some. Out of the blue he stopped walking and asked, "We haven't talked about Burt. How's he doing?"

"His mother got really ill. He went to Australia right before you—" Silence crackled between us as I searched for the words to finish my sentence.

"Before I tried to kill myself, Kat."

"He left me a number if I needed to reach him. He called a few weeks ago to let me know his mother died. He's been helping his dad."

"You didn't tell him, did you?"

"No."

"Good. He should take care of his family," Jake sighed. "He's taken care of me long enough." Jake stopped walking and looked into my eyes. "And you have, too."

The topic of what would come next could no longer be avoided, but I lacked the courage to bring it up alone. I had requested a shared session with Dr. Malmstrom. After we'd finished our ice creams and our walk, we headed back to meet with her.

Jake talked to me without regard to the therapist in the room, while I was constantly aware of her presence. "I want to come home. I've got this thing, this fucked up thing. I know that, but I need to know if you can love me again."

I looked at Dr. Malmstrom, feeling oddly unclothed baring this intimate moment as she watched. I gnawed at my fingernails, feeling a sudden sting of new flesh being torn. "I didn't stop loving you."

"What then? What's keeping you from letting us start over? I'm better, right? It's good between us again."

Silence hung, a damp and heavy curtain in the small room. Thoughts of my father swirled around in my mind. How had he done it? How had he preserved Elyse Ryan's image so lovingly? Hadn't he been furious with her? Had he thought of leaving her?

"Go ahead, Kate," Dr. Malmstrom said. "If Jake's transition back to life outside of Serenity Glen is to be successful, you have to be candid about your concerns."

"I—" Words wilted in my mouth.

"Go on, Kat."

I looked for flaws in the nubby fabric that covered the arm of the couch we sat on. My voice was a whisper. "I can't believe you did that to me. Set me up like that."

"Set you up? I don't understand."

"The flowers. The music. Like it was a romantic evening. I had been missing you. I'd been so alone. You set me up for the—" I closed my eyes and swallowed hard. "For the *scene* that you created upstairs. With the blood matching the wine and the orchids. It was like a seduction to get me upstairs. It made a mockery of—" I looked up to see Dr. Malmstrom's eyes fixed on the two of us. She glanced away, honoring the small privacy I needed to continue. "It was humiliating."

Jake slid from the couch down onto the floor, putting himself into the line my gaze. "Oh, Kat." His face melted as though it were made of wax, melted by the heat of my disclosure. "Is that what you've been thinking? That I did all of that to humiliate you? That I planned it?"

"Not *what* you did, Jake. *How* you did it. You damaged your body, but your plan cut me up, too."

With his eyes looking straight into mine, he shook his head. "No. No. No, my darling. No."

For the next half-hour, Jake explained to me that he had awakened that morning feeling a little energy for the first time in weeks. After I'd gotten the page about Allison Bennett, he'd sat there, looking at the Golden Gate through the arch of our kitchen window. He'd thought about how stupid it had all been. He'd risked everything he loved for some obsessive idea about an installation. As he walked around the house, he'd seen the signs of my sleeping on the chaise and eating take-out. Filled with remorse, he'd decided to make it up to me.

He'd wanted to make the house beautiful again. An act of repentance. He'd cleaned everything until he was exhausted, then he'd gone to the flower market and bought orchids. He'd uncorked the wine and poured a glass, pleased with how it looked next to the flowers. He'd loaded a stack of my favorite CDs into the player, turned on the music, and gone upstairs to take a shower.

"That was my plan. Honest to God. But when I got upstairs I was so tired. I started remembering how I'd screamed at Ryan, crumbled her branches, terrified her while your dad held her. Hurt you by telling you about Alice. The look on Ryan's face that night. Jesus. The look on yours. I remembered it all. Ryan's tears. Your pleading with me. Burt holding me back. You all looked at me like I was a monster." He continued to shake his head. "I knew I could never allow myself to do anything to cause those faces to look that way again. I went into my studio and got that scalpel you gave me for cutting leaves."

Jake had pressed the blade to his throat first, intending a single but effective slash, but found he was unable to press it in. He'd undressed and put his clothes away. He'd already showered, but something in him wanted to be even cleaner, so he'd begun shaving the hair on his chest, his legs, his genitals. "I wanted to change myself. Purify myself, maybe." He'd lain down in the tub, trying to summon the courage to plunge the blade into his throat.

"I started with a shallow cut across my right thigh," he explained. "The blood trickled and ran off to the right, and somehow it seemed that I had to cut the left to create a balance. The pattern of it began to... fascinate me."

The hundreds of cuts and the sting of the blade had made him feel more human, more alive than he had felt for a long time. "I felt so guilty for everything," he said. "I couldn't put you and Ryan through anything more." That's when he'd held his breath and gouged his right forearm as deeply as the strength of his dominant left hand would allow. He'd watched the rhythmic gushing for a few minutes and marveled at how quickly the pool of blood grew beneath him. With what strength was left, he'd sliced his left forearm to satisfy his disturbed sense of symmetry.

"I swear," he sighed, "the thought of you coming up the stairs never entered my mind. I was too far gone. You've got to believe me." I lifted the cuffs of Jake's sleeves, revealing the purple scars that disappeared beneath the fabric. With the tips of my fingers, I pressed the tender new skin there. His pulse, strong and even, throbbed beneath my fingertips. Surgeons had pulled his shorn flesh and stitched it together. The cells had found a way to reunite that which had seemed irreparably parted.

"I believe you," I said. And I did.

Jake's body went limp and he closed his eyes. "I know you have to leave me. You have to. It's the right thing for Ryan... and for you."

Knowing that Jake's violent acts were directed only at himself only managed to change my anger into sadness. I still had to leave him. But even with his volatility, his unpredictable behavior and mood, my biggest fear was that Ryan was losing the far better parent in the exchange.

* * *

"Daddy!" Ryan squealed as she ran through our front door. I set my keys on the entryway table, along with the folder of drawings that she had made for him. Jake lifted her and spun around in a slow circle, burying his face in her neck. His chestnut curls blended with hers, making it impossible to tell where she stopped and he began.

"I missed you so much. Wait until you see how great I can read now. Miss Debbie says I'm the best reader in my class. I'm reading *Little House in the Big Woods*, and when I'm done there are six more books about Mary and Laura Ingalls. I can read them to you."

"Slow down, honey," I said. "Let Daddy catch his breath. You haven't even let him say hello."

"Sorry, Daddy." She placed one small hand on each side of Jake's clean-shaven face. He'd put on weight since the last time he'd been home, the deep lines in his face softened with the added flesh. "Your turn to talk." She pressed her forehead to his.

"It's okay," Jake whispered. "I could listen to you talk for a hundred years."

* * *

We slept in our own house that night, though there was a canyon between Jake and me in our bed. We acted like strangers with one another: me being cautious, and him respecting my inability to relax and be close. Medication plunged Jake into an undisturbed sleep, but I lay there with my eyes wide open, listening to his breathing.

Why couldn't I just tell the people who loved me what was going on? Pride. Stubbornness. Shame. But part of me also knew that none of them could understand the whole picture of Jake and why I loved him the way I did. They'd support me, I knew that. But only one other person on the planet knew and loved Jake the way that I did—knew his genius and his goodness, but also his capacity for destruction.

I wandered into the kitchen and found my handbag. From my wallet I pulled the scrap of paper Burt had given me before he left for Australia. In the stillness of the night, in the blue glow of the moon, I dialed the number of Burt's sister's home in Sydney.

Slippery Slope

For the first time, on the phone with Burt, I told the whole truth.

While Jake and Ryan slept, I poured out every detail of all that had happened. I wasn't managing my words to protect Ryan or sculpting my image in front of another medical professional. My story was not altered by wanting to cocoon Jake's image to my family or to keep Mary K from judging him. Every time my story slowed or I got afraid of telling it, Burt would sigh reassuringly, or ask me how I was coping with it all. After over an hour, I felt I'd excised the last of all I'd been holding in for so long.

"I love him, Burty, I do," I said through salty tears. "And I feel like the most disloyal person in the world. He's ill. Who leaves their husband because he's ill? For better, for worse, right?"

Though he was a hemisphere away, it felt like Burt was at the kitchen table beside me. "It's not like that. We're not meant to wreck ourselves out of loyalty. That's not love, that's masochism. And you've got Ryan to consider."

I thought I'd choke on my next words. "But Jake is better

with Ryan than I am. I don't know how to be a good mother by myself." I closed my eyes, shielding myself from the shame of my confession. I told the ugly truths about how I'd all but abandoned her and sat drinking at the bar until I passed out each night.

"Oh Kate. You didn't abandon Ryan. You took her home to the folks that love her best. You've been suffering too. This drinking and avoiding Ryan, that's not who you are. This secrecy is killing you. Jake loves Ryan. He's a wonderful daddy when he's not having one of his—well, his episodes. But he can't be that daddy anymore. You've got good mothering instincts. Jake's just upstaged you, that's all. He does that. His light is so bright it's easy to forget who you are around him."

I knew Burt's words were as true for himself as they were for me.

"Ryan knows who her mum is. She gives you her fits because she knows you'll be strong enough to handle her. She never acts up for Jake because he's too fragile."

His words were a balm. As he spoke, the muscles in my shoulders relaxed. As I listened, I watched the sun break, casting a tangerine glow over the Golden Gate. "You forgot who you are, too, didn't you?" I asked.

"I did. But you helped me to remember. That's the friend you are. That's the mother you can be for Ryan."

Unfamiliar hope was a butterfly within me. "Thanks, Burty."

"I'll book my flight home straight away," he said.

I wiped my tears and felt myself smile for the first time in a very long time.

✳ ✳ ✳

After spending that first night with Jake at Sea Cliff, Ryan and I went back to Murphy's. It was early morning, and the pub was empty. I was surprised when Ryan seemed happy to be going back to the flat upstairs from the pub, and further surprised when she said she needed more sleep and wanted to go back to bed. I tucked her safely into bed, then went downstairs.

The bar was empty. I made a pot of coffee, poured myself a cup, and sat on Dr. Schwartz's stool. I heard my dad's footfalls on the stairs behind me. Saying nothing, he poured himself a cup and refilled mine, pulling a stool up beside me. Andy Williams crooned from the jukebox.

Buoyed by my conversation with Burt the night before, I told my dad everything. They veil of my silence had been pierced. He listened, nodding as I spoke. When I told him about the night Jake tried to kill himself, silent tears streamed down his face.

"I should have let him die, Daddy. And sometimes, I wish I had. That sounds pretty selfish to you, I bet."

"No, Kitten. It just sounds human. Watching someone you love suffer, and suffering yourself, is no way to live."

"But you stayed with Mother. It feels so disloyal, but I don't think I can—"

He patted my hand. "Jake is getting good care. You've seen to that. You've got to think of yourself and Ryan. There's nothing disloyal about that."

Andy Williams sang the final line of his song: *My huckle-berry friend. Moon River and me.*

"You know, Katie, I need to say just one thing to you. No problem ever got better by emptying a liquor bottle. I know this firsthand. I searched for answers and for a cure for heart-ache in the bottom of a glass. It can't be found there. I'm sorry for the pain you've been in. For the pain you're all in. Some of it I inflicted, I know that. I'd give anything to go back to our cucumber days."

"Huh?"

"Something my mother used to say. You can make a cucumber into a pickle, but you can't turn a pickle back into a cucumber. Once you know something, you can't go back to not knowing it. It changes things. I wish I could turn back the clock. I wish we could be back in our cucumber days. It wasn't right to deceive you. I should have told you the truth when you were old enough to understand." Dad's cheeks went slack. "But if you respect my fathering at all, I need to say something. I'll say it but only once." He wiped his lips with his palm. "Tully and Alice and I will help you and Ryan as long as we're needed. This is your home. But there are some things only you can do. She needs your comfort. She needs you to be available to her—body, mind, and soul. Ryan's without her father, she shouldn't be without her mother, too. You'll regret it if you leave that child alone to deal with all of this."

Without another word, my dad pushed his stool away from the bar and climbed the stairs, leaving me with my coffee and my thoughts.

* * *

The corridors of UCSF's Moffit Hospital rejuvenated me. More restful than any feather bed, more refuge than any sanctuary, work was where I could reclaim my more powerful self. At the hospital, I knew what to do.

Julio Juarez, or JJ, had been born with multiple birth defects—a cleft palate and severe facial and nasal deformities—that made it difficult for him to breathe and nearly impossible for him to talk. At seven years old, JJ had already undergone twelve surgeries. I was performing the thirteenth to repair his septum and soft palate, a procedure that would improve his breathing.

"Hi, little man," I said as I entered the pre-op examination room.

JJ sat on the edge of the exam table turning a Magic 8-Ball over and over. He looked up at me, his black eyes shining. "*Cómo?*" I could hear the whistle of air going through his nose as he breathed, a sound that had earned him the nickname "harmonica boy" from the cruelest playground taunters.

I looked into Mrs. Juarez's worried face, then to JJ's teen-aged sister, Theresa, to interpret. "He asked the 8-Ball if thirteen is an unlucky number for his surgery," she explained.

I looked into the black ball that JJ clutched. The phantom message bobbed in the blue liquid. I waited, letting the tri-angled answer float to the surface.

"Signs look positive," I said, showing the ball to Theresa, who interpreted the response. Heat rose to my face as I imag-ined the lie I'd have told if the ball had offered a bad omen.

"You see, Senora Juarez," I said. "Even the Mattel Company agrees with my medical advice." Theresa interpreted my words, and the proud woman gave me her delayed smile of under-standing. Like any worried mother, Imelda Juarez was desper-ate for confirmation that she was making the right choice.

I explained the procedure JJ would be undergoing, being careful not to describe so much that the boy would become frightened. "He'll go to sleep and we'll repair the hole in the wall that is in his nose. Then we'll build it up so that it will show his handsome face." I smiled. "Air will pass through without making the whistle sound. He'll sleep better and not have so many sore throats." I looked at JJ and whistled, moved my hands in a *kaput* gesture.

I looked into the golden brown face of the child in front of me, imagining that, as a teenager, he'd take his earliest chance to grow a mustache to cover the scar on his upper lip. After bowing her head for a moment, Imelda Juarez made the sign of the cross and then hugged me. Without a glance to Theresa she asked, "*Tiene hijos?*"

"She wants to know if you have children," Theresa translated.

I nodded. "A daughter."

Without waiting for the translation, the worried woman responded. "*Por favor, trate a mi hijo como lo haría su propio bebé.*"

"She wants you to treat JJ just as you do your own child."

"*Sí,*" I said. I took JJ's smooth chin in my palm. "*Sí.* Just like my own child."

But what I thought was, *Even better than that.*

* * *

That night in the lowered lights of the pediatric floor, I stood at JJ's bedside. From under the edges of the bandages on his face, deep purple bruises surrounded his swollen eyes. The pharmacy had provided him with his peaceful, painless sleep.

I thought about the bottomless glass of scotch that awaited me at the pub and wondered if the pharmacy might offer me simpler relief. I'd seen physicians try to navigate that slippery slope of writing their own prescriptions. Surrounded by medications, more than a few nurses and doctors sought escape from what troubled them with the capsules and tablets that passed through their fingers every day. For the first time, I sympathized with their inability to ignore the temptation.

Looking into JJ's peace-filled face, how could I blame Jake for searching for the sense of serenity that came from being without pain? Maybe the heroin had offered that for a short time. Maybe he thought death would provide serenity forever. Medicine had failed Jake. Art was a fickle helper. Love was not enough. My treatment of JJ would repair his defect. Drugs eliminated the pain he would have suffered from the process. If only Jake could have such an outcome.

"Sleep well, *mijo*," I whispered.

* * *

Wind whipped around me as I watched the swarm of six-year-old girls scurry down the soccer field in Larsen Park. This cold January day, the constant traffic on 19th Avenue provided only a distant hum behind the final championship game between Girl Power and The Skittles. An old Vought F-8 Crusader that served as playground equipment guarded the playground against invasion.

Two minutes remained, with the score tied. Mary K paced the sideline. The wind whipped strands of hair from her ponytail. Her thick glasses were speckled with mist.

"Come on, Girl Power!" Mary K shouted. "Teamwork. That's it! Way to pass."

Despite her efforts to hide it and the near-perfect prostheses Andra had designed, I could still detect the slightest hitch in my friend's step as she paced. When the ball was kicked out of bounds close to Girl Power's goal, Mary K signaled for a time out. She stood barely taller than the huddle of girls around her. "Sanchez, McAllister—" she scanned the group, "and Ryan, you're in for Simon, Frist, and Abernathy. Switch up, ladies. This is it." In unison, hands clasped in the middle of the huddle, the team belted out, "GIRL POWER, GIRL POWER, GO TEAM—HUP!"

The girls positioned themselves on the field, awaiting the kick from the sideline. They passed the ball, maneuvering it away from the hungry opposition.

"What a pass!" Mary K cheered. She turned to the on-looking parents with her arms spread wide. "That's what I'm talking about!" The ball reached Ryan where she waited near the goal.

"Look alert, Ryan!" Mary K shouted.

I chanted under my breath. *Kick it. Kick it.*

Ryan power-kicked the ball. The goalie dove. When the ball whizzed past her grasp and into the net, the ref blasted the horn. "Game!" he shouted. "Game and championship to Girl Power, 4-3!"

The team exploded, screaming and flinging their arms around Mary K, her fists raised in victory. She broke away and jogged to the other side of the field, where she gave the other coach a hearty handshake. While the rest of the girls offered a chant of appreciation to their opponents, Mary K lifted Ryan onto her shoulders in a single sweep while parents snapped photographs.

Ryan caught my gaze, then scanned around me. I watched as her grinning face slumped. Ryan slid from Mary K's shoulders until her feet returned to the ground.

She stomped toward me. "What did you do?" Her words were arrows shot from a taut bow. "What did you do to make Daddy not want to come to my game? He said he would come today." After Burt arrived, he'd taken Jake to New York to see his original therapist and adjust to our separation. The best support that Burt could provide to me was to take care of Jake so that I could focus on Ryan. They'd been due to return, but flight delays had kept Jake from getting back in time.

I held out Ryan's sweatshirt, indicating for her to put it on. "His plane got delayed. I had nothing to do with it."

She grabbed the sweatshirt and flung it down to my feet. "He doesn't want to be near you. You're always mad at him for something." Her face was twisted into a contemptuous smirk, her arms folded in front of her chest. I felt simultaneous urges to comfort her and to slap her.

Before I could lodge another defense, Ryan turned and marched away, her dark curls a frizzy corona, bouncing as she stomped. She arrived at the distant swing set, sat down with her back to me, and dangled there.

"Bloom's a no-show again, I see," Mary K said as she stepped up behind me. Welby, now thigh-high to Mary K, followed obediently at her heel.

It struck me as ironic that the one person who I could not yet talk to about all that had happened was Mary K. My pride still silenced me around her.

Welby sat at our feet and looked up, his furry face full of adoration. Mary K gave him a pat, then reached into her pocket for her pack of Marlboros. She lit a match and shielded it from the wind with the cup of her hand.

I looked back to the passing traffic. "Yeah, well. Things have been pretty bad between us."

"No shit."

"We're separated. Selling the house. I'm looking for a place for Ryan and me."

"I know." She shrugged. "Kids talk. No state secret that things haven't exactly been hunky-dory in the Murphy-Bloom household." Mary K nudged me with her shoulder, her attempt at affection. "Look, my only long-term romance ended like a wet fart. Who am I to judge, huh?"

Changing the subject seemed easier than trying to explain everything that had transpired in the months since Jake was hospitalized, released, and moved out. "Can I ask you something?" I said, wrapping my icy hands in Ryan's discarded sweatshirt.

"Free country."

"Why did you and Andra break up, anyway?"

Mary K untied the windbreaker from around her waist and put it on. She drew deep on her cigarette. "Straight question, deserves a straight answer. You probably think it was because I cheated or was an asshole or something, right?"

I shrugged.

"Thanks for the roaring endorsement," she said, exhaling a stream of silver smoke. "Littleton wanted babies. Biological clock started ticking so loud we were nearly going deaf from it."

"So," I said. "Lots of lesbian couples—"

"Don't be a retard, Murphy. I know about turkey basters and sperm banks. I know it's possible. I just didn't think it was such a good idea in our case."

"But you're great with kids."

The vapor of Mary K's breaths hovered in front of her face. "I'm not exactly a great long-term gamble. Littleton is the whole package. Beautiful, brilliant, kind, sexy. *Healthy*. She should have kids. Funny thing, but we almost did the whole baby thing. It sort of unraveled when it came to the sperm donor."

"Is that right?"

"Her first idea was to ask one of my brothers." She let out her one-syllable laugh. "That way the kid would at least be biologically related to me."

"And?"

"Picture my four brothers standing in front of their kids' first communion pictures and their statues of the Virgin Mary at their houses in Queens when my Texas beauty-queen girlfriend and I ask them to give us just a little of their jizz so we can make a baby."

"I guess that wouldn't go over so well," I sighed.

"Like a turd in holy water. But you want to know the kicker, Murphy? And you of all people will appreciate this. Littleton had an idea for the perfect donor."

I pulled Ryan's sweatshirt tighter around my hands and waited for Mary K's punch line.

"Bloom," she said with a chuckle. "Thought that since I was

so into Ryan it would be cool if our kid was a half-sib to her. Then you'd be like an aunt or something. Said since Bloom is a brilliant artist and everything, we might even get an artistic kid. How's that for a kick in the head?"

I looked toward Ryan, who still sat dangling limply from the swing.

"Kid's giving you a tough time, huh?"

"Jake's the saint and I'm the villain."

"They always hate the one that plays the grown-up."

"I'm sorry about you and Andra."

"Thanks for that." She snuffed her cigarette with her toe. "Back to work for me. I'm up to my B-cups in stiffs."

"On Saturday?"

"Holiday weekend. Extra big batch of drug overdoses."

"Why?" I asked.

She shrugged. "Seems like the dealers bring in extra pure stuff for the holidays. Regular junkies know their dosage. Purity causes a bunch of ODs. So, like my dad always says, I'm like the butcher who backed into the meat grinder." Mary K looked at me with a half grin. "Got a little behind in my work." Mary K chuckled at her own joke.

On impulse, I leaned over and wrapped my arms around Mary K despite her stiff response. She pulled away. "A little discretion, huh?" She began to walk away then turned back to me. "We wouldn't want people to think we're queer or something." Her eyebrows twitched, then she turned and walked toward where Ryan sat on the swing. She waved good-bye to me over her shoulder. Welby trotted at her heel.

Mary K sat in the swing next to Ryan's. The two dangled there for a while. Welby plopped his head in Ryan's lap. After a couple of minutes Mary K stood, nudged Ryan with her shoulder, and walked toward the road, her dog bounding beside her. I watched as she boarded the MUNI bus, her arms waving wildly as she negotiated passage for Welby. The door closed and the bus joined the river of vehicles.

Ryan sauntered toward me, her head hanging. "Can we go to Just Desserts for carrot cake?" she asked, her voice still pinched but her facial expression softened.

I turned to see the back end of the bus as it disappeared over the hill. "Carrot cake sounds pretty good to me."

Purgatory

"Whoa!" I said as I opened the front door to the house. Jake stood in the foyer looking as surprised as I felt. He'd been home from Serenity Glen for nearly a month. I'd seen him only during visitation with Ryan and to sign papers with the realtor for the final sale of the house. "I thought you'd left for New York already," I said.

"I leave in a few hours."

"Yeah, well, I just got off work and thought I'd get the mail and—"

"I put it all in the bowl on the sideboard."

"I'll put in a change of address."

We spoke like awkward unfamiliars. The discomfort of it made my scalp itch.

He looked past me. "Where's Ryan?"

"Sleepover at a new friend's house."

"Good," Jake said, studying the floor at his feet. "She seems to be making friends."

"She should be with kids her age instead of just hanging out at the pub all the time."

"Murphy's is a pretty nice place for a kid." It registered as he said it that Jake was losing not only Ryan and me, but the family that had adopted him as well. Another loss. "So the house sale is finalized? When does it close?"

"A long close. Forty-five more days. I'll start packing this week. Just tell me what you want."

"I can't have what I want."

We stood there in the silence. It had been nearly six months since we'd been completely alone together. Even our walks in Napa had been to public places. A feeling of being overexposed ran through me.

"Cup of tea?" he asked.

I attempted a nonchalant tone. "Sure. Why not?"

We sat at the kitchen table where Ryan's highchair had once crowded the space and we'd pried stuck-down Cheerios from the terra cotta floor; where we'd worked crossword puzzles on Sunday mornings. Now Jake and I balanced the awkwardness of strangers with the gravity of the history we'd shared.

At first we exchanged niceties—my work, Ryan's smooth entry into the first grade, updates on the gang at Murphy's. As each topic waned, it was replaced with a palpable silence that throbbed behind my eyes.

"This is weird," Jake said. "How are you, Kat? Really?"

I looked back out the window, searching for anything familiar that might anchor me but finding nothing but a horizon veiled by fog. "So you're doing a commissioned installation, Burt tells me."

"Burt set it all up. Hired an assistant to work with him since he's doing more of his own work right now. But you know Burt. Delegating isn't his strong suit. Did you know he's painting?"

I wrapped my fingers around my teacup and felt myself smile. "His gallery show, remember? It was great. Especially the portraits."

Jake nodded and looked off into the foggy distance, his face lined with remorse. "I always knew he was talented, but—"

"So tell me about this New York installation."

"Burt sold it big, I guess. A temporary sculpture in Central Park. More than an acre, actually. Big sponsors, so I can help pay off—" The words seemed to catch in his throat.

"What will the piece be?"

"It's not fully planned. Burt's going crazy, of course, wanting to know the details. It's all still forming. I've been thinking a lot about cracks, though."

I found myself smiling. "Cracks?"

Jake laughed his deep giggle that was both manly and childlike and always delighted me. He explained how cracks in stone, ice, wood, glass, and earth can at first appear random, but how they actually follow along a predictable path of least resistance, like a river cutting its course. A crack in a rock or a log or even in the earth searches for weakness and creates itself there. "Kind of Darwin in reverse, with weakness overcoming strength."

"Maybe not in reverse," I said. "The strong is still surviving, right? From the perspective of the crack."

"Exactly," Jake said, smiling. "Exactly."

We talked for a while longer about the installation, his first in two years. Jake dropped his gaze down to his lap.

"It's getting late." I said. "You've got your plane, and Alice is expecting me for supper."

Jake looked into my eyes. "Stay with me for just a little longer. I'll make you dinner. Ryan's garden is full of vegetables and fresh herbs." He donned his pitch-perfect imitation of my dad's brogue. "It'd be a sin to let 'em go to waste now, wouldn't it, Kitten?" His eyes flashed.

Ignoring the small voice of hesitation, I nodded.

Fragrances of fresh ginger, cilantro, and garlic rose through the kitchen from the sizzling wok on the stove. I found myself watching Jake's fluid movement as he chopped vegetables. He moved like a dancer, his body flowing with purpose and intention. "You look better. What meds are you taking right now?"

He spooned vegetables from the wok onto my plate. "They were throwing the whole pharmacy at me for a while. Antipsychotics, mood stabilizers. Most of it just twisted me up, messed up my sleep and my memory, gave me stomach cramps, night sweats, dry mouth, tics. The plagues of Job. I started looking over my shoulder for locusts and floods."

Science had always seemed to me like the solution for every malady. For Jake, it was a cruel temptress, mocking and deceitful.

The first bite of the stir-fried vegetables filled my senses all at once. He'd just thrown it together, but it was as sublime as any meal I'd ever eaten. "And now?" I asked. "What's your medication regime?"

With the back of his fork, Jake moved food on his plate. His face dropped, and without looking up he spoke in a level voice. "Can we not, Kat? Can we just enjoy this little sliver of time right now without the medical exam?"

"I'm sorry. I guess I'm like the crack, huh? Always pushing through, looking for the weak spots I guess."

We talked about my reunion with my family, Jake's treatment with Dr. Gupta. JJ's surgery. Mary K's new house. But mostly we talked about Ryan.

Jake sighed. "I've missed so many things." His regret was a dead thing—a carcass rotting in the room. "I'll do the installation in New York, then come back and help pack up the house. You can sell anything you don't want. The money can go to pay off some of the debt." Jake pushed his barely-touched plate aside. "I've arranged to sell some of the art. Do a few commissioned pieces. That should get us out of the hole. The new assistant is managing the sales. Checks will all come to you."

"Thanks. I know this is hard."

Jake's shoulders rose with a deep inhale. "Seeing me just wrecks Ryan, doesn't it."

"She loves you, Jake."

"I know, but I confuse her. I scare her. My mood cycles are more frequent than ever, more... volatile. I can't tell from minute to minute what I'm going to be like. They call it a *maturing* of my disorder. Ironic name, huh? Sedatives help me sleep, but then I wake up and the pain of losing you and Ryan is right there with its fist in my face ready to give me another punch."

"I don't want to keep you from Ryan, it's just—"

Jake put up his hand to halt my words. "You have to."

I looked at the sleeves that covered Jake's arms. "Jake, the heroin. Are you still using?"

He took off his glasses and rubbed his eyes. "Sometimes, when nothing else works," he sighed.

We'd had hours of discussion with Dr. Gupta and Dr. Malmstrom about how Jake, like so many with manic-depressive illness, used street drugs to moderate his moods. And though sometimes there was a dual diagnosis of addiction in cases like his, Jake was not a classic addict. This had been his first foray into needle use. I'd never been a prude about casual drug use and had imbibed my share of pot before Ryan was born, but the idea of heroin made my stomach turn.

"I can't have Ryan alone around you with even the possibility of drug use." Fear and anger clung to my words. The vision of Ryan holding a syringe was a scar in my mind.

He put his glasses back on and looked at me again. "You can't let me be alone with Ryan at all, Kat, even without the drugs. Ever. We know that, right? If I was just a junkie I could recover, but—"

"The needles. I got tested and I'm fine, but maybe you just got lucky. You're playing with another kind of fire."

He opened the drawer in the old sideboard next to the table and moved the stack of table linens aside. He removed a mahogany box where the good silverware was usually housed. The flatware had been replaced with a Ziploc bag filled with syringes, each still in its sterile packaging, and the rest of the paraphernalia I'd seen before. He picked up a carton of sterile syringes. "I guess I still had a modicum of sense; I used clean needles. AIDS is probably the one thing you don't have to worry about."

He reached for my hand. Gently, he turned the platinum bird's nest ring I'd tried a dozen times to stop wearing. He still wore the ring of platinum twigs he'd designed to match. He brought my fingertips to his lips and kissed them one at a time. His lips were a creamy balm.

"I don't want to mislead—"

The sweet tarragon on his breath and the citrus of his shampoo formed a haze around me. "I know it's only for just right now. I'm not asking for anything more than just this."

I closed my eyes and remembered seeing Jake's ice sculptures on Ocean Beach. I'd wanted them to stand forever in their shimmering crystal beauty. Words of our years together flooded my mind. *What makes them special is that they'll only be here for a flicker of time.*

We wrapped our arms around each other. His body's vibrancy radiated through me, down to my bones. We swayed there, like dancers to our own inner music. Without speaking, we walked together to the living room.

We came to rest together, like the first night we shared together, on the smooth suede chaise. Our bodies fit together like a well-worked jigsaw puzzle. I felt my heart, not racing wildly as it had when we'd first met, but beating with steadiness and strength. We lay there fully clothed and yet somehow utterly exposed.

Jake stroked my cheek with his fingers, like a blind man reading brail. His voice was pinched with pain. "It kills me to give us up."

His words were needles puncturing my skin. "Things will seem better when you're feeling stable again."

Even in shadow I could see sorrow on his face. "I'll never be stable. I've been like this since I was fourteen. My father hired every shrink on the East Coast. I've taken every legal and illegal drug known to man. I've meditated with gurus in Tibet. I've cleansed my chakras, purified my *chi*." He let out a low chuckle. "I even got exorcised by a priest in Spain once. Then I met you and we had Ryan. I thought you were my cure. But I was only, what would you call it? In remission?" He sighed a ragged sigh. "I don't want to be a disease in your life."

I closed my eyes, willing tears back. "You're not a *disease*."

In that moment, it seemed impossible to remember why we had to part. This man loved me, loved his daughter, and we loved him back. It all seemed so cruel.

The only sound in the room was the crashing of the surf below and the aching bellow of a foghorn. Like the waves outside, the relentless force of my grief pounded at me. Jake wrapped himself tighter around me, holding me until the intensity of the wave subsided. The moon appeared, showing its gauzy face in the window. "Your flight," I whispered.

"There's always another flight."

I leaned into him and caressed his freshly shaved cheek, its softness yielding to my touch. I pressed my lips to his. Like the first sip of water to an aching thirst, his kisses, his touch, his embrace all made me crave more. My deepened breaths drew in the rich scent of him: ocean and earth. His erection hardened against my thigh and he uttered a soft moan as my hand slipped beneath the waistband of his jeans.

Jake unbuttoned my shirt as though he was opening a gift, and when the wrapping was off, he paused to look at me in the blue half-light. His kisses formed a trail of heat down my throat and between my breasts—the same path he'd once formed with cool, black stones. We couldn't find enough ways to touch each other: with fingers, with thighs, with lips, with tongues. We moved slowly, two starving people savoring a last meal.

Our clothing peeled away. My fingers found the fine lines of the mesh of scars on his chest and arms. I wanted to trace every scar and make it disappear. Jake found the eagerness between my legs. He rolled on top of me and slid inside. My body offered no resistance.

For those moments there was only us in that room, unfettered by the past, unworried by the future. In the power of that slice of time, I understood Jake's art more deeply than ever. For art and for passion, the power of the immediate, the *instant*, is enormous by comparison to any monument made in remembrance of it.

We lay there, our bodies braided around each other. I looked down at us, my pale limbs entwined with his darker ones. "Marble rye," I said.

When I woke, the space beside me on the chaise was cool to the touch. I was covered with the soft chenille throw, and my clothes lay folded neatly on the couch.

Silent as a dream, Jake had risen from where I slept. I blinked, trying in vain to see through the inky blackness that had swallowed all but a single beam of moonlight. I lay there, an ache deep inside of me, hollowed by the absence of him, fearing the moment when sunlight would split the dark.

∗ ∗ ∗

Heat from the OR lamps pressed down on me as if it were made of lead instead of light. Rivulets of sweat trickled down my back, conspiring, along with the ticking clock and the pacing parents I knew were in the waiting room, to distract me.

My eyes remained on the rectangular opening in the surgical draping that let me see the flesh I was repairing. Nothing was allowed into my thoughts but what existed in that rectangle: tissue, tendon, blood, bone, and the percussive accompaniments of pulse and respiration.

Molly McInerney's throat and chest had been so badly burned when her hair snatched the flame of her birthday candles that her airways had grown blocked with scar tissue, requiring her to use a breathing tube through her trachea. She'd been only four when it happened, and in the two years since she'd endured unimaginable pain and more surgeries than most people would have in two lifetimes. The skin on the side of her neck had stiffened to taut, shiny leather that tugged at her head, keeping it tilted to the left. She was missing an ear and the hair on one side of her head. This was the last surgery on her throat.

I checked in constantly with Mark Goldman, the anesthesiologist. His job was to monitor the patient, to titrate just enough medication to keep her completely pain-free and unconscious. Molly's eyes were taped shut and a tube projected from her lips, yet she appeared completely tranquil. The magic of chemicals having their effect.

On the faces of the sleeping and the dead I had often encountered the appearance of peace. It was a look I could not even imagine on Jake's face. He waited every conscious moment for the next betrayal of his mind, never knowing when it would come. It had cost him everything that mattered, and medicine offered him no promise of relief.

Reentering the present moment, I became aware of the monitor that beeped with each of Molly's perfectly paced heartbeats. Then it came to me: *Death would free Jake.*

Like a dog shaking off water, I shook my head to rid myself of the germs of thoughts that had begun to plant themselves in my mind. *I could help him.* I had certainly let death come to patients, ceasing intervention that would only prolong agony—altered our course from medical intervention to "comfort care." I had removed life support and allowed others' loved ones to slip away. But to actually *cause* death was anathema to me: a line I had never imagined crossing.

My hands worked independently of my thoughts; I completed the surgery and nodded to my surgical partner to close. I rushed out of the OR, afraid I might scream out loud.

* * *

Usually my work at the hospital absorbed me completely. But once the sour thoughts of helping Jake die had seeped into my awareness, my haven was destroyed. Every corner of the place held reminders of the comfort medicine offered—comfort unavailable to Jake. Death became not the enemy I'd always fought, but the relief I'd denied Jake by rescuing him from what he'd truly wanted.

Images of Jake's suffering were my waking nightmare: lying in a creamy white bathtub, his body a hatch-work of wounds; strapped by leather restraints into a hospital bed, more animal than human; his eyes fiery with fury, setting fires on our hillside. My daydreams—and my nightmares, too—were flooded with the piercing sound of breaking glass.

Divorce was for those who no longer wanted to share a life together. There was no name for what Jake and I had become.

But what if Jake just went away? Disappeared from our lives to some far-off patch of the globe, never to be heard from again? Such abandonment would scar Ryan like no other wound. And for Jake, such a leaving would also subject him to living as an emotional amputee, with no opportunity for healing.

I walked the hospital corridors listening to the moans of those for whom medication provided inadequate relief. I'd thought myself compassionate, but now I knew just how insulated I'd become from the suffering that surrounded me. Orderlies pushed gurneys that concealed dead bodies so that visitors wouldn't notice. Charts of the expired sat stacked, awaiting final signatures. Doses of medication lay unadministered because death had won the race. I had never been numb to pain and loss, as some of my colleagues had been. But now I knew that I, too, had shielded myself from the most agonizing images. I'd focused on the solutions I could provide—the treatment plan, the medication regime, the surgery—and I'd blurred the pictures of pain.

Like a cat burglar, I became obsessed with planning, researching security systems and drug-custody protocols, determining how to avoid detection. I would never deny patients by taking what was intended for them. Nor would I rob a meds cart, which might result in a pharmacy tech being blamed. I began to imagine myself palming leftover drugs and slipping them into my pocket, just to see if I could.

Almost involuntarily, my eyes scanned every surface, every cart, and every cabinet, like I was on a macabre Easter egg hunt. I was surprised at how quickly and easily my basket could be filled. A hospital provides enough distraction and chaos that miscalculations occur more often than anyone would ever admit. Equipment gets lost. Papers get misfiled. Medication gets misplaced. In almost no time, I could have a cache of pharmaceutical-grade narcotics. Even with the protocols, it would not be hard to gather what was needed. I was trusted. I had a backstage pass to the medical theater.

Doubts droned like the dirge of bagpipes at Irish funerals. Shouldn't Jake's disease be allowed to take its course? Who was I to intervene? Another suicide attempt seemed all but inevitable. Why not just wait?

It was a gradual knowing that came upon me. The only *real* end to Jake's torture was death. He'd tried to hasten it, but I'd denied him that relief. If I contorted my thinking and looked at it through just the right lens I could see that helping him die would simply be righting a wrong I'd caused.

My father had assumed when I was small that the accidental death of a parent is something a child can withstand. Nearly every fairytale starts with a child who's lost one or both parents to illness or accident. Bambi. Cinderella. Dorothy. But fairytale characters are never orphaned by suicide.

I could slip my stolen booty, pure and potent, into the supply of drugs that Jake had shown me in the kitchen drawer. It would be only a question of time until he'd seek comfort there. Like Mary K's holiday overdose cases, Jake could die an *accidental* death. A death that Ryan could understand. A death that would bring her no shame.

I'd have to be careful—no, flawless—in my execution. I couldn't just write a prescription for narcotics and pick them up at the pharmacy. If discovered stealing drugs, I'd lose my job, my license to practice—my daughter.

I could not allow myself to shield my intentions with the pretty words of rationalization. What I was considering would be called murder by many, including the courts. *Murder. Murder. Murder.* The word, though accurate, had nothing to do with the actions I contemplated. Murder was about rage, revenge, greed. I sought only mercy for Jake, peace for myself, and safety for Ryan.

I reasoned that it would be easier for Ryan to lose Jake completely than to lose him a thousand times to bouts of madness. *He didn't mean to die*, I'd explain, teaching her the tragedy of drug use.

I could see only one possibility to free us all.

Eggs in One Basket

Even the engine of a chartered jet and my third tumbler of scotch failed to drown out the roar of my conflicting feelings about going to New York to see Jake's installation. My father's admonition rang in my ears. *You'll not find your answers in the bottom of a bottle, Kitten.* But his voice grew dimmer with each glass I emptied. And the scotch now had another duty; to drown the obsession I now had with Jake's death. Ryan, wearing headphones, had her eyes glued to a large TV screen, watching *Little Mermaid*. Another orphan's tale.

It had been nearly a month since I'd shared that night with Jake, and we hadn't spoken since. Burt, who called each night to speak with Ryan and me, had arranged our travel and urged us to come.

The plan I'd begun to form was a bruise, its aching silence another barrier to my talking with Mary K. I'd managed to gather a small cache of narcotics, which I'd housed in a safe-deposit box. The cache grew, a malignant, unseen cancer.

I looked over the top of Ryan's head to find Mary K spreading brie and caviar on a cracker. She caught my eye. "Thanks for coming," I said.

"What? I'm going to turn down a private jet to New York, my own room in a penthouse suite in Bloom Tower, and a chance to watch the Mets whip the Yankees from box seats? Mr. and Mrs. Kowalski didn't raise a fool."

When Aaron Bloom had gotten wind of Jake's installation, he'd begun his shower of offers. Jake, vulnerable and alone, had reconnected with his father and accepted his gifts on our behalf. New York was a place especially fraught with hazards for Jake. Aaron Bloom's presence loomed as large as the towering buildings he'd erected in his own name. The press would swarm. Expectations following Jake's two-year hiatus would be enormous.

I reluctantly agreed to go, just wanting Ryan to see her dad doing something positive.

I could not face New York and Jake alone. He'd agreed to stay at another of his father's hotels, but I needed Mary K with me as my wingwoman. With her there, I'd be safe from the hypnotic poppy field of my love for Jake. Ryan had finally settled into our new, lopsided homeostasis. Her tantrums had ebbed. She'd grown accustomed to seeing Jake only with either Burt or me present. She'd made new friends and was functioning way above grade level in all of her subjects. Much like Mary K's prosthesis, the new artificiality of our arrangement had become our norm. But Jake and I still suffered the acute phantom pain of what we'd lost.

Through the window of the jet, I spied the Statue of Liberty surrounded by the mercury-colored waters, her muscled arm unwearied by the weight of the torch she held. I'd seen her on my first trip to New York when Mary K and I had retrieved Ben Casey so many years before. Lady Liberty had seemed so powerful and noble when I'd seen her at eighteen. But at thirty-three, I saw her as utterly alone, suffering the cruelty of the elements.

Our pilot's announcement pulled me from my thoughts. "We have clear skies, so enjoy the ride as we take a smooth wide curve around the island of Manhattan before we head toward the airport. We'll arrive in about thirty minutes. As you can tell, we're just beginning our descent."

No, I thought. *My descent began a very long time ago.*

* * *

Morning cartoons and Ryan's squeals from the main parlor of the hotel suite stabbed like so many needles through my skull. My head pounded me with insults. Both the plane and the hotel suite had been outfitted with full bars, and I'd taken advantage.

Mary K entered my room with a loud kick to the door, carrying a newspaper and delicate china cup smelling of coffee. She sat on the edge of my bed, eyed me through her thick glasses, and took a noisy slurp from the cup. "I favor a sturdy mug to this daintiness, but the grog's pretty good."

I sat up and squinted at the cup. "I thought that might be for me," I croaked past the dust in my throat.

"Them that drink themselves to sleep fetch their own morning coffee."

"Since when did you get so self-righteous?"

"Just acknowledging a fact. Seems you've been hitting it pretty hard. You were higher than our airplane for most of the flight."

Fighting with the snarl of blankets, I sat on the edge of the bed. "When I want to wake up to a lecture from Nancy Reagan, I'll let you know. If you're not bringing coffee, why are you spoiling the raucous time I could be having alone with my hangover?"

"Jesus, you're pitiful. Here." Mary K held out her cup.

The coffee offered its sympathies with its rich aroma. "We shouldn't have come."

"That's just your hangover talking," she said. "The kid should see her dad's work. He's a major fucking artist, after all. Now get your ass in the shower, because you look like shit and I'm not going to be seen with you. New York is my town. I've got a reputation to maintain."

I looked my friend in the eyes. I'd longed for years for her to see Jake as I did, to notice his talent and his qualities as a father. Part of me wanted to tell her about the putrid plan that had begun to take shape. But how could I? How could I look into those steady eyes and confess that I was thinking of ending the life of the father of my child? That I'd already amassed enough narcotics to do the job? I could make no one my accomplice. "You're something, you know. I never know whose side you're going to be on."

Mary K stood and walked toward the door. "It's simple. I'm always on your side, Murphy." Her lips formed a crooked smile. "Look, I'll take Ryan out for the morning. Show her some sights. Give you a little time to fix the disaster you're wearing on your face. Show opens at three. We'll be back by two."

I gave a grateful, if painful, nod, and Mary K was out the door.

* * *

After my shower my head still drummed, my brain trying to fight its way out of my skull. Coffee, a lavish room service breakfast tray, and a half-hour of quiet brought me back to feeling near human again. I wrapped myself in a plush, white, terry cloth robe with *Bloom* embroidered in gold on the breast pocket and settled myself on the silk sofa with the Sunday *New York Times*.

Jake's photo gazed up at me from the front page of the Culture section, which featured a huge article about him and the "Wounded Mother" exhibit's opening. Jake's works seldom had titles, and this one intrigued me. I knew the photograph well. Burt had taken the brooding, black-and-white image for Jake's exhibit in British Columbia, just before Ryan was born. Jake's handsome face and soulful eyes made him appear mysterious and haunting. *It's so artsy*, I'd said. But now I saw it with new eyes. Jake's pain. His potential for rage. His darker self lurking beneath the handsome, photogenic image. Burt had seen it all and, with a single click, had preserved it. The Jake I saw back then had helped me discover love and passion. The Jake I understood more fully now had taught me about love's agony and heartache.

The article featured Jake as New York's prodigal son, returned home for his fatted calf of adoration. It lauded his importance to the world of art and the city's good fortune in hosting his reemergence. The article's writer alluded cryptically to "troubled times" in Jake's early adulthood, but framed him as "settled and secure" since marrying and becoming a father. Aaron Bloom's press secretary had done his job well.

I lay my head back onto a luscious, down-filled sofa pillow. No sooner had I done so than a knock came at the door. Maybe Mary K had forgotten something—couldn't find her key. Or room service was arriving with yet another "compliments of the hotel" basket.

When I saw Burt's ginger beard and ruddy face through the peephole, it felt as if my whole body smiled. The distortion of the lens gave him a funhouse look that made me laugh out loud. "Burty!" I cried as I opened the door. "What a surprise. I thought you'd be running around like a madman today, working all your magic for the exhibit."

Burt wrapped his burly arms around me and delivered a squeeze that left no doubt I'd been properly hugged. He kissed me on the forehead. "Nothing left for this madman to do, I'm afraid. No need for my tricks. It seems Jake-O has taken over the whole bully thing. Running with his own muse without me. I'm the lame duck, after all. Thought I might have a visit with you and Ryan instead of wringing my hands all day."

"Ryan and Mary K are out on the town until early afternoon. But I'd love a visit. Come on in," I said, realizing we were having a conversation in the doorway. "Have a coffee with me." I grabbed his beefy hand and pulled him toward the couch. "What do you mean, lame duck?"

The spacious sofa looked dainty under Burt's massive form. The coffee cup was miniature in his hand. "This will be my last Jake Bloom installation." Burt's voice was a mix of melancholy and excitement. "We decided together. Jake saw my paintings, and well—" Burt's face reddened even further. "Said he'd feel guilty keeping me as his sidekick now that he'd really recognized my talent. Said I should be fully devoted to my own art." He raked his fingers through his beard and looked up at me with a sheepish shrug. "A little grandiose, that one." Burt reached toward the food tray on the coffee table and plucked a grape from the stem, popping it into his mouth.

"He's right, you know. It's your time, Burty."

"So the new assistant has managed most of this. Jake hasn't let me see a thing, so I'll get to be a spectator just like the rest, I suppose." Burt tipped his head toward the raspberry Danish on my tray. "You having that?"

"Help yourself."

Our conversation was a warm blanket. He peppered me with questions about Ryan and laughed at the story of her losing two teeth in the planetarium. I got caught up on all the news about his family in Australia. His dad was getting on well, adjusting after losing his wife of fifty years. His youngest sister was having a new baby soon. He missed them all, but was glad to be back in the States. "Over here an Aussie accent is a novelty," he said with a laugh. "There, I'm just another big-footed oaf from Sydney."

He munched the Danish, crumbs landing on his beard, then dug into the chocolate croissant. He ate like a giant child, licking his fingers and wearing sugary pleasure on his face. Thoughts of Jake pierced the warmth of the moment. "How's he doing?" I asked.

Burt stopped eating, wiped his face with a napkin, and turned toward me, but cast his eyes downward. "He misses you. And Ryan."

My heart grew leaden. "Can I ask you something?" His open face invited my question. "Why didn't you tell me about Jake's history when we were in Japan?"

"I've asked myself that so many times. At first, I thought it wouldn't last, so why spill the beans? Then, I could see that he was different around you. It was his chance at happiness. How could I spoil it? When it looked serious, I thought I should warn you. But I just couldn't do what Aaron Bloom had always done." I waited while he coaxed the words from their hiding place. "I might have prevented so much pain if I'd told the truth."

"I'm afraid about leaving him," I confessed. "Afraid of what might happen."

"No," he said, waving his hands to stop my words. "Don't begin with the *what ifs*. *What if* is a dangerous, roundabout road to absolutely nowhere. I've gone round and round it myself. I think I've stayed right at Jake's side for all these years because I was afraid. As if somehow, if I was just a good enough friend to him, I could save him from himself." Burt pulled a handkerchief from his pocket and blew his nose with a honk that instantly reminded me of my dad.

"Train's in," I said. We smiled at each other.

"I realize now that Jake will do what Jake will do. All of

that control I thought I had was just an illusion after all. If love alone could protect him, I gave him enough. You gave him enough. Ryan gave him enough. It's not in our control, Kate. You just have to do what you know in your heart is right. You've got Ryan to think about."

"None of it seems fair somehow."

"Nothing fair about it, Love."

We sat together in silence for a while, occasionally sipping our coffee. I coaxed Burt to tell me about his paintings. He asked about my family and my work, and about Ryan's progress in therapy. "I don't know if I've ever thanked you well enough for all you've done," I said. "It's meant a lot to know someone truly understands. And Ryan, well, she adores you. You've done so much for her." I suddenly ran out of words and tears pooled in my eyes. "Will you look at me," I croaked. "I'm a mess."

"You're lovely," he whispered.

My heart began to pound and my mouth went dry. A rush of sensations passed over me like an electric current, leaving me feeling both weak and exhilarated at the same time. Under the image of this comical giant was a man I'd come to admire. A sweet, kind, generous, smart, talented man. Though I'd never thought of it, I'd always seen Burt as some kind of extension of Jake. *His* friend. *His* supporter. *His* manager. Out from under Jake's shadow, I could see the gentle glow of Burt's own light.

With a movement so swift that neither of us had time to think, I was no longer on the opposite end of the couch. I tucked myself into the gentle nest of Burt's strong arms. I felt delicate and small, cradled by him. For one split second, I let myself read the confusion on his face, but I ignored it and brought my lips to his. At first, it was only me doing the kissing, a monologue of sorts. Burt sat statue-like, neither responding nor pushing me away. But then his lips softened. He began to return each kiss with one of his own design— tentatively at first, and then the monologue transformed into a conversation, a tender exchange of affection discovered in that instant. His beard was softer than I'd imagined, and I could feel the thrum of his heart beating against my own. The taste of sugar on his lips made me want to laugh, but the strength of his arms around me made me feel that it would be all right to cry, too. He could hold me. All of me.

We pulled back from each other at the same time and looked into each other's eyes as though we needed to see— really see—one another.

"Kate, I—"

I stopped his words with another kiss. It did not seem the time for words.

In Burt's arms I felt a new and unfamiliar kind of passion. I was completely present, wholly myself and conscious of every touch. I felt every hesitation about what we were doing, but also felt free—with each kiss, with every embrace—to choose each next movement.

Trust. It dawned on me. That's what this new feeling was. Burt would never transform into something I couldn't recognize. I trusted him without a single molecule of fear. I *knew* him, what he was made of, what he was capable of, without the threat of some unknown force lurking beneath the surface.

I knew, even as Burt and I kissed, that I loved Jake. I loved him in that moment, and knew that I would always love him. Burt loved him, too. But the trust I felt with Burt was an element I knew I had never felt with Jake and never could.

I pulled myself away from him and began to untie the sash of my robe. Almost instantly, both of his hands were over mine. "Kate," he sighed. His head hung and his shoulders slumped. "I'd feel as if I was taking advantage. It's hard

319

enough to look at this kisser in the shaving mirror every day. I just couldn't face myself if I—"

It was a dousing of ice water, but my face and ears were instantly hot. Soon all of our fluid motion was transformed to awkward shuffling while I pulled my body from his and tugged the lapels of my robe more tightly closed. "I'm sorry. You must think I'm—"

"No, no," he said. "I think you're wonderful." He lifted his head and kissed me sweetly. "I want to, believe me. Every part of me wants to."

"I'm so sorry," I said. I buried my face in my hands, wishing they could swallow me completely.

In a smooth, gentle motion, Burt pulled me back close to him and rested his forehead against mine. His low voice became a whisper veiled in kind affection. "In all the years I've known Jake, for all of his talent, his family name, his genius, his charm, his good looks, I've been jealous of him for only one thing." He then brought his lips tenderly to mine. His kiss was full of melancholy and longing. I didn't know whether to cry or scream in frustration. Burt took both of my hands into his. "Even though every cell of me wants to go ahead with what we've started here, it just doesn't feel like the right time. I couldn't face Jake again if... and he's a friend in trouble. I just can't add more trouble to it."

As we sat together, a calm washed over me. Relief? Comfort? I didn't know what to call the feeling, but I knew that Burt was right. Betraying Jake was simply not something he was capable of. "Ironic, huh?" I said. "Your devotion and loyalty are what I love most about you. It's not really working on my behalf today, though."

Burt squared his shoulders. "I've been reckless when it comes to women. I've been called a rat bastard more than once, I'm afraid." His face wore a shy smirk. For years I'd heard about this woman or that in Burt's life, but no one serious. "I don't want to be reckless with you. The kitty's got too many chips in it."

"You're right. I know. I guess I wanted to be reckless, just for a moment. It's not like me. I'm so embarrassed."

"Darling, Kate, no, no, no," he said, bringing my head to his shoulder.

I rested my head on his shoulder as his fingers stroked my hair. I hadn't thought of being with anyone but Jake in so long. Numbness was the predominant feeling I'd had for months. These new feelings, full of both pleasure and pain, let me know I was still alive. "Promise me something, will you?" I said.

"I'd promise you anything."

A panicky desperation came over me. "No matter what happens, please don't stop being my friend. That would just kill me right now."

Burt cocked his head to the side and his bushy eyebrows came together. "That'll be the easiest promise I've ever kept." He leaned toward me and kissed me on the corner of my mouth.

I had no idea what might be possible between Burt and me, if anything at all, but he would not be my white knight. I'd have to serve that function for myself. Perhaps Burt and I were just two people in mourning, seeking comfort from someone else who had suffered the same loss. Or perhaps it was something more.

I watched Burt as he stood and gathered his jacket from the back of a chair, admiring the gentle power of his body. "What time do Ryan and Mary K get back?"

"Not for another couple of hours."

"I'd think it's best if I hurry along then. I'll see you there at the gate, but I don't want you to think I'm one of those blokes that—I've never been in this position before."

"I know. Believe me, I get how strange this is for you. For me, too. I understand," I said, not quite sure I really did.

He leaned over and kissed me sweetly. "My sweet, beautiful friend." Then he walked toward the door. When the door closed behind him, I knew I had discovered a brand new kind of loneliness.

* * *

From every window in the 5th Avenue penthouse I could look over all of Central Park. Clad in autumn finery, the treetops were explosions of crimson, saffron, and sunflower. When they returned to our suite, Mary K and Ryan were full of stories.

"And then Mary K bought me the best bagel ever, Mommy." Ryan was nearly spilling over with excitement. "And then we saw these people doing this beautiful dance in the street with ribbons that swirled all around them. Then we saw a man going number one on a bridge and another man that wasn't wearing any pants."

Mary K pulled a stick of gum from her backpack. "What can I say? I showed the kid all of the highlights. You're certainly looking new and improved."

"So you're willing to be seen with me now?"

"You'll do, Murphy."

While Mary K showered, Ryan came to the window of the suite where I stood looking out over the jewel-toned trees. "Where is Daddy's show?"

"Right there," I said, pointing to the spot where I knew the Conservatory Garden to be. "We can walk there from here."

"Is Daddy there already?"

"I don't know, honey. But you know that he has to concentrate right before his pieces are shown."

Mary K entered the room. Wearing her blue jeans and Mets

T-shirt, she seemed as incongruous to the palatial surroundings as I felt. Though clad in her usual attire, there was something new about her. She still wore the bygone summer in the sunny spray of freckles on her face and the sun-bleached shimmer in her hair. But there was something else.

"You guys ready?" she asked.

I scanned her, puzzling.

"Take a picture, Murphy. It lasts longer." Mary K clicked her tongue and shot a finger pistol at Ryan.

"Yeah," Ryan giggled. "Take a picture, Mommy."

Then it hit me. "You haven't smoked a single cigarette since we picked you up yesterday morning."

"Nope," Mary K said, her eyebrows rising nearly to her hairline. "Not for a month. And I owe it all to the munchkin."

The irony of the nickname was apparent as Mary K stood beside Ryan. Though Ryan was just six, the difference in their height was mere inches. Mary K lifted the sleeve of her T-shirt to reveal a shiny square of adhesive bandage. "I owe most of it to Ryan, and a little to the nicotine patch."

Ryan's lips spread into a grin, revealing a smile that was more holes than teeth.

"Did you know, Dr. Murphy," Mary K explained with a playful singsong in her voice, "that smoking increases risk of lung cancer and stroke?"

"Why yes, Dr. Kowalski, I did know that."

"Yes, but did you also know that for diabetics, cigarette smoking causes problems in the circulatory system that can increase the likelihood of infections in the extremities?"

"*Ex-trem-it-ies,*" Ryan explained with a nod. "That's hands and feet and fingers and toes. I told Mary K what I read in my health book about smoking. Now that she has Welby, she needs to stay healthy to take care of him and take him on walks. Plus, because we love her and want her to be alive for a really long time and to keep her one good foot. Right, Mommy?"

"It's debatable which is my good foot, Squirt. The good Dr. Littleton made me a pretty good one, and I don't even have to clip the toenails." It was the first time in a while I'd heard Mary K mention Andra.

Ryan laughed and the two exchanged playful punches.

Andra Littleton had created a series of new and improving prototypes of foot and ankle prosthetics over the years, with Mary K as her alpha tester. With interchangeable feet for different uses—walking, running, swimming, skiing, and even an arched foot that would have fit into a high heel, if Mary K had ever been so inclined—the prosthesis, with its hydromechanics and computerized responses, had become the subject of medical journals and had won Andra research grants for further development. More importantly, it had restored Mary K to the athlete she had once been.

"And hey, check it out." Mary K lifted her T-shirt, revealing a swath of skin above her waistband. "I'm the bionic woman, huh?"

"Look, Mommy," Ryan said. "Mary K's turning into a robot."

A thin tube emerged from a small plastic port, and Mary K wore a miniature insulin pump in her front pocket.

"Robot, funny," she said, ruffling Ryan's hair and lowering her shirt. "The pump reads when sugar gets low and automatically injects me with the right dose." Mary K looked up at me. "Keeps my levels steady. Seemed kind of stupid to be doing all of this and then smoking on top of it. I guess I decided to stop being a pain-in-the-ass patient."

"No more syringes?" Ryan asked.

My heart pounded, remembering the day months ago that she had found Jake's *shotters*. It seemed that years had passed since then.

"Nope, no more syringes," Mary K said.

Ryan grinned. "That's so cool."

"Enough mush. Let's hit it," Mary K barked. "Burt called while you were in the shower. Says we're to be the first ones let in at the exhibit and there are already a thousand people in line. We do *not* want New York pissed off at us."

His name had a new sound to it, and I felt myself flush at hearing it. I turned away from my friend for fear my color might tell her more than I wanted to reveal. Ryan scrambled to the door with Mary K right behind her. Unexpectedly, my legs had turned to stone. Was it stage fright, given that so much of what I was about to do was performance? I was Jake's wife in name only. How could I pretend that I had not spent weeks planning to end the life of the very artist everyone had come to admire? And to top it all, I'd just spent the morning kissing my husband's best friend in my father-in-law's penthouse suite. The buoyancy of the pleasure of his kisses now felt weighted by the reality that lay outside the room. I wondered if the balloon was sinking for Burt.

"I get to push the buttons!" Ryan shouted from the hall.

Without realizing that she'd moved toward me, I felt the warm touch of Mary K's hand on mine. "It's okay, Murphy. We can do this." We walked toward the door together.

On the way to the ornate lobby in the glass elevator, Mary K sucked in her breath and exhaled with a whistle. "I've been looking at Aaron Bloom's architectural hard-ons in this city since I was a kid. But I never thought I'd be riding the elevator in one of 'em."

"What's a hard-on?" Ryan asked.

I crossed my arms and looked at Mary K. "Thanks a lot."

Full Bloom

Acres of silk partitions fluttered near Central Park's Conservatory Garden. In hues of green, blue, and autumn gold, the billowing curtain blended near-invisibly into its surroundings. A simple copper sign read: WOUNDED MOTHER. Neither Jake nor his name were anywhere in sight. The area was crowded with people. Overhead, kites floated and the air was filled with the bitter fragrance of autumn mums.

Mary K's scanned the crowd "You'd think this was a fucking Springsteen concert."

Fresh-faced docents guided us toward the narrow opening of the silken path. Burt stood sentry. His face was pinched with worry I'd not seen there earlier. He gave me a smile, then focused on Ryan, who ran to him with her arms wide open. She all but disappeared into the mass of him. "How's my favorite little ankle biter, ay?"

"Uncle Burt, there must be a million people here," Ryan exclaimed.

He set Ryan gently down on the ground. I put my arms around him, trying to imitate how I might normally greet him. He returned with an equally studied hug.

"Mary K," he said, his voice full of warmth, extending his hand to meet hers.

"So, what can we expect?" Mary K asked.

Burt lifted his bulky shoulders to his ears. "Not a clue. No one besides Jake has stepped a hoof in there for over three weeks. It's taken round-the-clock guards, all courtesy of Bloom Industries, to keep people at bay. His new exhibit manager, Jeremy Lyon, has taken care of most of the details. I've been out of the loop. Haven't even photographed it."

Ryan began to jump. "So we'll be the *very* first ones to see?"

"Right-O," he said.

Mary K's eyes began to reflect the trepidation I felt.

"Is he here?" I asked.

"Not hide nor hair."

I leveled my voice, not wanting to alarm Ryan, though Jake's absence was setting off alarm bells in my brain. "Any clue where he is?"

Before Burt could answer, a pale, studious-looking man stepped up beside him. They exchanged handshakes. "This unassuming genius here is Jeremy, Jake's new right-hand man. Jeremy, meet Katie and Ryan Bloom and their dear friend, Mary K."

Jeremy delivered a warm but weak handshake and pushed oversized glasses up his nose. He looked like he could use some sleep. "So nice to meet you, Mrs. Bloom," he said, his eyes darting through the crowd, presumably looking for Jake.

I suddenly felt about ninety years old. "Please. Call me Kate," I said. "I hear you're doing a marvelous job."

"I try. But I must say, I've never worked with anyone like your husband. It's quite an honor. And, well... an experience." At the sound of the word *husband* my eyes met Burt's. Was the twitch at the corner of his mouth a wince of regret?

Conversation with the very fretful Jeremy gleaned that

he had also not seen Jake all day, nor had he seen what was inside the silk curtain. Those alarm bells in my head were ringing louder.

"Not to worry," Burt said. "Jake's one of those blokes that works himself silly and then goes off like an old bear and hibernates. You'll learn that soon enough, Jeremy. The exhibit is already over for him once he's got it done. Doesn't care much about the hoopla."

Mary K took Ryan's hand. "Ready?"

Burt placed his hand on the small of my back and its warmth radiated through me. Was that a gesture he'd done before? "I think I'll stay out here and help Jeremy with details. I'll see you all later," he said.

My stomach roiled, but I remembered Jake's past installations. Jake's art had always been a thing of wonder—beauty he was able to find everywhere. The sweetness of his soul always emerged in his art.

I parted the curtain. Once inside, the silken pathway served to guide us. Despite the thousands who waited to enter, it seemed no one existed but the three of us.

We meandered separately, at first finding nothing out of the ordinary.

Ryan made the first discovery. On the ground along the path's edge lay a female form about four feet long. The grass had been clipped short, revealing the gentle topographical curve of hip and shoulder in the earth. "Look, Mommy," Ryan squealed. She ran ahead pointing out one and then another human shape along the path—some male, some female, some childlike in shape. At first they were mere suggestions, but they became larger and more detailed as we proceeded. It was as if some distant call had pulled sleeping spirits—both magical and eerie—from the earth, and we were witness to their emergence.

Then I spotted something new: a crevice, just millimeters wide, two feet long, in the ground. It was lined in crimson. Unmarked, this crack in the earth would go unnoticed. But draped with brilliant red, the gap took on the image of a wound, moist, ripe, and ready to bleed. The dewy flesh had been added, of course, though it was impossible to discern the ingredients. Perhaps it was a pulpy mash of the red mum petals and maple leaves. It emitted an earthy, decayed smell, at once plant and animal.

Steps ahead, at eye level, another scar appeared on the side of a boulder. It, too, glowed blood-red, moist, and raw. Each gash lured us to the next until more unmistakable human forms rose. Anatomical curves of hips, shoulders, breasts, and thighs gave the appearance of bodies in repose strewn about the lawn, emerging from the roots and trunks of trees and rising from stones. These human forms had not been created, but discovered and exposed. Gnarled tree roots became elbows and knees, stones became shoulders, soft mounds of earth formed hips, jaw lines, and cheekbones in profile.

Each body bore a shimmering crimson slash, a slice across the torso, throat, or limb. Whether supine, prostrate, or climbing the twisted trunks of trees, the bodies became larger in scale—their corresponding wounds more gruesome in proportion.

We reached a clearing so vast that the curtains that surrounded us seemed to disappear in the distance. My eyes were assaulted with the destruction of wounded bodies and tangled limbs. It was a battlefield of bodies ravaged and torn by some force of otherworldly violence.

The fiery heads of mums and falling maple leaves conspired with Jake's work to complete the composition. Under the beauty, behind the glory, alongside the delight of blossoms, everywhere Jake had found the flaws—the cracks—the

carnage—that lay just beneath everyone's everyday awareness. He'd marked them so that everyone else could see what
he knew existed all along.

The scene of slaughter overwhelmed me. How could he
move leaves, mash flower petals, and crush patterns in the
soil and grass to create such a scene? The paralysis I'd felt in
the penthouse had been my warning. This scene was the same
that had met me in the bathtub of our home—the same beautiful destruction.

Then I spotted it.

Because of the sheer scale, I didn't at first recognize what
I saw. In the center of the clearing, tucked among the soft
swells of lawn, with a torso a dozen feet long, lay the body
of a woman. From the line of her chin to the curve of her
thigh, she'd been revealed. Her breasts were inviting mounds
of earth. Her hips a gentle swell. Her shoulder the exposed,
gnarled root of a tree. The lines of her tortured body pulled my
eye to her core, where her abdomen lay splayed and glistening red, her womb raw and torn. Her chin in profile screamed
her anguish, her mouth agape. The redness of her exposed
womb seemed to throb. She seemed not only to bleed from
her wound, but from her soul.

My vision blurred with my tears. I was unaware of Mary
K's presence next to me until she spoke. "Fuck me sideways,"
she whispered. "I've seen autopsies less wrecked than this."

Ryan's scream felt like a slice into my own skin.

The sound of my daughter pulled me from my stupor and
I ran toward her where she sat covering her face. Expecting
Jake's whimsy and finding this carnage was more than she—
and I—could bear. She hid her eyes in her hands and I rocked
her, unable to take my eyes from all that surrounded me.

"She's sleeping," Mary K said as she sat beside me in front of the fireplace in our suite. Only Mary K had been able to calm her, and only many hours after we'd returned to our suite. Burt and I sat on the couch. "I exercised medical privilege and gave her a dose of Benadryl. That'll help her sleep through the night," Mary K sighed as she fell into a chair by the fireplace.

"Poor angel," Burt whispered, shaking his head. "My God, Kate, if I'd known. I'd never have—"

Ryan's screams had instantly summoned Burt into the exhibit. He'd snatched Ryan into his arms.

"Shut it down," I said to Burt as we fled. "He can't be exposed like this." Jake's art had always revealed his inner beauty. This exposed the depth of his disturbance.

"I don't even know if I have the authority. We don't own this. It's the property of the museum."

"Just look at her," I said nodding toward the bundle in Burt's arms.

The curator would not close the show, but Burt convinced him to post signs that warned of the graphic nature of the exhibit and that it might not be what families expected for their kids to see.

Police managed the crowd. Press swarmed, barking questions at us as we made our escape. Burt charged through the crowd carrying Ryan. Mary K and I followed in the wake he created. His presence and the fury on his face repelled attacks. In mere moments we were through the crowd and in the sequestered safety of our suite.

With Ryan asleep we could finally speak with candor.

"I should have prevented this," Burt said.

"If anyone should have known, it was me," I said.

The door of the secrets I'd held about Jake had been blown off its hinges. In the hours that followed, Burt and I revealed all of the small details I'd held back from Mary K about Jake's decline over the past two years.

"Jeez, Murphy. Why didn't you say something to me?"

"I just kept thinking that it would pass. That he would get better if we just found the right medication. That I was smart enough to figure it out. I guess I felt ashamed, too. What must you all think of me, with my life so out of control?"

"It's fucked up logic, but I get it. Not so great at asking for help myself. But, Jesus Christ on a raft." She looked at her watch. "I know you said to go ahead to my folks' place tonight, but I should stay. It's no big deal."

"Your family invited you. It's been so long since they welcomed you home. Go. I can't bear the thought of causing you to miss an opportunity to reunite with your family."

"I'm staying right here on this sofa," Burt offered.

"I'd rather be alone." I squeezed Burt's ropy forearm. "Can you try to find Jake? See if he's okay? That'll make me feel better."

"Anything," he said.

"You're sure?" Mary K asked. "I should get back about midnight."

"I'm sure." I refilled my glass from the scotch bottle on the coffee table. "I'd like to go home tomorrow, though. Ryan should be home."

"No problem." Mary K stood but seemed reluctant to move toward the door. "If you need me, you know. You've got my cell number."

"And I'm here in two shakes. Just give a jingle," Burt said, giving my forehead a kiss.

They both moved toward the door. With a sudden burst Mary K leaned down and embraced me. With her cheek against mine, she whispered in my ear, "I love you, Kate."

I could not remember Mary K ever uttering my first name,

and the tenderness of it stunned me. Just as suddenly as she had embraced me, she disappeared out the door.

Though I knew she couldn't hear me, I whispered my response: "I love you more, Mary Louise."

✷ ✷ ✷

With a bang and a burst of light I was jerked from sleep. I shielded my eyes from the glare and read the bedside clock. Twelve-thirty.

"Murphy, wake up. Where's Ryan?" Mary K shouted. She's not in her bed."

"The bathroom—"

"I looked. She's not here."

My heart ricocheted against my ribs.

Mary K dialed the front desk. "Yes, this is the penthouse. Have you seen Ryan Bloom tonight? She's almost seven years old, but tall for her age. Pale skin. Dark, curly hair." I searched her face for clues to the answer from the other end of the phone.

"How long ago?"

Another pause. I could hear my own blood surging through my eardrums. Bile rose in my throat. I prayed to no one in particular. *Please, please, please.*

"Thanks," Mary K said, hanging up the phone.

I searched for my shoes. "Where is she?"

"They saw her leave around eleven. With Jake."

For a millisecond her words disintegrated first into syllables, then into a jumble of unintelligible sounds. "Ryan would never leave without telling me. How did Jake get in here?" I jammed my feet into sneakers.

"We're in the fucking *BLOOM* Tower, Murphy," Mary K spat. "I think they'd let Jake Bloom into the penthouse where his wife and child are staying, don't you?"

The next seconds were a blur. Mary K called Burt, and then the police, who told her they could do nothing if the child was with her father. "Motherfuckers!" she shouted as she slammed down the phone.

I grabbed Ryan's jacket from a nearby chair. I held it to my lips, taking in the fragrance of baby shampoo. I allowed myself only the hastiest glance around the room—a few heartbeats to gather my thoughts. Her suitcase rested on the floor, garments strewn as she'd left them. Sketches of princesses and white horses lay on the writing desk, pencils and markers scattered on top. The rumpled sheets and pillow bore the impression of her but they were cool to my touch. The only thing missing, besides Ryan herself, was her love-worn stuffed lamb.

"Come on," Mary K called from the entrance. "Let's go! We've got to see what they know downstairs." Her jaw was set and her eyes squinted into a warrior's expression.

Fending off the greetings from doormen and desk staff, Mary K and I sped through the lobby. I'd fallen asleep in my clothes, or I'd have fled in my pajamas. The concierge tipped his head as we approached. "A night outing, Mrs. Bloom? Can I get you a car?"

Mary K spoke up when words failed me. "No. Thank you. We're meeting Mr. Bloom." Her eyes dipped to take in the gold nametag on the lapel of young man's navy blazer. "Byron, did you happen to notice if they took a cab or remained on foot?"

Oh God. My brain was too addled to come up with such a cogent question. Give me a patient in cardiac arrest, an emergency C-section, or a compound fracture, and I'd know how to respond. But with Ryan in the balance, hysteria nearly erupted in me.

The eyes of the concierge darted between us. "It seems that Mr. Bloom and Ryan were going for a walk as well."

I wanted to pound him with questions. *Was she okay? Did she seem scared? Was she crying? Did Jake seem crazed, high—dangerous?* Instead, I wrangled my voice from the dusty column of my throat. "Did you notice which way they were going?"

"A little nighttime scavenger hunt," Mary K said, turning her full attention to the doorman. "Help us get a jump, will you? And might we borrow a flashlight?"

Nothing in the young man's face said he was buying the ruse. "I believe they crossed the street and proceeded toward the park," he said, pulling a flashlight from his drawer and handing it to Mary K. "It's a beautiful night. Lots of moonlight. Mr. Bloom was carrying your daughter since she was sleepy and had forgotten her shoes."

Shoes! Oh God, Ryan has no shoes. I thought of her pink feet stepping on sharp rocks. I silently wished for such small injuries.

I stilled myself and drew my first full breath. A single thought floated through the haze of my confusion. "I know where to find them," I said, with a calm that surprised me.

As soon as we were out of the sight of the concerned concierge, we bolted toward the "Wounded Mother" exhibit. Breathless, head throbbing, I ran beside Mary K. Our path was awash in blue light, the glowing moon above us our beacon. Seconds seemed like days as images of my daughter broken or bleeding played as a movie in my mind. I huffed as my feet pounded the ground. *Please, please, please.*

When we arrived at the edge of the clearing, the silky labyrinth in the distance, its curtained border glowed with bright light emanating from deep within. We stopped, resting our hands on our knees and panting. After a few restoring breaths, we resumed our run toward the eerie glow.

At the entrance stood two night guards wearing Bloom

Industries badges. Only then did I notice that guards patrolled the entire perimeter. A barrel-chested guard placed his body between us and the entry. "I'm sorry. Exhibit's closed."

I held my side. "I'm Katherine Murphy," I panted. "Uh— Katherine Murphy *Bloom*. The wife of the artist. Is my husband in there with our daughter?"

My heart slid down into my belly while I waited for a reply. The security guard stepped up and held his hands wide, blocking our path. "Mr. Bloom insisted on privacy. He's making modifications to the exhibit."

Modifications. I thought I'd scream.

"Look," Mary K barked. "Has he got a kid with him in there?" When he said nothing, she said, "I take that as a yes."

Another, more portly, guard approached and began to confer with the first. Each second's tick was an explosion of panic. "I'm going in!" I said, pushing my way past the guard's outstretched arm. Mary K followed, and the guard grabbed her sleeve.

"Don't touch me, asshole," she said as she stepped beyond the width of the guard's arms.

"My daughter's in there!" I screamed. "She's been missing for hours. We're going in to see if she's all right."

"Have you got any ID?" the second guard asked.

"Fuck this," Mary K said, grabbing my hand. "New York's real cops will not be happy when they find out that a couple of rent-a-cops prevented a mother from protecting her kid. Move aside."

We ran, leaving the two guards with their heads together. They mumbled amongst themselves and let us flee without chase. The beam of Mary K's flashlight searched our course. The moon's light illuminated the wounds that seemed even more grotesque in the shadows of night. My own voice pierced the darkness. "Ryan? RYAN?"

Mary K's voice echoed mine.

As we made our way through the silk-banked hallway, the light we'd seen from the distance grew brighter. We wound through the maze.

Mary K stopped. She held her fingers to her lips. "Shh."

From over the crest of a small hill came a soft and repetitious sound. *Tch-shoosh. Tch-shoosh. Tch-shoosh.* Mary K and I whispered and mimed our unified plan. I would step toward Jake alone to try to reason with him while Mary K would survey the scene and try to find Ryan. We slowed our pace, stepping lightly to avoid alerting Jake to our presence.

Mary K signaled to me from the perimeter of the huge meadow. She held her palm to her chest, a gesture that I knew meant she would stop at nothing to get to Ryan.

Jake stood at the center of the clearing, illuminated by searing white light from four floodlights. Shirtless and thrusting a slim spade into the ground, his shovel pierced the belly of the woman in repose, widening her wound with each thrust. He tossed soil into a wheelbarrow at her side, not a crumb of it mussing the pristine area that surrounded the incision he was making. Next to him, on a tarp on the ground, lay an enormous mound of moist, red pulp that resembled entrails and flesh. *No.* I would not let my imagination run wild. I had to stay calm. The only odors I could detect as I neared were those of newly turned earth and Jake's perspiration, not the familiar tang of human blood.

I inched toward him, searching the lit area for Ryan. Glancing to my right, I saw Mary K, barely visible in the shadows.

The muscles of Jake's sinewy body flexed with his efforts. The lattice of scars on his torso glowed red and angry in the cruel light. Beads of sweat flew from his hair like discarded diamonds in the cruel, white light. *Tch-shoosh. Tch-shoosh.*

My skin tingled with fear. Still clutching Ryan's jacket, I stepped close enough that I could reach out and touch Jake's elbow. "Jake," I whispered. He continued his digging. A little louder, "Jake."

He froze.

"Jake, what are you doing?" I asked, forcing into soothing tones. I wanted to grab him, to scream, *Where's my baby?* Instead I stepped slowly, no sudden moves.

His head swayed back and forth. He gripped and released the handle of the shovel.

"Where's Ryan? It's cold out. She forgot her coat." The heat from the floodlights penetrated my scalp.

"She's pure," he groaned. "She can heal all the wounds."

Acid rose to the back of my throat. "Where's Ryan, Jake? Did you hurt her?"

He looked up at me for the first time, his irises fire-flecked with yellow-gold and icy green. "She's perfect. Flawless. That's why she can heal the wounds. Don't you see it, Kat? It's a cancer, all around us. Beauty is a distraction from all of the pain. It's everywhere. Everything is diseased. I've tried and tried to heal it. I've looked for beauty, but now it's taken over. It's everywhere now. See?"

I had to keep him talking, keep his focus on me so that Mary K could find Ryan. With a jerk, Jake flung the shovel to the ground. "I'm so black inside."

"That blackness is not you. That's your illness. Where's Ryan? We don't want her to be up too late. You know how crabby she gets when she doesn't sleep." My words sounded absurd, but I had to keep talking or I'd explode into fragments.

Jake gestured down toward his feet. "She has to stay here. She has to go *here*, to heal this place." I was close enough to look directly into the gash in the earth and see its hideous shape. Nestled in the belly of the woman, Jake had carved a hole—an unmistakable, life-sized, Ryan-shaped hole, her silhouette curled into the fetal position—an empty womb. Down to the profile of her upturned nose, the cavity's likeness to my daughter was eerie. Perverse in its detail, the possible purpose of Jake's sculpture sent a ripple down my spine.

Almost apelike, Jake lunged to the pulpy heap and sank his hands into the moist mass—its acrid odor finding its way to me. He leaned down and began to line the Ryan-shaped gap with the glistening ooze.

"You see. She will heal all of the ugliness that's everywhere. She doesn't have my blackness. She's been spared." Jake looked up at me like a child pleased with his creation, awaiting my approval.

Vomit threatened to rise in me. My heart pounded a new rhythm of panic as I scanned the clearing. What if we were too late? What if this grotesque gash was a grave for my already dead child? My ragged breaths became panting. From the inky distance came the sound of footfalls against the moist ground. More than one set of feet—Ryan's?—no, too heavy for Ryan's.

"Let's take Ryan for a hot fudge sundae. She'd like that." I was saying anything, trying to sound normal. Trying to reach the gentle daddy within the madman before me.

Jake's head fell forward and he slipped down to his knees. He held his moist, red dripping hands in front of his face. "What have I done, Kat? What have I done?"

His plaints amplified my terror. In a sudden flurry, a dozen guards exploded from the edge of the darkness and surrounded Jake and me, guns drawn and aimed directly at Jake's head. "Don't move!" one shouted. Jake showed no startle response, he just knelt there, examining his hands.

"Jacob." A rich, baritone voice floated from beyond the ring of light that surrounded us. When he stepped into the brightness, I recognized the distinguished form of Aaron Bloom as I'd seen it in newspaper photographs. Even with his slicked-back hair and precisely groomed goatee, I could see Jake's features on the older man's face. "Jacob, I've brought some people to help you," he said in a voice both calm and commanding.

I looked into the eyes of the man who Jake had so reviled. In his features, so like Jake's, I hoped to find compassion, kindness, love—all the emotions of which Jake always claimed his father was devoid. Instead I saw only steely determination and utter control.

Jake looked up at the pistols aimed at him. He held his arms out wide, closed his eyes, and leaned his head back. "Please," he whispered. "Tell them to end this for me, Father. Tell them to free me from this horror. It's my only way out. Make them shoot me. Please, please. For God's sake."

I was molten in the presence of Jake's pleas; as though if I let myself, I would become nothing more than a warm puddle on the ground. I thought of the narcotics I had stored in a safe-deposit box—enough to end his agony. I looked up at Aaron Bloom. My voice was small and trembling. "Ryan. We have to find Ryan?"

Aaron Bloom stepped close to Jake and rested one hand on his son's shoulder. With the slightest motion of his other hand, he directed the guards to remain where they stood. "Come now, Jacob. Tell us where the child is."

Jake looked up into his father's face, then back down at his hands. "Ryan. Oh, God. What have I done?"

I thought my heart would seize. My vision blurred at the edges, leaving only Jake and his father's forms clearly in focus.

Piercing the darkness from beyond my view, Mary K's voice rang loud and clear. "I've got her! I've got her!"

With the slightest jut of his jaw, Aaron Bloom directed his

guards to grab Jake. Blinded by the floodlights but flung by another force, I sprinted toward Mary K's voice. "Over here! I've got her!" Then I saw the beam of Mary K's flashlight. My feet were thunder, pounding the ground until I reached them. Mary K gently transferred Ryan into my arms. All I could feel was the warmth of Ryan's body next to mine and her steady pulse against my lips. I wanted to fall to my knees and weep, but knew that my daughter needed me to stand, strong enough to hold us both.

Mary K whispered as she wiped her eyes with the back of her hand, "She's all right, Murphy. Smart girl. Slipped away and hid when things got scary."

I looked over Ryan's shoulder at Aaron Bloom towering over Jake's crumpled form. In his face, in his stiff-shouldered posture, I could see the older man's revulsion for his son. As impassively as if he were directing them to sweep unwanted crumbs from a linen tablecloth, he directed his squadron to manage Jake. The security officers encircled Jake, guns still poised.

For a flicker of a second, the mythical mogul turned and his gaze caught mine. At first it was a cold stare—the look of a general overlooking his battlefield. This was the man who had warned me, tried to bribe me away from his son. Aaron Bloom, the great strategist, had achieved his success because of his ability to see many moves ahead of his competitors. So, too, he had seen this inevitability when I was too blinded by love to believe it.

He stepped toward us as the security guards carried Jake away. I tucked Ryan's head into my shoulder. She wilted, allowing me to cradle her, clutching her lamb to her face.

As he neared, Aaron Bloom extended a hand toward Ryan. All I saw was Jake's hand—the long, tapered fingers, gently curved—in his father's gesture. The creases at the edge of his eyes softened as soon as he made contact with Ryan and a small tremor, barely visible, appeared at the corners of his mouth.

He rested his hand on Ryan's heaving shoulder. Instantly, she was calmed to stillness, and she looked up into her grandfather's face. As he touched her, he seemed to be trying, in this single contact, to absorb every moment of her life that he'd missed.

With Jake shouting nonsensically in the background, his father retracted his hand. He cleared his throat and his face returned to its former, stony expression. His voice was a piece of ramrod steel wrapped in billowy cotton. "We'll take Jacob to the Beaumont Spa in Vermont, if that's all right with you, Katherine."

"Jake needs more than a spa."

"Perhaps my euphemism isn't apt. Beaumont is a locked therapeutic facility. He's been there before. In his youth. It's restful, quiet, and completely discreet. Exceptionally qualified staff. I can assure you he'll receive the best possible care."

I nodded, unable to summon my voice.

"The bills will be managed, of course. I've arranged for helicopter transport from here so that the press can be avoided. I could arrange transport for you as well."

"No," I said. "I think we just need to get Ryan out of here."

"Then at least allow my security staff to escort you back to the hotel." As if calling for a sommelier to refill his champagne glass, he lifted his finger and three uniformed guards were at our sides. He reached into his hip pocket and retrieved a sleek platinum case. He withdrew a business card bearing only his name in embossed gold against glossy black and a telephone number, identical to the card I'd received and discarded nearly eight years before. "If you or the child needs anything, Katherine." He said, extending the card toward me. He reached out once more and rested his hand on Ryan's shoulder.

Though he had been right about Jake's condition from the start, I saw no sense of triumph on this man's face. He drew no joy from the spoils of battle.

I took one more look at the womanly mound of earth, my daughter's silhouette her empty womb. A picture of Ryan, pale and lifeless, appeared in my mind. Then, mercifully sparing me from the worst horror of my imagination, Ryan curled her body, tucking her head more deeply into my caress, reminding me that my living, breathing daughter was safe in my arms. I rested my chin on her head and looked back. Beefy guards flanked Jake as they walked to where I supposed the helicopter would land. He turned toward me, his eyes pleading.

Without turning for another look, I carried Ryan out of the clearing, back toward the maze, guided by the beam of Mary K's flashlight, her arm at my elbow steadying my steps. We exited, three guards at our sides, just as Burt arrived, his face an etching of every fear and pain I'd felt. He looked into the distance where Jake was being put into restraints, all the while ranting and screaming, "Help me! They're going to take me away! Help me! You can see it! You can see it too! I know you can!"

Burt looked down at me, his eyes pleading. Holding Ryan tightly in my arms, I rested my head against Burt's shoulder.

"Take us back, Burty," I whispered. "They're taking care of Jake. I have to take care of Ryan now."

Mary K wrapped her arm around my waist. Where I felt molten before, I could now feel that my flesh and bones were firm and intact. I was a pillar, standing by my own force. I had my daughter in my arms and my dear friends at my side. With this, I knew that I could make it.

I felt the *whump, whump, whump* of a helicopter approaching before I heard it. Leaves and flower petals churned around us, and the silk partition huffed and heaved. Only someone with Aaron Bloom's clout could arrange for a helicopter to land in Central Park in the middle of the night, and I was grateful he had.

Looking up, I spotted bold block letters, gold against the black of the approaching helicopter. BLOOM INDUSTRIES. I had a vague sense of Jake calling out to me, his voice being swallowed by the sound of the machine that would take him away.

I moved first one foot, and then the other, with Burt and Mary K in lockstep beside me. Jake's screams disappeared. As I walked, the only sensations I was aware of were Ryan's heart beating against my chest and the sounds of the footfalls of the loyal friends beside me.

Bless Me Father

After we returned to San Francisco, Ryan didn't speak. She didn't cry. Her muteness terrified me more than if she'd been screaming. I'd take her to Mary K's, and she'd mindlessly sit, petting Welby. At the pub, she mutely watched while Alice baked an endless array of her favorite treats while Rian held Sausage, the latest of my dad's fat cats, in her lap. She held my dad's hand while they walked around Stow Lake or the Arboretum and he chattered on about the flowers and plants along their path, mute beside him. Tully did magic tricks. Dr. Schwartz read poetry. All with Ryan as a mute observer.

I held her, rocked her, told her how much I loved her, and begged her to talk to me. But she looked out the window or stared at unturned pages of her favorite books. Each night I wrapped myself around her as we shared my childhood bed.

With Ryan sleeping upstairs, Mary K and I sat with my family at our familiar table and told them all that happened in New York.

I had only one secret remaining: the contents of the safe-deposit box and the pull I felt to help Jake. Yes, that's what I'd begun to call it, *helping Jake*. He'd begged his father to let the guards shoot him in Central Park. He'd gouged his wrists to end his life. How many times had Jake wanted his agony to end? How many times had someone intervened, prolonging his pain, keeping him from the serenity he craved?

But could I actually help him die? Would I? Jake's suffering haunted me. My private plan was an indescribable ache with no outward sign of injury, but it was hobbling me nonetheless.

"Poor baby," Alice said over and over as she listened to the story. It didn't even matter whether she was referring to Jake, Ryan, or me. We were all poor babies, I supposed.

* * *

Ryan and I crossed the Golden Gate Bridge three times a week to see Dr. Rachel Gross, a child psychologist who specialized in trauma. Her office was filled with art supplies and shelves of miniature figurines. Aaron Bloom offered to pay for the therapy, and because the house had not yet closed, I gulped the hot coals of my pride and accepted.

At first, Ryan went into the sessions alone while I leafed through copies of *Parenting Magazine* with its irrelevant articles about summer camps and how to get children to eat green vegetables. After the third session, Dr. Gross had Ryan sit in the waiting room while she talked to me inside.

Rachel Gross was a petite woman of about fifty with soulful brown eyes and a rich, soothing voice. Dressed simply in soft gray linen, she seemed intentionally nondescript. "Ryan would like you to join our sessions from now on," she said.

"She spoke to you?"

The therapist nodded. "Not with words. Just with the scenes she creates in the sand tray."

In tidy rows, on dozens of shelves, stood thousands of figurines—fairies, soldiers, characters of all kinds. Vehicles, trees, animals both domesticated and ferocious. Fences, buildings, stones, and shells. Mountains and tunnels. Houses, caves, and bridges. The elaborate menagerie stood at the ready.

"But she's not talking," I said. "Shouldn't we try to get her to talk about everything that's happened? I just have to know she's going to be all right."

The therapist's face exuded kindness and patience. "It's our job just to witness what Ryan has created in the sand tray," she explained. "Over time we'll begin to see transformation in the scenes. That's how the process becomes reparative."

"And you've begun to see transformation in Ryan's trays?"

Dr. Gross nodded. "The first two sessions, Ryan put her back to me and buried figures. Now she's allowing me to watch. That's progress. She wants to be witnessed."

When I heard Dr. Gross say that Ryan *buried* items in the sand, the image of the hole that Jake had created in her likeness rose to the forefront of my mind and sickened me. "Dr. Gross. I've researched manic-depressive disorder. There's a strong genetic component and—"

"You want reassurances. All that can be known from Ryan's behavior right now is that she is a child reacting to a trauma. We can help her through that. Let's take things one step at a time."

How many times had I given similar information to terrified parents? Only in this moment did I appreciate the inadequacy of such explanation.

Dr. Gross opened the door and invited Ryan back into the room and toward her completed sand tray. In the middle of the tray stood a collection of figures, all centered around a tall pewter wizard who held a scepter in one hand and a clear, crystal orb in the other. In front of the wizard was a hole, and in it a small, ceramic rabbit completely buried but for its nose and ears. Miniature stone walls had been placed around the wizard, and just outside the wall was a warrior woman on horseback bearing a bow and arrow.

Ryan looked up at me for the first time since we'd come back from New York. Silently, her eyes pleaded with me to examine what she'd created.

I kneeled so that the tray was at eye level. The rabbit was so small. The pewter wizard, who seemed benevolent and magical from the outside, appeared menacing from the perspective of the rabbit.

"I see, baby," I whispered. "I see."

$$* \quad * \quad *$$

I consulted with an attorney who gave me the news that I could do nothing to keep Jake hospitalized against his will once he was no longer an imminent risk. I could get a restraining order to keep him from Ryan, but whatever naivety I'd once been guilty of had died. No piece of paper would protect us. The attorney even warned that, after a period of stability, Jake could even be awarded visitation or partial custody by a sympathetic judge.

Medicine had failed Jake.

The law offered me nothing.

I submitted for a leave of absence from work. I had a more important job to do. While Ryan stayed with Dad and Alice, I went to UC for one morning to transfer my patients to able colleagues. I was unable to focus on the stack of medical charts on my desk. The words blurred together, the details leaving me as soon as I finished reading a sentence.

On my desk sat a framed photograph Burt had given me for my birthday the year Ryan was born. Jake and I lay in the grass, our limbs entwined, and between us—all baby fat and smiles—was Ryan, cozy in the nest our bodies made for her. I turned the photo over, unable to look at the perfect moment now gone forever.

I pulled my wallet from my bag. Tucked in the thin,

zippered section of the wallet was the business card I'd placed there. My fingers traced the gold-embossed letters. Quickly, before I lost my nerve, I dialed the number.

"Aaron Bloom," the voice answered after only two rings.

"Uh—" I'd expected a receptionist or a recording.

"Aaron Bloom here." The words were clipped and impatient.

"Mr. Bloom. This is Kate. Katherine Murphy."

A softer voice continued. "Katherine. How are you? How is the child?"

"She's still struggling. I think the psychologist is helping. I don't have long," I lied. "I need to ask you something." I licked my lips, trying to summon the courage for my question. "Why did you try to stop Jake from marrying me?"

I could hear the tight swallow from the other end of the line. "It wasn't you. I've always known that anyone he married would have to endure the effects of his... illness. If there were children, the suffering would be tenfold."

Silence hummed.

"Jacob's mother climbed to the edge of a thirtieth-floor balcony when he was two. She had my son in her arms. Were it not for a quick-witted nanny, you and I would not be having this conversation."

"Does Jake know?"

"Would it change anything?"

I closed my eyes. "No. I guess it wouldn't."

* * *

My consultation with the attorney and my phone call with Aaron Bloom blanched me with hopelessness. My path back toward Murphy's surprised me when I found myself in a back pew at St. Anne's Cathedral. I'd not been in the sanctuary since I'd left for college. With knees resting on the worn kneeling rail, I took in the flickering light of the candles and the aroma of Wood Oil Soap and incense. Footfalls of the faithful coming in and out for confession echoed against the stucco walls. I rested my forehead against the back of the wooden pew before me.

St. Anne's had been a spiritual refuge for my mother, but it had proved impotent to help her find relief in her earthly life. Still, it was in the tranquil courtyard of this church that she had chosen to spend her last living moments.

I wondered if I should I pray for guidance. Or if I should seek forgiveness for the murderous intentions that still haunted my dreams each night and bullied their way into my waking thoughts. Experts had offered me little help. Was God the expert of last resort?

I knelt until my feet grew numb. I looked down at the surgical greens I wore under my coat. How many times had they been cleansed of the blood of patients? Could I be so cleansed after I got blood on my own hands?

Seeing the light glowing above the confessional, I moved toward it, parted the heavy crimson curtain, and entered the chamber. The air was thick and still, tinged with the lingering, sweet aroma of a woman's cologne. Had her fragrance been applied to buy God's favor? What sin would be pardoned on account of Chanel No. 5?

The priest slid the miniature window open. I recognized his profile. Father Sean was no longer the jovial young priest playing basketball on the churchyard courts who I remembered from St. Anne's Elementary. He was somber in this formal role. He made the sign of the cross and kissed the rosary he held.

Father Sean sat silently, unmoving.

A whisper escaped my lips. "I've made so many mistakes."

In a soft voice, the priest replied, "Our Heavenly Father knows our hearts. He loves us without condition. Nothing we could do could alienate him from us or deny us of his forgiveness."

"I probably shouldn't be here. I don't even know if I believe in God, Father."

"But still, you're here. Some part of you must be seeking guidance? Forgiveness?"

Tears dripped from my face, joining the decades of repentant tears that must have fallen on that very spot. "I don't know what to do. I have allowed my love for a man to keep me from protecting my child. He's... mentally ill." The words were acid on my tongue. "He's dangerous. My love for him blinded me. I allowed him to do harm."

"You're not responsible for the actions of others, child. Is your daughter safe now?"

Had I mentioned that my child's gender? "I'm doing everything I can to take care of her now."

"Good. And what of your husband?"

"He's in agony. Tortured by his condition." I paused to search for the words. "He almost died once by his own hand, but I rescued him. An act I now regret. It's my fault that he's still dangerous to our child and that he continues to suffer. I don't really pray, Father, but I've *wished* a thousand times that he would die."

"Wishing is the doubter's name for prayer. God hears them both. Your prayer comes not from malice for your husband, but from a desire to end his pain and the danger he poses. It is also your own pain that you wish end." Silence buzzed in my ears.

A picture of Burt popped into my mind. "My husband and I have been apart for some time, Father. And I recently... well, I recently tried to... I didn't, but I almost—"

"You were unfaithful?"

That word, *unfaithful*, swirled around my mind like a

cyclone. "No, not technically. I would have been, but the other man stopped it."

"You know this man well?"

I nodded.

"Then perhaps you chose him because you knew he would have the strength to resist temptation."

"That's pretty generous, Father."

"God's love is generous, and more understanding than you might imagine, my child. You love your husband?"

I nodded.

"Loving him is an expression of the promise you made in your vows of marriage. Pray not for the death of your husband, but for clarity. Without God, we are left with only our intellect to determine our path. Intellect is a dull knife when cutting through the grisly matters of living this complicated life. God sees you. His guidance will come."

Father Sean moved his hand in the sign of the cross. "In the name of the Father, the Son, and the Holy Spirit. Go and sin no more. Bless you, child."

* * *

Ryan began to talk a little, and, as recommended by Dr. Gross, she returned to school. I returned to short days at the hospital and brought her to daily sessions with Dr. Gross.

Just as Dr. Gross had predicted, the scenes in the sand tray began to morph. Figurines once buried began to interact on the sand's surface. The tray began to blossom with plant life, and some of the more threatening figures began to be excluded. Soon Ryan abandoned the burial rituals in favor of domestic scenes with furniture and gardens. Still, the figure of the wizard lurked in the corner, though sometimes his back was turned.

One day during our fifth week in Dr. Gross's office, Ryan

stopped her play with the figurines. She looked up at me with a strength of presence that I had not seen in weeks.

"Mommy?"

The sound of her voice, calm and steady, startled me. "Wh-what, honey?"

"I want to go back to our house."

I looked up at Dr. Gross, whose only change of expression was her lifted eyebrows. Her kind eyes encouraged me.

"To Granddad's?"

"No, Mommy. To *our* house. I know Daddy can't live with us anymore because he's too sick. But I think we should go home for just a little while. You and me. In *our* house. To say good-bye to it."

I searched Dr. Gross's face for how I should respond, but just as she had with Ryan, she offered me no answers, letting me find my own. "You know we can only stay there for another week or so. Then the people that bought it will move in."

"Daddy won't be there, will he?" Fear edged her question.

"No. He won't be there anymore." I looked up at Rachel Gross, whose focus remained on Ryan.

"Then I want to go. Even if it's just for a little while."

"Okay, honey. We'll go home, then."

✳ ✳ ✳

Even in the brittle days of December the bougainvillea vines blossomed magenta against the creamy stucco of our Sea Cliff house. The exquisite house had become haunted for me, but for Ryan it meant familiarity. It meant Jake, and she needed to say good-bye.

After Ryan went to bed, each night for the next week, I wrapped glasses in tissue and sorted through books and the general flotsam of the years we'd been a family. I packed up all of Jake's clothing and the supplies from his studio, though I had no idea if he'd even care about any of it. Movers would arrive soon to cart things to a storage unit I'd rented for him. I had mailed him a key so that he could retrieve his belongings whenever he wanted them without coming to the house. I cared nothing about the house or its contents—only about Ryan.

Finally, with one empty box remaining in the foyer, I found myself alone in the kitchen while Ryan slept upstairs. Moonlight afforded a perfect view of the towers of the Golden Gate, strong and powerful against the night sky.

I opened the drawer of the sideboard beside the kitchen table and removed the mahogany silverware box. I examined its sickening contents—syringes, rubber tubing, a blackened spoon, and several plastic bags with traces of white powder. Just as Father Sean had foretold, clarity came to me. Now, sitting at the breakfast nook with Jake's belongings stacked in the foyer, I steeled myself for what I knew I must do.

I picked up a parcel, wrapped neatly in brown paper. I opened the lid of the mahogany box and tucked the parcel inside. Resting my palm on top of the box until my heartbeat slowed, I closed the lid. I then packed it into one of Jake's cartons of clothing. With a thick black marker I labeled the box JAKE'S CLOTHES. Then I added the words MAHOGANY SILVER BOX to guide Jake specifically to the box and its contents. I sealed the box with layers of tape, assuring myself that I'd have to work hard to change my mind and open it again.

I turned off the kitchen light and lingered there in front of the window. It had been weeks since I'd had a drink, and in that instant I knew I was completely sober and clear-thinking for the first time in a very long time. I wasn't drunk on scotch or inebriated by guilt, or worry, or fury, or fear. Passion and love were no longer my intoxicants. Work was no longer my anesthesia. Secrecy could alter my thinking no more.

Fully conscious, energy coursing through my veins, I pulled away from the window and climbed the stairs. I sat in the dark at the edge of Ryan's bed, simply watching my baby sleep.

Jake-in-the-Box

When I was three, Tully gave me a jack-in-the-box. A tinny version of "Pop Goes the Weasel" plunked as I turned the toy's crank. My family hovered, awaiting the moment of my delighted surprise. When the lid popped open and out came the clown, I screamed and burst into tears. Tully cranked it again, thinking that because I knew what to expect I'd enjoy it, but I was terrified every time anyone brought it near me. Tully felt so badly that he made great theater of throwing the toy into the dumpster behind the bar and covering it with garbage.

In the weeks of waiting for Jake to reemerge from the hospital I often thought about that jack-in-the-box. It was not the atonal music or the pop of the lid that frightened me. It was the anticipation—the pluck of every note, each turn of the crank, bracing myself for the shock of it.

It was a wintry weeknight a week before Christmas. We'd returned from New York ten weeks before, and Jake had been in the hospital in Vermont ever since. Ryan was just beginning to resemble her old self again.

The pub was filled with regulars. Dumpling and Sausage,

Dad's fattest cats ever, sashayed across the bar, one following the other. Holiday lights hung outside and the pub was trimmed with red poinsettias. Outside, the night roared with wind and driving rain. As new customers entered, an icy gust blasted into the bar, inciting a chorus of, "Close that door!" Nat King Cole sang of chestnuts and Christmas cards. Aromas of cinnamon and apple rose from the Crock-Pot where mulled cider brewed.

My dad greeted me as soon as I came in from the hospital, his face creased with worry. "Burt called this afternoon. He tried to reach you at the hospital."

"I've been in surgery all day."

"Jake discharged himself last night."

My knees weakened under my weight.

"Chin up, love." I could see that he was tempering his own fears to calm me. "We're all in this together now. You and Ryan are safe and sound. Go have a look at the decorating your daughter has done, why don't you, Kitten?"

I worked my way to the storage room to find Alice and Ryan unpacking the last of the holiday boxes. Just as I had when I was small, Ryan stood on the balcony of the storage loft, a bird's perch that afforded a full view of the entire bar. She wore a Santa hat and a garland necklace.

Just as I'd wiggled my way past the boxes to help Alice, another chorus of "Close the door!" rose from the crowd.

My blood turned to ice when I looked over and saw Ryan's frozen face. She stared, transfixed, at the front of the bar. As I scrambled through the clutter, I watched Ryan thaw. Her brow crinkled and she tipped her head to one side, as if evaluating what she saw. Just as I neared her, I could almost see an electrical charge pulse through her, reanimating her muscles and limbs. "Daddy!" Ryan's shrill scream sliced the room.

Ryan ran, her lean body weaving around the pool table

and the sagging sofas, past the dart game and the clusters of patrons, past the jukebox, until she launched herself at Jake in a desperate embrace. He pulled off her Santa hat and showered her with kisses.

Every muscle in my body prepared to protect my daughter, ready kick and punch until Jake lay motionless at my feet. When I reached them, Jake gazed at me in silence through the veil of Ryan's curls.

"I missed you so much," he said. He spoke to both of us.

Jake wore new glasses and his face was freshly shaved. The shoulders of his jacket were soaked and his hair hung in ringlets, glistening with rainwater. He'd gained some weight, and his face bore the boyish softness it had when we'd first met.

Gone was the wild, fire-flecked look of threat I'd seen as he'd boarded the helicopter. In seconds, Tully, Alice, and Dad surrounded Jake. My motley army of defenders. Dad stepped up to Jake and with a firm grab of his forearm pulled Jake aside. Jake towered over my father, but he leaned down to listen as he spoke. Jake nodded and Dad released his grip, patted him on the back, and stepped aside. Jake returned to Ryan.

Alice reached for Ryan's hand and smoothly pulled her from Jake's side. I exhaled. Alice's eyes were kind, but her lips were set in a straight, bothered line. "Come now, sweetheart. Let's let your daddy get out of that wet coat and go fetch him something to drink." Alice then reached Jake and embraced him and kissed his cheek. "What'll it be, Jake? Hot cider is good on a cold, wet day."

Jake stammered. "Sounds great, Alice. Thank you."

"I'll get it," Ryan chirped. "Go sit at the family table and I'll bring it. Just like a real waitress." Ryan scurried off to the end of the bar, where Dr. Schwartz sat nursing a brandy. He offered a reassuring pat to her head.

The rest of us stood, not quite knowing what to do. Finally, Tully extended his hand to Jake. "Good to see you."

Soon, it was only I who had said nothing. Jake turned to me. "You look wonderful, Kat."

I broke my gaze from his as if it was a solar eclipse I'd already looked at for too long. Jake, Ryan, and I sat in the family booth where Ryan chattered, regaling Jake with all of her pent-up stories of schoolmates, teachers, the tricks Welby could do. Her smile was overstretched, her voice extra exuberant. I tugged at small hangnails with my front teeth until all my fingertips smarted. Jake listened while Ryan's words twirled around us. The others left us alone at the table, but my father peered at us. Tully paced the room like a nervous guard dog. Alice popped over repeatedly under the guise of offering food and beverage.

"Plenty of fish and chips, Jake. And a good lamb stew. Can I fix you a plate?"

"No. Thanks, Alice. I'm good."

In a few minutes she'd be back, refilling Jake's cider or warming my coffee.

The evening wore on. Ryan's chatter was a whirlwind, a vast contrast to the wordless child of a few weeks before. Anxiety was a near-visible glow emanating from her. Her superficial babbling was a performance she was delivering for an audience of one. With her every word, I felt her longing. She was searching for the daddy she'd been missing—finding him here, now, in this familiar place, so different from the terrifying figure he'd been when she'd seen him last. She needed to face this wizard as she had in so many trays of sand. She needed to recognize that her loving daddy and the frightening wizard were co-inhabitants of the same form.

Jake sat calmly, listening, with creases at the corners of his eyes. His squint gave him the appearance of looking past

Ryan's performance, trying to see the happy and confident daughter he knew.

Time was a concertina, expanding and collapsing all at once. I looked at my watch. "Ryan, it's nearly midnight. You've got school tomorrow."

"Please, not yet," she begged, but her weary eyes told me that the "happy girl" show had exhausted her.

"Mommy's right," Jake said. "It's very late and I need to get going." He looked back at me with unspeakable grief in his eyes.

Ryan's face wilted. "You're not staying?"

Jake never broke his gaze from Ryan's. "I'm sorry, I can't." He moved so that Ryan's face was only inches from his own. "I can't stay with you and Mommy anymore, Ryan. I never want to scare you again—the way I did. I'm really sorry about that."

Ryan's voice was muffled and soft. "You're not scary right now, and I know you didn't mean it."

"I would never hurt you on purpose. But I can't always trust myself to—"

"But you're okay now. You're better now. I can see you're better."

"I am better right now. And nothing makes me happier than seeing you... and Mommy. But I can't count on myself to stay this way. I have a sickness, Ryan. In my mind." Jake looked up at me, his eyes cool green. "When I'm well it's easy to forget that I can get sick again. It tricks me and everyone else. So I can't live with you anymore, even though I want to more than anything. My sickness makes me dangerous sometimes. I never, ever want to hurt you or Mommy."

Ryan's chatter was quieted and she spoke between sniffs. "Are you going away forever?"

"I'm doing a project. Then I'll be gone for a while."

I expected Ryan to fly into a fit of rage, but the most

surprising look came over her face. I didn't recognize it at first, and it seemed foreign to her. It was the look of utter relief.

Ryan nodded. She wrapped her arms around Jake's neck then kissed his cheek. Jake loosened, then tightened, his hold around her before finally releasing her from his embrace.

Alice appeared at our table and took Ryan's hand. "How's about you and I go have a cup of chamomile tea to call the old sandman?"

Ryan nodded. She labored to take each heavy step away from the table.

"Sleep well, my darling," Jake said. "I love you."

Just before she turned away, Ryan looked back at Jake. "I love you more, Daddy."

Jake watched her until she disappeared up the stairs. Then his lips turned downward and creases of pain appeared across his brow. Squelched sobs escaped his throat. The sounds of a wounded animal.

Frank Sinatra's voice floated from the jukebox. At last it seemed that Jake and I were alone—or as alone as we could be under the circumstances.

Jake sniffed and pressed the heels of his hands to his eyes.

"I wish you'd called," I whispered. "It would have been nice to prepare her."

"I wasn't sure I'd actually come in," he said. "I walked around outside for an hour." He swiped his nose with his sleeve. "She's a stranger—" His voice caught and the rest of the sentence was pinched. "All of that babbling. She's so nervous around me."

My resolve to berate him melted away. He was already doing that to himself. "She'll settle down."

"I just want her to be okay, Kat." He looked toward the steamy window, his ghostly image reflecting back. "Thanks for packing the boxes for me. I went to the storage unit this afternoon."

My heart dropped to my belly.

Sinatra's voice filled our silence. *Please have snow and mistletoe.*

"It means a lot to me that you would—" I looked into the darkness outside the window.

He reached across the table for my hands. It was the first time he'd touched me since we'd last made love months ago. But this time there was no electric charge of passion, only the throbbing ache of resignation.

"I'll be fine." Jake's body was limp with defeat.

From the jukebox the melancholy song continued. *Christmas Eve will find me. Where the love light gleams.*

Aching, I pulled my hands away and stirred my cold coffee, reminding myself of the distance I needed to maintain. "So you're doing a project? Burt didn't say anything about it." Saying Burt's name to Jake felt newly odd on my lips.

Jake removed his glasses, wiping them with his shirttail. "It's something I'm doing independently. Nothing, really. It doesn't matter."

We sat with no words to rescue us from the residue of what we'd lived through together. Jake stood. "I should get going. You've got work tomorrow."

"Actually," I said, pulling myself from the booth and standing beside him. "I took tomorrow off to bring cider and cookies to Ryan's class holiday party."

A smile broke across Jake's lips. "Dr. Room Mom, huh?"

"Just plain old Room Mom."

"Nice."

On his way out, Jake stepped toward my dad and extended his hand. "Thank you, Angus, for welcoming me tonight. And thanks for taking such good care of my girls. Would you extend my appreciation to Alice? And Dr. Schwartz and Tully, of course."

"So you're off, then?" Dad asked, shaking Jake's hand.

"I think that's best."

Dad pulled Jake into a firm embrace and patted his back. "You take good care of yourself now, son."

"I'm going to step outside with Jake for a minute, Dad. I'll be right back."

Dad gave me a look that told me he'd be waiting for me, right where he sat.

As we stepped out the door, Sinatra's voice followed us: *I'll be home for Christmas—if only in my dreams.*

The storm had quieted. Silent rain fell. Jake and I stood in the shelter of the entryway, surrounded by holiday lights. He pulled me to his chest in a hungry embrace. After a while he allowed a small space to creep between us. Clouds of breath hung before his face. "I thought the love we have would be enough, Kat. Honest to God I did."

I shivered from the chill and Jake pulled my sweater around me.

"You're a great mom," he whispered.

"I make mistakes every day."

Cars passed on Lincoln Avenue, tossing rooster tails of water from their tires. Headlights sliced through the darkness, splashing light onto us as they passed. "What did my dad say to you?"

Jake's laughter rang out into the night, full and hearty. I couldn't help but laugh with him. He donned an exaggerated version of my father's brogue. "I love you like a son, Jacob. But make so much as a move to harm the ones I love and the sole of my boot will be across your throat before your heart has a chance to pound its next beat."

"And Tully," he added. "I thought that scrawny little guy

was going to clock me for sure. He can deliver some serious stink-eye."

The sound of my own laugh surprised me. "Alice deployed a hydration strategy. Maybe she thought you couldn't do any damage with an over-full bladder."

The sparkle of our laughter faded. We stood with only crackling silence between us, broken by the sounds of traffic and rain. "Good-bye" was a poison I could not inflict. Jake leaned toward me, then stopped with his mouth just millimeters from mine. Only when I moved toward him did he kiss me. Our tears mingled, flavoring the sweetness of the kiss with their salt.

His fingers traced the line of my jaw. When he pulled away, it felt that a piece of my own flesh had been torn. He stood for a moment, just outside of the alcove where I could hear the raindrops plopping onto his shoulders. The streetlight lit him from behind, denying me the details of his face.

I watched until he was swallowed by the night.

Rain

The overnight rain cleared, leaving behind a biting chill and a cloudless sky. The towers of the Golden Gate Bridge stood like powerful shoulders against the moody wind that shook my car and snapped the scarves of tourists as they posed for pictures along the railing.

Jake's surprise visit the night before had left me feeling raw. I wanted Dr. Gross to help Ryan to manage it all. I wished she could help me manage it, too. Even in Friday, holiday traffic, I was glad to be on the way to her office. "How you doing, Noodle?" I asked as we crossed the bridge. In my rearview mirror Ryan's reflection shrugged and stared, expressionless, into the distance.

I gripped the wheel tighter against the wind that tugged at the car. "It was a nice party in your class. Your friends seemed to like Alice's cider."

Another shrug.

"How about we have supper at Pacific Café on the way home? You always like the crab there."

"Sure. Whatever." Ryan's voice contained no petulance, only sorrow.

* * *

Wordlessly, Ryan designed a scene in the tray of sand. She scooped sand, moving it until it formed mountains separated by a canyon. She selected the small paper rabbit from the cigar box she'd brought that contained the gifts Jake had sent to her from the hospital. She placed the rabbit atop the highest of the hills. On the hill next to the rabbit she placed four figures: a jester, Glinda the Good Witch, a bear, and an armored knight. At the canyon's edge, she erected a fortress of seashells and stones. Then she placed a second, larger rabbit next to the small one. She added the warrior princess to the scene, a sentry at the river's bank.

The wizard remained on the shelf. I wondered if he would be forgotten today.

In a single, decisive movement, Ryan snatched the wizard. With a jerk she snapped the scepter held in his left hand and broke the crystal ball from his right. The muscles in my jaw tightened and I held my breath, startled by her silent violence. She replaced the wizard on the shelf next, but with his face turned to the wall. Then she dropped the scepter and sphere into a hole she'd dug and smoothed sand over the top. Lastly, she adorned the hill with a circle of colored stones. She stood to the side.

"So the wizard isn't in your tray today," Dr. Gross observed softly.

"No," Ryan said. "He lost his magic powers."

"And the rabbit has some company on her hill."

Ryan nodded. "She likes it better when she's not alone."

Ryan's face smoothed and her breathing deepened into a calm rise and fall. Her brows lifted. She looked up at me. "It's done, Mommy. I'm hungry. Can we go to Pacific Café now?"

* * *

We drove along Bridgeway in Sausalito. It was only six-thirty, but winter had already dropped its dark curtain on the day. Tourists with their shoulders scrunched to their ears bustled on the sidewalks, ducking into art galleries and trinket shops trimmed in holiday lights. We snaked toward the bridge behind a slow trail of cars.

"How come it's so slow?" Ryan asked from the back seat.

"Friday night, I guess. Holiday traffic. And this crazy wind makes everybody nervous driving."

"How long till we get to Pacific Café? I'm starving."

"I don't know, baby."

I wanted to talk to her about the sand tray, to let her know that I would always protect her. But I resisted interpreting the scene she'd created, as Dr. Gross had advised.

After only a block, the traffic came to a halt. I turned the radio to KGO for a traffic report. "... worst disaster in Golden Gate Bridge history..."

"What happened, Mommy?"

"Shh. I don't know yet." Just then my pager went off, buzzing at my hip. I squinted, reading Mary K's telephone number. I turned off the radio and pulled my cell phone from my purse, fumbling to dial.

"Are you okay?" she asked. Her voice was shrill. "Is Ryan with you?"

"Fine. We're just trying to leave Sausalito. Traffic's miserable."

"So you haven't heard?"

I turned to look at Ryan, who sat in the backseat manipulating a strand of yarn into Jacob's Ladder.

"Look," Mary K said, her voice softer but still insistent. "The Bridge is closed. Pull off and get a room. Whatever you do, don't turn on the TV. I'll get on the ferry and be there within the hour."

"What is it?" The note of alarm in Mary K's voice raised smoky fear within me.

"Just do what I say, Murphy. I'll be there as fast as I can. Call me when you've got a room. Keep Ryan away from the TV. I'll let everyone at the pub know you're okay."

The traffic was my excuse to Ryan for renting a hotel room. As soon as we got a room, I called Mary K with our location. Ryan drew pictures of nesting birds in her sketchpad. I stared out the window toward the bay with San Francisco's twinkling skyline in the distance. Every cell in me itched to turn on the TV, but if I'd learned nothing else, I'd learned to trust Mary K.

A firm rap came at the door.

"I'll get it!" Ryan squealed and bounded for the door.

"Yay! You brought Welby to our sleepover." Mary K entered the room. Her shoulder sagged under the weight of the same knapsack I'd seen her carry into our Stanford dorm room twenty years before. My throat clutched when I saw my ashen-faced friend. Welby pranced toward Ryan, his collar tags jingling.

"Can we have dogs in the hotel?"

"Welby's no dog, kid. You know that."

"I know. I know," Ryan said with a roll of her eyes. "He's a wise old soul in canine form." She took the leash from Mary K and led the dog across the room.

Mary K ruffled Ryan's hair. "Hey, keep an eye on the mutt, would you? There are training treats in my pack. I want to talk to your mom for a minute."

A cloud passed in front of Ryan's eyes. Usually curiosity would make her pester us for details. Instead she squatted down and nuzzled Welby, but her smile faded.

Mary K and I stepped into the bedroom and closed the door behind us. She patted the end of the bed, inviting me to sit down to sit next to her. She drew a deep breath. "It's Jake."

I waited for the mallet of pain. I closed my eyes and listened. The pulse of helicopters sounded in the distance. I could not force my eyes to open. Looking into my friend's steady blue gaze might break me into pieces. "All this traffic. The helicopters. The sirens. It's Jake?"

"'Fraid so."

Slowly, I looked at her. "Is he dead?"

Mary K nodded, her unblinking eyes locked onto mine. "They just confirmed it on the news. Bastards didn't even wait to notify next of kin."

Everything in me went slack, every muscle conspiring to crumble me to the floor. Mary K grabbed onto me, keeping me from sliding off the edge of the bed.

I pulled myself to standing, then held onto the corner of a bureau to steady myself. "Take Ryan and Welby for a walk. Buy her dinner," I commanded flatly. "She loves that waffle cone place just down the block. Buy her an ice cream after. Take her Christmas shopping. Anything."

"But Murphy, I—"

"Please. Give me some time. I've got to sort this out and figure out what to tell her."

"You're sure? You don't want me to stay here with you?"

"I'm sure. We're going to need you and that furry friend of yours right here with us."

"You can take it to the bank, Murphy."

* * *

With the click of the door I snatched the TV remote. In a box behind Tom Brokaw's shoulder perched the same black-and-white press photo that had been in *The Times*. Across the bottom of the screen a caption floated: "Jacob Bloom, 1952-1997." In his steady baritone, Brokaw described the horror. I could absorb only pieces. "... renowned artist." "... rare visionary." "... tragic loss." "... as beautiful as it is horrifying." "... artistic vision run amok." "... madness of a brilliant artist." "... dramatic history as part of one of America's wealthiest families." "... possible suicide or drug use." "... pending autopsy."

I willed myself not to blink as I stared at the images before me. The screen filled with shaky, water-speckled footage taken by a weather helicopter crew of a strangely colored helicopter flying above the north tower of the Golden Gate. The bridge sat eerily empty of cars because of wind warnings. The copter lurched, suddenly tilting ninety degrees. From the open door, dozens of pale blue bags fell. Seconds later, they burst apart, letting fly thousands of fluttering sheets and shards in greens, blues, silvers, and golds that floated in a spectacular shower of color.

Tom Brokaw's voice told the end of the story. "... then, quite suddenly, things went hopelessly awry." I could listen no more. All I saw was the calico helicopter tossed by the wind, tumbling over and over until its propeller hit the top of the bridge's tower. Like a wounded sea bird, the chopper spiraled downward, tangling its crumpled wings in the cables of the bridge until wind dragged it off of the screen toward San Francisco's rocky shore. Flames from burning fuel lit falling sheets of paper and vellum.

For one brief instant, all of the falling debris cascaded in front of the bridge and I recognized the image as familiar: a perfect, shimmering waterfall spilling from the side of the bridge, backlit with the fiery orange sunset.

Jake's preposterous image was now real. Fire and water in the same place, at the same time. With shaking hands, I switched the channel, watching it from new angles—trying to catch a glimpse of the pilot's face.

Film crews shot footage of the second phenomena that emerged in the current. The enormous swatches of foil, paper-thin sheets of glass, and opalescent vellum joined together in writhing forms, moving in undulating, underwater choreography. The creation became a school of glittering fish as the current beckoned it out to sea.

On the TV screen was everything I'd feared and everything I'd prayed for. Jake was finally freed from the torment of his madness. He'd left in a torrent—a beautiful destruction—a storm that left a swath of ruin in its wake.

But had he left in a cloud, intoxicated with narcotics? Had he planned this whole thing as an elaborate suicide—a death with a vivid and spectacularly artistic exclamation point? Each possibility was a firefly, lighting itself in my mind, then fading back into the darkness.

Jake, what have you done?

Post Mortem

By the time Mary K brought Ryan back to the hotel, I had watched Jake die countless times. When I heard the cheerful tinkling of Welby's tags outside the door I clicked off the TV.

As I waited for Ryan to settle Welby down, I hoped that the perfect words would find their way to my lips. Mary K and I exchanged glances. "Hey Squirt," she said, "Why don't you come over here so your mom and I can talk to you awhile?"

Together we told Ryan of what had occurred. Prepared for tears and screams—or worse, a slip back into the silence from which Ryan had so recently reemerged—I braced myself. Instead, she looked up at me, her eyes unblinking. "Daddy's dead, then?"

The simple truth of her words pierced my heart. "Yes, baby."

There it was, the look of relief I'd seen on Ryan's face at the pub the night before. The unmistakable calm that comes when a long fight is at last surrendered. Ryan closed her eyes and sat still as night.

"What are you doing, baby?"

She opened her eyes and in them I saw the cool green tones I'd first seen in Jake's. "I can still see him," she said. "So he's not really gone. And he's not sad anymore because he doesn't have to be lonely without us."

I felt a sudden and odd sense of calm even amidst my grief. For the first time, there was nothing left for me to do. No choices remained.

I remembered the first date I'd had with Jake, when he'd created gourmet pizzas at The Front Room. I'd told him about my Jane Doe who had died in the ER that day. "Her pain is over now," he had said. "You'll be the keeper of the last memory of her."

"No, my darling. Daddy's not sad anymore." I said to Ryan. "His pain is over."

* * *

We all slept together that night in the king-size bed, Mary K and I wrapping our limbs around Ryan, Welby an extra blanket at our feet. Though the bridge was reopened by morning, we took the Sausalito ferry back to San Francisco, leaving my car at the hotel. I just couldn't drive across the Golden Gate.

"You'll take care of Welby for me, right, kiddo?" Mary K said to Ryan when our cab reached the pub. "I've got a lot to do, so he'd just be in my way. He'll have more fun with you." Ryan's hands had not been off of the dog since she'd learned of Jake's death the night before. She nodded.

"Great," Mary K said, handing over her knapsack. " I'll bring more food tonight. I know you'll take good care of him." Mary K. knelt down. She rubbed Welby's ears and hugged Ryan. She stood, grabbed me, and hugged me hard, then broke away and rushed into the cab.

* * *

That afternoon Ryan and I sat cuddled on the couch in my dad's flat, watching *The Land before Time* videos and avoiding all broadcast TV. Alice pulled out an old jigsaw puzzle. She and Ryan sat at the kitchen table, filling in the pieces. Now and then my eyes would meet with Alice's. Seeing her and Ryan together transported me back in time to when she sat at that very table doing a puzzle with me after the death of my mother—or at least the woman I'd known then to be my mother. I could now feel, as if it were my own, Alice's anguish at both losing her friend and acting as a substitute mother to the child she'd given birth to.

After eleven, Ryan was finally asleep, her arms wrapped around Welby. I slipped down the staircase to the bar. Dad's rumbling snore emanated from behind his bedroom door.

Tully sat at the end of the bar, a mug of tea in front of him. With a pat, he invited me to sit on the stool next to him. Alice sat at the family table with an embroidery hoop, sewing sequins onto felt New Year's hats.

TV pundits squawked about Bill Clinton and Monica Lewinski.

"Do people really care about this?" I muttered.

Tully shrugged. "Gossip. People love it."

I nudged Tully's shoulder. "Thanks for picking up my car."

Tully patted my arm. "Least I can do."

The local news then began replaying film from earlier in the day of Jake's body being pulled from the rocks at the base of the bridge on the San Francisco side. My gut knotted when the black body bag sagged with his weight as officials hoisted it onto a gurney. The charred helicopter was a crumpled bit of cellophane on the rocky shore.

"Mikey, turn that shit off, will ya?" Tully grumbled.

"Please. I have to see this," I said.

Together we watched until Jake's body had been placed into the coroner's wagon. The newscaster commented on Jake's "fatal masterpiece." That's what everyone had begun to call it.

A Santa Rosa farmer then spoke, revealing that Jake had rented his large barn. The farmer hadn't known who Jake was. Jake had hidden a used helicopter, which he'd stripped and repainted, in the barn. For over two years he'd amassed explosives and the rest of the materials for his "project." He'd painted the helicopter silver with swaths of tangerine and blue to disappear against a sunset sky. The contents of the bags were released mid-air by the detonation of small, explosive devices timed perfectly to burst just as they reached the cables of the bridge.

Watching the footage dozens of times made it no more real.

From behind me came Dad's voice, gravelly and deep. "You can shut it off now, if you would please, Mikey?" His hand rested on my shoulder and I felt its warmth penetrate into my bones. "Haven't you've seen enough, Kitten?" His hair was misshapen and his fleshy cheeks bore the crinkled impressions of his pillowcase. His feet were clad in his worn leather house slippers. He pulled up a stool and squeezed in beside me. Mike brought him a cup of tea.

"You're a good lad, Mikey," Dad said as he lifted his cup. Mike poured a second cup and then I felt Alice's gentle kiss on my cheek. The two men scooted aside and Tully pulled up a stool. The three of them could not sit close enough to me.

"All of us here know a little bit about grief," Dad said. "And we know what it is to be unable to save someone you love. It feels like you die along with them. But here's the truth of it, Kitten. Tomorrow and the next day and the day after that, your heart will pump and your lungs will pull in the air they need and let go of what they don't." Alice dabbed her nose with a tissue tugged from her sleeve as Dad continued. "You'll keep on living because you've a daughter to care for. I know this path. But don't let this phase of deadness go on too long. In one blink Ryan will be driving a car. In two, she'll be leaving for college. In three, she'll be a mother herself. You don't want to miss all that."

"I hope we get some more cucumber days, Dad. I'm sort of over this pickle thing."

"We will, darlin'. That's a promise."

I stood and looked at the love-filled faces at the end of the bar. Newly exhausted, I climbed the stairs knowing that, just as they had for my whole life, they were watching my every step.

The following day I accepted the condolences of loved ones and visitors, but all of it seemed like a hazy dream. Only one thing would make it all seem real.

I had to see Jake's body.

* * *

Chewing my cuticles, I sat in a plastic chair outside of a door labeled CITY AND COUNTY OF SAN FRANCISCO MEDICAL EXAMINER. The sting of the pink flesh around my thumbnail and the bead of blood that erupted reminded me that despite the numbness I felt, life still coursed through me, just as my father had said it would. The mingled odors of antiseptics and floor wax and the harsh glow of fluorescent lighting gave me an odd sense of familiarity.

After lengthy protest, Mary K had agreed to arrange for me to see Jake's body, but not from behind the viewing window. I'd already seen him through the distance of a camera and a television screen. I needed to be closer.

The door opened and Mary K peeked out. "You're sure, Murphy?"

I nodded.

"Okay," she said. "But this is some grisly shit."

"I've seen dead bodies before."

"Not Jake's."

Mary K escorted me to the morgue. Jake's body had been drawn from its holding drawer and he lay on a stainless steel table, covered with blue surgical draping. The chill of the room wrapped itself around me. I tried to identify Jake's profile under the blue sheet.

"Can I have a minute?" I asked.

"I can't leave you by yourself in here. The coroner would shit a Maytag. He already chewed me a new asshole, warning me not to let you touch anything." Mary K guided me to where Jake's body rested. She studied me until I nodded, and then she pulled back the draping.

At first nothing of Jake was recognizable. His hair was pulled straight back from his face, revealing the pale swath of his forehead. Sooty smudges lined his jaw. His face was more grotesque catcher's mitt than human face: gray and misshapen, covered with abrasions. His nose bore cuts deep enough to reveal shining white cartilage. The lips I'd kissed a million times were no longer full and ripe, but colorless and twisted.

On his torso, beneath the feathery tufts of chest hair, was a sutured, T-shaped incision, starting at the hollow of Jake's throat, disappearing beneath the drape that covered his lower body. Like it was her signature, I recognized the perfect evenness of Mary K's surgical handiwork that closed the gash. Across his chest, where so many times I'd rested my head, Jake now wore a gaping wound that no stitching could disguise. The flesh was shredded and pulpy; its resemblance to the gashes in his New York exhibit caused me to feel lightheaded.

I hoped to see his wedding ring; the platinum wreath of twigs that was the perfect mate to mine, but Jake's left arm had been severed at the elbow—lost to the sea.

Nothing of this body before me conjured Jake for me until I spied the fine white crosshatch of old scars over his arms, chest, and abdomen. I looked up at Mary K, whose expression told me that we were both looking at the same perversely beautiful pattern.

"That's a fuckload lot of scars, Murphy."

In the thick of his bushy, dark eyebrow, I found the single small scar, offset from the symmetry of the others. It was an insignificant white line—nothing by comparison to the gouges that now riddled his body, and miniscule in comparison to the elaborate mesh of self-inflicted scars. For an instant I was no longer standing in the morgue. Instead I stood beside an examination table in an ER, yellow wires protruding from Jake's ears and the buzz of music, while I stitched his brow. A sideways smile. His cocky swagger. His penetrating gaze.

I reached out and touched the fine white line. His skin was cool, but I felt the warmth of recognition radiating through my fingertips.

Mary K looked over her shoulder. "Murphy."

I jerked my fingers away and stepped back. After one last look I closed my eyes. Mary K picked up my silent signal and pulled the draping over Jake's face.

"Let's go up to my office," she said. "You look a little green."

* * *

Mary K pulled out her desk chair, inviting me to sit. She drew a plastic bottle of orange juice from the fridge under her desk. I welcomed its sweetness in my dry mouth.

"You gonna puke or faint?"

"I'm all right."

"Look Murphy, I took a look at the tox results just before you got here. They're going to release them to the media."

My heart galloped. I had exhausted myself wondering if the cruel blows of the helicopter crash had been softened by a pillow of narcotic numbness. Was it a drugged haze that clouded his judgment and slowed his reflexes, causing the crash? Was it all just another colossally impulsive act that had gone awry? Or had Jake been fully conscious, fully intending all of this?

"Clean," Mary K said.

Surely I had heard her wrong.

"Nothing?" I asked. It seemed impossible. "Not antipsychotics? Not antidepressants? No speed, barbiturates, heroin?"

"The boy didn't have so much as baby aspirin in his system."

I pulled in a great swallow of air.

"I double-checked the labs myself."

"So did you conduct the autopsy?"

She shook her head. "Nope, wouldn't be ethical. I know the deceased. Given the high profile, the brass wanted everything by the book with this one."

"But the stitching—"

A shy look crossed Mary K's face. "They usually staple up a body that's going for cremation. I asked to close. Thought Bloom would appreciate being sewn up right, even if it will only be for a couple of days."

This macabre act of kindness flooded me with gratitude and sorrow. I steeled myself, preparing for my friend's answer to the next question. "Cause of death?"

Mary K looked at me, the directness of her gaze penetrating past my skin and looking deeply into me. "Massive impact to the chest," she said. "The steering column crushed right through the sternum. He hit the bridge tower head on. Punctured the heart and lungs. I'm guessing he didn't even have time to say *oh shit*."

The moment it was lifted, I knew the weight of the worry I'd carried that Jake's suffering had been prolonged. We sat together in silence while I absorbed the meaning of all that I'd just heard.

Mary K wiped her palms on the front of her jeans. "Kind of weird timing here, Murphy, but... you ready for some good news?" She lifted one eyebrow and gave me a slanted smile. "Looks like you're going to be Auntie Kate. Andra's got a baby on board. Found out today."

Joy rose effervescent, like bubbles rising from the bottom of a deep pool. "Baby? You said *baby*, right? So you're together?"

"What can I say, Murphy? She couldn't live without me." Mary K gave a low chuckle, then her smile faded. "Straight up? You and Bloom got me thinking. Maybe this love stuff is a pretty rare thing. You walked through hell for it. All I've got to do is say yes. We're all only here for a little while, right? Who knows how long any of us has?"

I glanced around the room at the bulletin board plastered with grotesque photographs of mutilated corpses. "No kidding."

"The tick of Andra's biological clock just got too loud to ignore, with or without me. She went to a clinic, picked a daddy from a book, and got herself knocked up. Called me to let me know right before we went to New York. She's kind that way. Didn't want me to hear it through the grapevine. When I saw her... all happy and glowing, well—"

"You didn't tell me."

"I planned to, but then things went haywire with Bloom. But things are good. She moved into my house last week. We're fixing up a nursery. All that gooey mommy stuff."

"Mary Louise Kowalski, in love and with a baby on the way. As I live and breathe."

"We'll be Mommy Squared, or something like that. I guess we'll make like *Leave It to Beaver*." Mary K's mouth twisted into a sly grin. "But with double the beaver."

I couldn't help but laugh.

"News of my impending motherhood ought to get me

disowned for good by the rest of my family. Glad I've got you and yours. Takes a village, right? I'm going to need the help of some great moms. You and Alice will be my first line of defense."

It felt like my heart was being knit back together. Mary K still regarded me as a good mother after everything she'd seen, and I could think of no better mother than Alice. "And the baby? Details, Kowalski. Details."

"Due in mid-May. Don't know the gender yet, but I'm hoping for a shortstop with a gun for an arm. Look, Murphy. I wanted to tell you, but I just couldn't seem to find the right time."

"And the morgue after viewing the corpse of my husband is the perfect moment, I suppose." Mary K's hoarse laugh joined mine.

Finally, my strength returned. "How about we go to Murphy's? There's a crew of people there that could use some good news. Ryan is going to flip. Alice will never stop crocheting booties."

Mary K grabbed her keys from her desk drawer. "I've had enough of this tomb. What's say we blow this pop stand?"

* * *

Three days later, two days before Christmas, San Francisco Bay's gray waters matched the mood of all on board the luxury yacht, Latitude. The unseasonably warm day was a kindness. The captain cut the engine and dropped anchor just south of Angel Island. The Golden Gate stood luminous, cinnamon against a moody sky. A cold breeze blew to remind us that it was winter. All of us stood in a circle on the deck of Latitude. Tully, Alice, and Dad together, as always, with Dr. Schwartz sitting in a deck chair beside them. Father Sean wore white robes of celebration as I'd requested. Mary K and Andra stood together, Andra's lean body just beginning to soften with pregnancy. Dahlia de la Rosa gave me a small smile from across the circle. Beside her stood Dr. John Marshall and Maggie Simon, the nurse who had helped deliver Ryan, looking unfamiliar in street clothes. Burt, big as a redwood, held Ryan's hand and she held mine. I was surrounded by a circle of friends and family that had been with me at every step, though I'd lost track of them along the way.

Father Sean spoke of God's mercy, love, and forgiveness. "We are human," he said, "endowed with the gifts of our humanity as well as its frailties. The God I know is big enough to understand it all and love us with all of our flaws." He looked at me with kindness in his eyes. As he spoke on about understanding and forgiveness, I looked around the circle. These people had taught me so many lessons. They'd taught me about unconditional love. They'd taught me about devotion and generosity and gentleness. But my family had also taught me about secrecy—a lesson that, when combined with my pride, had become my worst flaw.

I let the soft warmth of the sun find my face, and with it I felt washed clean, the mistakes I'd made vanquished. I looked over to see Burt's glowing face. I returned his smile and lifted Ryan's hand to my lips, giving her hand a tender kiss. Burt repeated my gesture with her other hand.

Next to the urn that held Jake's ashes sat a bundle of twisted willow branches wrapped in yellow flower petals, Ryan's way of showing her dad that she'd forgiven him, too.

At the boat's stern, outside the circle, stood Aaron Bloom, his gaze locked onto the bridge in the distance. As though gravity tugged harder where he stood, the distinguished man's face was pulled downward. Despite an impeccably tailored suit and his enormous influence, this icon of a man was simply a father who had lost his only child. He appeared as destitute as anyone I'd ever seen.

Tully cleared his throat, straightened his clip-on tie, and stepped forward. "I don't never know what to say at times like this," he said. "But my old friend Ivan has been coaxing me to read some of his books now and then. And I read them sometimes, at least when there's no good ball game on."

Smiles cut through tear-stained faces. Tully cleared his throat again. "Ivan helped me out by marking some of his favorite poems to guide me along. This one might work for today. 'A thing of beauty is a joy forever. Its loveliness increases. It will never pass into nothingness, but still will keep. A bower of quiet for us, and a sleep full of sweet dreams, and health, and quiet breathing.'"

Tully pulled a small white stone from his pocket. "We always leave one of these on Elyse's grave when we go to see her." After a gentle kiss, Tully set the stone next to the vase of willow branches.

Burt's eyes were hooded and red. He squatted down next to Ryan and smoothed her curls as they blew around her pale face. She leaned into him and stroked his auburn beard with her long, slim fingers.

Father Sean nodded to me. I lifted the urn and held it to my chest. I expected a rush of memory, an explosion of tears. Instead, I felt only the sensations of my body: the sway of the boat; the steady beat of my own heart; the smooth inhale and exhale of air through my lungs. Jake had been a flicker of brilliance, made more vivid by how quickly it had passed, but the fog-cloaked sun reminded me that my light and Ryan's still shone behind this veil of sadness.

Burt walked forward with Ryan. She picked up the bundle of branches. Her eyes reflected the calm of the gray sky. "Now, Mommy?"

I nodded. "Now, baby."

One at a time she tossed the branches into the water below. We watched as the current embraced them, stripping the petals from the limbs until they became a yellow ribbon winding through the water. I tilted the urn over the bow of the boat and poured. At first the ashes were a smoky cloud, but the breeze shifted again, letting them flutter to join the petals. The ash and petals wound their way across the water's surface toward the west—toward the Golden Gate.

* * *

After the memorial everyone returned to Murphy's. The pool table held a feast of ham, three-bean salad, and Bundt cakes provided by the ladies of St. Anne's. The table was covered with a clean, white cloth, decorated with embroidered lilies, roses, and ranunculus. "Blooms," Alice explained. "I thought Jake would feel honored."

With his topcoat neatly draped over his forearm, Aaron Bloom and I found a quiet corner.

"Katherine," he said, his voice muted and tender. "I'm grateful to be included today. Your family has been extraordinarily kind."

I wanted to reach to him, to soothe him, but something stopped me.

In his father I could see the face that Jake would have eventually worn; his eyes the same amalgam of grays and greens. And I could also see the flecks of gold, the lion lurking behind the mossy camouflage.

"There was a great deal that Jacob and I did not understand about one another." His lips stiffened. "But I did love him, Katherine. Perhaps I loved him as much as you did, but not nearly as well."

A swell of pity filled me for the man the world regarded as

impenetrable. In the last weeks of Jake's life, Aaron Bloom had done what he never had before. He had been present. Burt told me that Aaron Bloom had spent every visiting hour at the hospital, flying back to Manhattan in his helicopter to handle business overnight, then returning the next morning with *The New York Times* and fresh bagels. He and Jake had sat in the solarium solving crossword puzzles and sharing walks surrounded first by the falling leaves and then the first snow.

In the sequestered halls of a residential psychiatric hospital, Aaron Bloom had become Jake's father.

"Jake knew you loved him," I said.

Aaron Bloom pulled a crisp white handkerchief from his breast pocket and dabbed his nose. "Missing out on so much of my son's life will be my biggest regret."

"Jake didn't believe in regret. Just be glad you came together." A sudden impulse made me lunge forward to hug him. At first, the father felt as his son had—tender, open, vulnerable. Then his body stiffened and he pulled himself away. He looked around the bar with its holiday decorations and the crowds of milling loved ones.

"You're sure you won't reconsider my offer to get you a house. I'd like you and Ryan to have a home."

"No. Thank you. Taking care of the debt is more than I could ever hope for. And arranging for the boat today. It was a blessing to have privacy."

"Jake and I enjoyed a few lovely outings on boats when he was small. I don't suppose he remembered. I thought that—" Suddenly the stately man stopped speaking. His face crumpled a bit and he pulled his handkerchief across his lips. "You're sure you won't reconsider. About the house?"

"Thank you, no. I rented a nice little bungalow between here and the hospital, just a few blocks from Mary K and Andra's place. I want a place that I can manage on my own. We'll move in after the New Year."

He scanned the surroundings. Murphy's Pub, with its twinkle lights and jukebox, its scuffed floors and sagging couches. His lips curved ever so slightly upward. "This reminds me a lot of a watering hole my friends and I frequented in our college days. I can see why you wouldn't want to be far from it and your family and friends. Ryan is a fortunate girl."

Over Aaron Bloom's shoulder I spotted Ryan sitting across from Tully at the family table, a Shirley Temple with a half-dozen cherries in front of her and her fingers entwined with a strand of string. She held her perfectly formed Cat's Cradle out to Tully, who fumbled until the string was in knots. Alice untangled the mess while Dad snickered into his sleeve. Tully put his hands up in surrender.

"Yes," I said. "I think Ryan should grow up with lots of family around."

"I'll be on my way. I'm glad to have spent a little time with Ryan. She's as brilliant and as lovely as her mother."

"I hope she has a chance to get to know her other grandfather."

"I'd like that. Thank you, Katherine." He leaned toward me, planting a gentle kiss on my cheek. "If you ever need anything—" And then with one smooth movement he stepped away. The door of the pub swung lazily in his wake.

* * *

Burt sat at the family table. He ran his fingers through the condensation on his beer glass. I scooted into the booth across from him.

"First time today I've seen you without Ryan clinging onto you."

He took a sip of his beer. "Oh, I'm not sure she was the one doing the clinging."

"We haven't had a minute alone since—"

"No," he said. "That was a lovely moment. I've thought about it a lot."

Even in the midst of the sadness that surrounded us, I felt a small bit of joy rising in my body. "It was lovely." He sipped his beer again, coating his own mustache with a frosty foam.

I believed that Burt would keep his word. I would not lose his friendship whether more ever developed between us or not. I needed to be on my own for a while, to heal, to help Ryan to heal, and to see what I wanted to become without Jake as a force in my life.

"What now? I mean, for you?"

Burt raked his fingers through his beard. "I've been thinking about that. I've been holding on to the tail of Jake's comet for almost twenty years. I've liked building my own artistic muscles again. I'll still manage the publication part of the business, if you don't mind. The books and whatnot are still a tidy business and they need minding. You and I are partners in that now, I suppose."

"We could hire a manager, so you don't have to—"

"No," he sighed. "I'd like to see things through. If that's all right with you."

"Of course," I said. Burt seemed like a humble giant before me: shy and awkward. He tucked in his lips and wrapped his hand around his beer mug. "I've been dipping the brush a lot since New York. It's been a comfort. I've decided to get my own studio."

"In New York? Sydney?"

Burt pushed his beer glass away and looked at me through his eyebrows. "I know Ryan's got you and her family. But I was wondering if you'd mind if—well, if—I um, I'd like to still be a part of Ryan's life. My family's scattered around the globe. Mum's gone and Dad won't be long to follow. New York is... unhappy for me now. I'm thinking San Francisco might be a nice place for me. Maybe I could retire my suitcase to the attic for a bit. But perhaps having me around would bring up too many bad memories for you, so I'd understand if—"

My heart tripled in size. "Nothing would make Ryan happier than having you near us."

Though his eyes were still filled with sadness, Burt's lips curled into a grin. "Let's make Ryan happy, shall we?" He sniffed and straightened his broad shoulders while I fought the urge to throw my arms around him.

"Oh!" he blurted, "I nearly forgot. I brought you a little present a while ago, and with all that happened, I just kept forgetting to give it to you. Would it be all right now? I mean—" Burt scanned the room and gave a one-shouldered shrug.

"I could use a present," I said. "Though really, you shouldn't have—"

He dismissed my hesitation by slipping out of the booth. I could not suppress a smile as I watched the mountain of a man actually scamper to gather a string-handled bag from behind the bar. He returned, sliding into the booth beside me. "I'm not one for fancy wrappings and all. Hope you don't mind."

I tilted my head, as if looking at this man from a different angle might tell me more about him. He was uncharacteristically giddy, and I saw in his burly expression the same look of whimsy and bubbly elation I'd seen on Ryan's face so many times.

"I just can't imagine," I said, lifting the bag that felt nearly empty. As I sifted through the newspaper that filled the bag, I finally found my surprise. Pulling it from the bag, I felt my face flush. Safe from within the nest of crumpled newsprint, I pulled a perfect oval, almost as big as my head. Holding my breath, I held the orb gingerly in two palms.

"Don't worry," Burt said, smiling. "Ostrich eggs are good and strong."

The shell seemed made of tempered glass rather than calcium carbonate. Its thick shell was pierced at the bottom end where the contents had been drained, and its slightly golden surface was smooth to the touch and shiny.

"I noticed you have eggs on your mantel," Burt whispered. "Thought a specimen from Down Under might be a nice addition."

I pulled the egg to my cheek and felt its smooth surface against my skin. "It's a perfect addition, Burty. Just perfect."

* * *

After the guests had left the pub, the ladies from St. Anne's washed every dish and packaged every leftover. Finally, the gray-haired swarm of them departed.

"Can I ask you a favor?" I asked Mary K. "If Andra wouldn't mind, would you and Welby come home with Ryan and me tonight? We're going to say good-bye to the house. Ryan asked if we could have you there with us."

"You know me. Always good for a slumber party."

We spent the evening in front of the fireplace in snuggly pajamas, listening to the foghorns. Welby lay on the floor, enjoying lavish petting from the three of us at once. We rocked easily back and forth between laughter and tears. "I'm going to miss my daddy," Ryan said.

"I know, baby. Me too."

After she'd wept awhile, Welby licked Ryan's salty tears and turned her crying into laughter once again.

"So will your new baby be my cousin?" Ryan asked Mary K.

"Not by blood, but sure."

Ryan scratched Welby's belly. "Blood doesn't matter. That isn't what makes you family."

I smiled at my wise daughter. "No, baby. It doesn't really matter much at all."

Peace washed over me. Ryan was Jake's daughter, and I could see that she had his quicksilver mind and his eye for beauty. She had his sensitivity and his kindness. But I could see that she also had an ability—even as a child—to put things into perspective; something Jake had never had. In Ryan I could see the best parts of Jake. But I saw Alice's resilience and my father's wisdom, Burt's humor, and Mary K's love for animals. I was even starting to recognize qualities of my own in her. She was stubborn and willful. She withdrew when she was afraid. I wished I had not passed these qualities on to her. But I could also see a quiet strength—a strength that could easily be underestimated, but which emerged when she needed it most. Perhaps these were qualities I also had. She had inherited a legacy far greater than her genetic code.

Ryan would have scars from all that had happened, but as I watched her cry, then laugh, then cry again, I knew she would not be disabled by her experiences. She would be made stronger by them. And so would I.

Once Ryan and Welby were tucked securely in bed and sleep had pulled them both safely away, I wandered the house while Mary K took a shower. Tully had retrieved Jake's boxes from the storage unit. Movers would come for it all the day after New Year and take it to our new bungalow on Irving Street, where I could take my time sorting through the items, selecting mementos for Ryan.

The cloud-wrapped moon spilled light through the atrium windows. I found the box labeled "Mahogany Silver Box" and opened its overlapping flaps. On top sat the box, just as I had placed it. I stroked the smooth wood finish.

As I opened the lid, it let out the softest whine. I paused, not quite sure of what I was seeing. Gone were the charred spoon and the lighter. Gone were the rubber tubing and the crumpled plastic bags. Gone were the syringes. The box had been relined with plush royal blue felt. The only object inside was the parcel I had placed there, rewrapped with rice paper embedded with yellow flower petals.

The day before I'd packed this box, I went to the bank and opened the safe deposit box where I'd stored the collect of pharmaceutical grade narcotics I'd pilfered. I stuffed them into my coat pocket, looking all around me like the thief I'd become. I'd already risked my career by just taking drugs out of the hospital. The next steps would be far riskier.

Surprising myself, I removed the ring Jake had given me. It slipped off my finger more easily than I expected. I pulled an envelope from my purse and tucked the ring inside, placing it into the safe deposit box where it would remain safe. As clear as a movie, I could see myself giving the ring to Ryan for her high school graduation. A future was beginning to form.

With the drugs in my pocket, I drove myself to Ocean Beach. I'd walked that patch of sand countless times growing up, nearly every Sunday morning with my father. I'd fallen in love with Jake there when I'd first laid eyes on the miracles he'd created with ice and stone. Without removing my shoes or rolling up my surgical greens, I waded into the icy water, standing there until my feet and shins were numb. The sickness of my secrecy stared right at me and gnashed its ugly teeth. I imagined myself telling Alice, Dad, and Tully about the drugs in my pocket and my plan to help Jake die. I'd plead my case well. *He's suffering. Medicine has failed him. Ryan can't live this way.* Then I imagined telling Mary K and imagined her response. *Have you fucking lost your mine, Murphy?* And how could I ever tell Burt that I had provided his friend—his brother by choice—with the means to take his own life? Worst of all, I imagined facing Ryan when the truth of what I'd done inevitably emerged. Whether she was a child or had become a grown woman by the time she found out, there would be nothing to say to justify what I had done.

I decided right there; Jake had to make his own choices, just as I had made mine.

I pulled the plastic bag of drugs from my pocket and opened it. As I poured the contents of the bag, the morphine compound disappeared into the lead-colored water at my feet. Relief washed over me, confirming the rightness of my choice. My burden was lifted. I couldn't resist romping, splashing briny water with each dancing step.

When I returned to the house, the photo on Ryan's bedroom wall that Burt had given me almost audibly called my name. I wrapped the photo that our friend had titled "The Nest" in brown paper and inserted a notecard in a small envelope. Inside I wrote, "I'll always love you." It was this parcel that I placed into the mahogany box. I wanted Jake to have one lasting image of the family he'd helped to create.

Opening the rice paper wrapping, I had no idea what I might find. The envelope I'd placed there was gone, replaced with a new one bearing my name in Jake's unmistakable flourish. I traced the letters of my name with the tip of my finger and imagined Jake's pen making the strokes.

With my heart pounding, I opened the flap of the envelope. It said only, *"I loved you more."*

Author's Note about Manic Depression and Bipolar Disorder

This story portrays a character struggling with manic depression, which today is referred to by mental health professionals as Bipolar Disorder (BPD). Many advances have been made in recent decades (after this story would have taken place), both in treatment and medication, which have helped to improve the lives of those who live every day with BPD. Many of those with this condition are able to manage it successfully through a variety of treatments, medications, and healthy living options.

But BPD remains one of the most baffling of disorders. There is no one-size-fits-all solution for BPD. Some people withstand medication well, are helped by it, and are so dedicated to their wellness that they continually search for the right combination of practices that will help them to function and live satisfying lives. Others find that holistic health and meditation practices help them best. Still others want better lives but find the rigors of managing their condition daunting, its mysterious qualities perplexing. For nearly all with BPD, working with qualified, skilled, and insightful professionals and receiving the support of loved ones is a crucial part of the management of their condition.

While advancements have been made, some people with BPD still fare better than others, and for some it can be a life-threatening condition. This is a highly baffling condition, and its management seems to require as much art as science. Medication, while vital for many, is not helpful to others. BPD is often misdiagnosed and under-diagnosed, and those who have it are sometimes abandoned as hopeless. Loving someone with mental illness, particularly BPD, can be heartbreaking, infuriating, and wildly frustrating.

In no way do I intend to say that the experiences of the characters in this story are necessarily those of everyone with BPD or their loved ones. As a licensed therapist who has practiced for more than two decades, I have seen a wide range of experiences for both those who struggle with BPD and their family members. I've seen the frustrations, and I've also seen people so dedicated to having a happy life with this disorder that they do all they can to create such a life for themselves. I've been deeply inspired and moved by all of my clients—by both their struggles and their successes.

What I know for sure is that if you or a loved one struggles with mental illness in any form, support and information are vital. The National Alliance on Mental Illness (NAMI) is at the forefront of those providing information about mental illness to individuals, their families, and mental health professionals. Their website provides a wealth of information about mental illness—in all its forms—as well as help in finding resources beyond what they provide. NAMI is available on the web at www.nami.org. Their helpline, which is staffed with amazing, compassionate people, can be reached at 800-950-NAMI.

Acknowledgments

I love watching the Oscars. Not for the clothes or to see the celebrities, though that's always fun. I love the acceptance speeches. Tightly polished or frantic, tearful or funny, I always like to witness the famous and the obscure oozing with gratitude for all who have helped them and those whom they love most. Given that I'm over fifty and can't act, I'll likely not find myself at such a podium with a weighty statuette in my hands, but as an author, I have this acknowledgements page. Before the music starts to play me off the stage, I have a few folks to thank.

Every writer needs a tribe of other writers who really get what is required to get words out of your head, onto the page, and shaped into the story you want to tell. Most central around the campfire in my tribe are the other three members of my writing critique group, Bella Quattro: Linda Joy Myers, Christie Nelson, and Amy Peele. My Bellas, you are scarecrow, tin man, and lion on my journey. Each of you is so generously endowed with courage, intelligence, and heart that I'd never have found Emerald City or my way back to Kansas without you. My work may have gotten written without the Bellas, but it wouldn't be as good, and it would have been way less fun. *Grazie!*

I found my Bellas among the Fourth Street Writers in San

Rafael, California. The other four of these fabulous women are Lum Franco, Colleen Rae, Kathy Rueve, and Barbara Toohey. Ladies, all of you helped me to find my voice and feel that my stories might just be worth sharing. Plus, you're a blast! Guy Biederman, thank you for being the writer's Pied Piper and the one we followed to find one another.

Early readers of this story endured it when it was a couch potato of a book—flabby, out of shape, and needing to drop quite a few pounds. Joan Keyes, your kind support and keen eye proved invaluable, and I'm so glad that a love of words brought us together and made us lifelong friends. Dianne Grubb, you shared the reactions of your heart and let me know which parts rang truest. Eileen Rendahl, you shared your vast experience with writing and publishing books, and told me the things that are brave to share and absolutely golden. Mark Schatz, you gave me the much-valued guy's perspective. Thanks for telling me that men would like the story too, and for encouraging me to ditch the girly title. Sorry the Stanford section didn't make the cut. Suzie Zupan, when I was lost and thought I'd have to scrap the whole thing, you used your brilliance and your candor to help me restructure, reshape, and rebuild the entire story into something that ultimately proved to be the shape of the book. I'm so grateful that it aches. Elizabeth Appell, no one could ask for a better writing role model or a more enthusiastic cheerleader than I've found in you. Julie Valin is a woman of such vast kindness and generosity that I can't believe it can be contained on just one person. Julie, not only did you give me your critique of that flabby draft, you have become a partner with me in launching this book. To top it off, you shared your beautiful family with me while I lived far away from mine. I love every layer of our friendship, darlink!

Brooke Warner, it's impossible to fully express my gratitude for your masterful editing, your insight into the essence of this story, and your sheer wizardry. It seems that, once again, my writing life has brought me not only a fabulous resource in you, but a lovely friend as well. I look forward to our next chapters.

Thank you to the readers and the audience members of the Women's Writing Salon in Nevada County, California. Every time I watch a new writer shakily unfold her story and share it with the audience, I'm newly empowered. The audiences of the Salon have taught me that stories become three-dimensional only when they're shared, or, as I once heard the awesome author Dorothy Allison say, "The words rise to glory when I give them away." Thank you to Patricia Dove Miller, who co-produces the Salon with me and is kind enough to praise my stories when I am brave enough to read them. To my students of memoir writing (more teachers than students, and therefore I shouldn't charge you a dime), your bravery has encouraged me to stretch beyond my comfort zone, not just in writing, but in everything I do.

The first pages of this book were nurtured in the cozy living room of author and writing teacher Jessica Barksdale Inclan. Thank you for supporting the story in its natal form. Heather Donahue, thank you for your kind support. I'm inspired by your ballsiness and willingness to "go there" in writing and in life. I think I'll try me some of that. Deep appreciation for Sands Hall, who is not only a skilled word wielder and a champion of writers but who has written an absolute bible of resources in *Tools of the Writer's Craft*, which helped me to finally understand point of view. Kim Culbertson, I thank you for your instant willingness to support this book. You are a force, girl, and I've been watching you and learning for a long time. Verna Dreisbach, thank you for nudging me toward that last round of edits. I thought I was too tired to go there.

I'd like to offer a special thanks to the fabulous artist Andy Goldsworthy. I glimpsed photos of his work many years ago, and that was the seed of inspiration for the art of Jake Bloom in this story. After I'd completely written the book, I allowed myself to look at more of Goldworthy's books and to watch *Rivers and Tides*, the documentary about his work. I was happy to find that he was a tranquil, peaceful man—quite different from the character in whose hands I placed his artistic genius. I only hope one day to see his creations in their real locations. It would be a thrill.

To the members and organizers of Sierra Writers, California Writers' Club, Sacramento Valley Rose, the Women's National Book Association, and countless writing conferences, I thank you for providing me with more resources than I'd ever have imagined existed, for bringing me together with other word-slingers, and allowing me the opportunity to meet and get to know some of my rock-star author idols.

Every tribe needs a keeper of the flame. The amazing women at She Writes Press are doing just that. The publishing industry is currently gasping and coughing, contracting and consolidating. A lot of naysayers say, "The book is dead." Unless you're an author with an established track record, you've won American Idol, slept with a celebrity, or birthed eight babies at once, it's hard to get a book published these days. I'd like to thank the truly visionary women of She Writes Press. Co-founders Brooke Warner and Kamy Wicoff didn't just bang their high chairs about the frustrations of the publishing industry; they decided to create a new model for helping authors—in this case women authors—to share their books with the world, and to do so with a perfect combination of power and femininity. They are pioneers. I'm honored down to my bones that they've allowed me to be among the first-year littermates of this revolutionary indie publishing company. Krissa Lagos, thank you for keeping me from sharing my comma addiction with the world. Kiran Spees, thanks for the book's interior design. Sheila Cowley, thank you for your patience and collaboration while working with me on the cover design. I just love it.

I am blessed in my life to have friends who feel like family, and family members I regard as the best of friends. Dianne Grubb, your heart and your love have always been my anchor. I'd most truly have lost my way a thousand times without you. You are so much more than a sister to me. Jim Grubb, you could not be more brother to me if we shared DNA. I thank you for your burst of enthusiasm when I told you this book was coming out. I can't remember ever being so touched. I have stolen shamelessly from your prosaic profanity and bawdy humor, finding some of your words coming out of my characters' mouths. Keep up the good work. I've got another foul-mouthed character in my next book. Matthew Grubb, your photograph proved the perfect background for this cover. I love you for your imagination and your heart. Love overflows for Megan Shell, whose playful and delightful blogging nudged me into the cyber world. (Check out Megan's blog, *Gourmet or Go Home*. Fun!) Michelle Verity Colvin, child of my heart, I love you ever and always. Linda High, for your authenticity, your generosity, and your big laugh I love you more each day. Richard Day, friend of my youth, we've weathered a few storms together. How I wish you were nearer. Gary and Sally Bauman, Tom Cline, and Curt Carnes, thanks for the music and the laughter. My next book features a musician; I'm going to be calling on you guys. To those friends and family not mentioned by name, please know that you are woven into the tapestry of who I am. I am beyond grateful.

My husband, Tom Fasbinder, is a man of few words—about twenty-six a day unless he's had a few beers. But Tommy, you have taught me in these decades of loving each other the value of demonstrating love through simple and quietly generous acts. You gave up your dream shop and moved to where I got a writing studio. You show me love in your steadfast honesty, simple devotion, and tender touch. I hear you, Fas, I really do *hear* you. Max and Sam, mothering you has caused me to grow new chambers in my heart to accommodate love bigger than my former heart could hold. As boys you delighted me. Watching you become men fills me with such massive love and pride and gratitude that I feel I will burst.

My favorite of Oscar speeches are the ones that go too long and now I know why. I am grateful to many more, for much more than can be said in this rare opportunity to gush.

Oh, and I'd like to thank The Academy.

About the Author

photo © Tom Fasbinder

Fire & Water is Betsy Graziani's debut novel. She has been published in journals and anthologies and four of her fiction and memoir pieces have been produced as Readers" Theater in the historic Miners' Foundry Theater in Nevada City, California. Betsy lives nestled in the soft hills of Marin County, California with her husband, one son on the launch pad, and one out on his own in a neighboring town. Her Golden Doodle, Edgar is her faithful writing companion.

You can find Betsy at the following social media sites:

Website: www.betsygrazianifasbinder.com

Twitter: @WriterBGF

Find her under her full name on Goodreads, LinkedIn, and Facebook.